Looking Glass Sound

NIGHTFIRE BOOKS BY CATRIONA WARD

The Last House on Needless Street
Sundial
Little Eve

Looking Glass Sound

CATRIONA WARD

NIGHTFIRE

Tor Publishing Group

New York

LOOKING GLASS SOUND

Copyright © 2023 by Catriona Ward

A Nightfire Book
Published by Tom Doherty Associates / Tor Publishing Group
120 Broadway
New York, NY 10271

www.tornightfire.com

Nightfire™ is a trademark of Macmillan Publishing Group, LLC.

Library of Congress Cataloging-in-Publication Data

Names: Ward, Catriona, author.
Title: Looking glass sound / Catriona Ward.
Description: First U.S. edition. | New York : Nightfire/Tor Publishing
    Group, 2023.
Identifiers: LCCN 2023002336 (print) | LCCN 2023002337 (ebook) |
    ISBN 9781250860026 (hardcover) | ISBN 9781250860033 (ebook)
Subjects: LCGFT: Novels.
Classification: LCC PS3623.A7315 L66 2023 (print) | LCC PS3623.A7315
    (ebook) | DDC 813/.6—dc23/eng/20230203
LC record available at https://lccn.loc.gov/2023002336
LC ebook record available at https://lccn.loc.gov/2023002337

Our books may be purchased in bulk for promotional, educational, or business use. Please contact your local bookseller or the Macmillan Corporate and Premium Sales Department at 1-800-221-7945, extension 5442, or by email at MacmillanSpecialMarkets@macmillan.com.

First published in Great Britain by VIPER, part of Serpent's Tail, an imprint of Profile Books Ltd

First U.S. Edition: 2023

Printed in the United States of America

0 9 8 7 6 5 4 3 2 1

For Edward Christopher McDonald

The Dagger Man of Whistler Bay

From the unpublished memoir by Wilder Harlow
June, 1989

I'm looking at myself in the bathroom mirror and thinking about love, because I plan on falling in love this summer. I don't know how or with whom. Outside, the city is a hot tarry mess. There must be someone in New York who . . . I wish I wasn't so weird-looking. I'm not even asking to be loved back, just to know what it feels like. I make a face in the mirror, pulling my lower lip all the way down so the inside shows on the outside. Then I pull my lower eyelids down so they glare red.

'Hello,' I say to the mirror. 'I love you.'

I give a yell as my mom bursts in without knocking. 'Mom! Privacy!' A startled roach breaks from behind the pipes and runs across the cracked tile floor, fast and straight like it's being pulled by fishing line.

'You want privacy, you lock the door.' She grabs me by the arm. 'Come on, monkey. Big news.'

She drags me to the living room where the air conditioner roars like lions. Dad holds a piece of paper. 'Probate is finished,' he says. 'The cottage is ours.' The paper trembles; I can't tell if it's from the air-con or whether his hands are shaking. He looks exhausted. Good and bad can feel like the same thing, I think, if they're intense enough.

Dad takes off his glasses and rubs his eyes. Uncle Vernon died in April. Dad really loved him. He goes up every summer to visit – well, he did. We never went with him.

'Vernon's crabby,' Dad always said. 'Doesn't much like women or kids.' Uncle Vernon was the last of that side of his family. We Harlows aren't much good at staying alive so Uncle Vernon did better than most; he made it to his seventies.

'We have to list it right away,' Dad says. 'Sell while the summer's still fine. I know that.' We all know that. The envelopes with red on them come through the door all the time.

'Tell you what,' Mom says. 'Let's go up there first, OK? Before we sell.'

'What?' Dad keeps wiping his glasses. His eyes are pink and naked.

'Let's have a vacation,' Mom says. She tucks a strand of imaginary hair behind her ear, which is a sign that she's excited. We haven't had a vacation since that trip to Rehoboth Beach when I was seven. 'What do you say, Wilder?'

'That could be fun,' I say, hesitant. The ocean sounds like a good place to fall in love. Plus, if we take a vacation maybe my mom and dad might stop fighting. They think I don't hear but I do. In the night a certain kind of whisper sounds louder than yelling.

'You deserve a vacation, monkey,' she whispers. 'We're so proud of you.' The phone call came yesterday – Scottsboro Prep are renewing my full-board scholarship. I let her hug me. The truth is that things at Scottsboro got pretty bad by the end of term. I was at break-ing point, walking to class as quickly as I could so as not to be caught in the hallway by others, or taking a book to lunch so no one could catch my eye. That way I could at least pretend not to hear what they said about me. My hands got red and sore from wringing out clothes, ties that were soaked wet with toilet water and bleach, sometimes other stuff.

My scholarship makes it possible for me to go to Scottsboro, which is very expensive. All I have to do is hold on for a couple more years. It has to end one day. *Just hold on*, I tell myself over and over, in my head. I'll go to college and from then on, everything will be different. I'm going to write books.

I don't tell my parents about what happens at Scottsboro. It might make things even worse between them.

We leave the city in a warm June dawn that promises another sweltering day, and drive up through the woods. We move backwards through the season, travelling through time, the summer growing younger and cooler as we make our way north.

In the late afternoon we leave the highway. The grass gets tall and green. There are wildflowers I don't know, the sound of crickets. The warm wind is full of salt.

Evening's falling as we pull over at the foot of a green hill marked by a shingle path. The cottage perches above like a gull on the cliff. We walk, sweating, up the green swathe of land, suitcases leaving tracks in the rough grass. The house is surrounded by a white picket fence with a gate. It's white clapboard with blue shutters, and I think – *I've never seen anything so neat, so perfect*. There are rows of seashells on the porch and twisting silver driftwood hangs above the door. The leaves of the sugar maple whisper – under it, there's a high-pitched whine, a long shrill note like bad singing.

This is the first time I hear it, the whistling for which the bay is named. It sounds like all the things you're not supposed to believe in – mermaids, selkies, sirens.

I come to with my mother's hand on my shoulder. 'Come on inside, Wilder,' she says, and I realise I've been just standing there, mouth open.

'What's that sound?' It seems like it's coming from inside me, somehow.

Dad pauses in the act of unlocking the door. 'It's the stones on the beach. High tide has eaten away at them, making little holes – kind of like the finger stops on a flute – and when the wind is in the east, coming over the ocean, it whistles through. Neat, huh?'

'It's spooky,' I say.

'Come to think of it,' Dad says thoughtfully, 'the way Uncle Vernon was found was pretty spooky, too. He was just sitting up on those rocks as they whistled around him, eyes staring. Like he'd been taken before his time, whistled to death by Whistler Bay . . .'

'Dork,' I mutter as I follow him inside. I know Uncle Vernon died in hospital of a heart infarction.

Inside the cottage everything is bare and white and blue, like a shore washed clean by the ocean. My room has a single bed covered in rough wool blankets, and a round window like a porthole.

'Keep the windows closed at night,' my father says. 'There have been some break-ins around here. I'll get locks in the morning.'

'And careful in the water,' my mother adds, anxious. 'There's a drowning almost every year.'

'Yes, mother dearest.'

She slaps my arm. Sometimes she gets mad when I'm what she calls *fresh*, but mostly she likes it.

I open the porthole and fall asleep to the sound of the stones and the sea.

In the morning I wake before my parents. I realise as soon as I put them on that my swimming shorts are way too small. I've grown a lot since last summer. I didn't think of it before we left New York. So I put on some underwear and flip flops, grab a towel and slip out the back door.

The red ball of the morning sun is burning off the last sea mist. I go down the path, gravel skittering from my sandalled feet, towel slung over my shoulder.

On the beach the pebbles are already warm from the sun. I take off my glasses and rest them gently on a rock. On an impulse I slip off my underwear too and go into the sea naked. The water takes me in its glassy grip. For a second I wonder, *riptide?* But the sea is still and cool. It's a homecoming. I think, *I'm a sea person and I never even knew it.* Even underwater I can still hear the wind singing in the rocks. And I hear a voice, too, calling. I break the surface, coughing, water streaming from my head.

A girl and a boy stand on the shore. I think they're about my age. She wears overalls and a big floppy hat. Her hair is a deep, almost unnatural red, like blood. She wears a man's watch on her wrist, gold and clunky. It's way too big and it makes her wrist look very slim. I think, *frick that was fast,* because I am in love with her right away.

I see what she holds: a stick, with my underwear hanging off the pointed end. She wrinkles her nose in an expression of disgust. 'What kind of pervert leaves their underwear lying around on the beach?' Her scorn mingles perfectly with her accent – she's English. Not the sunburned kind who throng round Times Square, but the kind I thought existed only in movies. Classy.

The wind billows in the fabric of my shorts, filling them. For a second it looks like I am still in the shorts – invisible, struggling, impaled.

'Hey,' the boy says. 'He didn't know anyone else was here.' *Heah.* Is he British, too? He's tall with an easy, open look to him. I think, *it's boys like that who get the girls.* As if to confirm this thought, he puts a hand on the girl's back. 'Give 'em, Harper.'

Harper – it seems an odd name for a British girl but it suits her. Maybe her parents are big readers.

Reluctantly she swings the stick around at him. He takes off his shirt, plucks the underwear off the end of the stick and wades into the shallows. He doesn't seem to mind his shorts getting wet. 'Stay there,' he calls. 'I'll come out.' He swims out in long slow strokes to where I bob in the centre of the cove.

'Here you go.' *Heah ya go.* Not British. He hands me my shorts. Then he swims back towards the shore. I struggle into the underwear, catching my feet in the fabric. I begin the endless swim back.

The boy is talking to the girl – she's laughing. I think with a bite of fear, *they're laughing at me.* But he puts another gentle hand on Harper's back and turns her away, pointing inland, towards something on the cliff. I realise he's being kind to me again, making sure I can get out of the water in privacy.

I huddle, cold, in my towel. I'd thought there was something special about this place this morning but there isn't. The world's the same everywhere. It's all like school.

'See you around,' I say and make my way back up the path. I feel their eyes on my back and I stumble on the incline. The rocks make their evil whistling and I hurry away from the kids' gaze and the sound, which seem part of each other. I go straight indoors and stay there until long after I hear them come up from the beach and past the cottage, long after their footsteps have faded away down the hill, towards the road.

I wonder what the relationship between them is, if they're dating, if maybe they're doing *it*. I don't know enough about *it* to tell. He touches her with a casual assurance but they didn't behave romantically towards one another – not the way the movies have led me to expect.

I had planned to journal each day, here. But I don't want to write down what happened this morning. I wash my face over and over again with cold water before breakfast, so Mom and Dad don't see redness around my eyes or any other traces of tears.

I want to go home so badly I can taste it. I think of my usual seat at the library in the city, near the end of one of those long tables, the lamps with their green glass shades throwing circles of warm light. Everyone helps you understand things, there.

'Come on, sport,' my father says. 'Good for you to get out. You can't sit in your room all vacation.' So I go with him to run errands in Castine. What else am I going to do?

Waiting for him to finish at the post office, I gaze glumly at the sacks of chickenfeed piled outside the general store, wander up the main street. It's lonely being with family sometimes.

A pickup pulls up with a screech on the other side of the street, outside a cheerful white and blue shop. *Fresh Fish*, reads the sign overhead. The truck is battered and rusty with panels beaten out badly where they've been staved in by collisions. Probably a drinker, I say to myself, knowing. A line comes to me. *Living by the sea is tough on paint, and just as hard on the mind.* Maybe I'll write it down later.

A thin man in a vest gets out of the truck. He busies himself with coolers and crates, and a moment later, the rich smell of raw fish reaches me. I watch the man with interest. He's so easy in himself, unloads the truck in quick, decisive movements, every now and then spitting a thin vein of brown juice into the gutter. *A man of the sea*, I think. He's weather-beaten, skin as brown as shoe leather, but his eyes are a warm blue, striking in his worn face. I imagine him living in a board shack, bleached silver by the sun and salt, down by the water, going out in his boat every day before dawn. Some tragedy lies in his past, I'm sure of it. He has a rough, sad look like a cowboy in a western. But he's a sea cowboy, which is even cooler. I back into the shadow of a little alley. I don't want to be seen staring.

A bell jingles, and a young woman comes out of the blue and white store and greets him, friendly. He nods back. Her eyes are swollen, her nose red. She's been crying, I realise, and I feel a spurt of hot sympathy for her. Or maybe she has a cold. She blows her nose heartily and stuffs the Kleenex back in her pocket. She takes the crates into the jingling doorway and brings them back empty, swinging from her hand. The bell announces her exits and her entrances, jaunty. It isn't a cold; she's been crying, for sure. In fact she's still crying. Fresh tears shine on her face. She dabs them dry with tiny movements.

'Sorry,' I hear her say to the fisherman, as if she's offending him somehow. The man nods gently. The world is full of sorrow, his silence seems to say. *Maybe they were lovers*, I think, excited. *Maybe he left her.*

When the contents of all twelve crates are inside, she hands him a wad of bills. He takes them and turns back to the truck. As she goes into the store for the last time the Kleenex she'd dried her tears with falls from her pocket. He must see it in the corner of his eye, because he turns quickly, and picks it up before the wind can take it. The man slips the tissue into his pocket. I feel how kind it is, his act of humility, to pick the tissue up for the crying girl and take it away, so it doesn't blow down the street and out to sea.

As if feeling my eyes on him, the man looks around, slowly surveying the street. When his eyes light on me he smiles, amused. 'Hey,' he says. 'Who you hiding from?'

I come out from behind the house, bashful.

'You want to take a ride? Help me get the next load from the dock?'

He indicates the passenger seat in a careless, amiable way. People around here don't seem to talk much but they like to do small kindnesses.

'I can't,' I say, regretful. 'I have to wait for my dad.'

He nods slowly, and then he gets in the truck and it roars away, up the street, in the direction of the ocean. I wish I'd gone with him now. It would have been fun to see the dock.

Someone says 'boo!' and I jump.

The boy from the beach says, 'You took off pretty quick the other day.' He looks even more relaxed and golden than I remembered. 'I'm Nat,' he says. 'Nathaniel.'

'Like Hawthorne?'

'My last name's Pelletier.'

'I meant, Nathaniel Hawthorne the writer.' He looks uncomfortable. I go on quickly, 'I'm Wilder. It's a weird name. You can call me Will.' I've been waiting to try 'Will' out for a while.

'Nah, it's cool. Like a wrestler or something. You're wild, but I'm wilder!' He bares white healthy teeth in a snarl. It sits oddly on his friendly features.

'I'm *Wildah*,' I repeat, and really it doesn't sound so bad, the way he says it. Like something from a play.

He punches me on the arm, fake mad and I laugh and he grins. 'Don't worry about Harper,' he says. 'She's rich so she doesn't need manners.'

I laugh again because he seems to be joking, but I think, *she really didn't seem to have any.*

'You want to swim with us later? We're going late this afternoon. We'll make a fire, sit out.'

I hesitate. I want to go but I'm scared too. I don't really know how to talk to people.

I start to tell Nat no, just as my dad comes out of the post office and beckons to me.

'I've got to go,' I say.

'We'll come by the bay around five,' he calls after me, and half of me is so happy that he seems to want to be friends, and the other is unnerved because it all seems to be settled without my doing anything at all.

I won't hang out with them, I know better. I'll pretend I'm busy when they arrive.

Nat, Harper and I sit on the sand, silent and a little awkward, watching the tide go out. The wet sand of the bay is slick and grey. It's obscene like viscera, a surface that shouldn't be uncovered. Behind us on the beach, the bonfire smokes half-heartedly. As it turns out, we aren't any of us much good at lighting fires. Harper looks even more beautiful in the long, low light. She has the smooth, angular face of a fairy or a cunning child, I think, and then immediately wish I could write that down to use later. I feel the beginnings of stirring in my chinos and after that I purposely don't look at her again. I feel her presence next to me, warm like a small sun.

'I'm sorry,' Harper says. 'I was horrid the other day.'

'Oh, no problem,' I say, cautious. 'I mean, it was just kidding around.' That's always the best thing to say to people who might hurt you. It takes the pressure off of them.

'No, it was mean. I get these moods. I try not to but I do.' She pauses. 'It was also somewhat confusing; you have very unusual—' She pauses, and I feel sorry for her; she's trying not to be rude again.

'I know,' I say. 'I get it all the time.'

People form opinions of me quickly because of the way I look. My eyes are very big, which is supposed to be good. But they're too big, like a bush baby's. And they're pale. So pale it's hard to even tell what colour they are. They almost blend in with my skin, which is also really pale. I'm planning to get a tan this summer – to look more like a regular guy and less like some kind of insect.

'Yeah,' Nat says. 'The guy who lived here before you had the same eyes, the same – colour.' He squints and leans away, looking at me. 'You look like a younger version. He swam here in the mornings too.' He pauses. 'He was nice, we talked sometimes. He liked taking pictures of the coast around here.'

'I thought he died,' Harper says. 'Are you a ghost?'

'That was my Uncle Vernon,' I say. 'He *did* die.'

'Hey, Harper.' Nat's voice is easy but she looks up and flushes.

'Sorry,' she says. 'I get a bit personal sometimes.'

'It's OK. I didn't know him. My dad calls it the Harlow look. Big bug eyes, white skin.'

I risk a surreptitious glance at Harper. Her skin is white too, but creamy, scattered with golden freckles. She looks like a human being, at least, whereas I'm aware I kind of don't. She shivers and I want to give her my sweater but I don't. I've seen it done in movies, giving a girl your sweater, but I've never done it myself, or really even spoken to a girl, and I feel shy.

'Where do you go to school?' I ask them.

'Edison High, in Castine,' Nat says. 'We live on the shore.' I've seen those houses on the shore. They're bleached silver, roofs often patched with aluminium.

Nat wears ragged denim cutoffs and a faded Red Sox t-shirt that's too big for him. I feel the hot poke of shame. The kids at Scottsboro call me poor so often I've got used to it – my mom takes the pants on my uniform down each year instead of buying me new ones. I get a bursary for schoolbooks. But I am reminded now that I'm not poor.

Harper says, 'I'm starting boarding school in the autumn.' She sighs. 'It's a good one, and I'm so bad at school. I probably won't last long there. I'll probably end up at *Fairview.*'

I've heard of Fairview. It's where rich people dump their daughters when there's nowhere else left.

'I belong at Fairview really,' Harper says gloomily. 'It's a crap school for people who are crap at school. Everyone knows it. Even I know it.' She frowns and pokes the sand with a stick. 'I want to go home.'

'Oh. Well, goodbye.' My heart sinks. But I've had an hour with her.

'I mean to the UK.'

'I don't think you'll make it by dark,' Nat says.

'Funny.' She sighs. 'I don't want to go to boarding school. I'm going to miss Samuel so much.'

'Who's Samuel?' I keep my tone casual, even though jealousy is a hot lance in my side. I can't tell if I hide it well or not.

'Oh. My dog,' Harper says. 'He's a dachshund. He's small but he doesn't act like a small dog. He's got dignity. They're giving him to the housekeeper, or that's what they say. It's probably a lie. Mama's probably having him put down. He's so lovely. He always knows when I'm scared. He always comes.' She gets up and dusts her palms free of sand. 'I suppose I do have to go now. It'll be dark soon.'

'Walk you back?' Nat says.

'Better not,' she says. 'They wouldn't like it.' They exchange a look. I burn with envy at the natural intimacy between them. Once again I wonder if they're doing *it.*

We both watch her pick her way up the path in the fading light, crest the clifftop, and vanish into the purple sky.

Nat settles back down into the sand. 'Harper got kicked out of every school in England.'

'What for?'

'What not for? Everything. She *mistrusts institutionalised authority structures.*' His mimicry of her cut-glass tones is pretty good.

'Have you two known each other long?'

'A couple years. Her folks come out every summer.'

'Is – are you two, like, involved?'

'No.'

'I thought maybe you were.'

'No. But I'm in love with her,' he says.

'What?' It is a shocking thing to say out loud, like someone taking off their clothes in public.

'I said, I'm in love with her. I'm going to make her love me, one day.'

'But you don't just – *tell people* stuff like that.' My fists are balled. I can't hang my anger on anything rational, and that makes me angrier still. 'That kind of thing is private, you keep it to yourself . . .'

'Maybe you do, or try to,' he says with a sudden flash of anger. 'But you're not so good at it. You look at her all the time when she isn't looking. But you can't even look her in the eyes; it's embarrassing. Like you've never seen a girl before.'

'You're not getting anywhere either,' I say. 'How long have you been thinking about, like, holding her hand?'

'I'll still get further than you,' he says, confident, and I know he's right.

Before I can think my palm hits his cheek with a crack. He puts his hand up to the red print mine has left behind. 'Did you just *slap* me?' he asks slowly.

I rear back as his fist comes at my face and the punch lands on my breastbone just above my heart. My chest explodes into pain and I gasp. I go for him now, raining blows on his face and chest and everywhere I can reach. I'm not great at fighting but I don't think Nat is either, because neither of us lands many good ones. But he gives me a black eye and I get him one on the side of the face.

We fight until we cough sand and it's in every crevice of our bodies, until we're panting and exhausted. Neither of us seems likely to win so we just kind of stop by common consent, roll away from one another and lie on our backs, spitting grit.

'Sorry.' I hesitate. 'I really thought you two were – you know – together.'

'Nope,' he says. 'We're friends.' He sighed. 'I thought at first you and me could be friends.'

'I know,' I say. 'I thought that too. But it can't work if both of us are in love with her.'

'I think we have to be,' Nat says. 'Friends, and in love with her.' He's right, it isn't possible to stop either thing.

'We can't fight all the time.'

'We have to work out some kind of, like, agreement.'

'OK,' I say, thinking. 'So, rule one, no cheating, no going behind the other's back. We have to agree that from now on, neither one of us tries to get her. Agreed?'

'And we can't ever tell her about it,' he says. 'That's a rule too. Deal?'

'Deal.' I shake his hand.

He touches his cheekbone with a tentative finger and winces. 'Good thing my dad's night fishing. Sleeps in the day. He won't see me in the sun 'til a week.' He pauses. 'That was fun, though. Good fight.'

We kick sand over the smouldering remains of the bonfire and go up the path.

'See you tomorrow,' he calls behind him.

I'm apprehensive about my parents seeing my black eye. I needn't be, as it turns out. My mother puts arnica on my face and makes tut-ting noises.

'It's OK,' I say. 'We're friends now. Me and Nat.'

'You usually make friends by roughhousing?' she asks, amused, and I realise she thinks it healthy for a boy my age – *roughhousing*.

The next day Harper and Nat are at the white fence after breakfast.

Harper stares at my eye. 'Gnarly,' she says, then, very English, 'What a shiner.' A sour scent hangs about her.

'Like I said,' Nat says, 'I stumbled, grabbed Wilder and we both wiped out. Rolled down the path.' Turning to me he says, 'We're going out on the boat. It's down on the water.'

Harper picks her way down the shale path with exaggerated care. 'Mustn't slip,' she says as if to herself, shooting me a look under her lashes.

The boat bobs on the water in the morning sun. She's chipped and scraped all over, and you can see every colour she's ever been painted, her past written on her like a record. *Siren*, reads the shaky black lettering on her stern. The outboard motor at the back leaks a narrow trail of oil into the water.

There are only two life jackets so after some argument we agree that the only solution is for none of us to wear one.

'One dies, we all die,' I say. It's pleasing.

'Seems like you two are doing a pretty good job at killing your-selves,' Harper says. She watches me with bird-like focus. She takes off her big, clunky gold watch and puts it carefully in a Ziploc bag, then stows it in the locker beneath the bench.

The little outboard engine chugs against the waves. We put her nose out into open water, go out of sight of land, looking for great white sharks. When navy-blue water surrounds us in every direc-tion Nat stops the engine. We take turns jumping off the side into the deep, gasping with shock at the cold, our breath coming fast, picturing monsters moving slowly in the depths below us. We don't see any sharks and soon it gets to feeling lonely, nothing but water everywhere. When we sight the shoreline again we yell with relief, as though we've been adrift for many days.

We make our way slowly up the coast, passing houses perched on cliffs, hillsides rugged with dark pine forest, green meadows studded with ox-eye daisies. On a lonely stretch we surprise a family of seals sunning themselves on flat rocks in a sheltered cove. They watch us, tranquil, with their strange round eyes but don't move. They know we're no threat – we're part of the ocean now.

Harper talks about Grace Kelly. She loves Grace Kelly. It's like the words fill her to breaking point and have to be released. It seems almost an impersonal act, her talk – a mechanical release not meant as communication. 'Such control,' Harper mutters to the sea. 'As an actor, as a woman. She told the truth all the time, but she was a castle of her own making. No one could reach the real her. It was perfect. She made herself safe in a dangerous world.'

'Harp?' Nat touches her gently with his foot and she starts.

'Sorry,' she says. 'I just think actors are holy, you know?'

Harper talks about her dog, too. 'The thing I miss most about Samuel is the way he protected me from my dad,' she says. Then she sits up abruptly and scans the cliffs. 'Do you think the Dagger Man is watching?'

'Ah, we don't need to talk about that,' Nat says. A rare flash of discomfort crosses his friendly face. 'It's freaky.'

'I think he's watching. I think he's waiting for us to come ashore somewhere really remote and then he'll come for us, quick as a shadow, holding his dagger above his head ...' She raises a fist behind her head as if to stab. Her red hair falls about her face, which has become dark and frightening.

I ask, 'What are you talking about?'

'The guy who breaks into houses round here,' Harper says. 'The Dagger Man. Don't you know? You're not local, so I suppose no one tells you anything.'

I don't point out that owning a large house you visit for a month a year is hardly being local. 'You tell me, then.'

'It happened last year,' Harper says. 'There were break-ins. Always visitors, no one local. But the thing is—'

'—he takes pictures of people asleep,' Nat says. 'It's not as big a deal as she's making it sound.'

Harper says, 'He only takes pictures of the kids. And it *is* a big deal. They think he does it to children because they'd be easier to overpower if they woke up. Then he leaves. He doesn't take anything, that they can tell. The family don't even know they've been broken into, even.'

'So how—'

'He sends the photos to people,' Harper says. 'The Polaroids. At least, that's what I heard my dad say. The police, the families. Sleeping children. And they say that in the Polaroids there's a kind of dagger at the child's throat. It happened to the Masons, and the Bartletts, I think some other family but I don't remember who. Anyway it stopped when summer ended. But everyone's wondering if it'll start again.'

'We're not kids,' I say. 'We're probably going to be ok.' Unease is all through me. And some other feeling, too. I stare at her hand, which often squeezes her knee or thigh for emphasis, or as if for stability. Her nails are bitten to the quick and she has an old, greying Band-Aid wrapped around her thumb. There are tiny golden hairs on her legs, which occasionally catch the midday sun like fine wire. When I look up, Harper's eyes are fixed on me.

'His name,' Harper says dreamily, looking at me. 'I think of it as all one word. Daggerman, daggerman . . .'

'Don't. . .' I feel like something's going to happen if she says the name a third time.

'Got one!' Nat yells from the front of the boat and we both jump as if waking from a dream.

Nat pulls the writhing fish from the hook and hits it against the prow until its brains spray out in the bright air. Its body is long and beautiful and bloody. 'Striper,' he says, putting the fish in the cold box, laying the pole carefully down in the bottom of the boat.

We pull into a tiny white beach, no more than a spit of white sand. Nat finds oysters growing waist deep on the rocks beneath the surface. He opens them carefully with the oyster knife. 'My dad carved this,' he says proudly. 'Cool, huh?' The handle of the oyster knife is walnut, worn smooth with use, chased with a pattern of tiny fish. 'He gave it to me for my birthday when I was, like, seven.'

'My dad would never let me have a knife,' I say, enviously.

'He's pretty cool,' Nat says. 'He catches seals sometimes, in the shark rig. That's why he always keeps a boat hook in the *Siren*. What you do is come up beside it, knock it out with the hook, snare it in the shark rig, then pull it along beside the boat for a time, until it's ready to do whatever you want. Then you take it somewhere else on shore to finish it.'

Without hot sauce or lemon the oysters are disgusting but I still eat two. We build a fire from driftwood. We're a little better at it, this time, don't put too much wood on at once to start. We gut the sea bass, wrap it in aluminium and cook it on the coals. The fish's flesh is charred to black in some places and almost raw in others, but we devour it anyway. Spider crabs scuttle near on delicate legs. We throw them the fishbones and they swarm over the skeleton, picking it clean. We lie on our backs on the warm white sand, watching the thin corkscrew of smoke rise into the air. The sun burns above and our skins grow pink and sore.

'This is the best day of my life,' I almost tell them – but I don't. I want to keep all this life corked tight inside me, bubbling and dangerous.

Harper pulls a bottle of Jim Beam out of her bag. It's maybe a third full and we pass it between us, sputtering as the heat strokes down our gullets. 'You might as well tell me,' Harper says into the quiet. 'Why you fought.'

'We didn't fight.' I'm dreamy with whiskey. 'Nat fell on the path, took me down with him.'

'Whatever. You're both terrible liars.' Harper holds up the empty whiskey bottle. 'Let's spin it,' she says.

My heart crawls up my throat into my mouth, a warm lump. I've never played spin the bottle, never kissed anyone. I wonder what it would be like to kiss Harper. I wonder if I'm going to throw up. Nat's watching me. I wonder, through a white haze of panic, what this means for our deal.

'Harper,' he says, but she hisses 'sssssssh!' and glares at him.

Harper puts the bottle on a flat rock in the middle of the three of us. She spins. The bottle gleams and whirls like a propeller in the glare. It slows, then comes to rest. The top points at me, and the other end points out to sea.

'You have to kiss the ocean,' she says.

'But those aren't the rules—' I start to say, helpless, then decide to leave it. Maybe I misunderstood the rules; it's not like I've ever played before. Harper would know how to play better than I do. 'Spin again?'

'No,' Harper says, squinting at me. 'These are our rules, Wilder. You have to kiss who it says.'

Standing up is like being a kite, I'm billowing around on the end of a string. How much whiskey have I drunk? I go to the shallows where they wash bright over the pebbles, turning them into jewels. 'Nice to meet you,' I say to the sea. 'That's a lovely blouse you're wearing.'

The water rushes in over my feet. 'Right down to business, huh,' I say, resigned. 'Whatever you say, ma'am.' I kneel and kiss the sea. It kisses me back, stroking my mouth like a cool tongue. I imagine for a moment that it's salty skin beneath my lips.

'More tongue!' Harper yells. 'Give her more tongue!' And I realise she's had even more to drink than I have.

The game is that we have to make out with whatever object the bottle tells us to. Nat embraces a rock passionately. Harper drapes herself in seaweed, spitting and gagging.

'The bottle is the rule,' I say to her, sententiously. 'The only rule. More tongue.' She pushes me hard and I fall backwards onto the sun-warm shale, laughing so hard I feel like I'll die.

We wake with our feet in the water. The tide is almost in; we have to swim out to the boat with clothes and bags held above our aching heads, the waves slapping salty and cold into our open mouths.

Harper sits at the back of the boat, staring at the water. Her hand trails in the cold blue.

'I don't know how Harper does it,' Nat says. His voice is low, under the cover of the engine and the waves. 'Whenever we play that game it only ever lands on like, a tree. Or a rock.'

I pause in the middle of pulling on jeans. 'You guys play spin the bottle – just you two?'

'Pretty dumb, huh?' He sees my face. 'Not anymore,' he says quickly. 'Now we wouldn't play without you, Wilder.'

By the time we make it back to Whistler Bay we're moving through a swamp of exhaustion.

*

That night I float above my bed, hot and strange, like the sun has entered my body. I can still feel the boat dipping under me, moving with the waves. *This is what life is really like*, I think. *It's this intense.* Then I stumble out of bed and run down the narrow cold hallway to the bathroom, and throw up violently, chunks of half-cooked fish riding on a hot torrent of old Jim Beam.

In the morning my parents leave early for some craft fair or maybe a seafood market, or maybe sightseeing, I don't know. I groan and turn over. 'No,' I say through the pillow. 'I'll stay home. Do some vacation reading for school.'

'Well all right then,' says my dad, pleased. I drift back into the dark, head pulsing.

At last, at about ten, I wake up properly. The day is already noon-hot outside. I make coffee and go out into the sun with a fistful of granola in my hand.

Harper's sitting on the grass outside the gate. She looks drawn and I suspect her night was even worse than mine. I feel a stab of excitement. She came to find me.

'How long have you been here?' I ask, casual. 'You should have knocked or yelled or something.'

She shrugs. 'I'm not in a hurry,' she says. 'Just bored. Nat's got chores. Can I have some coffee? Can I hang out with you today?'

I am excited and terrified at the prospect of spending the day alone with her. 'OK,' I say. 'Yeah, I mean, sure! We can stay here, if you like. My parents are out.'

She nods. 'It's nice to be near a house sometimes,' she says. 'I'm kind of tired of the sea.'

I hold out my hand. 'Want some breakfast?' We eat dry granola from my open palm.

We climb into the branches of the maple. We're just kind of sitting here, awkward, and I'm searching for something to say when she reaches across towards me with a twig.

'What really happened between you and Nat?' She pokes my thigh. 'I think you were fighting. Does he like me?' I think I hear longing in her voice.

'I got questions for you too,' I say. 'Why was that bottle of whiskey you brought on the boat two-thirds empty?'

We glare at each other. I cave first. 'Sorry,' I say. 'I'm being a dick. I've never had a friend who's a girl before. In fact I've never had friends before.' I stare at the ground, waiting for her to say something crushing and smart, or just leave, maybe.

'I don't have any friends except Nat,' Harper says, matter of fact. 'Everyone hates me. All year I wait for summer when we come here. What's your excuse?'

'You first,' I say. 'Why does everyone hate you?'

'I'm not good with people.'

'Why? Truth for truth.'

Harper goes pale and waves her hand, like, *no*.

'Come on,' I say. 'Your British is showing. What are you afraid of?'

'Nothing, stop it.' She brightens. 'Do you have anything to drink?'

'My parents don't drink.' There's a bottle of sweet vermouth on the shelf in the store cupboard. My mom likes a small glass with a lemon slice before dinner. I'm not giving it to Harper. When I look again she's crying. She does it in complete silence, tears gleaming on her face in the dappled shade of the tree.

'Oh . . .' I slide down from my perch in a panic and go over to her. I reach up to where she sits in the crook of a branch. I don't know what to do so I kind of pet her side, like you would a pet a horse.

She shifts away from my touch. 'I just really miss Samuel,' she says thickly.

'Your dog.' I'm pleased with myself for remembering.

'He was so kind and good. He looked after me. He would only eat French fries if they had mustard on them. Isn't that weird?'

'I'm sure he's a great dog,' I say. 'I'm sure he's happy, wherever he is.' I wonder if her parents have already had the dog destroyed. She's talking about it in the past tense today. Could they have done it that quickly?

'Let's just hang out,' she says, tired. 'OK, Wilder?'

'OK,' I say.

So that's what we do. We find a backgammon set in the cupboard beneath the stairs and she teaches me to play. I'm terrible at it.

'Frick,' I say as I lose another game to her.

'You can say fuck, you know. I'm not your mum.'

'Uh,' I say, feeling shy. 'But then I might get used to it and say it in front of her by accident.'

'You are such a weird guy.' She sounds approving.

We crawl inside and eat Cheez Whiz on crackers in front of the TV. It's old, there's a constant rainbow sprawl in the corner of the screen, but eventually we find a movie to watch, something about a friendship between two bartenders. And only once does that peculiar electricity roar up my spine. Only once, all afternoon.

'Do you ever wonder if you're imaginary?' Harper asks dreamily, putting her head on my shoulder. 'Not a real person?'

'You're real,' I say, every sense alive.

She yawns. 'I'm so sick of this movie.'

'I thought you hadn't seen it before.'

'I hadn't.' She starts. 'Sorry, I'm falling asleep. I'd better go.'

'Let me walk you.'

'Why? Nothing's going to happen to *me*,' Harper says.

She still sounds kind of out of it so I start to insist – but then she gets mad so I back down.

I watch from the window as she goes along the clifftop in the low light.

I'm putting away the Cheez Whiz when I notice the bottle of vermouth is gone. When did she take it? While I was in the bathroom?

I'm afraid my parents will notice, but when they get back they're distracted, unnerved. Not, for once, fighting. There's a problem in Castine. Someone went swimming this morning at dawn, and she hasn't come back. A local business owner who has lived here all her life. The coastguard is out.

'I hope they find her,' my mother says, face white. 'Christy's the most neighbourly soul in Castine, everyone says so.'

'No swimming outside the bay, sport,' my father says to me, placing a hand on hers. I try not to notice that she flinches. 'If you go out in the boat with your friends you stay in the boat. Always take a spare can of gas. The riptides around here are lethal.' His spectacles reflect the lamplight and his beard is messy from the wind.

'I have to see my friends.' I'm anxious but it comes out sounding mad. I'm afraid he'll tell me not to go.

'Just be careful,' he says. 'Did you get any reading for school done today?'

It takes me a moment before I recall my lie of the morning. 'Oh, tons,' I say. He looks so happy that I hug him tightly.

Dad pats me gently. 'I've got to pick up that spare part for the mower,' he says and slips out the front door. My mom's eyes follow him.

He comes in late; the sound of the front door opening blends with my dreams.

*

Some days Harper's busy with her parents or in trouble for something or other and it's just Nat and me. On those days we talk about her feverishly, about her eyes and hair and how cool she is. We talk about how we'll never love anyone else but her. We feel closer to one another for it. It's strange maybe but it bonds us, being in love with her. It lends security to the whole thing. It means we can be doubly sure that nothing will ever happen.

At first I lend Nat my favourite books. He's such a great friend and if we could only talk about books together he'd be *perfect*.

'But do you *like* Tom as a character?' I ask, as we wade out through the pools at low tide. 'Did Dickie deserve to die?'

'No one deserves to be murdered,' Nat says, handing me a shrimping net.

'I'm not sure,' I say, thinking of school. I feel disappointed. I don't think he even read the book.

'Periwinkle snail,' Nat says, showing me a small shell with a beautiful curve. Inside I glimpse a delicate, shining thing. 'You can cook and eat them,' he says.

'Are – is that what we're going to do?'

'Are you hungry?'

'No.'

'Then no.' He puts the snail gently down in the tide pool.

I don't know much about his home life, or even exactly where on the shore he lives – he keeps that to himself. He always comes to the cottage to collect me, and won't come inside, even when my parents ask him to. He seems most comfortable outdoors, under the sun, beside the ocean.

I never once, throughout our friendship, see him indoors. Until that last time.

We walk together along a cool pine trail. Nat carries the BB gun over his shoulder. We're supposed to be shooting rabbits but I secretly hope we don't find any. Sometimes we stop to line pinecones up on logs and shoot them. I'm pretty good for a beginner.

It's a long, sunlit day. I give Nat half the sandwich I have in my pocket because he didn't bring anything. To my relief we don't see any rabbits. He teaches me to recognise plants – trees and flowers. 'City boy.'

As we near home, we stop in the sloping meadow above the bay where you can see over the beech tops down to the sea, which is bright aching blue today. A stream runs through it, chattering. We drink with cupped hands. Dandelion clocks whirl up around us as we sit down in the grass.

'My folks are fighting a lot.' It feels good to tell someone.

'What are your parents like?' Nat asks.

'They're OK,' I say, surprised. 'My dad is kind of a dork.'

'Do you guys like, hang out?'

'Sometimes,' I say. 'Not as much as we used to.'

'I miss my mom. She ran away and left us. It's OK,' Nat says, seeing my face. 'It was a long time ago.' He opens his battered Velcro wallet. 'My dad doesn't know I have this. He wouldn't like it.'

A woman with a shock of shaggy blonde hair, that her son will later share. She's in a bar, pink with beer and the warmth of the room. Nat has folded the photograph in two, so it fits in the clear plastic sleeve in his wallet where the driver's licence is supposed to go – so that he sees her every time he opens it, I guess.

'She's called Arlene,' Nat says. 'I wonder where she is, sometimes.'

'Maybe one day you'll go find her,' I say. 'Go into the big wide world.'

'Nah, I won't leave. Why would I?' He gestures at the sea, the meadow, the summer sky.

'You feel about this place like Harper does about her dog,' I say. 'She misses it a lot, right?'

Nat shakes his head. 'She doesn't have a dog. Never did.'

'What do you mean?'

'It's not my story to tell.' And I can't get him to say any more than that. Instead Nat says, 'My pa's letting me off chores again tomorrow. We can take the boat. Harper and I will call for you at seven.'

'In the morning?' I'm incredulous.

'We have to get out early to hit the god weather.'

'The good weather?'

'That's what I'm saying.'

I'm nearly sure it wasn't what he said.

I shiver, and everything goes a little dim, as though there's a cloud over the sun.

Nat's watching me. 'What's up?'

'I've got to get home. My mom's expecting me.' My dad probably won't be there. I know that. He's not home much, these days.

But it's not that. I just suddenly don't like this place. I don't know why. It's a beautiful meadow full of flowers overlooking the sea, what kind of person doesn't like that? But I can't wait to get away from it. I feel like I might throw up.

He slaps me on the back in a friendly way and I don't stop to say goodbye. I hurry down towards the sea and Whistler Cottage.

As soon as I'm through the beech trees and back on the cliff path I feel better. There's no way I can explain the feeling that overwhelmed me just now. Like a hand was squeezing my insides. *Get a grip, Wilder*, I tell myself. *Just a place.* But I hated it. I felt like it was looking at me.

The early morning is grey and flat, pressing down on the horizon. In the bottom of the boat is rope, a grappling hook and the oyster knife. My eyes return to them again and again, as we push out of the bay and around the headland.

'What are those for?' I ask eventually.

'We're going somewhere special,' Harper says. She seems worked up, her eyes glassy. I realise that she's been drinking. I feel unease for her, but it's also a little exciting. She's troubled and needs my friendship. Once again there's a stirring in the depths of me.

The sea tosses and spits, black with rims of white.

'This doesn't seem like good weather,' I say.

'It's god weather,' Harper says. 'It's the best weather to see the god in.'

'What god?'

'She's just kidding around,' Nat says. 'Harper pretends she thinks something lives in the back of the cave. And when you call her, especially when the weather's rough—'

'She wakes up,' Harper hisses, eyes on the horizon. 'The woman in the sea. The god.'

I'm scared and I think about telling them to take me back, but I don't want to in front of Harper. Perhaps this is what they've been planning all along – befriending me to lure me here as a sacrifice. My palms slip and slide where I grip the side of the boat.

'Hey,' Nat says, gentle. 'Relax. It's just a trick of sound and light on the water. There's nothing really there.'

'Why take the knife if it's not real?'

'To be scared,' Harper says. 'Being scared is fun. But you have to make it feel real – to be properly afraid.' She puts her hand on mine. 'Don't worry. It's play-acting, I promise. But you have to *commit*.' Her hand squeezes mine urgently. 'We're going to find Rebecca.'

I can tell she wants me to ask, so I do. 'Who's Rebecca?'

Harper smiles. There's just a hint of slurring round her consonants. 'So, like, twelve years ago there was this young actress named Rebecca who was just about to have her big break. She was going to play an Olympic swimmer in some big Hollywood epic. She came up here for the summer to practise, tested herself every day, swimming further and further from shore.

'Rebecca was married to this perfect guy. Every day at dusk, her husband hung a light out for her at the end of the pier, a lantern with a blue bulb, to guide her home. She'd swim to the pier and he'd pull her out of the water, and rub her down in a big fluffy towel, take her inside to warm up and draw her a bath and give her a glass of wine and make dinner and they'd go to sleep.

'One day at dusk, he went down to the pier and hung the blue light. He drew her bath as usual and poured a glass of wine ready for her. He waited patiently. He waited and waited, but Rebecca didn't come. Night came, the stars came out, and she still didn't come.

'As for Rebecca, she swam towards the blue light, looking forward to her bath and her dinner and her warm towel and her warm husband. She felt happy, knowing she was near home. Her limbs had that nice heaviness that comes with tiredness, knowing that you'll rest soon. But the minutes passed and the light didn't seem to be getting any closer. The tiredness in her arms and legs was turning to heavy weight. But she swam on. She was starting to feel afraid.

'The night got dark. But somehow, she couldn't get any closer to home. The blue light stayed there, in the distance. Rebecca swam harder and harder, her breath coming in gasps. She tried not to think about all the big shapes moving far below her, how small her body was in the big black sea. She strained and swam towards that little pinpoint of blue. Still, it didn't come any closer. Rebecca felt the tears running down her face, into the cold sea around her.

'Now it was completely dark, except for the blue light shining in the distance. When she looked up, there were no stars, no moon. Solid black. And the sound of the water was different. It sort of lapped, and echoed.

'Rebecca saw that she wasn't in the open ocean anymore. There were stone walls on both sides of her and over her head. She was in a cave. And ahead was the blue light, reflecting on the shining black walls, on the water. She was crying really hard, now; her body was exhausted and she was afraid. She turned and swam again, swam for her life, into the dark, away from the blue glow. But her fingers met stone. There was no cave mouth. She was alone under the rock and the tide was rising. She knew she was going to die. The blue light pulsed and brightened, like it was enjoying itself. Finally, at last, it came nearer. She stopped swimming, but still the blue light approached. It wasn't one light, she saw now, but two. Eyes that shone in the dark like St Elmo's fire. It came closer and closer. She clawed again at the wall, looking for any opening that could save her. Under the water, she saw the body of the thing was vast, filling the cave like ink spreading in water. Rebecca was surrounded by the god. It tugged lightly at her limbs. Then it took her, drew her down and down and away for ever. It took her and they became part of each other – Rebecca and the god.

'She's strong, though. Even though she's dead, Rebecca never, ever stops trying to find her way back to shore, back to her life and her husband. But all that swimming makes her hungry. So if you feel something grab you by the leg, beneath the water, you'd better say your prayers. Rebecca's got you.'

A pleasurable shiver runs between my shoulder blades and down each vertebra.

'You feel it?' Harper's eyes are bright and fixed on me.

'Is any of that story true?' I ask Nat.

'People do drown out here,' Nat says. 'Like Christy Barham who owned the fishmonger. Everyone's pretty sad about that. And there was a woman called Rebecca who disappeared years ago. Or they say so. Maybe there wasn't and they've just got used to saying it. Harper made all the rest of that stuff up.'

'OK then,' I say. 'Let's go wake the god.'

'Are you afraid?' Harper whispers.

'Yes,' I say and she quivers with pleasure. I finger the wicked, long blade of the oyster knife. 'But if she's dangerous, we'll get her with this.' I fumble and almost drop the knife overboard.

'Careful,' Nat says, anxious. 'That was a birthday present. My dad still borrows it sometimes, he'll know if I lose it.'

We moor the boat to a tall rock like an obelisk. Beyond is a narrow channel lined with rock. The water swells are steep peaks and falls like a rollercoaster. At the end is a dark mouth in the cliff. A cave.

'My dad showed me this cave when I was little,' Nat says. 'It's kind of special.'

The water lashes white against the cave mouth.

'Is this safe?' I ask, with a strong return of my unease.

'We've come here loads of times,' Harper says. Her gaze is fixed on the opening to the cave.

'Not when it's been this rough,' Nat says, reluctant. Harper looks at him in surprise, and then with fury.

'You stay here then.' Before we can move or reply she's gone over the side, into the heaving flanks of the ocean. The thunder of the sea is so loud in the narrow channel, I don't even hear the splash.

'I think we have to go, now,' Nat says. He wriggles a broad elasticated band onto his head. It has a light fixed to the front. 'Don't forget the knife.'

'Wait—' But he's gone too. I'm alone in the boat.

I take a deep breath, grab the oyster knife and jump. The water seems colder, saltier than on that first day. It feels solid, like a hard hand slapping my face.

The temperature plummets as we come under the rocky ceiling, the quality of sound changes. Light plays all over the cave walls and roof. The cave narrows to a tunnel. We move into single file. Here the ocean breathes up and down; the swell throws us against the rough walls, leaving bloody scratches. I raise a hand – my fingers just graze the rough stone overhead.

The swell lifts us gently. The tide is high and rising. I try not to imagine our legs from below, kicking tiny in the black. The narrow tunnel opens up into an echoing space. We're inside the cliff now, I can feel the weight of rock above our heads. I can't see much until Nat's headlamp blinks on and he shines it around.

It's large, the cave, it goes back and back. It's loud, too, like being inside an engine. A big stone looms over the lashing water. The top of the rock is flat, just about big enough to stand on.

'Let's call her up!' Harper yells, her voice echoing and eerie.

'Yes!' Nat yells. His voice is filled with a strange energy. 'The cave is filling up,' he says, coming up beside me. His head flashlight is blinding. 'Right up to the roof. So let's make this quick.'

'Tell me what we're doing.'

Harper's face is just a gleam of wet cheek. She swims close. 'Some say she's that woman who drowned. Some say she's always been here. We call her Rebecca but who knows what her real name is? She tries to kiss you.' Her face is close to mine, now. 'If you let her kiss you, it's the last thing you'll ever do.' Her breath fills my ear, runs down the spaces of me. Despite the staleness that lingers, it lights my groin with fire. 'She wraps you in her arms and drags you down with her, into the cold depths of the sea. You drown, but in ecstasy.'

Here, now, in the cold dark cradle of the water, it feels real. I see what Harper means, now, about commitment to the story. I feel Rebecca below us, waiting.

Nat says, 'I think Wilder should call her.' I can't see his expression; his voice is friendly, but some feeling emanates from him.

'Why?' I ask.

'You don't want to?'

'I'll do it.' I don't want Harper to think I'm not committing.

'Get on up there, tiger,' she says. I hand her the knife and swim over to Nat.

He helps me up onto the rock with the flat top which sticks up out of the waves. 'I'll hold your arms,' he says, taking a wide stance. 'You lean forward and tell your secret.'

He takes my arms in a strong, solid grip. I lean forward slowly, testing. My breath comes shorter as my arms go taut, pinned behind me.

Harper's voice carries over the water. 'You have to tell a secret. The god only comes for those.'

'I don't have any secrets.'

'Everyone has secrets.'

She's right, of course. I could tell them the big one. The one I've been slowly realising, this past year, about myself. For a moment I'm exhilarated. *I'll do it*, I think.

I don't know how to say it, this new idea – that it might not be just girls that I like. But these are my friends, I'll find the words.

'Fine,' I say to Nat. 'Lower me down.' I lean out, perilous, over the water – like a ship's prow. I hear Nat grunt with the effort of holding me back. There are rocks down there, under the shining surface. Suddenly, I realise that I can't move. My arms are pinned behind me, my muscles and chest are burning.

I forget about the secret or anything but getting back up. The pressure on my lungs and ribcage becomes unbearable. I'm having trouble breathing. I gasp, 'Up, up!' Water laps at my face. I think, *he wants to suffocate me.*

'Pull him up, Nat, pull!' I hear Harper's voice as if I'm already underwater. 'This was a stupid trick.'

'I'm trying!' Nat yells and as he does his grip on my arms slips and the black water rushes up. It closes over my head, a sharp rock scrapes along my side. The sea presses on me, smothers me like at school, like the sweatshirt they pressed to my face to stop me yelling. Water dashes cold into my throat. I choke and cough, manage to turn my head and grab a breath.

Four hands scrabble at my slick flesh; Harper's grip is as strong as a monkey's, her fingernails dig into my arms. But I slip down through their hands and inhale more mouthfuls of cold salt. Harper and Nat scream at each other – *I can't pull him up! Let him go! The rocks!*

Someone grabs the back of my shorts and hauls me up away from the water, onto the narrow rock platform. There's not enough room for three here and Harper falls. Nat staggers, holding me; I cling to his wet flesh, breathing fast.

'Sorry, Wilder,' he says in my ear. 'Sorry.'

'You brought me here as a trick,' I say.

'Harper was meant to be waiting underwater for you,' Nat said. 'And then she'd burst up and kiss you. It was supposed to be funny. It was supposed to—'

'Don't be angry, Wilder!' Harper calls from somewhere below. I ignore her.

'I was yelling at you to pull me up, but you wouldn't, you made me stay down, I couldn't breathe—' I hear the sounds coming out of my mouth, I understand that they're words but I can't connect them to meaning. Fear and adrenaline course through me in strong, black pulses.

I shove Nat and we both fall into the black. The cold sea closes over my head. I break the surface to the sound of screaming; it echoes on the cave walls, seems to ricochet off the water. At first I can't tell where anything is – up or down, or where the screaming is coming from. Then I see the sun dancing on the waves, a narrow band of blue day at the end of the tunnel, and I strike out hard, heading for the light. I hear the others following behind. The rough roof is even closer over my head and I don't have any breath left for screaming, I'm breathing too fast, hyperventilating as I reach the bright blue. Harper and Nat are behind, calling to me, but I don't wait.

The rising water has narrowed the cave mouth to a slender crescent of light. We were nearly out of time. I dive below the surface and swim out – when I break up into the sun I just bob there, clinging to a barnacled rock, letting the day stroke my face.

My muscles seem to have dissolved into liquid. I can barely pull myself up and into the boat. Shock, I guess. Nat tries to help but I push him away.

'I couldn't hear you, Wilder,' Nat says. 'By the time I realised . . . I swear. I'm sorry.' He shivers, looks smaller than usual, hunched, hair plastered flat to his head.

I just shake my head.

We go back along the coast in silence, to the sound of the motor and the lapping of the sea. Harper touches my leg. 'It was only supposed to be a bit of fun,' she says. 'It went wrong.'

I can't look at her. It's like the day we spent together never happened.

I leap out at the mouth of Whistler Bay, not waiting for the boat to reach the shallows. 'Wilder,' Nat calls after me.

I swim hard for the warmer shallows. The sea now seems unfamiliar, a big spreading thing waiting to kill me. I can't wait to get to land. I think, *yes. There's something in these waters that eats people.*

It's fun to feel fear, Harper said. Is it more fun to make others feel it?

When I reach the shore and turn they're still there, watching from the boat. 'We nearly died back there,' I call. 'You realise that? How could you both be so stupid?' Then I yell, 'Frick you both.'

I turn and go up the path. Friends can break your heart, it seems, just like love.

In the next room, my mom and dad are hissing at one another again. It's been bad these last couple of days. The car starts in the middle of the night and my dad isn't here some mornings. I was so dumb to think that a vacation by the sea would fix things between them. I've heard Nat and Harper's voices at the door, too. I told my mom to say I wasn't home. I never want to see them again.

'Don't you dare,' my mother says furiously to my father. 'I'll deal with it.' The door to my room flies open. 'Come with me, Wilder.'

I groan and pull the covers over my head. The sheets and I have the same musty smell, as though I have fused with them in some way.

The darkness is whipped away and I lie in the blinding light. I cover my eyes.

My mother's hand is firm about my wrist. 'Come on, monkey,' she says. 'I've got you new swimming shorts.'

The wind and the day feel sharp, like my skin is being scraped off. I follow my mother's slim shape down to the water. The towels she carries flutter in the wind.

On the shore I shiver in the breeze. My new shorts are slightly too large, but bright blue with a pattern of anchors on it, like something you'd buy a kid.

My mother wades out of her depth, swims out a couple of strokes then turns. 'The water's fine, Wilder. Come on.'

'I don't want to.'

'Do as I say, please.' There's an unfamiliar steel in her voice. 'When did you last have a shower, monkey?'

The water slips over me. And it is nice – somehow comforting to be a small shape in the vast sheen – to be reminded of my smallness by the large world.

Mom ducks beneath the water and comes up red-faced and breathless. Her hair is a wet mop, her face bare of makeup. I rarely see her like this. She's always so neat, every hair in place. We bob.

'Your friends have been calling for you,' my mother says.

'They're not my friends,' I say.

'What happened, Wilder?'

'They played a trick on me. A prank. It was mean.' Some obscure residual loyalty prevents me from telling her what it was actually like – about the water covering my face, about gasping for air. I know they didn't really mean to hurt me. I know that. But they tricked me and it hurts so bad I could die.

'It's difficult, being sixteen,' my mother says. 'You don't know what's a big deal and what isn't. I remember.'

'It's a big deal to me,' I say curtly and turn to go ashore. I've done as she asked, haven't I?

'Stop a moment.' She sighs. 'Your father doesn't want me to tell you this. But I think I have to. I had a – thing – where I went to bed for a time. It started when I was about your age. I felt this great weight on my chest and I just couldn't get out of bed.'

'For how long?' I'm fascinated. My mother rarely talks about herself.

'Six years, on and off.' She takes a deep shuddering breath, as if feeling that weight on her chest again. 'It was like seeing the world from far away, through dark glass. There were five of us to support, you know, us kids. My parents didn't know what to do with me. That generation buttoned everything up. They'd never heard of depression.'

A darkness, a coldness seems to pass over me with her words. A shadow covering the sun.

'A doctor gave me pills to take,' she says. 'And they helped, eventually. Or maybe I just got used to it. I don't know which. I got out of bed and got that job at the high school, and of course I met your father. But I missed lots of summers like this.' Under the water, her hand finds mine. 'I don't want you to miss anything, Wilder. Ever. I want you to be happy. I think if I'd resisted it from the first, if I'd never let it start, I might have been able to fend it off. So, can you try? Can you try to be happy for me?'

'Yes,' I say, determined. I have never seen her cry before, it's awful. Her face is pink and shiny.

She hugs me, and I cling to her; her flesh is cold and slippery against mine in the water. *Like a corpse*, I think before I can stop the thought.

'I don't know if Nat and Harper will come over again,' I say. 'Maybe they won't.'

'They'll come,' she says, stroking my head with a cool hand. 'Kids are optimists.'

And Nat and Harper do come, just like my mom said they would. When I answer the door they look startled and unprepared. We all stare at the ground, awkward. We've all seen too deeply into one another; it's hard to come back up to the regular surface of things.

'Let's go to the beach,' I say.

It's better down by the sea; if we feel shy there's always something to kick at or pick up or look at. The sea lying in the background like it's watching over us or something. The afternoon is dying so we start to build a fire.

38

'It was a really dumb joke,' Nat says suddenly. He kicks at the sand and draws a semi-circle with his toe. He throws an armful of driftwood, white like bone, onto the pyre. The tide is going out, leaving a network of glassy pools in the dusk.

Harper says, 'It went too far.' Her eyes are red and I realise she's been crying. 'We just wanted to give you a little scare, just for a second. Then Nat couldn't get you back up.' She shivers. 'It was so scary.'

I am glad they're sorry. But it feels disappointing somehow. The glamour that surrounded them is cracked open. They're just kids like me, after all.

Nat says, 'The fire's ready.' He lights it carefully with a lighter and tinder of dried grass. It glows red and curls in hot filaments, then licks up flame. Beyond its warm circle the sea stretches out into the dark. I think about how big and old the world is compared to us. We're just little fires burning in the night.

'We'll never lie to you again,' Nat says. 'I swear. It was so dumb.'

'I swear too,' Harper says. Her hand slips into mine. 'We've decided,' she said, 'that you get two forfeits.'

'What do you mean?'

'At any time, you get to ask one of us to do something. And we have to. It's for ever, it doesn't expire. We could all be like, eighty, and we would still have to do it.'

'Anything?' I ask.

'Anything,' Nat says urgently.

'Ha,' I say. 'You don't know what torture I can devise.'

Harper laughs even though it's not a great joke. We watch the fire leap and crack.

'I know we made it all up,' Harper says. 'But I was afraid – in the cave. I kept seeing things – like pictures – like writing on the dark. I'm so sorry, Wilder. It was all my idea – I thought that you liked me.' She's bright red, now. 'I thought maybe you'd tell us that, as your secret. Then I'd come up from below and pretend to be Rebecca and kiss you. I thought it would be fun. No, I didn't think.'

'We're not very good at pranks,' Nat says. It seems funny to me, because it really was the worst practical joke, and I laugh a little, weakly.

'I want to tell you something.' Harper takes off her big wristwatch and hands it to me. 'I don't have a dog,' she says.

'Harper, I couldn't—'

'I'm not giving it to you, you idiot. Look on the back.'

The engraving on the back of the man's watch she wears says *Samuel*.

'Sam, my brother,' she says.

'Why would you pretend it was a dog?'

'I like talking about him,' Harper says. 'But it's kind of a bummer to keep talking about your dead brother. It's a way of talking about him and not talking about it, both at the same time.

'He was only a little older than I am now when it happened. He took a corner too fast on his motorbike. Maybe that's why I feel so weird this year. Soon I'll be older than he ever was. He only ate fries with mustard. He always knew when I was upset.'

I pat her awkwardly. I have to learn something better to do when women cry. It seems to be happening to me a lot lately.

'We don't have to go on about it,' Harper says, smoothing her hair. 'I just thought – after what we did, you know, in the cave – that you deserved the truth.' She sighs. 'You can bring dead people back sometimes, with witchcraft, you know. I tried to bring him back but it didn't work.' She sways, watching something we can't see. I realise she's drunk again. 'What was the secret you were going to tell, Wilder?'

'I didn't have one,' I lie. 'What about you Nat? Anything you want to share?'

'Uh,' Nat looks anxious, as if he doesn't want to disappoint. 'I don't know?'

'Natty,' Harper says, amused. 'The world's open book.'

'No,' he says, stung. 'I have stuff.'

'Like what?' I ask.

'It doesn't matter what,' he says after a pause, with some dignity.

We both look at him and smirk.

'What?' The annoyance on his honest, handsome face just makes it worse. One of the few things that irritates Nat is being laughed at. Harper giggles, which makes me laugh. By the end Harper and I are rolling around in the sand, coughing.

'Why is it funny?' Nat keeps saying. 'I don't get it.'

We don't stop for a long time.

It's the kind of laughter that only comes to kids, I think. Grownups are too used to the absurdity of the world.

The days that follow are golden and quiet. We go out in the boat again when we can, but we're careful. We don't go in any caves, and we avoid the open ocean, hug the coast with its sheltered coves. I can't stop thinking about Christy Barham who went missing while swimming near Castine.

I cut off the legs of a pair of my jeans to make denim shorts. As I get more tanned and haircuts become a distant memory, I enjoy how much like Nat I'm starting to look. I imagine that people might mistake us for brothers. I even start flattening my 'a's a little when I talk – before his look tells me that I'm not doing it right.

I think about my forfeits. I want to choose carefully. In the meantime, I'm trying to come up with something we can all do together that's a little dangerous, a little out there. I feel like it'll make us all equal again.

I have my big idea as I'm helping my dad clean out the tool shed behind the cottage, and I come across cans of spray paint. They're old

41

and rusty and I wonder if they work. But when I depress the nozzle a jet of bright green shoots out, making a rough circle on my bare leg. I blink in surprise, and then it comes to me.

'Can you get the boat tonight?' I ask Nat. We're roasting marshmallows on the coals of our dying fire. I have to go up the cliff path for dinner with my parents, soon. But I'm hoping this is just the beginning of the night.

'Yes,' he says. 'My dad's been on the water all day, he'll be sleeping. As long as we're back by sunrise? That's five-thirty, for you folks from away.'

'I can come too,' Harper says. 'I'll pretend to go to bed early.'

'Oh,' I say, 'you're assuming you're invited?'

She punches me absentmindedly, then pulls her warm marshmallow out into a long string of goo. Before I realise what's happening she has placed it gently on my head, where it clings stickily to my hair.

The porthole swings open silently, letting in the warm night air and the song of the rocks below. I slip out into it.

'Let's go south some,' I say. The spray paint rolls around in the cooler where I've stashed it. 'Where's a place with a big seawall cliff, where lots of boat traffic passes?'

'Penobscot Point, I guess,' says Nat. 'What are we doing?'

'You'll see.'

The point is a sleeping tiger against the night. The cliff wall rears beside us. It's fairly smooth, perfect for my purposes.

I stand up in the boat, wavering with the bobbing of the water. I don't want to risk a flashlight. Trusting to instinct, I take out the can of green paint.

'Wilder,' Harper's voice. 'What are you doing?'

I spray my message on the cliff in the dark. I can only hope it will be legible. I write in capital letters, swaying with the movement of the boat.

A swell tosses me off my feet and I fall into Harper's lap with a yell. From the clifftop above, there's a spurt of yellow – a light coming on. Nat guns the outboard engine and we speed off as a man yells indeterminate things, a flashlight raking the dark waters around us.

'What did you do?' Nat says, when we slow up out of sight. 'What did you write, Wilder?'

'I wrote "THE DAGGER MAN WAS HERE".'

'What?' Nat says on an indrawn breath. 'What did you do that for? Ah, shit.' Nat rarely swears.

'It's from the story,' I say, surprised at his intensity. 'The one you made up about the Dagger Man. Like the thing in the cave.'

'That story's not made up,' says Harper quietly. 'It's real. Wilder, you shouldn't have done that.' The dark reveals a lot. It's harder to hide things in your voice. Harper's afraid. Not the kind of shivery dramatic fear she likes, but the quiet, real kind.

I feel uneasy for a moment, but I quash it quickly. 'It's just some graffiti, right?' But I wish I'd known it was real. That he's real.

There's a picture of my wavering graffiti on the cliff wall in the paper the next day. The fishing boats saw the message at first light. I have brought the Dagger Man back from the dead. Harper brings the paper over to show me. She climbs high into the maple above me as we talk. She always needs to be doing something. It's not so weird, I tell myself. But I can't help the feeling she's like a lookout up there, scouting for danger.

43

I stare at the headline.

'Don't be scared, Wilder,' Harper says from above. 'I mean, it was pretty stupid of you. But people will forget about it eventually.'

'I'm not scared,' I say, absentminded. I can't stop staring at the picture. And it's true, I don't feel afraid, just kind of numb.

If I'd paid attention to the local paper my father got delivered every day, I would have known that the Dagger Man was real. If I'd listened to the conversations in the general store in Castine instead of zoning out and thinking about stories, or maybe Harper's skin, maybe I would have heard talk about the happenings last summer. Maybe if I hadn't been so desperate to move on from what had happened in the cave, and had asked Nat and Harper questions, I would have understood what was truth and what was fiction. I'd assumed it was one of their made-up stories, like Rebecca.

'Maybe let's do normal things for a while,' Harper says. 'Daylight things – things regular teenagers do.'

'No problem. I never, ever want to do anything like that again,' I say. I feel slightly sick, like I've eaten something bad.

'Hi, Mr Harlow!' The leaves shudder as Harper waves energetically at my dad who's at the open kitchen window. He waves back. Despite my misgivings about letting them meet her, my parents like Harper. It took me a while to understand that they think she's my girlfriend. I let them; it makes me feel good. They don't know Nat so well, especially as he doesn't like to come inside. He's shy of parents, I think. I've never met his dad, Mr Pelletier.

I decide to journal today; no more wasted time on pranks and sneaking out at night. I'll write, read a great book, get my dad to take me out in the car, do some practice on these quiet roads, get ready for my test in the fall. Normal things like Harper said.

I pull on clothes. My mom's outside hanging laundry on the line. She just shakes her head when I ask where Dad is. Her mouth is a narrow line around the clothes peg. When I look down the hill I see the car is gone.

I go to kick my brain into action with caffeine. As I'm hunting for the coffee I see there's something propped against the window, behind the little aloe vera plant Mom keeps there. I pull it out. It's a Polaroid – a fuzzy image taken in bad light, but it's clearly the view from the window of the cottage, out to sea. There's the cliff, with the sugar maple in the background. There's a shining path of light across the ocean. The sky is dim, perhaps a storm's coming. There's also a long pale shape across the bottom – a finger, I think.

It sets off a weird train of thought in my head. How many people around here own a Polaroid camera? Harper's voice is in my head. *Daggerman.*

'Vernon loved that thing,' Dad says gently, and I jump. I didn't hear him come in. 'We used to go on walks together, find stuff to shoot.' He sees my face. 'You OK?'

'Yeah, it just made me think about the thing with the – with the kids.'

'Don't worry, sport. All that Dagger Man stuff happened last summer. It's over now. Just some drifter who's moved on. Neighbourhood kids playing around, maybe.'

That afternoon I try to read in my room. Instead I think about Harper. A sharp, deafening tattoo breaks into these thoughts. It's hammering, coming from the side of the house.

When I go out to investigate I find my father putting restrictors on all the windows, so they don't open more than a couple of inches. He reinforces the door to the cottage with mortice locks. 'Finally getting around to it,' he says to me cheerfully. 'Just so your mother doesn't fret. Better safe than sorry.' The local paper lies beside him, open at the picture of my handiwork on the cliff. I suddenly realise how distinctive my handwriting is – even when I'm spray painting in the dark. My 'M's have soft curves at the top instead of sharp triangle points. Dad follows my gaze; his eyes rest gently mildly on the picture, and then on me.

'Hooligans,' he says in a resigned voice. 'Don't think any more about it, Wilder.' He takes up the drill and the last screw goes home. He tests the window, makes sure it only swings open a hand's breadth.

'We're all safe and sound now,' he says and picks up the drill. He wanders on to the living-room window. 'Nothing in or out,' he says through a mouthful of screws.

I watch him pick up the drill, humming some old French song. Serge Gainsbourg maybe. He likes all that stuff.

My mom brings out the big box of Uncle Vernon's Polaroids from under the stairs. I'm bored so I sit with her and look through. Maybe I'm not bored. I wouldn't admit it but I want to sit near my mom for a little bit.

'You've grown three feet just this summer,' she says. 'Oof, and I can hardly get my arm around these broad shoulders!'

'Come on, Mom.' But I'm surprised to find, sitting next to her, that she has a point. Either I'm taller or she's got smaller. I hope it's the first one.

Uncle Vernon's photos are really pretty bad. There are so many of them, too. The still lifes are even worse than the landscapes.

'What do you think this is?' Mom holds up something pink, striated with lines of light.

I tip my head to one side. 'It's a hand over the lens. Fingers, anyway.'

A bag full of groceries, a blurry foot striding along a sidewalk, a tabletop with nothing on it labelled 'my pen' in shaky ballpoint. There's a stifled sound from beside me. My mom has a hand over her mouth.

'Mom?' She makes that little smothered woof again. Then she takes her hand away and releases a short shriek of laughter.

'It's *art*, Mom,' I tell her as she lets out those little barks. 'Have some respect.'

She screams and slaps me weakly.

'What's up, folks?' My dad beams from the doorway.

'Oh not much,' Mom says, wiping her eyes. 'Wilder was telling me a joke.'

She knows Dad wouldn't like us making fun of Uncle Vernon. Taking the piss, as Harper would say.

But in the following days I catch her sometimes with a gleaming look on her face. Once at the dinner table she snorts mashed potato in the middle of some conversation. She meets my eye and I know she's thinking about Uncle Vernon's 'art'.

Unbelievably, August is here – and then it's halfway done. The summer is coming to an end.

It's the hottest day of the year so far, deep in the dog days. My father and I take refuge from the heat under the maple. The leaves shush gently in the breeze above our heads. One or two leaves are turning already, taking on a deep, burnt orange hue.

My father has the *New York Times* over his face, his breathing regular. I fidget. It's only an hour until I meet Nat and Harper on the pine bluff. The time I spend away from them has begun to seem vague and unreal. My last days here have become unbearably precious.

The cottage goes on the market in the fall and I'll never come here again. Some other family will come and live here. Some other teen-ager will watch the stars through the porthole, listening to the sound of the stones singing in the bay below. Where will Uncle Vernon's pictures go? I somehow can't imagine that we'll take them back to the city. They'll probably get thrown out. For some reason this both-ers me intensely. The new kid will probably be really cool, maybe have his own car. Nat and Harper will like him more than me.

The newspaper moves gently with my dad's breath. *If he died*, I think, *would I inherit the cottage?* Or Mom would, maybe. I'm nearly seventeen; they couldn't make me go back to school.

I start. My father is sitting up, watching me. How long has he been awake? 'Summer's nearly over. You keeping up with your summer reading? Fall semester will be here before you know it.'

'Yeah, I'm on top of it.' I'm not. The thought of Scottsboro turns in my gut like a knife. Sometimes I feel like I'm not in love with Harper, but with Harper and Nat as a pair. This thought makes me feel uneasy and excited in equal parts. Other times I wonder if you can be in love with a place, just like with a person – this stretch of coast, the bright long days here where you can lose yourself. It's private, this part of the world. Like each cove or copse is a secret.

'You know, the rental market's not bad in these parts,' my father says.

'Good for the rental market, I guess?' I'm furious that he can be so casual when my heart is breaking.

'You've really come out of your shell here, Wilder. This life seems good for you.'

'It is.' I wait, heart beating. You can't hurry my father. Ever. I've tried.

'It's a little nest egg, too. Uncle Vernon got quite the return on it. So what we're thinking is,' he places his large, hot hand on my shoul-der for a moment, 'we could keep it. Not sell it. We could come out here every July. Rent it out the rest of the time. What do you say?'

My heart's pounding. So I just hug him quick and hard.

I skid down the path to the sea to tell my friends.

It feels like no more than two heartbeats before my last day arrives. We spend it by the water as usual. Afterwards Nat starts to build a fire on the beach but I say, 'I'm over bonfires on the beach.' I want a fire, really, but I can't stand it, that this is the last one.

Harper and Nat both look at me and I see they understand. That makes it worse in a way. 'Ugh, so boring,' I say, turning away. Then, staring at the ground, 'Sorry.'

Harper's hand is cool on my sunburned shoulder. 'Let's go up to the meadow?'

'Yeah,' Nat says, 'I'm bored of the beach too.' I love them both so much.

It's cool and green as we go under the trees; sunlight and shadow chase across our faces.

The meadow looks beautiful. Black-eyed Susans peer from the long grass, which stirs in the late afternoon breeze. The air is full of butter-flies, birds sing in the nearby copse of beech. *Cuckoo, goldfinch*, I say to myself, thinking of the first day we came here. I didn't know the names of these birds or flowers then.

One thing's the same though. I hate it here, no matter how pretty it is. Every time I sit a little voice in my head goes, *no, not there*. I don't want to say anything – it's better not to go to our favourite places today. Better put the sad memory here, in a place I don't like.

Harper sits on a log and produces a bottle of Havana Club

from her bag. Her parents don't keep tabs on their liquor cabinet. They really should. As I drink she watches me with a combination of interest and amusement. 'What is it with you and this spot, Wilder?'

'I don't know,' I say, shifting on my feet and swatting at the midges that swarm above the grass. Is the itching I feel from them, or coming from inside me? 'I feel like someone died here or something.'

'Someone died almost everywhere,' says Nat, practical.

'I've thought of my forfeit,' I say. 'But I don't know if it's possible.'

'We have to do it,' Nat says. 'That's the rule.'

'Well, this one's for Harper, because you live here.'

Harper raises her head and looks at me. Her red hair is bright, the colour of flame, her skin pale, and for a second it seems like a different person is looking out from inside her. 'Go on,' she says.

'You have to promise to come here every summer, even when we're grown up. All three of us have to get together.'

'Sure,' says Nat, eagerly. 'Sure.'

'How can I promise that?' Harper asks, exasperated.

'I don't know. But you swore. So you have to.'

'Do the thing,' Nat says.

'But . . .' She sighs. 'OK. Maybe. If that's what you really want, Wilder. You both have to do exactly as I say. But first I need some stuff. Give me a couple minutes.'

We trade tiny sputtering sips as we wait for Harper. We're talking loudly about dirt bikes so we don't hear her soft approach through the meadow.

'Do you know what this is?' We jump. She holds a plant, uprooted, shedding loose soil. It's twisted, looks like a withered white carrot, maybe, or a ginger root. Harper grips the stem through a handkerchief, because she doesn't want to get dirty, I assume.

We shake our heads.

'Hemlock. Don't touch it, not even a little. We're going to put it in the spell, to make the promise last to death and beyond.'

I shiver. 'Is that really – cool, Harper?'

She just shakes her head as though she's too busy for me and scans the land. She goes to a place a little ways away where the earth dips, forming a natural bowl.

Nat puts a warm hand on my back. 'She'll be OK,' he says quietly. 'She gets like this sometimes.'

Harper fetches stones and lines the dip in the ground, making a fire pit. She builds a cone of dry twigs and sticks. Then she puts the hemlock at the heart of it, handkerchief and all. 'Blood,' she says, without turning around. 'We need blood. From all three.'

We both step forward and give her our hands. I can't even see what she holds that does it, but there's a feeling like a click and a moment later our fingers drip crimson.

'Don't waste it,' she says, impatient. 'Put it on the fire.' So we all hold our dripping hands over the wood and kindling and watch it become spattered with red.

Harper puts a match to the fire which crackles up right away. It's been a dry summer. She pushes us upwind of the smoke. 'Don't go near it,' she says. 'The hemlock's burning. I don't know if it's danger-ous to breathe it in.'

'Maybe don't burn it if you don't know stuff like that?' I say, nervous.

'Oh be quiet, Wilder.' She smiles and I blink. For a second it looks like she has too many teeth. 'We have to stay here until the fire dies,' she says. 'So that the spell works.'

'Also to make sure we don't set the woods on fire,' Nat says. He becomes more and more comfortable the weirder things get, I've noticed.

'I'll put something in the spell that will help you with school,

Wilder,' Harper says. 'It'll stop anyone bothering you.' She hugs me. It's unexpected. Usually she shies from touch like a cat. Except Nat's.

'I'll miss you,' I say. 'Can you put something in to help you get sent back home, away from school?'

She shakes her head. 'That's the one thing about magic,' she says. 'You can't do it for yourself. Only for other people.'

'Where do you get these rules?' Nat passes her the Havana Club.

'I just know them.' She looks sad and drinks. When she passes the bottle to me it's got a lot more air at the top. Harper wants to believe in something so badly. In Rebecca, the cave, in magic. Whatever is available. I really love her right now, and also kind of want to shake her, yell at her. But I don't do any of these things. She takes my hand and squeezes it.

The little bonfire gives off heavy plumes of smoke. It billows like thick liquid on the still evening air. Some of the wood must be damp. I hope it smoulders on for a long time. I don't really believe that Harper can stop what happens at Scottsboro. I don't think we'll always come back here every summer. So I want to make it last – the fire, this moment.

Pearl

Pearl's first memory of her mother is her voice raised in the wind, calling. They were on a mountaintop, Pearl doesn't know where. She was little, her legs hurt, her ears hurt because the wind was strong. She was crying, stranded on a crag a way away from her. She didn't know how to get down and go to her mother.

Her mother strode across the rocks, leapt over gaps like a deer. When she got to Pearl she bent and put both hands over her daughter's ears, warming them. 'Hold on,' she said.

Pearl wrapped her arms around her mama's neck and her mother picked her up and folded her inside her jacket. Then she put her down and led her down the mountain. It seemed to take hours. 'You're OK, you're cool,' she bent and said into her daughter's ear. 'You're as cool as a long drink of water.' And Pearl giggled and felt better. It always calmed her down, this saying of her mother's.

Maybe it wasn't a mountain. It was probably a hill. It probably took a minute or two, not hours. But every time Pearl thinks of her mother, she remembers being saved.

She's named after her mother's favourite jewel. She has never felt equal to it – has never felt valuable, since her mother went.

You can't get to know people after they're gone. All you have are memories, moments, and that doesn't make a whole person.

Pearl was five. It was a bright, gleaming morning. They were staying in Castine up the coast, and they came down to the sea each day with a picnic. They already had a favourite spot, a little cove where the rocks made this weird sound when the wind blew in from the sea. Pearl's daddy would explore the rock pools with her, swim, make sandcastles.

While they did this Pearl's mother swam out for forty-five minutes or so. There was a cove by a sea cave where she stopped, got out and stretched, and then went back in for the return. She did it every day. By the time she got back, they had set out lunch on the blanket. Afterwards they would get in the car and go home, feeling sea-dazed and lovely.

Nothing about that day was different, at first. They drove along the green roads to the sea. Mama put a hand to her ear and said, 'Oh, dammit, I've lost one of my earrings.'

'It'll be back at the bed and breakfast,' Pearl's daddy said. 'We'll find it later.'

They parked, climbed the hill and descended the path on the other side. Mama was strong and tall in her black bathing suit and swimming cap; she seemed made for the sea, like some kind of dolphin or fish. They had chosen this beach specially because it had soft sand for Pearl to play in, not like most of the rocky ones around here.

'See you at lunch.' Pearl's mother strode into the water, struck out and soon was just a black skull, bobbing in the waves.

Daddy paddled with Pearl, then got hot and retired to the shade of the cliffs. He napped briefly with a hat over his head. She explored the farther pools, making sand angels in the wet slurry by the water-line. Mama would be back soon, and they would have lunch.

Pearl wanted her sandwich. Daddy woke and started dressing the salad, humming. Crushed garlic, a spoonful of mustard, lemon juice, white vinegar, olive oil. Mama was very particular about her salad dressing. Daddy made it fresh just before eating, every day.

Pearl fell down in the damp sand once more and scrambled her arms and legs. Suddenly there was a searing agony on her breast-bone, like fire, the worst pain she'd ever felt. She thought she was dying. Her scream came from very far away. She was paralysed with pain.

Cheek in the damp sand, chest on fire, she watched Daddy's feet racing closer, sending up sprays of sand. He picked her up and the pulsing pain got worse. If she looked down, she could just see a red welt on her chest, above the line of her bathing suit.

He scooped cold handfuls of sea water over the red mark, then carried Pearl over to the picnic cooler and poured white vinegar over it. The tide of pain receded, and he hugged her carefully and rocked her. Pearl cried even harder then. The comfort was worse than the pain somehow.

'It was just a jellyfish,' he said. A dead one buried in the sand, probably. 'Don't worry kiddo, it's over now.'

But it was only just beginning.

They waited but Mama was late, so Daddy let Pearl eat her sand-wich. Something round and hard was in her mouth. She spat it out and excavated it gently from the bread, peanut butter and jelly. It was a single earring. It must have fallen in somehow while Mama was making the sandwiches.

Mama didn't come back. The red welt on Pearl's chest healed and every day it did was another day she was gone. Daddy kept up hope, but Pearl knew it wasn't a jellyfish she had felt there in the sand. It had been her death. She was only five but Pearl knew. Rebecca had drowned, swum too far out, and left them.

Sometimes her mother talks to Pearl in the night. She learns to keep herself awake, so she can hear her. It always happens the same way, Rebecca's coming. It starts with the sound of the wind, roaring in Pearl's head, just like that day on the mountain. And then Rebecca's warm hands close over her cold ears. Then she hears her voice muffled by her hands. Pearl loves her touch but she always wishes she would take her hands away so she could hear her mother clearly. But Mama never does. She only ever says one thing.

Stay cool, sweetheart. Cool as a drink of water.

Pearl keeps the lost earring in her locket. One day the other one will show up, she knows that too, just like she knows it won't be a good day when it does.

[ ]

Heat
Hat
What

Here
Where

Ham
Am

Hit
Hi
Is
I

The Dagger Man of Whistler Bay

From the unpublished memoir by Wilder Harlow
June, 1990

I get to Whistler Bay first – I take the train to Portland then a bus to Castine and a cab out to the cottage. My parents are coming tomorrow but since they had some adult stuff to do in the city we agreed I could come straight here and spend the night alone. I'm nearly eighteen, after all. Totally an adult.

I haul my bag up the hill. I haven't brought much. All I need are shorts and t-shirts, flip flops, sneakers. Swim shorts. Harper arrives next week. Nat's coming to the cottage tonight. I wrote to him weeks ago via the Castine post office, the way he told me to, and let him know I was coming. I don't have his address. When I passed through Castine earlier I found his reply waiting, just as he promised I would, written in careful, childlike cursive: OK. *I'll bring dinner.*

I think of all the things we'll do. I'm glad Nat and I get to catch up before we see Harper. It'll give me a chance to test the ground. I'm kind of nervous about whether the agreement we made still holds. Isn't a year enough to change everything? Because I'm determined to get a girlfriend this summer, and part of me hopes against hope that it could be Harper.

And if the agreement does hold, it will give us a chance to get tight again, me and Nat, before she comes. So I won't be tempted to break our pact.

I hope this logic is sound. It's all so confusing.

There's a figure ahead on the path, silhouetted against the sky. A tall man. He crests the hill and stops, leans against the white garden gate. I wonder who this guy is and what he wants – my heart sinks at the prospect of having to deal with some kind of adult business, when all I want to do is dump my bags and be ready for when Nat comes to get me. I'll tell him to come back tomorrow after my parents get here.

The man turns around in the warm sunset. He holds up a hand in greeting. He's even more handsome than I'd remembered. It's Nat.

We hug briefly and then stand back, examining one another. 'You're, like, a foot taller,' is all I can say.

He smiles. 'You too, Wilder,' he says politely.

Until this moment I'd been so proud of the three and a quarter inches I've shot up this year.

Nat pokes me. 'Go on,' he says, impatient. 'Dump your stuff and come down to the water. I've got beer.' His cheekbones seem even more pronounced beneath the stubble.

I drop my bag in the kitchen. I lean against the wall and breathe, without turning on the lights. Through the kitchen window the sunset is a greenish line on the horizon over the ocean. I know Nat's waiting for me out by the gate – I can almost feel his impatience through the walls. Still, I take time to go into every room of the cottage. For some reason it feels important that I fill the house with my presence, my breath, make it mine again. It's like magic, the kind of thing Harper would do. I wonder how much she's changed, this past year.

The house seems to breathe back at me, a long, slow breath of relief.

I slip into swimming shorts, grab a sweater and go out into the dusk. I'm home.

On the way down to the sea Nat stops. 'Wait,' he says. 'Follow me.' He leaves the path, wincing at the sharp rocks on his bare feet.

The long grass of the meadow is pale in the moonlight. A shimmering fractured moon shines from the sea below. I still don't like it here.

'Come on,' I say. 'What's the hold-up?'

'I got to get something.' Nat shines a flashlight on a tumble of stone by a small escarpment. He reaches a careful hand into a dark crevice and withdraws a six-pack of beer. 'My hiding place,' he says. 'I leave stuff here sometimes. You can help yourself when you want,' he adds. 'Just don't drink it all, OK? I have to pay that dumb Sonny at the auto shop five bucks each time he buys it for me. Or catch him lobster.'

On the beach we build a fire and Nat pokes the potatoes under the greying coals with a stick. He's proud of making the dinner himself, of doing something to welcome me home.

We're still being a little cautious with one another, he and I, getting used to it all again. Because it's the same as last summer, but different too, like looking at two exposures of a photograph.

'You look older,' he says, echoing my thought. 'When I saw you coming up the hill in that blazer, those Oxfords.' He smiles at me, tentative. 'I didn't recognise you. And you looked at me like I was a stranger. Time to eat.' He takes the oyster knife from his belt and plunges it into the blackened carcass of the potato. Steam shoots up into the night sky. 'Potatoes make everything OK,' he says, appreciatively.

The potatoes are too hot so we hack them apart with the knife, stabbing at the flesh with the forks I brought from the cottage. Nat takes a small aluminium parcel from the cooler and unfolds it carefully. A small pale pat of butter. He handles it carefully, divides it between the potatoes with precision. I feel a start of guilt. I could have bought butter in Castine or Bar Harbour, any of the towns I passed through on my way here, we could have bathed the potatoes in it until they dripped gold. But he wanted to do this for us. I'm not always smart about people but I have enough sense not to try to help.

Nat finishes his potato and starts to eat the skin so I do the same. It tastes charred and chewy.

I look up and my flesh walks on my bones. A girl stands at the edge of the firelight, pale as a lily, her eyes two pits of shadow.

'I thought we were meeting at the point,' she says to Nat. 'I been waiting an hour.'

'I forgot.' Nat's shoulders hunch with guilt or maybe resentment. He holds out the remains of his baked potato on its bed of blackened tinfoil. 'You hungry?'

She takes it from him and sits, starts to eat with long delicate fingers. 'Who's this?'

Nat says, 'Wilder. Wilder, this is Betty.'

'Hi,' I say.

Betty looks at me for a moment before turning her attention back to the potato skin. 'Let's go,' she says to Nat when it's finished.

'Hey,' Nat says. 'Wilder just got here.'

She wipes the back of her hand across her mouth then licks it. Her lips still have a buttery sheen. 'Let's go.'

Nat turns to me and shrugs as if to say, *what can you do?*

'You go ahead,' I say. 'Good to see you, man.'

'I'll come by tomorrow,' he says.

Nat and Betty walk away into the dark. She puts an arm around his waist. As they go I see her lift his t-shirt and trace the small of his back with an index finger. I flush and look away.

I pick up the bottles, our trash, then I fill Nat's cooler with seawater and pour it over the remains of the fire. Steam hisses, the stink of charred wet wood sits heavy on the clean night air. I go up to the cottage and dry the cooler, put it by the door, so I can remember to give it back to Nat tomorrow. I change into pyjamas, brush my teeth and use that facewash that's meant to prevent zits. I sit up in bed with *The Heart is a Lonely Hunter* open in front of me. I don't take in a word of it. After a while I turn off the lamp and lie in the dark, the sound of the sea coming in with the moonlight. But I don't sleep. Ever since Betty appeared out of the dark on the beach, my heart's been beating so big and splashy that I can hear it in my ears. Nat has a girlfriend now. He's not in love with Harper anymore.

Faintly, from down in the bay comes a long, narrow high note – and then another. The stones begin to sing. The wind must have changed.

The next day my parents arrive shortly after 10 a.m. They come in quietly and seem surprised to find me awake and reading in the kitchen, the cottage neat and orderly.

'We were afraid you'd have some buddies round,' my father says. 'Have a party.'

I shrug. 'I just saw Nat. We went for a swim.'

'You're a responsible kid, Wilder,' my mom says. Maybe it's my imagination but I think she sounds a little disappointed.

*

A week later I sit in a low crook of the maple, facing out to sea, trying to get into Carson McCullers. I keep a pencil behind my ear but don't make any notes. I read the same sentence a hundred times, it feels like.

Suddenly everything goes dark. There are hands over my eyes, cool fingers stroke my eyelids. My heart hammers. I go very still, which is sometimes how I deal with danger.

'This is how you die,' a voice breathes in my ear. Something narrow slides across my throat. I know it's my pencil, I felt it slide out from behind my ear, but still my breath hitches, my throat goes dry.

I grasp a narrow wrist. I feel a thick metal watchband on it. The hands are small, I can tell that now. I stick my tongue way out and by straining, I just manage to lick the heel of one of her hands where it sits on my cheek.

Harper leaps away. 'Gross,' she says. 'Ugh.' Then she grabs my book and licks it, drags her tongue all the way down the page I'm reading, watching me as she does it. 'Now we're even.' The page is divided by a wet trail, as if a slug has crawled across it.

'Welcome back, Harper,' I say.

'Thanks.' She tosses my pencil over the cliff.

'I need that,' I say.

'No you don't. You're bored of reading. You want to come swimming with me.'

Unlike Nat and me, Harper doesn't seem to have changed at all. She looks the same – that wide gaze, that impossible almost blood-red hair. She doesn't look older or taller. Maybe she really is a fairy. Love fills me as I look at her. She's not a fairy. She's just herself.

I prop *The Heart is a Lonely Hunter* open with stones so it can dry out in the sun and we go down to the beach.

First we go up to the meadow that makes me afraid of death, to get a beer from Nat's secret stash in the rock. When I put my hand in it's warm and damp like a large mouth. I wait for the jaws to close on my arm, take it off. I can almost hear the crunch of bone, feel the hot gout of blood springing from my shoulder.

There are four bottles in the hole. I offer one to Harper, but she shakes her head.

'Not for me.'

She seems different. Her eyes are clear.

We wade in, bob pleasantly in the water. I'm so happy to see her, I can't keep my eyes off her face.

'How's the new school?' I ask.

'It sucked. I'm not going back. I missed a lot of class this year.'

'Are you—'

'Yup,' she says. 'It's Fairview for me.'

'I thought that was just a joke,' I say.

'In typical fashion, that joke has become my life.' I'm ready to be upset for her, but she smiles. 'It's OK, Wilder.'

'You do seem – OK.'

'Yes. I missed school because I went to – well, a place for troubled young ladies who self-medicate. A very expensive place, of course. I don't want to talk about it, Wilder. It worked, that's all.'

'OK,' I say. 'Do you miss it? Is it hard – not to?'

'Drink? Actually, it's a relief. I mean, it's boring, but it's much less stressful. I have coping mechanisms. They teach you those.'

'Like what?'

'Hobbies,' she says, suddenly shy. 'They encourage us to develop interests – knitting, basket-weaving.'

I'm trying to stop my smile but it just breaks through all the same. 'What?'

'I'm imagining them trying to make you like knitting.'

'I know!' She laughs. 'I told them I already had a hobby – witch-craft. It's really interesting, you know. More like psychology than anything else.' She strokes the water with gentle fingers. 'I miss him less when I'm with you. My brother. Samuel.'

'Good.' I want her to be OK, so badly.

'I guess you remind me of him.'

And suddenly I'm not enjoying myself anymore. I swallow to rid my mouth of the sudden sour taste.

'Let's get Natty out tonight,' Harper says, flicking the water with her fingertips. 'I haven't seen him yet. He must be busy with his dad. He usually finds a way to say hi on the day I arrive.' She nibbles a nail. 'I got here yesterday; he's slipping.'

'Yeah, he does seem busy.' I'm not sure whether to mention his girlfriend. I think *no, don't*, because it feels like a violation of the agreement, I'm not sure why, and then the moment's gone, I've waited too long and missed it. 'Come by tonight,' I say. 'We'll sit out, the three of us, catch up.'

Harper turns her eyes on me now, gives me once again that intense focus. I had forgotten what this feels like, the completeness of her attention – it's almost narcotic. 'How are you doing, Wilder?'

'I'm OK,' I say, surprised to find that I mean it. 'It was . . . an OK year.' And it was. Solitary. Lonely, even. But quiet. I studied, read, wrote. The guys who made last year so terrible seemed to forget about me this year.

'Yeah, I know,' Harper says. 'You owe me. Big time.'

'Oh, really?'

'I did magic to stop them bullying you, Wilder.'

'Well, thank you.' I cup my hands and throw water at her head.

She dodges it, effortless. 'Nice try.'

'You want to see me really try?' I launch myself at her.

I wish Harper would cool it with the magic stuff – it makes me uneasy. It's like a tiny clinging remnant of old Harper, who's so desperate to feel, who drinks in the mornings, who makes Nat play tricks on me in a dark cave that nearly kill us all.

Nat comes by shortly after she leaves. 'How's Harper?' They keep missing one another; it's like one of those old British farces – in one door and out the other. Also, it occurs to me, I haven't mentioned she was here – how does he know? Has he been watching us?

'You haven't seen her yet?'

He shakes his head.

I have the feeling of life being just a little out of sync. It's disquieting but also somehow exciting – in the past Nat and Harper were the core of our friendship, a unit, an indivisible pair. Now they seem severed, adrift. Everything is reorienting – with me at the centre.

'Come by tonight,' I tell him. 'Then we'll all be here together.'

My parents are going out to dinner so Nat, Harper and I will hang out at the cottage. I get soda out of the refrigerator, load a cooler with cans to show them that's what we're going to drink. And we will, I tell myself, or at least Harper will, so it's only two-thirds a lie.

My dad is wearing his dumb cufflinks made of Coke-bottle caps, with a safety pin glued to the back. Uncle Vernon made them for him as some kind of joke when they were little.

'Dad, do you have to wear those? They are *so* embarrassing.' I'm anxious that maybe my friends will see them.

'I think they're cool,' he says, striking a pose.

I am almost in an agony of dread. 'Just *go*,' I say. I walk out with them to the gate.

'Hey.' Nat melts out of the dusk. I feel again that quick moment of unfamiliarity. Who is this tall man? Nat looks like he's been running. His shirt is half unbuttoned, a fine sheen of sweat covers him, though the night isn't that warm.

'Hey,' I say. 'Mom, Dad, you remember Nat.'

'Sure,' my dad says, holding out a friendly hand to shake. Last year Nat was a kid, now he's a guy my dad shakes hands with.

Nat just stands there, looking confused. He stares at my dad's hand like he's never seen a hand before. Then I see that he's staring at the cufflinks. I was right, he's horrified; they're so dorky.

'Nat,' I say, and he starts.

'What?' he asks. 'Wilder?' Then he shakes himself like a dog and takes my dad's hand. 'Good to see you again, sir.'

Harper comes up the path. My mom gives her a hug and Harper goes pink. Her eyes stay on Nat the whole time.

'Have fun, you kids,' my mom says, breathless. She pushes an imaginary strand of hair behind her ear even though there's no wind. She's excited about dinner.

'You too!' I say, 'You *crazy* kids.'

They go down the path. We hear the car start and drive away.

'Hello, Natty,' Harper says.

Nat ignores her, frowning – and I see with surprise that he's shaking the tiniest bit. Harper sits down with a thump and puts a hand to her cheek like it's warm.

'Did you get sunburn today?' I ask her. She doesn't look burned but it's getting dark so I can't be sure.

She shakes her head. 'You OK, Natty?'

'Sure.' Nat flicks the nails of his thumb and index finger together. I've learned that this means he's lying about something.

Nat takes a beer out of each pocket and offers one to Harper.

'No,' says Harper with an edge in her voice. 'Natty. I wrote you. I don't do that anymore.'

'Come on.' There's something strange in his voice. 'Wilder's having one.' Though I haven't said I will.

'No,' she says. 'Stop it.'

Nat hands the beer to me but I shake my head. I don't want to make things harder for Harper.

'Fine,' he says, tips his head back and drinks it all. Then he raises the second one and drinks that too. His brown throat moves as he swallows. He wipes his mouth. 'Spin the bottle?'

I look at him. 'I thought—'

'What, Wilder?'

I can tell he knows I'm about to mention the pale girl. So I don't. 'No spin the bottle for me,' I say. 'You have to take me out for dinner before we get to the hot stuff.'

He looks at me, sullen. 'You took all my beer, Wilder. I had to get more at the gas station. You're not supposed to clean me out.'

'I didn't,' I say, startled. 'I took one this afternoon, that's all.'

'Don't be mean, Nat,' says Harper.

'Aww, you guys can eat it,' Nat says.

'What's that mean?' I ask.

'Yeah, what?' Harper says. 'Did you mean to say suck it, Natty? Or maybe suck it up?'

He says, confused, 'Eat it. That's an expression.'

'No,' I say.

'No,' says Harper.

'Shut up,' Nat says, but he's smiling.

And it feels like things will get easier from hereon in, but then Harper screams. A pale shape hovers behind the gate, tall and slender as a candle flame.

'What are you doing here?' Nat says, annoyed. 'Don't follow me around.'

'I was bored,' Betty says, walking into the light.

'Hi,' Harper says.

Betty looks at her but says nothing. She just stands there. Nat gets up abruptly.

'See you guys tomorrow.'

Their footsteps fade down the path. 'What is up with him?' I ask. 'He was being *seriously* weird.'

Harper shrugs. 'Get the backgammon board,' she says. 'This'll be nice – the two of us.'

My heart jumps painful and hard inside my chest.

Harper stays for two games then she says she's tired. I walk her as far as the point. She is quiet as we go but I feel her, like always, as a warm sun at my side. I think about what it would be like to take her hand, to touch her in some way, but it seems impossible. She's wrapped in her own isolation. When we come in sight of her house she stops.

'I'm OK from here.'

'But I should take you all the way . . .' I don't want to leave her; I want to find some little thing to hook into her attention so she notices me.

'The less parents know, the better,' she says. 'Mine aren't very trusting. Maybe,' she adds in a spurt of honesty, 'I haven't given them much reason to be.'

I can't help feeling she's just taking the first opportunity she can to be alone. To get out of my company.

I walk back along the cliff, under the moon, flashlight off. It's been a strange evening and I'm filled with a frustrated energy. I almost wish for an accident; I want some kind of damage done to something or someone, even if it's myself.

Whistler Cottage rears out of the dark. My parents' car is still gone. As I turn the corner, I see that light is pouring from the living-room window, glowing red through the drapes. Someone is in my house.

Dagger Man, I think. I shake myself, that's dumb. But someone's in my house, someone who shouldn't be.

I go quietly down the side of the cottage and get the rake that leans against the wall. Holding my breath, I open the door and slip across the dark kitchen. Someone is sitting on the couch; I can just see the top of a dark head. I raise the rake. It's the heavy kind with teeth.

The head starts to turn and I get a really good backswing going. I ready myself for the blow, for blood.

My mom screams. Her pale face is startled. 'My god, Wilder!' she says. 'What are you doing?'

And I swing wide so the rake hits the couch harmlessly. But I am almost crying with panic at how close I came to hitting her over the head with the vicious metal jaws.

'Why are you sitting in the dark?' I ask.

'I was waiting for your dad,' she says.

After I've put the rake back outside I find her in the kitchen.

'Let me make you some tea,' I say. 'I know that raspberry-leaf stuff you like.' We take cups into the living room.

'I wondered where you'd gone,' she says. 'All the lights were off.'

'I walked Harper home. Where's Dad?'

'He had a little indigestion. I think it was the lobster roll. He always orders it, even though he knows what it does to his insides. He dropped me off, went to find a pharmacy.'

'An open one? Around here?'

'The guy in Castine lives above the store. Apparently he opens up if he's in a good mood, and you ask nicely.' She smiles; I can tell she's tired.

As a guy you're not supposed to think about stuff like when your mom has her time of the month and so on, but it's not like I can ignore it; she gets quiet and pale and lies down a lot.

My sleep is filled with uneasy visions and the scent of stale beer.

Both my parents are still asleep when I get up.

The day is already warm though it's barely eight. I eat a pop tart as I head down the hill. I'm going towards the woods for a change. It's nice to be alone. In the city and at school I feel lonely, even though in those places I'm always surrounded by people. But here, being on my own just seems right.

On the road below the house I see there's something white – either paper or plastic, I can't tell, lying in the middle of it. Litter dropped by someone, or blown here on the wind. I feel a sense of outrage. This is my place, people don't get to leave their trash lying around. I hurry down to get it.

The breeze lifts a corner, flips it. The thing tumbles down the road a couple of feet. I hurry to pick it up. As I draw closer I see what it actually is. The fluttering square is a photograph, a Polaroid, face down. My mom's been looking at Uncle Vernon's 'art' again, I guess – one must have blown away.

I pick it up, looking forward to seeing which of Uncle Vernon's bad attempts at photography has made a bid for freedom. The one of the pine tree where the tree is at a drunken slant? The one of the sea where a big thumb obscures the left-hand corner of the photo? The one with a figure standing in complete darkness, except for one bright point like a star? Mom and I think this is a self-portrait taken in the mirror, but the flash got confused by its own reflection, and didn't go off.

But it isn't any of those.

The face is white, washed out by the flash, as pale as if they're lying on a mortuary slab. Boy or girl, it's hard to tell. They're curled up with a fist under their chin; a tendril of hair, blond or brown, lies on their cheek. The curve of their small ear is perfect.

The sheets have a pattern of teddy bears. The pyjamas are yellow with rockets on them which might suggest it's a boy – or not. Girls like rockets too. There's no comforter thrown over the small frame, which sends a lance of fear through me. I think this is recent. It's been way too warm for covers at night for the past week.

And I guess he doesn't put the knife at their throats, not always. In this picture, the long, shining blade is by that small pink ear, perpendicular. It almost rests against the lobe, just by the place where the ear joins the skull. A slight movement, a quick twitch and it would be off. I imagine the ear coming free like a pinch of pink cotton candy pulled from the stick.

Maybe it's an old picture, I tell myself. Maybe it's been lying in a ditch or caught in a tree for months and the wind just blew it into the road yesterday.

But the Polaroid isn't old. Its shiny surface is pristine, the image sharp and unfaded. The white strip at the bottom is unblemished. I knew that was a vain hope.

I drop the photo quickly. But I can still feel the touch of it on me. Thinking quickly, I get a small rock and weigh it down. The edge still moves slightly in the stiff breeze, but the rock stays firm.

I run up the hill towards the cottage, yelling for my dad, my mom, and just 'help, help!'

They run down towards me, faces white.

'A picture,' I say, breathless. 'A Dagger Man picture. It was lying there in the road. He must have been here!'

My mother's mouth sets in a grim line. 'If this is a joke, Wilder—' she says. But her tone is frightened.

'Are you sure, sport?' my dad says.

'Please hurry,' I say, agonised. 'Please.'

'I have to respect my knees on a downhill, Wilder,' Dad says, reproving. 'You know that.'

As we near the bottom, I see the little white square, still held fast under the stone. I run the rest of the way.

I get that unpleasant feeling in my fingertips as I turn the Polaroid over, slowly. Behind me I hear my mom's indrawn breath.

Teddy bears, rockets, shining blade.

Dad comes with me to the little police station at Castine. 'But I just found it on the road,' I say over and over. My fingerprints are on it, of course, so they have to take those for elimination. They ask my dad if he touched the picture. He tries to remember.

'Did I?' he keeps asking me, bewildered. 'Did I touch it, Wilder?'

I can't remember if he did or not. My memories of everything that has happened since are static, single scenes. A stack of bright still moments with no narrative. Like a stack of Polaroids.

They take my dad's prints too, for elimination.

I'd thought it might be exciting, being at a police station and involved in a real crime, but after the first surge of novelty it's not. It's long drawn out and boring and scary all at the same time. Throughout the questions and the taking of the report and the fingerprinting all I can think about is that kid in the picture. There are three or maybe four cops in the station, two old guys, a woman. I can't keep their names straight in my head.

'Is it the Abbott girl?' I hear one of them ask. 'The younger one. The Abbotts who took the Salter place this summer?'

'Looks right.'

'Ayuh,' the older man says.

The woman's notebook sits open the whole time, and every so

often she writes something in it very, very quickly. It can't be more than a word or two. It never seems to be in response to anything particularly significant that we or they say. Maybe she's making a grocery list. I guess cops have lives just like anyone. They must get their milk from the store in town, like everyone else. Watch TV at night, kiss their families. Normal stuff.

But I see the woman officer biting her lip. Her eyes are miles deep. Nothing's quite normal, or will be ever again. Not for us, because we've seen the Abbott girl sleeping. We've seen those long lashes, the teddy-bear sheets, the fist curled so trustingly under the chin. He has made us see through his eyes, and we can never forget it. To this day, I can't.

As we leave I glimpse the page the woman cop was writing on in her notebook. Over and over the page is scrawled with *stay calm stay calm stay calm.*

I just want my mom to hug me now, and I'm not even embarrassed about it. I've had enough of adult stuff – even the adults have, it seems.

The next day the woman cop is on the dirt road behind the cottage. She places yellow markers gravely at certain points. A photographer comes. Someone else in a white hazmat suit. They don't find anything good, though. I can tell by the forlorn slump of their shoulders. My parents and I watch from the window. The place doesn't feel like ours anymore.

The cop picks up an object with gloved hands, produces a plastic Ziploc bag and drops it in. It looks like a cigarette butt. Reality and imagination blur and shiver. Did *he* drop it? I feel crazy, because I imagined the Dagger Man smoking, in exactly that spot, and it makes me feel responsible, like somehow I've created him or am controlling him or something.

'I'm going down there,' I say.

'What do you mean?' my father asks. His beard is particularly wild today, a good indicator that he's upset. 'Just let the authorities do their job, Wilder. No need to interfere. We've done our part.'

'I'm just—' I look around wildly for inspiration. 'I bet she could use a cup of coffee.'

I carry the steaming coffee delicately down the hill to where she stands, lips pursed in a thoughtful pout. Her face is broad, her eyes too, black like buttons. She looks like one of those old-fashioned dolls knitted from wool.

'Hm?' she says, thoughtful, taking the mug of coffee from me. Then she starts. 'Oh. Hi again. Thanks. You put sugar in it?'

'No.'

'Good.' She drinks the coffee in two swallows. It must be very hot but she doesn't show it, just wipes her mouth with the back of her hand and hands me back the coffee cup.

'Do you think you can catch him?' I ask.

'How do we know it's a him?'

I shrug. 'I think it's a him.'

She sighs. 'Me too.' I still can't recall her name so I look at her name tag which reads *Trooper Harden*. I do it covertly, but her bright button eyes follow my gaze.

'Yes, I've heard all the jokes,' she says. 'You can just call me Trooper.'

'Um, OK.' Right away I can't stop imagining some of the jokes and I feel myself going pink.

'You're freaking out,' she says with certainty. 'I get it.'

'Please can you tell me the truth,' I say. 'I need to know. Would he get a long sentence, if they caught him? I'd freak out less if I had some facts. No one will tell me anything.'

'You're a kid,' she says. 'Don't need to be worrying about this stuff.'

'I'm seventeen.' I take a deep breath. 'I could be tried as an adult, for example.'

She looks at me with her black round eyes. 'So you could,' she says. 'OK then. Facts. They're thin on the ground, right now. But OK. Breaking and entering is a Class B crime – if we can prove it. Then we've got him for taking a picture of a kid which is – what? Child endangerment, sure. Violation of privacy? Probably. And there's the knife. He might get eighteen months. When really, he should be put away forever.

'So even if we figure out who's doing this – maybe nothing much even happens. But we have to try anyway. We *are* trying. Can't wait until he does something worse. Because he will. In the end. That factual enough for you?' She takes a card out of her pocket and hands it to me.

'You gave us one of those last night,' I tell her. 'A card.'

'And I'm giving you another one now. Put one by the telephone, keep one on you. You call us if you see anything else. I mean, anything.'

'Do you think he'll come back here? Like, retrace his steps trying to find it?'

'Maybe. But we'll keep an eye on you. Get a patrol car to swing by in the evenings. You're not his usual type, thank goodness. Good you don't have kids in the house.' She thumps her heart with a clenched fist. 'Oof. I drank that coffee too fast. Couldn't sleep last night, so I was keen for the caffeine. Anyhow, I'm parked up the road a ways.'

I watch her go, feeling strangely bereft.

He must have dropped the Polaroid in the night or early morning, not too long before I found it. That picture wasn't in the road yesterday evening.

Will he come back for it?

That night I lie in bed listening to the sea, the crickets, some night bird calling in the dark. At length I hear it, faint, the sound of a car approaching in the lane below. This is unusual; the road is really quiet. *It's the patrol car*, I think, *they're checking up on us.* I imagine Trooper Harden's serious face behind the wheel, her button eyes scanning the woods for dark figures. Even the memory of her makes me feel safer. I think about getting up and going to the kitchen window, which overlooks the road, to watch her pass. But I don't.

Because what if it's not Trooper Harden. What if it's him?

'Watch your step,' someone says and I blink, startled out of my thoughts. I'm walking tightrope along a groyne that's sunk into the tarry shingle of the oily beach that skirts Castine like a dirty fingernail.

My mom is running errands in town and I've come down to the shorefront. There's not a lot to do here. It's a place for work – rusting hulks stand up on hurdles, yards of net festoon the pontoons. It smells like gasoline and bloody fish. It's not like Rehoboth or Coney Island, not built for fun.

'Watch yourself,' the voice says again, more urgent, but I've already lost my balance. My foot sinks into a pile of slimy seaweed. The ground has a spongy swollen texture and I sink further and further. I yell; all the memories of old black-and-white movies and Sherlock Holmes books run through my mind like tickertape, all those stories I ever heard about quicksand. Struggling makes me sink deeper, and I fall forward. My hands sink into the soft, stinking stuff; I can't help thinking of it as rotten fruit. I'm gasping; each panicked breath seems to send me deeper, deeper; it clings and sucks at me.

A firm hand grasps my shoulder and hauls.

'You OK?' It's the fisherman with the blue eyes who picks up Kleenex. 'Got a little stuck there?'

I smile, embarrassed.

'Come aboard and have a soda,' he says.

His boat bobs off the little jetty.

The boat smells like gasoline but also like carbolic soap. It's very clean. My mom would approve. 'It's like a house,' I say. It reminds me of Whistler Cottage – so neat, everything in its place. I imagine living here, never coming to shore again, just living surrounded by peaceful blue, no people, no worries. No school.

'A floating house,' he agrees, pleased.

Two metal canisters sit on the countertop in the tiny galley. One says *tee*, the other *cofee*. He gets the soda from the cooler. The bottles are still frosted. He lifts the caps from them with a *pop*. The precision of his gentle brown fingers is wonderful to watch.

'Wilder,' I say. 'Sorry, I should have said before.'

'And I'm Mr Pelletier, I guess, but only the bank calls me that. Alton, or Al, to my friends.' He sees my face. 'You know my son. You're a friend of Nathaniel's.'

'Yes,' I say. 'Sorry, I didn't realise.'

'He's not proud of me,' Mr Pelletier says. 'Well, children should want to be more than their parents. It's only right.'

I don't have anything to say to that. To cover the silence I take a deep swig of soda. I cough and it streams out my nose.

'Can I keep the bottle caps?' I ask when I can breathe again. They make me think of my dad and those dorky cufflinks. Maybe I could make my dad another pair; his have gone missing.

'Sure,' he says. 'Why?'

'It's kind of hard to explain, but it's a present for my dad.'

'That's good,' he says, approving. 'Love in a family. That's good.'

The bottle caps make little cold nuggets in my palm.

'You want to see the shark rig?'

I do.

The shark rig is a hydraulic pulley, the line gleams with wicked hooks. I shiver as I look at it.

'I know,' he says. 'Cruel-looking thing. Honestly, I'm losing my stomach for shark fishing, these days. They've got smart eyes, sharks. Last time I got a whitetip I put him back. I could see his pain. Now, bluefin. That's a different story. They're some sons of bitches. I'll drag a bluefin along on the line for as long as I need, no regrets.'

I laugh. He shows me lobster pots, and the tooth he keeps around his neck from a great white. 'Nathaniel gave me this,' he says. 'He's a good boy. Didn't catch it, found it on the beach. But you won't tell him I told you that.' His thumb strokes the tooth. 'He's a real good boy. He's growing up. Not home so much, these days.' He brightens. 'I've got some squashed-fly biscuits,' he says. 'Made with real flies. I get you one.' But I see the flash of sadness on his face. There are certain unmistakeable expressions, no matter how quick they pass. Nat's father is lonely. I think about how my father doesn't seem to want to be around us at all and what a waste it is.

The squashed-fly biscuits are buttery, falling apart at the touch. The 'flies' are plump raisins. 'I'm the baker since my wife left,' Mr Pelletier says. 'This is my gram's recipe. Someone should keep making it, I thought. Can't let a good thing go to waste.'

'When did Nat's mom leave?' Then I quickly say, 'Sorry.'

'It's all right.' Mr Pelletier crumbles another biscuit between his fine fingers. 'Seventeen years ago, now that's a long time, isn't it? Arlene had just birthed Nathaniel. What kind of woman leaves her newborn child? "I'm not coming back," she told me, and I said, "Fine. Let me keep the baby. Raise him right."' He stops. 'She'd fallen back into some bad habits – things she swore she'd quit, when we married. So I let her go and Nathaniel stayed with me, and we've been just fine, us two, ever since.' Again that look crosses his face. 'I just wish he spent more time at home.

I look at my watch. 'Shoot,' I say through a mouthful of crumbs. 'Sorry, Mr Pelletier. I have to go.'

But when I get back to Main Street my mom's car is gone.

I ride in the flatbed of the truck which is great and Mr Pelletier drops me at the foot of the hill.

My mom is drinking raspberry-leaf tea on the couch when I come in. 'Where the hell were you, Wilder? I waited an hour in town.'

'Sorry,' I say. 'I met a friend.'

'You never do that to me again, you hear? I was worried sick. *Sick*. You ungrateful boy.' Her voice drops from a yell to a whisper and she leans back on the couch, pale.

'Are you OK, Mom?'

'Yes,' she says. 'I made sandwiches for lunch but there aren't any left. There's cereal if you're hungry. No milk though, your dad's gone out to get some.'

'Of course he has,' I say.

I grab a handful of dry cereal. I kind of like it like this anyway. And I'm full of squashed-fly biscuits.

'Don't eat it like that,' my mother says, annoyed. 'And don't use that tone about your father. Have some respect.'

'Fine,' I yell. I slam the door on my way out.

I stomp along the cliff path. The wind cuts in sharp, it's cold and miserable. Everything is just fricking *crappy*.

Ahead of me is a hiker dressed in neon yellow. The wind is against them, they don't hear me. I can tell, just from the relaxed set of their back, a glimpse of their profile as they turn to look out to sea, that they think they're alone.

I could run at them, I think. *Catch them off guard. I could push them off the cliff - watch as they bounce off the crags, become a little limp yellow figure, and then vanish into the roaring surf at the bottom. Fricking yuh!*

I can't tell if it's a man or a woman yet. I speed up, close the distance between us, my sneakered feet quiet on the rocks. *If it's a woman,* I think, *I'll let her live. If it's a guy—*

The hiker turns seawards again. This time a ponytail comes out of the collar of her jacket, and flies free in the wind.

Ha, she lives.

I'm on the section of path that winds along below the meadow, I can tell, because I get the bad feeling. Ugh. I really hate that place. But I'll put up with it; I want a beer from Nat's hidey-hole. He keeps accusing me of stealing them - so I may as well do it.

I hear something like a hoot in the meadow above. As I move through the trees I see a shape in the long grass ahead that doesn't make sense. It looks like a monster. Limbs, eyes. I squint and come closer. I use the same quiet feet I used for sneaking up on the hiker.

It writhes. Those breathy sounds come from it. Hoot, hoot. So this is why I get a bad feeling here. I knew, somehow, that something terrible would happen in the meadow.

I stare, but my mind will only take in isolated detail. Hair red as an alarm, the ragged hem of denim cutoffs. His hand on her back, brown on white. Her shirt has fallen off her shoulder.

Nat's eyes meet mine over her shoulder. They are unfocused and then sharp. Her back is to me, she doesn't see. Nat and I look at one another for a moment and then I turn away and go down the hill. Nat has broken our deal.

I climb the maple tree and stare out to sea. The sea doesn't care about stuff like love, does it. The sea doesn't even know about promises, so it can't break them.

I don't hear my mother calling me for supper. I start and yell as she tugs on my sneaker toe. My father is not home again. We eat macaroni and cheese from a box. I can't finish it, even though it's my favourite.

I know what Harper would say if she knew about the agreement Nat and I made. I know she'd hate it. Would she hate it enough to stop whatever is happening between them? I could find out. And I know he's still seeing Betty. I can ruin it all with a word.

I have the power now, I tell myself. But it doesn't feel like that.

I lie awake with the porthole window cracked open as wide as the restrictors will allow. The Dagger Man can't get in that way – I'm starting to suspect he doesn't need to.

The boat engine idles, the sea beckons. We're going out to one of the little rocky islands. Harper wants to watch the seals.

Nat's shorts only have so much life left in them; they're frayed almost halfway up his thigh. I swallow as I remember the long grass tickling them, the hooting sounds.

'No,' I say. 'Let's not go to the island. I want to go to the god again.'

'What?'

'I have a secret to tell.'

'Wilder—' says Harper, annoyed. She really wants to see the seals.

'It's my forfeit,' I say. 'I'm calling it in.'

'We have to, Harper,' Nat says.

The boat speeds out of the bay.

'You OK, Nat?' Harper asks.

'Sure.' But he's lying, doing that thing where he flicks the nails of his thumb and forefinger together. A tic, you might call it.

'What's going on?' Harper asks me. I raise my eyebrows and cup a hand at my ear, like the engine's too loud even though we usually yell over it. Harper sits back, watching me with narrowed eyes.

The boat bounces on the waves like they're solid matter, the sun grows hot. The growing day refuses to reflect my mood, is set to be burning bright.

The tide is halfway in, the cave entrance visible, like lips politely parted. We swim into the dark. I hold the long shining blade of the oyster knife carefully. Behind, the half-moon of daylight beckons. It would be so easy to turn around, swim back out into the warm air, the light.

'Come on, slowpokes,' I call. 'Hurry up.' Cold salt washes into my mouth and I cough.

In the big chamber water trickles down the cave walls, shining. It's quiet in here today, still as looking glass.

'Hold me up,' I say to Nat. 'I've got something to say to the water. A secret.'

'Please, Wilder,' he says. 'Please don't.'

'My forfeit, remember?'

He climbs up behind me and takes my arms.

Nat lowers me, down, down until I'm almost kissing the water. I welcome the pain in my arms, my back. I feel like crying.

I take a deep breath. I'll ruin it for him. For both of them. They deserve it.

'I think my father is the Dagger Man,' I hear myself say. It's not the secret I intended to tell; this bursts out of me instead. I'm so tired and worn out.

Harper says, 'What?'

Nat gasps and staggers. One of my arms slips through his hands, slick as wet rubber and then he only has me by one hand. We both swing perilously over the sea. Then Nat's grip slips, he drops me and I fall headlong.

Beneath me, below the surface of the water, something swirls and comes hurtling towards me, breaks the shining skin and screams into my face. The sound ricochets around the cave, high and ear-splitting. I see her arm reach out.

Someone's hitting me in the face and stars explode behind my eyes. *Stop*, I try to say, *stop*, and push her away but she keeps coming. Nat is yelling, he tries to put himself between us. I flail backwards in the water, and suddenly there's the smell of tin. I'm no longer holding the knife – where is it? Somewhere Nat is moaning, a bad sound that echoes off the water, the stone walls.

We get Nat out of the cave somehow. The light is blinding, a blow to our eyes. There's a trail of crimson in the water behind us, leading back into the dark. It looks like red cloth rippling beneath the surface.

'Sharks?' Harper whispers.

I don't want to think about that.

'How bad is it?' I ask.

Nat groans and lifts his hand. The knife has gone right through it, silver as a beam of light.

I climb into the boat and Harper pushes him while I pull. We try not to jog the knife where it protrudes but we're scared and clumsy. Nat is openly crying now which is hard to take. Eventually we're all in and I start the motor. Nat has gone extremely pale. Dark red gouts of blood continue to pulse from the wound. The knife is in the heel of his hand, almost, and I suddenly think of wrists and veins – how close is the knife to these things?

'Tie a tourniquet round his wrist,' I say to Harper. 'Try and stop the bleeding.' I'm just repeating words I've seen on TV shows, it's the only guide I have.

Harper rips off the bottom of her t shirt, and Nat groans and tries to push her away. She ties it tightly, and the bleeding slows some. But maybe that's bad too? Maybe the hand will go dead? I don't know what to do.

'Where do we go?' I yell at Harper. 'Where's the nearest hospital, or phone, or whatever?'

'I don't know!' Her voice is so high it's almost inhuman. 'Just follow the mainland back towards Castine and stop at the first house we see!'

I don't know how to drive a boat so our progress is slow and stuttering. It's incredible how little attention we paid to the houses on the trip out here. It hadn't seemed important. Now the empty shore passes in endless, agonising minutes. I have the brief conviction that everyone in the world is gone and we're the last three left, that we'll go on and on forever, Nat crying, Harper holding him and whispering, 'I'm sorry, Natty, I'm so sorry.' Then she whispers, 'I love you.' He doesn't reply. I see he has passed out. She cradles him carefully, trying to protect his wound from the jolting of the sea. Still the coast crawls by.

Eventually there's a distant glare ahead on the shore, a couple hundred feet inland maybe. As we approach, I see that it's a big, modern house made mostly of glass. A long boardwalk leads up to it, fenced with white. I pull the *Siren* into the pebble beach, leap out. Running up the beach is like running in a nightmare; time and again I sink, ankle deep in the sand. I think of Rebecca, swimming forever towards the blue light. But eventually I reach the walkway. The boards are good under my feet. I go full pelt but still it seems to take forever, the world dipping and swaying as if I'm still on the waves.

A startled couple are pouring their first cocktails of the day when I burst onto their pool deck, wet and bloody and wild-eyed, as if I've just been born from the sea.

Harper and I wait while they work on Nat. The urgent care centre at Castine is a small building, mostly used for getting things out of toddler's ears and tetanus shots. But Nat needs blood, there's no time to take him on to Belfast or anywhere else.

We curl up on some hard, plastic orange chairs. Occasionally someone goes out for coffee or the receptionist goes to the parking lot to have a cigarette and the doors wheeze open and closed like bad lungs.

'Why do you think your dad is the Dagger Man?' Harper asks. Her eyes are wide in her pale face.

'Little things,' I say. 'But when it's all put together it feels like – a lot. I found something. It was a picture of the Abbott kid, a Polaroid.'

'Where?' she asks sharply.

'Right by our house, on the road. There's no one else for miles – why would anyone be out there? My dad came out here every summer without us, to visit Uncle Vernon,' I say. 'So he was here at the right times. Plus, he disappears at night. There's always some excuse – he's looking for a pharmacy, or we've run out of milk, but it's a big fricking coincidence.' I clear my throat. Weird how even now this is embarrassing. 'Plus things with the Dagger Man happen at a certain time of the month. Like, my mom's time of the month. I don't know . . .'

'Serial killers operate on lunar cycles sometimes,' Harper says. 'I read that.'

'He's not a serial killer.' It's awful hearing it out loud. 'But Uncle Vernon liked to take Polaroids. Maybe they did it together, Dad and Uncle Vernon. Maybe he killed Uncle Vernon.' I put my head in my hands. 'Oh god, maybe he is a serial killer. There's something bad going on, Harper.'

'Do you really think it's him?' There's an odd note in her voice. It sounds like – but surely cannot be – relief. But she's scared too. I've spent a lot of time pretending not to be afraid – at home, at school, so I recognise when people are doing it.

'I don't know. I'm freaking out.'

'Do you think Nat will be OK?' she whispers into my shoulder.

'Of course he will.' But I don't know. His skin was the wrong colour when the ambulance arrived. By the time they carried him in here it was like there was no one in his body anymore.

The glass doors wheeze open. Outside, the sun is throwing low pale light across the parking lot. *Dawn*, I think, then realise, *no, sunset*. It doesn't seem possible, but it's still the same day.

'Hey, you two,' Trooper Harden says. She's holding a coffee taller than her head. 'Rough day? You stay here a moment. I'm going to need to talk to you for the report. Then I'll get you back to your parents.' She goes through the swinging doors to the ward, whistling something.

'We have to tell her,' Harper says. 'About your dad.'

I start to talk but she puts a finger over my mouth. 'Stop,' she says. 'This is a very important moment. Whatever you're going to say – think about it before you speak. Those words will be there forever, you won't be able to forget them. So make sure they're not something you'll regret.'

It's like she can see right into me. I had been about to say, *you can't tell anyone.* But that would be wrong. I've seen the little pink ear, the fist curled under the chin, teddy bear sheets. Whatever my dad is, he's dangerous. I can't let it go on.

I take a deep breath. 'OK. You're right. I'll tell her.' Panic rises. 'I mean, I don't have any proof or anything but—'

The doors to the ward swing open and Trooper Harden comes out. She's different. Her eyes are flinted and sharp. They don't even look round anymore, but have narrowed to wicked points.

I start to get up to talk to her. It's now or never. I know that if I think about it I'll find a reason not to.

Trooper Harden points at me with a sharp finger. Everything about her is suddenly sharp. 'You sit right back down,' she says. 'Neither of you moves a muscle until I say.'

I sit down. She mutters into her radio, watching us the whole time with those sharp eyes.

'What's happening?' I whisper to Harper. 'Do I still talk to her about my dad?'

'No, Wilder,' she says. 'You don't need to.' Her face is twisted with feeling.

It's the oyster knife stuck through Nat's hand that does it. Trooper Harden recognises it from the Polaroids. The picture I found in the road, of the Abbott girl – it doesn't show the handle. The Polaroids of other kids were never released by the police, but in them, the knife is clearly visible. The handle is distinctive; it was hand-carved by Nat's father, Alton Pelletier, from local walnut.

There is one, single microscopic millimetre of hair caught in the knife between the handle and the blade. It's the Abbott girl's hair. It must have been trapped there somehow when he snuck into her room. They think maybe the Dagger Man cuts some off while they're sleeping.

We have been using the Dagger Man's knife to shuck oysters and pry the lids off cans.

The police search the Pelletier property down by the sea. What they find there makes everyone forget about the Dagger Man, because it's worse, much worse than anyone could have imagined. The world breaks apart and we are shattered, all three. I don't think I've truly been whole since.

It was never the tide which was dangerous to swimmers around here.

In the Pelletier place, there is a cellar. The walls of that cellar are lined with carpet, which is stained rich and dark with old blood. Buried in the corner in a cigar box, the police find treasure. A driver's license bearing the name Christy Barham, wrapped in a tissue, stiff with tears. A plastic tortoiseshell barrette. A keyring with the word *Daytona* on it. A wallet-sized picture of a young woman with purple hair. A single pearl earring which is identified as having once belonged to a woman who went missing, presumed drowned, ten years ago. Her name was Rebecca Boone. All these objects are rusted or speckled with blood. Alton Pelletier's fingerprints are all over them.

They find cord from the shark rig, miles and miles of line, spikes with shining wicked hooks. They find Alton's aluminium fish box, six feet long and two wide. Alton made it himself. It seals tight with metal clips. There are traces of human blood inside.

The fish box was how the women were removed from the house after the end. That's how the police think it happened, anyway. No one will ever really know. It must have been a relief to them – the end.

Sometimes I wonder about that time when I drank soda with him – was the fish box on board that day? Was it empty? Was it full?

Alton Pelletier is arrested.

Both Nat and Alton's fingerprints are on the oyster knife. They both used it at times. *For what?* My mind repeats over and over. *For what?* Nat's voice repeats in my ear at night – *snare it in the shark rig, then pull it along beside the boat for a time, until it's ready to do whatever you want.*

Harper and I spend the next day on the narrow bench in the police station, as they interview us – together, separately, and then separately again. The small rooms are hot with late summer. We want to go home but we can't. We tell them, over and over, about our cave, and why we went there, everything we ever saw Alton Pelletier say or do, everything Nat ever said or did. I am so tired the world seems to ripple before my eyes.

As I look up a ghost is passing. But it's Betty, her pale face stained with tears. When next I look up, Harper is gone from my side.

I stagger out into the blinding light of the street, looking around wildly. 'Getting some air,' I say vaguely when someone tries to stop me.

Harper and Betty are standing very close together on the sidewalk. 'What did you tell them?' I see that Harper is holding Betty's little finger in what looks like affection. But the tip of the finger is turning purple.

'What did you tell them?' Harper says again.

'I told them the truth,' Betty says. 'Where to look – behind the skirting board in the living room. Now let me go or I'll hook your eyes out of your skull.'

Harper breathes fast, her face mottled red. She releases Betty's finger. 'Nat told me you were a snoop,' she says. 'He told me you saw his dad hiding that stuff. Don't lie about it. You know it wasn't Nat's.'

Betty looks at her. 'Yeah,' she says slowly. 'That's why he chose you. You still believe his lies. I can't anymore. You take care now.' Betty goes, holding her sore finger gently.

'She's the liar,' Harper says. Her eyes follow Betty down Main Street. 'Oh god.' Her mouth opens wider and wider into a rictus, an upside-down laugh. Tears gleam on her face. 'We've only had a few months together,' she whispers. 'Me and Nat. This can't be how it ends.'

I put an arm around her tentatively.

'Don't touch me, Wilder,' Harper says, savage. 'I never want anyone to touch me again.' Then she bends and vomits neatly into a sewer grate.

In the living room at the Pelletier house, in a hollow behind the skirting board, they find different items. A small sneaker, a brown apple core gnawed at by milk teeth. A ring made of candy, a t-shirt with Road Runner on it, still stained with egg from long-ago break-fast. Each thing is neatly Scotch-taped to a Polaroid photograph of a sleeping child. There are no fingerprints on any of these objects – as if they have been handled with gloves.

In the same hiding place, they find my father's Coke-bottle cuff-links. How they got there, whether Nat or Alton took them, no one knows.

Nat hovers, unconscious, between life and death. They don't move him from Castine. He lost a lot of blood. They think he'll lose his right hand. We're not allowed to see him; we don't know whether he'll live or not.

I don't know what to hope for.

The local papers report it, then the nationals. Alton Pelletier, Nathaniel Pelletier. The names are all over. The sound of them, the way they look on the page, is beautiful. Kind of reminds me of the coast around here, up and down, rising and falling.

I wouldn't have said it could get worse, but it gets much, much worse.

Three days later I stand on the clifftop in the dusk and watch the boats pass the bay, their blue lights flashing and faint. They're searching the caves along the shore with diving teams.

They search all night. I don't sleep. I stare at the ceiling, listening to the boat engines tool up and down the coast, sometimes a distant hum, then a near growl in the bay below. Then as pink light steals in the window, they fade west and don't return. They've found something.

I get up and go out into the dawn. I jog west along the headland until I see the coastguard boats. They bob in the narrow channel that leads to the cave entrance. The obelisk shines black in the morning light. I knew, somehow, it would be here.

I watch, hidden behind the jagged rocks of the headland. Two divers splash in. I wonder if the god will eat them.

The two divers come up and dive again, come up and dive again. They bring up detritus from the cave floor, unrecognizable things festooned with seaweed. Then, at around 11 a.m., they both surface at the same time. They're holding something between them. A guy on board lowers a winch with a platform on it. They lower the platform into the water, and the frogmen do something with chains. An engine churns, the chains go taut, and it begins to rise from the water. It's a metal barrel – an oil drum. Rusted orange, sides pitted with salt and time. One of the guys in a wetsuit takes up a crowbar.

'No,' I whisper aloud. 'Don't open it.' I know he has to, but I know he shouldn't – I have the feeling, the one that comes on like sickness, the one I sometimes get up in that beautiful meadow above Whistler

Cottage. My breath comes short, there are black blossoms all over my vision.

The guy very carefully inserts the crowbar beneath the rim and pries open the top of the drum. The metal lid comes away slowly, stickily, with reluctance. He looks down at the contents, puts his hand slowly over his mouth, walks to the side of the boat and vomits into the waves.

After twenty minutes, another drum is hauled from the deep. The divers lug it up to stand beside the first one on the deck. The drums are both crusted with weed and shellfish; they've been there a while. But I feel like I can smell what's inside anyway, even from here.

And another barrel comes out from the water, and another, and another one after the other. Then there's no more room, and a second boat arrives. They load all the new drums onto that. Eight in all. I learn later that the police think that there was once one more drum; they found the broken end of its chain. Somehow the oldest, the first drum was loosed, was swept gently out to sea by the tide, fell off the deep ledge of the sea shelf and into the deepest black.

By the end of the day both boats sit low in the water, heavy with their cargo of dead women.

Rebecca Boone has come home at last.

I read how her drum is the first one to be found, wedged into a crevice in a deep pool, concealed by floating weed. The oyster knife matches the marks on her bones. She was also the first to die, over a decade ago.

Then they followed the chain and found the next oil drum, and then the next. The bodies are intact – some of the drums are still watertight. These women have different marks on their bones – from a cleaver or an axe, they think.

Two more recently dead women 'deglove' as they are removed from their drum. I don't know what it means at first; I say it to myself a couple of times. It's a beautiful word, something a Victorian lady might do as she comes in from an afternoon stroll.

It's when skin becomes detached from underlying flesh and tissue – happens with drowning victims, or bodies that have been submerged for a time. The two women slip out of their loose skins as they are taken from the drums.

The police think that many of the oil-drum women were summer visitors reported missing over the years, presumed drowned, taken by the tides. But the tides aren't the dangerous thing around here, it turns out. All have blunt trauma to their skulls. The theory is that Alton got near them as they swam, stunned them and took them to the Pelletier house. When it was over he stored them in the drums, in the cave.

They identify two of the women quickly. The first is Rebecca Boone. Christy Barham is in the last drum. I saw her crying, once. Her murderer picked up her Kleenex. I wish I knew why she was crying that day outside the store but I never will. No one will, because Christy Barham is gone.

I dream about it sometimes. Their waterlogged grey skin sliding off them into a pool on a white tile floor somewhere. But in my dreams the women rise up out of their old hides. In my dreams they're new and pink, smooth as a young hand fresh from a satin glove. They walk away, leaving their old selves behind. I don't know where they go, the dream always ends there. I hope it's somewhere nice.

When we fetch the paper from town, there she is on the front page – Rebecca. She's real – not a monster or a story. I take it into the garden to read; it somehow seems better to do it outside. I can't stop staring at Rebecca's picture.

Rebecca leans against a windowsill in a garden on a sunlit day. Crimson flowers, tulips I think, bloom in the window box behind her. One hand shades her eyes from the sun and her arms are brown and corded with muscle. A swimmer, for sure. She's small, athletic, slighter than I'd expected, her face thin with an earnest look. She has big dark eyes and curly hair the colour of ripe straw. Dyed, maybe. It haloes her face like a dandelion, or the rays of the sun. There's a look in her eye like she knows, somewhere deep down, that her time will be cut short. It's strangely common, I have found, with photographs of the dead. It's there in their faces – what's to come. But of course that can't be true. It's us who are left behind who see it. Who put it there.

I think about Rebecca's family and what they must be feeling. They thought she'd drowned, presumably mourned her. Her kid would be about my age. Their past is rewritten, now. Time travel really does exist. Certain kinds of knowledge can change everything, even if it's already happened.

I think about my mother, how she tidies her hair when she's excited, even if it's already perfectly tidy. I remember how when I was little every time she went someplace nice she wrapped bread-sticks in a napkin and brought them home for me. I would wake to her silhouette, open my mouth and she'd feed me tiny pieces, whispering all the time how much she'd missed me.

Two weeks later the news comes that Nat is awake. I'm helping my dad paint the white fence. The phone trills from inside.

'I'll get it,' I say and go in. 'Hello? Harlow residence.' My mom taught me this dumb way to answer the phone when I was little, I guess she thought it was cute, and I can't seem to shake it now, it's a reflex.

'He's conscious,' a voice says. They take a quick inhale. A cigarette.

'What?' I've never heard her voice on the phone before, it takes me a minute.

'Nat, Wilder.' She's impatient. 'Nat's awake. We should go to see him together.'

'Harper, when did you start smoking?'

'Tomorrow, two p.m.,' she says, and I can hear it in her voice, how close she is to breaking. 'That's when visiting hours start.'

'OK.'

She hangs up without saying goodbye, leaving me holding the dead receiver.

I go out and take up the paint brush again, dip it in the can.

'You OK, sport?' My dad's concern is almost too much; his warm hand on my back makes me want to cry. It's so good to be able to love him again.

'Uh, yeah, Dad.' I shrug him off. I draw a long sleek line of paint along the scarred wood. It glistens white in the sun.

I'm at the hospital the next day at two. Harper is late. I wait for her for ten minutes outside, and then I go in by myself. I worry that all this has started her drinking again. But there's nothing I can do about that right now.

There's a state trooper outside Nat's room.

I don't know what I expect. Nat looks sick, but ordinary. He's grey, thin. His hair hangs lank around his pale face. He's lost all that golden glow. I realise in this instant that I was never in love with Harper, not really. It was a way of measuring myself against him.

I give Nat the book on rare coral fish that my mother got for me at Christmas. I think, liking the sea, that Nat will appreciate it. He looks at the cover and shivers. I put it back in the bag right away, stung with remorse. What a stupid idea.

I think Nat is feeling something similar, or maybe he sees my thoughts in my face because he says, 'Sorry, man. I'm so sorry.'

'It doesn't matter,' I say. 'I'm sorry about your hand.'

The stump is blunt and white in its bandage. It looks unfinished and is startling in the way that unfinished things are. I wonder what they did with the hand once they took it off. Burned it?

'It's going to be rough, getting nets in with one hand. But maybe that won't be a problem. Maybe I'm going to jail.'

'You didn't know, did you, Nat?' I say in a rush. Again I see Alton Pelletier's eyes, warm and blue, as he picks up a used Kleenex from the ground. I hear his voice. *Squashed-fly biscuits.*

'I can't talk about it,' Nat says. 'Don't ask me that.' Tears leak from the corners of his eyes. 'I'd rather be dead than go to jail – always inside, always locked up in a room, no sea, no sky. Like this place but worse.' Nat closes his eyes, weary as death, and turns his head to the wall. 'I always thought what a weird story that was, to tell me about clubbing a seal and hooking it in the shark rig.' He is crying now. 'He told me never to go down to the cellar, Wilder, that it wasn't safe.'

I think about how small the Pelletier house is. The cellar isn't deep. I think about how sound travels, even through bloodstained carpeted walls.

'He told you the cave was special,' I say.

'I didn't know why. *It's a place of reflection,* he said.'

'We swam right over them,' I say. A row of drums, connected like a daisy chain, deep beneath the water.

Nat moans softly. I have so many questions for him but they all make me feel sick. I picture him in the dark of Whistler Cottage, taking my father's cufflinks from the nightstand as everyone sleeps, breathing gently. Is that how it happened? I wonder why they were found with all that kids' stuff.

I stagger up, sending the plastic chair flying.

'Wait, Wilder,' Nat calls. 'Come back! I have to tell you something!' I run on down the linoleum corridor.

Sometimes, on the edge of sleep I still hear it – my friend's voice, asking me to come back. I can't help wondering what he wanted to tell me – I think I'm better off not knowing.

I crouch on the sidewalk outside the sliding doors of the little Castine urgent care centre. My heart is expanding and contracting, too big then too small for my chest. I gasp. Pain runs up and down my ribs. I know I'm dying.

Someone grabs my bicep and yanks me upright.

'Breathe,' Harper says. 'Just bloody breathe, OK?' She takes something out of a paper grocery bag and hands the bag to me. 'Here. Use this. I've seen it on TV.' The brown paper crinkles uselessly in my hand. 'You breathe into it,' she says scornfully as I fumble with it. Relenting, she takes it and holds it to my mouth. 'Here. In, out. In, out. Slowly, OK?'

I do as she tells me and strangely it seems to help.

'I don't know what's happening to me,' I say when it seems to have passed.

'You had a panic attack,' she says, lighting a cigarette. 'I've had a few, these last weeks.' She takes a deep drag and a woman coming out of the hospital doors frowns and flaps her hand in disapproval at the cloud of smoke.

'Are you OK?' I ask.

'You really messed everything up,' Harper says. 'Everything was all right until you came here. It was under control.'

I tremble again, this time with anger. I am swamped in sticky rage. 'What Betty said, the other day. Did you know? Did you fricking know about the stuff behind the skirting board? The pictures.'

'How can you ask me that,' she says, going flat against the worn hospital brick. 'I didn't know.'

'But you suspected.' I can see she's upset but I'm so angry, this has to be someone's fault.

'Maybe,' she says, and now she's crying, and I feel like such a rat.

'I'm sorry,' I whisper.

'We have to stick together, Wilder.'

I feel kind of unreal and I lean on the wall beside her. We both slide down to sit on the warm sidewalk. Harper gnaws her lip. 'I didn't *know*. But there were little weird things. Nat wasn't allowed to go home some nights. He had all these stashes of blankets and beer and food along the cliffs for the nights he had to sleep out. One morning I got up early and found him sleeping on the porch at my house.' She smiles through her tears. 'I thought it was romantic, but maybe it was just raining. He seemed to think it was normal. "My father needs his space," was all he ever said about it.'

'Those pictures, the Polaroids of the kids,' I said. 'Did Nat take them?'

'Alton's the murderer,' Harper says. 'He must have taken the pictures too.'

'They seem like two different things,' I say. 'The photographs of the kids and the murders. The cops think so. There's one up there, outside his room.'

She shakes her head. 'Just shut up, Wilder.'

'That story you told, the blue light, the monster . . .'

'A story. We make them up all the time.'

'But Nat *knew* she was there, Harper. He knew she was in the cave.' Nat's voice, the pride in it. '*My dad showed me this cave when I was little.*'

'Yes, he was a kid. He was a kid when that woman was killed, Wilder.'

'I know he couldn't have done . . . that.'

99

'You should feel sorry for him, being raised by a – you know.'

'What did it do to him, being raised like that? Maybe Alton was, like, training his replacement.'

Harper stubs out her cigarette, takes me by the neck of my t-shirt and pulls my face close. I think, though it's crazy, *she's going to kiss me.*

Instead she says through bared teeth, 'That's not how it was, Wilder. You won't go telling people that, will you?'

'No,' I say. My stomach writhes.

'OK,' she says. 'You remember.' She sighs. 'Goodbye. I don't think we'll see each other again.' Now she does kiss me – briefly, on the cheek. 'You're a sweet kid. Weird though.' She takes the paper bag from me and replaces the object in it. Aluminium foil glints in the afternoon sun. Something for Nat. *Is it a snack*, I think blankly, before her words sink in.

'What do you mean?'

'My parents don't want to come back here,' she says. 'Understandably. And nor do I.'

'Harper . . .'

'It's for the best. Nat's everywhere I go, here.' She goes into the hospital and the doors swish closed behind her.

Harper's right, I don't see her again – her family leaves the next day. No one tells me where they go. Sometimes I wonder if Harper ended up at Fairview or not.

I only wonder later what she was taking to Nat – the object wrapped in aluminium foil. A longish shape like a cigar but tapered, more like a carrot.

Maybe the way we three all loved one another these two summers will never happen again for me. Maybe I've had my share of love.

After I get home I sit on the cliff. The wind is up, and the whistling from the stones below is high and needling in my head. I suddenly realise how horrible it is, how it's the sound of wind in a cave, the sound of a metal drum dragging across the sea floor.

I shut myself in my room to get away from it. My parents are packing up for our departure tomorrow. Their voices are raised in their bedroom, querulous. They let me be. Everyone wants to get away from here. The thought of murder hangs over the bay like the scent of decay. I pack my things in ten minutes, leaving the little cabin room as bare and neat as I found it.

Everything is finished, here. The city waits, and then school. I wonder if I can survive it. But at least I'll be away from the whistling, and the sea.

I don't think I realise yet that you never get away from that kind of thing.

The air-conditioning unit roars. I'm in my room, staring at the wall. Outside, New York steams. The radio drones on. At around noon, the sidewalks will be so hot, you can fry an egg on them. Some team is playing baseball tonight.

My father is in the doorway. I start. He never comes to my room and my first thought is that there must have been a disaster, some bereavement.

'Is Mom OK?'

'I thought you should hear it from me,' he says. 'Nathaniel Pelletier died a couple of days ago.' First thoughts are often correct, as it turns out.

I feel that peculiar rearrangement of time and space that happens when you hear of death. 'Who killed him?' Harper's face is before me, a clever, cunning child.

'No one killed him. He had a cardiac arrest. It happens. His wound was infected, he'd developed sepsis. You run a high enough fever – the heart just stops. Maybe it's for the best,' he says, putting a hand on my shoulder. 'They're still finding things in that house, the cellar. They think the two of them might have done the killings together. Father and son.'

His hand squeezes my shoulder. From this angle I could bite my father's index finger off. For a moment I actually feel it, the crunch of bone between my teeth.

I turn back to the wall, shaking. I feel the give in the bed as my father sits down beside me.

'I know he was your friend, Wilder.'

'Nat wouldn't have hurt anyone,' I say. 'Wouldn't have.' If I keep saying this, it might come to feel true.

My father sighs. 'Maybe he was a good kid deep down. But there seem to have been other parts that were ... darker.' I can feel him thinking. 'I don't see any reason why you shouldn't know this,' he says, 'and maybe it will help. Alton Pelletier wasn't Nathaniel's father, you know. Couldn't have been, with the blood types. They weren't even related. In Castine they say the mother ran off to the city one summer. Alton went after and came back with the kid. He said the boy was his; she was bad news and he'd taken him from her. No one had reason to doubt him. She was a troubled woman. But no, it turns out wherever Alton got the boy, he wasn't his son.'

'So Nat was – what? Kidnapped? His mother might've been looking for him the whole time?'

'Maybe, sport.' My dad hugs me and that makes me really feel it – how terrible it is that my friend is gone. I think of Nat as he was, kind and golden like a young lion. Or Nat as I thought he was. Whatever the truth of him, it's all gone now.

'I thought it was you, you know,' I say into my dad's shoulder. 'The Dagger Man.'

'What?' he says quietly. 'Why the hell would you think that, Wilder?'

'You were out at weird times in the night, acting guilty, telling lies. You've been different these last couple years. I thought at first it was 'cause I'd grown up – but it's not just me that's changed.'

His face collapses. 'I'm sorry you were worried, sport.'

I can't stop thinking about Nat. Did he know he was a stolen kid? Did he think about running away, finding his family? I feel so bad for him. Then I feel cold because I think, *bad things give birth to bad things*, and they're often the same kind. Kids who were stolen might think about stealing kids. So Nat might have thought about that, or at least about sneaking into their rooms and looking at them while they sleep, like maybe someone once did to him. Maybe he thought about taking them.

Maybe he just wanted what they had, those kids. A home, a bed with a nightlight in a house where they slept safely with their family. I can understand that. I can almost feel it, twisting in my own gut – the longing he must have felt. Longing can become the urge to punish, even at seventeen I know this. Did Nat think about punishing those kids?

Or maybe everything I'm thinking is wrong and it was all Alton.

I hear the front door click. My dad going out. It's his birthday today. None of us are really in the mood for a celebration, but I do have a surprise present I made for him.

I've found a new way of dealing with my panic. The apartment is quiet. My mom must be napping. I go to the kitchen and look around for a suitable thing. I pick up a chopping board. I feel the weight of it, the heft. Then it seems natural to raise the board high and bring it down on my knee. Pain radiates up my thigh, down my calves, a hot racing stream, and it helps so much, feels so right, that I do it again. I remind myself to be careful. *My parents will have questions if I can't walk tomorrow.* I hear the crack as the board hits my leg as if from very far away. Black flowers bloom before my eyes. *Again,* I think, *just one more.* There is a whistling all around, and I recognise it as the song of the rocks, in the bay, when the wind is in the east. I hear Nat's voice in my pulsing head. *Good fight.*

When I look up my mother is standing in the doorway watching me, and her face is white like flour, blank as if there's no one behind it. Or a stranger behind it. She holds her bottle of sweet vermouth by the neck. Her nail scratches insistently at the label.

'Are you OK?' I ask.

'I can't do this,' she says, her voice high and small. 'I can't be in charge of this. It's not right, leaving me all alone to handle these problems.' She takes a ladylike sip from the bottle.

'Mom?' I whisper. I get up on aching legs and stumble towards her.

'No!' she says. 'I can't help you. I shouldn't be asked to.'

'No one's leaving you alone.' She's upset, it's terrible.

'Oh yes he is,' the stranger who is using my mom's face says. 'Your father is leaving us for a woman in Canada. He's down the block right now, calling her from a payphone. They met in Maine during one of those summers he spent with Vernon. She's not the first, she won't be the last.'

The front door opens. 'Hey, sport,' my father calls. 'How about going out for pizza? It's my birthday, after all.'

My mother throws the vermouth bottle at the wall where it shatters in a spray of glass.

'We agreed we wouldn't tell him,' my father says. 'Not right now. He's been through so much.' My mother has made herself as small as possible in the big armchair by the window. 'I won't lie for you anymore,' she says. She covers her eyes with one hand. I can only see her mouth, which is twisted into a horrible shape, a shape no mouth should be, one corner impossibly high, lips white and gone against her pallid face. Vermouth paints the wall in a long wet stripe and sweetness hangs heavy in the air.

'Dad,' I say. 'It isn't true, is it?'

'I . . . it wasn't meant to go like this,' he says, helpless.

'What's her name?' I ask. I don't know what difference it makes but it feels important.

'Edith,' my father says, then with a gleam of pride, 'she's named after Edith Piaf. That fancy French singer. Her mother is a quarter French.' It isn't Serge Gainsbourg he has been humming all summer, after all.

'I'm sorry, Wilder,' my mom says. 'I'm sorry.' She takes her hand away from her eyes and I wish she hadn't; the mouth was bad, but the eyes are worse. 'You were always slipping up,' my mother says to my dad, pleading now. 'You'll get bored of her like the others.'

My dad starts to cry. 'Edith's different.'

'It's OK,' I say automatically. 'It's OK.'

'If you're going,' my mother screams, 'then go! Stop dragging it out!'

'Please, Sandra,' my father says. 'Please, not like this.'

I take the Coke-bottle cufflinks out of my pocket. I tried to make them just like Vernon did. I even put a little dent in one of them, like the ones that ended up in the Pelletier place.

'Here,' I say. 'Happy birthday.'

He doesn't take them so I go to the kitchen and put them down the garbage disposal. The machinery grinds and screams. Something is happening to the room. The world goes very slow and dark, narrowing to a pinpoint of light which is vanishing into the distance.

'Wilder?' I hear my father say somewhere. The dark hole of the garbage disposal is like the mouth of a cave.

'You know,' I say, 'I think I would have preferred it if you'd been a serial killer,' and then everything is gone.

That is my first episode. Deep breathing can lower the anxiety, and medication dampens it all down to a neutral grey. But nothing stops them altogether. Stress brings it on, as do dark, enclosed spaces – and anything that looks like a lit window in the night, or daylight through a cave mouth.

My father leaves the next day, and I don't see him again until after he's married.

I go back to school and it seems so obvious to me, now, that this life is all there is. I'll finish Scottsboro and then become a teacher.

I do what I do best for the following year – stay low and survive. I get good grades. I'm offered a full scholarship to the liberal arts college I've always wanted to attend.

My father doesn't sell Whistler Cottage. He gives it to my mother in the divorce. He goes to live in Canada. I don't visit. He writes.

His new wife Edith has two teenage sons who blame him for the collapse of her marriage. He can't seem to keep teaching jobs, keeps falling victim to cutbacks. He doesn't feel at home in Ottawa, he misses New York. I think he misses us, too, but there's no way for him to admit that. When we speak occasionally on the phone he sounds so tired I almost feel sorry for him.

The income from my mom's job plus rental from Whistler Cottage keeps us going. The bay becomes a point of interest for people who are into all that stuff – murder. Dark tourism, they call it. It's always rented out for months and months in advance. So we do OK from it. My mother starts scrapbooking, and I'm glad she has a hobby but I worry about it. She cuts out endless pictures of birds and flowers from magazines. No people.

I don't think people should live by the ocean. It's too big to understand.

I think of it, sometimes, the empty Pelletier place – the deep cellar, its walls lined with bloodied carpet, doors crisscrossed with yellow tape, dust gathering on the boards. What ghosts walk there? I hope none. They deserve rest.

I think of Nat's kindness to me, a stranger and a lonely kid. He was my first, my best friend, and now he's gone. I will never know who he really was. And I can't help the feeling that Whistler Bay isn't finished with me yet.

[ ]

Cone
Done
Don't

Set
Let

Turn
Tern
Ten
Hen
Her

Set
Met
Meet

Ace
Race
Grace

Wilder and Sky

My dad drops me at the front entrance to my dorm, unloads my suitcase and stuff from the trunk. It sits in a forlorn messy pile. Mom would have known how to pack things so the cord of the lamp didn't get tangled, the book covers didn't get creased. I hope she's OK. I hope they're treating her right. She gets scared in new places.

Dad claps me on the back. 'Proud of you, sport,' he says.

'Thanks,' I say. 'I can take it from here. You've got a long drive.'

I accepted the ride from him – I had to, Mom was having a bad day – but I don't want him to think he's forgiven.

When he paid for gas just after Allentown a picture dropped out of his wallet. A confused-looking woman with grey hair in tight curls. She's smiling and wearing white. Edith, on their wedding day. I handed the picture back to him without comment.

Now he looks sad and lingers a moment. 'I'll help you get it all up to your room.'

'Really,' I say. 'I've got this.'

He nods, claps me on the back once more, gets in the car. I want to watch him drive out of the gates but I don't. I'm alone. I have to learn to deal with it.

I look around. Grey squirrels are chattering in the bare trees. There's a sound of water from somewhere. The sky is bright and clear. I feel like I can smell the mountains nearby. I wanted to get out of the city for college. And I wanted to be inland, as far as possible from the sea. There's only a small stretch of lake shoreline in Pennsylvania, and I find that comforting.

I take a deep breath and start to drag my suitcase up the steps one by one. Someone jostles me with their shoulder.

'Sorry,' the guy says. He's my age but tall, thin, his chestnut hair messy. He has a big nose and big dark eyes like a horse. He drags an old-fashioned steamer trunk up the steps by its handle.

'He's so clumsy!' his dad says. The dad is kind-looking with a big grey moustache and suspenders. 'Help your fellow student, Sky,' he says to the guy, who dumps the steamer trunk at the top of the stairs and comes back down.

'Oh, OK.' He lifts the other end of my suitcase.

'I'm fine,' I say.

'It's no problem.'

We're up the stairs in no time. 'All set?' the messy-haired guy asks, dusting his hands. People swarm around us down the corridor; we are a rock parting a stream.

'Completely,' I say, smiling, filled with alarm, and they're gone.

The hallways are so loud, full of yelling and people dragging suitcases and carrying pot plants. By the time I've finally fought my way to the bulletin board, found my room allocation, gotten lost in the maze of corridors twice, my heart is beating really fast.

I look at my watch. It's just 11 a.m. and I'm supposed to have them with food, but I take my anti-anxiety pill anyway. I do the deep breathing the counsellor at Scottsboro taught me.

Most of the college is built of old, mellow stone. My room is in the new wing, a network of breeze block and brown and green linoleum. The air is thick with the scent of instant noodles, mingling with the odour of meatloaf from commons. I find room sixteen through a thick fire door which slams loudly behind me, up a steep set of stairs, at the end of a long corridor. This can't be possible, but I feel like the corridor narrows, that the walls converge to a point. The handle of sixteen rattles; it's loose and there's a dent in the lower part of the door as though someone has tried to kick it in.

I go in, then start, because someone's already here – a guy lies on the bed by the window, tossing a tennis ball up and down. He watches as I drag my suitcase in, panting. The window overlooks the back of the kitchens. It lets in a grey, partial light. The smell of noodles in here is almost overwhelming.

'I'm Wilder,' I say.

'Doug,' he says. He's pink, thickset. An athlete, I would guess. Football maybe.

'Shitty room,' Doug says. 'Isn't it?'

'Oh, it's OK,' I say, suspecting some kind of trap.

'This is where they put the full scholarship students,' Doug says moodily. He throws the tennis ball hard against the wall. *Thwock.* His hair is wiry sand. *Maybe they group us by appearance*, I think. The weirdest-looking ones room together.

'Someone's come at our door with a steel toe,' Doug says. 'You see that?'

'I guess we scholarship types are an angry bunch.'

Doug stares at me, his face motionless. Then he gives a short hah. 'OK, you're funny.'

'Thanks,' I say.

'Maybe this will be OK,' Doug says. 'I like a funny guy.'

I put my fists on the sides of my hips and make a face like Groucho Marx, do a quick softshoe. I feel sorry for me and Doug – that we're both so grateful for my bad joke.

That night as I lie in bed, the scent of weed drifting up from the yard below, listening to the kitchen staff laughing, relaxing after their shift, I think, *well, I got through Scottsboro. I just have to do four years here. I get the grades and then I'll be free.*

I wonder when you stop marking time, as an adult – when life starts. What would I even do with it if I had the freedom – live?

It happens sooner than even my worst expectations – as in, the next day, in the middle of my first class. Everything's normal at first. I have a bad phone call with my mom after breakfast – she's in a manic phase – but I'm still excited for Introduction to Gothic Architecture. I want to study something real and solid, like buildings. Not stories or books.

I find the room, a seat; I have the correct books. Getting these things right feels like such a victory that maybe I relax my guard a little too much.

The professor has something on his tie, oatmeal maybe, there's a strong scent of coffee and bad breath in the room. But he's a good teacher. We're talking about the gothic, about architecture and the sublime; it's all very interesting. He pulls down the screen over the whiteboard.

He gets out a projector and even then I don't realise, don't worry. *I'm OK,* I think, pleased.

My first pulse of panic comes when he goes to the light switch, and the room goes dark. But no, it's just visual aids, surely this isn't a problem. I breathe deeply. The girl sitting next to me flicks a quick glance in my direction and moves an inch or two away.

The projector throws the image up onto the screen – an elaborately carved arch, with daylight behind. The archway glows like a lighted doorway, or a cave mouth.

That's the last I thing I know; dark comes down over me like a soft blanket, like night falling sudden on the sea.

His is the first face I see when I wake up. We're on a bench, outside in the cold air and the merciful sunshine. From somewhere behind us there comes the sound of the river running.

He's not looking at me, is frowning down at a paperback. He is familiar, though I can't in this moment recall why – messy hair the colour of turning beech leaves, dark russet. His eyes are big and dark. *It's very striking, that colouring*, I think vaguely, and the word strike must set off some kind of word association in my head, because now I remember where I've seen him before.

'You again,' I say. 'From the steps outside the dorm yesterday.'

'That's right,' he says, soothing. 'Hi. You're back.' He looks closely. 'Are you back? Really, I mean.'

'Yes.'

He looks into my eyes a moment longer. 'OK. Because you kept saying you were OK, earlier, when I could tell you weren't.'

I don't want to know, but of course I have to. 'What happened? What did I do?'

'You got up and left class. You seemed kind of confused, so I followed you.'

'Oh.' I'm relieved. 'That's not too bad. Sometimes I start—' I clear my throat. It's rough and sore as though I've been yelling. 'Sometimes when I get upset I have memory gaps.'

He is still looking at me closely. 'That must be scary.'

'Embarrassing,' I say, and I start to get up from the bench. 'Better get going.'

'Woah,' he says, putting out a hand that seems to simultaneously support me and restrain me. 'Hold on. Class is finished, in fact it finished a while ago.'

'How long?'

'An hour or so?'

'And you stayed with me all that time?'

'Sure,' he says.

'You didn't have to do that, I would have been fine.' I can't stand that he feels sorry for me.

'I'd got the point the guy was making,' he says. 'Gothic arches. Very gothic. Arches. Completely arched. No reason to draw it out.'

'That was nice of you I guess.'

'I thought someone should stay with you. So I told the professor I knew you. That we were old friends from back home.'

'Resourceful.'

'That's me. Can you walk? We should get you to the medical centre.'

'Please don't,' I say. The thought of roofs and walls and enclosed spaces is enough to speed my breathing up again. 'I can't handle being inside right now. I – just can't. Please don't ask me to explain.'

He nods and doesn't say anything, goes back to his book, which is great. His presence is relaxing. Most people's thoughts poke out of them, even when they're not talking, when they're trying not to bother you. Maybe especially then. His don't.

I find my pill case in my jeans pocket and take my afternoon medication early. After a moment's thought I take another one.

'I'm Sky,' he says. 'Well, not really. My name's Pierce. But I've decided to start over at college.'

'My name's Wilder.'

'Like Thornton Wilder.'

'Yes.'

'I feel my role as concerned citizen is to get you to a healthcare professional.'

'I just want to stay outside,' I say. 'Please.'

He looks at me, assessing. 'OK,' he says. 'Let's play a game. My dad used to make me do this when I came home late, so he could bust me if I was drunk. If you get this right we can go to the river and forget about the sick bay. If you mess up you have to come with me to medical, no complaints, no questions. OK?'

I think about it. 'What's the game?'

'I'll give you a word, and you have to change one letter, to make it into another word. You can substitute, move, remove and add. But only one letter. OK?'

'OK.'

He pauses. 'Indicate. So you see, what you do is—'

'Vindicate,' I interrupt.

'Very good, a quick study! Hmm. Fiend.'

I smile. 'Friend.'

'Oh, yeah, clever. But I can keep it going.' He smiles back. 'Fried. Are you good to walk?'

I am.

The river is cold, dark brown and rushing, the trees bare and spectral with a couple of clinging crimson leaves. Fall is underway early this year. Crows sit like sentries on the branches, black against the aching blue skies. It feels like there are too many of them. Why are there so many – and why are they so still, so silent? I shiver.

Sky takes off his jacket and holds it for me, expectant.

'You need to keep warm, you're in shock.'

I think about arguing, but in the end I just turn around and slip my arms into it because he's right, I am cold. It's tweed, expensive. The fabric smells of him, like bergamot and lemon, like a fragrant cup of hot tea. Earl Grey maybe.

'Wilder,' Sky says. 'That's an unusual name. Where have I heard that recently?'

My heart sinks. I shrug. 'I have no idea.'

Our names were in the newspapers – mine and Harper's. My mom was mad, but there was nothing to be done because I was over sixteen. I'm really hoping Sky doesn't remember where he heard it.

'We must have met in another life,' Sky says. 'Or a dream.'

'Ream,' I say absently.

'Team,' Sky says. 'I like you, Wilder, we should room together.'

'You don't really know me,' I say. 'Besides, I already have a roommate.'

'Do you like him?'

'Not particularly.'

'Mine eats egg salad sandwiches in bed. It's awful, I want to get rid of him anyway. So it's settled.'

Black wings burst forth from a bare tree, the still dark sentries become a ragged cloud of cawing. One black feather drifts down on the air, sidling, riding the eddies of the cooling day.

I jump. 'What scared them?'

'A cat? A fox? Or nothing, probably,' Sky says, soothing. 'It's just some dumb old crows being melodramatic.'

A giant black shape wheels on a thermal above our heads. The smaller birds scatter out of its path.

'Ah, wait, that one's not a crow,' Sky says.

'Raven,' I whisper.

'Craven.' I can hear a smile in his voice. 'You need someone to take care of you. I'm pretty sure you weren't supposed to take two of those pills together.'

I know he's only joking, and it might be a weird thing for a guy to say to another guy, but the thought of someone taking care of me is seductive in its strength.

But I can't get into the habit of depending on anyone. My mom got dependent on my dad and look what happened there.

'I don't think we can change our roommates now,' I say coldly. 'It's too late.'

I walk away quickly and don't look back.

My roommate Doug is talking on the payphone at the end of the hall. I recognise his hunched back, his corrugated hair.

'He's so weird-looking, too,' Doug says as I approach. 'Bug-eyed. Creepy.'

I flush and hurry past before he sees me.

It comes to me again that night, the dream.

It goes like this – I am swimming in the sea. I become aware that something is tugging on my leg. I'm not afraid; it's a game Harper and I are playing. She swims under and tugs my leg, then swims off before I can catch her. It's like underwater tag, I suppose. I don't know where we've come from, in the dream, or what we're doing there. There's no land in sight, just navy-blue water stretching out in every direction. No boat. No one else.

The tug comes again on my ankle and I dive beneath the surface to try and tag Harper.

But I was wrong, Harper's not here. I see, however, that I'm not alone. The thing tugging at me is a chain which is fastened to my ankle. It leads down into the depths. I follow it down, breathing easily in the glassy deep.

The first oil drum looms out of nowhere, too suddenly for me to back away. It's Rebecca, this one, of course, her blonde dandelion hair floating beautiful and white in the murky water.

I follow the chain on, I have to, it's the logic of the dream. Here's woman five. Her skull is bare, she didn't have any hair left when she was found – they were never sure exactly why. They think maybe it was burned off.

I'm gasping as I try to swim, muscles burning, but every time I pull away a current hauls me back towards it, the terrible daisy chain of oil drums hanging there, silhouetted against the waterlight. There are nine drums, of course, not just the eight they found. The last one is Harper. Her skin has slipped off her flesh. It floats by her like a dress rippling in the current. Degloved.

I wake myself by yelling.

My roommate Doug says, 'What the hell?'

'Sorry,' I say. 'Bad dream.'

'Come on,' he says, thumping the pillow with a fist. 'It's the third time in a week, man. Come on.'

The girls in the room next door are thumping on the walls with something, a shoe maybe. They're pretty sick of me too. They're French, foreign students come for the American college experience. I don't think they expected to be woken by so much screaming during this first week of their US visit.

I fumble for the paper and pen I keep beside the bed. I get my folder of clippings out of the cubby. I take everything out into the corridor. The hallways in this building are always reassuringly floodlit, night and day.

I flick through the clippings, scanning them. At length I have what I need, and I turn to a clean page in the notebook. I start to write the list, hands shaking.

Rebecca Boone loved semi-precious stones. Turquoise, lapis, pearls.
Woman two had a pale band on her finger, where a wedding
    ring probably once sat.
Louise Dominguez had five children.
Elaine Bishop was very short. Her hair was dyed purple.
Woman five had a hip replacement but it was done in Mexico so
    they can't trace her.
Carla Yap had recently had a small tattoo removed from her
    hip. It once read adam.
Maryanne Smith had unusually white, healthy teeth, with no
    fillings.
Christy Barham ran the fishmonger in Castine. Her favourite
    city was Paris though she never went.
        They never found woman nine, although they think she
    died first. Her barrel drifted off.

I refer back and forth to the newspaper articles as I write, to make sure I've got everything correct.

Gradually, as the list goes on, my breathing steadies, my hands stop shaking. This is the only way to keep the dream from taking me: I nail myself down with facts. I make them warm people once more. My mother hated it, my habit of clipping all the stories about each victim from the paper and keeping it. I hoard them, treasure each one like a priceless jewel. I have to; each fact about the oil-drum women is a delicate thread that tethers me to sanity.

Now I put all the clippings back in the binder. I like this binder, it has a picture of Aphrodite coming out of the waves on it. I keep the articles in plastic sleeves to preserve them but even so the newsprint's getting blurred with use. I'll go to the library tomorrow and look through the microfiche for recent articles. There might be something that I don't have, some little human detail. New information still comes out, though in trickles now. They identified Rebecca Boone and Christy Barham right away, but they only worked out it was Carla Yap a couple of months ago.

I worry about woman nine. Is she still lying lonely on the deep sea floor, year in and year out, with no one to make her real? I think about how every family whose mother or daughter or wife or sister went missing near Castine must feel. They may never know whether she's still down there or not, in the deep, curled up tight in her drum.

I never dream about Nat.

The next day I come back from class weary as hell. I didn't get back to sleep last night, I just watched dawn come in at the window, rising grey over the backs of the kitchens. All I want to do is collapse onto my bed and never get up again. I can miss art history in the afternoon, I tell myself. I can get someone's notes later.

Doug's stuff is gone. A steamer trunk sits at the foot of the bed. Instead of his aggressively non-ornamental black-and-white checked comforter, the bed is draped with a bright wool throw. I can tell it's expensive. A copy of *In Search of Lost Time* sits open on the nightstand. A green fountain pen with a gold nib lies across it. I can see that the page is closely tattooed with notes and underlining in emerald-green ink. I peer closer.

'Hey, roomie,' someone says from the doorway. It's Sky.

'What the hell? Where's Doug?'

'I told you I'd work it out. It wasn't difficult. Doug has had enough of you, I'll be honest. He wasn't difficult to persuade. My assigned room is pretty nice, too, overlooks the main quad; he was only too happy to swap. Even after I told him about the egg salad sandwiches.'

'You had no right to do this without asking me,' I say.

'I just figured neither of us was happy with their roommate—'

'It's creepy – moving in with someone without asking.'

'I thought you'd be happy—'

'Happy you gave up your big room on the quad to move in here, above the kitchens.'

'Well—'

'What's your name again? Sky? It's a real novelty for you, right? A big joke. You'll enjoy slumming it here with the scholarship students until you get bored, and then you'll bribe Doug to get your old room back. You'll feel all daring and tell your friends about what an adventure you had with the poor students, the kicked-in door, maybe say something about how you don't really *see* things like class or race. *It's not me who's rich, it's my parents.*' The anger lights up parts of me I never knew existed.

'I'm not like that,' he says.

I go close to him, look into his face. 'You are exactly like that. I know you. I went to school with hundreds of you. And I don't intend to spend college being patronised by you.'

'Sorry,' he says. 'You're right. I shouldn't have – sorry.' He opens

121

the trunk and stuffs the throw back in. 'I'll talk to Doug. I'll be gone first thing tomorrow morning.' His big dark eyes are hurt.

'Good,' I say, icy.

The water is deep and dark. I spit, my mouth is full of cold weed and small snails crawl over my face. My rotting hand reaches for the circle of light, the top of the barrel. Trapped, I scream and the water rushes in. My skin begins to slip from my body as I fight my way free of the barrel that holds me.

'Woah,' someone says; a warm arm wraps around me in the freezing water. I scream again and gasp awake.

I am in my room, trembling, drenched in sweat; it is pooled everywhere. Sky is holding me, pale with shock.

'Get off me,' I say, 'get off!' My throat is hoarse. How long was I screaming? He gets up. I lean over and fumble with the bedside table but my fingers won't grip. I can't get it open.

Sky reaches and opens the drawer. 'What do you need?' he asks.

I point to the pills in their plastic bottle. He twists the cap off, shakes out a pill. My hands are still shaking so he puts it in my mouth and holds the glass for me. My teeth chatter on the rim.

I say, 'I have to – I have to—' I gesture at the notepad, the folder of news clippings with Aphrodite on the cover. I have no idea how I would explain what I have to do now, so it's lucky Sky doesn't ask.

He puts the binder on the bed, opens it. 'I'll leave you to it.'

'Don't go,' I say. 'Please.'

'OK.' He goes back to his bed, picks up *In Search of Lost Time* and starts to read – green pen in hand, making the occasional note in the margin. He seems focused, doesn't seem to be paying me any attention at all.

Rebecca Boone loved semi-precious stones. Turquoise, lapis,
pearls . . .

At last I'm calm again, or the closest I get to it these days.
'What are those?' he asks. 'The clippings.'
'Nothing,' I say. 'Just research for a project.' Then, dreading it,
'You can put out the light now.'
'How about,' Sky says, 'we keep it on? I got some reading to do.'
'Sure, whatever.' Relief floods my body. 'Look, about earlier—'
'You were right,' he says. 'Simple as that.'
Sky doesn't sleep. I listen to his quiet breathing. It's regular
and deep. With that and the scratches of the pen it sounds like . . .
'Like a horse barn at night,' I say, hazily.
'Hmm?' he asks quietly.
But I'm drifting.

I wake to the sound of the alarm. I lie there blinking in confusion.
This is more sleep than I've had in days.
Sky is quietly brushing his hair before the mirror. It springs
back immediately into its original shape.
'See you tonight, man,' I say and turn over.
'See you tonight,' he says after a pause.
So Sky stays.

I get an envelope from my mom the next morning. Inside are
twenty or thirty pictures of flowers carefully cut out from magazines. Her medication is pretty heavy but they let her use safety
scissors.
I understand what she means, even though there's no letter.

The payphone at the end of the hall is free, and the hallway deserted for once. I lift the receiver gently. There's only an alarmed beeping. I see that the tongue of the cradle is stuck in the upward position, meaning the phone is off the hook. Someone has jammed it there with pink bubble gum. I grimace and hook the gum out in gooey strands with the tip of a pencil.

It makes me think of marshmallow in my hair, warm from the fire, hair red as an alarm. I know she said she wasn't going back there but I can try, can't I? I just want to hear her voice.

I still have it written down in my address book, the phone number for Harper's house on the bay, the big white one on the hill. I'm nervous, my fingers are clumsy and I keep misdialling. But at last I get it right.

For the first ten rings or so I can imagine that someone might pick up. But they don't. On and on it goes, but no one answers. Even after forty rings or so I can't hang up. I don't know what I thought would happen. I imagine the trill echoing through empty rooms. What a lonely thought that is, a phone ringing in a vacant house.

We've broken our promise to each other. Nat, Harper and I will never all be together at Whistler Bay again.

I replace the receiver with shaking hands and do my breathing. It doesn't help this time. No one told me that grief would feel so much like fear.

I wait until I'm ready, then I take a deep breath and pick up the receiver to call my mom.

There's a hollow tree stump at the summit of Pursing Hill. Sky and I meet there most days after class. From here you can just see the foothills of the Appalachians to the south, blue against the grey cloud.

'Why did you choose to come here?' I ask Sky. 'You probably could have gone anywhere.'

He doesn't answer, and I see that a rare flush is spreading up from his neck.

'I want to do the writing program when I finish undergrad,' he says. 'The MFA. They say you have a better chance of getting in if you do your bachelor's here – especially if you major in English lit. So that's my plan.'

The college has a graduate writing program. Occasionally, essayists or a novelist comes out of it. It's very highbrow and exclusive. We don't have much to do with them, but occasionally we see the writing students drifting around campus. They look stressed and like they need a shower.

'Oh.' I'm surprised. Because Sky doesn't seem that interested in the English lit seminars. He always wants things to be literal. He's still reading *In Search of Lost Time* after two months. *Maybe he really likes it*, I tell myself. *Maybe he's rereading it*.

'I write short stories sometimes,' Sky says. 'I want to write books.' His face is almost scarlet. He turns away towards the wind, which is the bracing November kind. I look away, too, let him have his privacy. We're good at that, he and I.

'Writing things down purifies them,' he goes on. 'This world is so hard. We need something better. We need books.' He scuffs his foot through the dry grass. 'I don't know if I'm the one to write them though.'

'I bet you write well,' I say, loyally.

He shakes his head. 'No. I don't. It's like – when I put my pen to the page all I can hold in my head is a single word at a time. There are no – it doesn't build anything. Ugh. I'm so blocked I can't even describe my own block. Whatever. Let's talk about something else.'

'I guess you found something money can't buy, rich boy.'

'You *asshole*,' he says, delighted, and grabs me in a chokehold.

At commons, Sky can hardly keep his eyes open. He yawns. All his sounds are gentle. But he looks tired, his nose seems particularly aquiline against his drawn face. I know he doesn't get much sleep because of me.

'Hey, Sky,' a girl says, passing. 'How was your weekend?'

'Hey,' he says back, easy. 'It was good.' I've noticed that everyone seems to know Sky already – people tend to say hi like he's an old friend.

When we get back to our room, I start putting stuff in a backpack.

'What are you doing?' he asks.

'You can have the room to yourself tonight.'

'You don't have to do that—'

'I wake you up almost every night. Afterwards I get back to sleep but you don't. It's not fair, you'll fail your classes.' I take a deep breath. 'Maybe you could write if you got some rest.'

'Wilder I'm fi . . .' His sentence is broken by another long yawn. 'But where would you go?'

'Not your problem,' I say. 'Maybe I'll get laid.'

'Who's the lucky lady?' he asks, smiling.

'Sleep well,' I say.

I close the door on the rest of his protests.

I don't really have a plan so I sit in the library until it closes, and then I go to the movie theatre in town. I get a ticket for the 1 a.m. showing of *The Last Picture Show*. I watch it, nodding gently. It's dark and I'm the only one in the audience, but the people on the screen feel like company, so I do sleep a little.

After the movie finishes I walk back to campus. A couple of windows are lit high up in the main quad. One swings open as I watch, releasing a blast of laughter. The coal of a cigarette glows brightly. A long ponytail swings in silhouette, a burst of Pearl Jam fills the cold air, before everyone says *shhh*. The cigarette arcs and falls like a red star into the dark and the window slams shut, cutting the laughter off, closing me out in the night once again.

I wonder what would happen if I knocked on their door. *Sounds like a party.*

But I won't knock, I know that.

The dark heads are silent behind the glass, they move in silent shadow theatre. I stay for a moment or two to watch. There is a power to it, observing them like this. I wonder if this is what he felt – the Dagger Man.

There's a shed behind commons I've noticed where the lock is loose – so I knock the lock right off it with a rock. I hold my breath after each blow but the night stays quiet, no one comes.

I crawl into the sawdusty interior. Woods and forests loom out of the darkness, painted on flats. This must be where they store the props for the theatre department. I sit on a dusty golden throne upholstered with red plush. The gold paint flakes gently onto my clothes, into my hair. My watch hands crawl slowly round the dial.

I sneak in at about 6 a.m.

Sky is reading in bed, the book upside down. He wears striped pyjamas. His skin is flushed, his hair damp. Has he just had a shower? He doesn't seem surprised to see me; he must have heard the heavy fire door at the foot of the staircase open.

'Hi, Wilder,' he says, turning *In Search of Lost Time* back the right way up.

'Did you sleep?'

'I did,' he says. 'But it was weird, being here on my own. I missed you. Buddy,' he adds quickly.

I get into bed and am instantly asleep – in fact I sleep right through my first econ class. I wake late and panicking. My pillow is covered in sawdust and paint chips which have fallen from my hair in the night.

I buy a padlock for the prop shed and keep the key. Now at least I have somewhere warm to go on those nights.

To a casual glance, the shed door looks undisturbed. If someone tries to open the padlock with the old key, obviously there will be a problem. But I think it'll be OK; the play is *Waiting for Godot* this semester. The director has set it among a regiment of US marines deployed to Vietnam. They're not using much scenery, it's just a blue backdrop and some sand.

I'm still getting more sleep overall than I have done since the bad summer so I don't mind. I figure the occasional night of this is a fair trade-off.

I can't find a pen anywhere so without thinking I open Sky's bedside cubby. A pair of little eyes stare at me from the dark and I gasp, heart hammering.

It's a small doll, made of something dark and wiry. Hair. Horse hair? It's finer than that. The eyes seem to be made of bone – when

I look closer I see that they're two small human teeth. I pick it up. There's a strange weight to it.

'What are you doing?' Sky is pale, his eyes wide. I put the doll back in his cubby and wipe my hands on my pants. I'm embarrassed, as if I've been doing something intimate.

'I didn't mean to – I was looking for a pen.'

He gives me a tight smile and offers me a ballpoint from his pocket.

'What is it?' I ask. 'The doll?'

At first I think he's not going to answer. 'It's magic,' he says. 'For the destruction of my enemies.' I can't help laughing, the words sound so strange in his gentle voice. Then I see his face.

'What is it, Sky?'

Sky sits down heavily on the bed. 'Something happened to me when I was little. I don't remember it, but my parents were really freaked out. And my mom swears it changed me. That I was different, afterwards. My parents are Bible people, you know? There's no room for any kind of different in our house. So when I was thirteen my parents sent me to this place. A camp. It was supposed to fix me.' He shivers. 'It's called reparative therapy, as in – *oh, I'm broken, I need repairing.*'

I've heard about those places. There was a *New Yorker* article. 'What did they – do to you?'

'They used to – no, it doesn't matter. That's not the story. It was winter and we had to sleep in these wooden huts, me and the other boys. It was so cold. In the mornings they let us into the bunk house where the counsellors slept, to do chores – make the beds and so on. It was heated so we all used to take as long as we could to make each bed – to get the numbness out of our fingers.

'I remember thinking, if it's possible that life can be this guilty and hard and sad, then it must be possible for the oppo-site to exist. Possibility. Magic, I suppose. So I decided I'd grow up, learn to do that magic, and punish all of them. I started taking the hair off the counsellors' pillows and braiding it together. People actually shed a lot of hair over the course of three months.' He picks up the doll. 'And I made this. The teeth are mine – two milk teeth I kept.' He puts the doll gently back in the cubby. Even after he closes the door, I can still feel the teeth-eyes watching me. 'I don't know why I keep it. Comfort for a lonely, sad kid.'

'I know someone who used to do magic like that,' I say slowly. 'Or said she did. It never worked for her.' I think of the doll, its teeth-eyes, its horrible hair-body. 'Has it worked for you?'

'Not yet,' Sky says. 'Come on, let's get out of here.' His com-posure has returned – his face once more wears an expression of benign confusion. 'Let's go to the woods. I think it's going to snow.' He pauses. 'Maybe they did me a favour, in a way,' he says. 'That place forced me to know who I am. And I swore I'd never let anyone hurt me like that again.' He squeezes my shoulder. 'Be fucked up, be free. Right?'

We go up onto Pursing Hill into the cold, and it does snow, it lands in stars in his hair and lashes. Moments afterwards they're gone, vanished in the warmth of him.

The flashlight shines into the dark, waves lap up, lick the cave walls. Harper's hand reaches out from the oil drum.

Don't, I say. *Please.*

It's OK, Wilder, Harper says. *It's safe. We're all degloved now.*

I turn over into blinding light. There's the scent of sawdust, of paint. I'm not back in the cave, I'm in the prop shed – and someone's shining a flashlight in my face. Behind I can just see a dark figure.

'What the hell?' A male voice. The security guard noticed the new lock at last.

I leap up and scramble backwards over some peeling battlements. The figure follows, the flashlight beam dances crazily. I've cleared a way through the old cottage frontages, the forests and plywood city skylines, in case this very thing happens. I'm familiar with it, can pick my way through in relative darkness. The security guard can't, it seems. I hear the report of bone on wood and a gasp of pain. I stumble around behind him, weave through the Egyptian pyramids and out into the night.

I can hear the crash of scenery behind me as I run through the main quad, around the back of the kitchens and up towards my corridor. I back into some bushes, out of sight of the quad, and stop to catch my breath. I'm bent double, laughing and panting, trying to do it quietly. I can't wait to tell Sky, it's the kind of thing he'll appreciate.

The heavy fire door swings. Someone comes down the stairs that lead to room sixteen. He has a kind face, a grey moustache. Unease crawls down me. I know him, recognise him right away. There's only one room up that staircase.

Why is Sky's father here – coming out of our building in the middle of the night?

Sky's hair stands upright in a russet crest; he looks childlike, startled. 'He's got some legal problems, he was kind of – a bad dad. My mother doesn't want me around him. When she found out he dropped me here at the beginning of the semester, she got a restraining order. He's not allowed near me. They'd send him back to jail if they knew he was coming here. But I can't not see my dad, can I. Even though he's bad?'

'But you could meet anywhere, Sky—'

'You won't tell, will you, Wilder? Swear you won't tell.' The expression on his face is sad. Even though I know that Sky is lying about his father, I don't say anything. The story doesn't make any sense. It's somewhat comforting to know that he's so bad at deceit. We respect each other's privacy.

I sit down on the bed. 'I had the dream,' I say.

Sky comes to sit next to me. 'Again?'

'Again.'

He pauses and I can feel him thinking. Then he says, 'Wilder, do you want to tell me what happened?'

'I can't.'

'You listened to me yesterday. Now it's your turn. It will help, I promise.'

'OK.' I take a deep breath and go to the binder with Aphrodite on it. At the back is a special folder. I take the pages out. I've been working on it on and off in the odd hours between classes and studying.

'You know,' I say, 'I used to write a little fiction. Short stories mainly. But I stopped after—'

Oil drums in a daisy chain. A hand, reaching.

I take a deep breath. 'After something that happened to me last year. It really messed up my head. That's when it all started. The dreams and so on.

'But I got the idea to start writing this after something you said the other day. Writing things down purifies them. I thought I'd give it a try. So this isn't fiction, it's – well, you'll see what it is. Here.'

He takes the pages from me, wondering, scans the title. '*The Dagger Man of Whistler Bay*, a memoir by Wilder Harlow.'

He reads. I flip quietly through a book, trying not to watch him. I think about leaving the room but that seems worse somehow. There's nothing I can do now, it's out of my hands.

I can tell when he's near the end; it's like I can feel the story moving in him as he reads.

Sure enough, he's on the last page when I turn back. He puts it gently on the stack. He's looking down, I can't see his face.

'So that's why I'm so weird,' I say into the silence. In the spirit of honesty I add, 'Actually, I was always weird. But I'm much weirder now. Not in a good way.'

'I had heard your name before,' Sky says. 'I knew it. You were one of those kids.'

'Yes.'

'What are those for?' he asks, pointing at the newspaper articles.

'It's everything I can find about them,' I say. 'The women.'

'You always read them after you have nightmares.'

'It helps, I don't know why. It makes them real. Helps me remember they were people. Not just nightmares.'

'Oh, Wilder,' he says, and when Sky looks up I see that his mouth is stretched down. He wipes the back of his hand across his nose. He's crying hard, really ugly crying.

'It's OK,' I say, desperate. 'Sky, please don't.'

I put an arm around his shoulders. He flings his arms around me like a kid and holds me tight. 'I'm so sorry,' he says in my ear. 'That all those things happened to them. To you.' We stay like that for a moment, I can feel his heart beating against my chest. I suppose he can feel mine, too.

Sky pulls away and slips a hand behind my head. His gaze is on me, we're inches apart; it's like being in a beam of sunlight. I can smell his tears, mineral on his skin.

'Reading that was like being inside you,' he says. I try and shift out of the floodlight of his gaze, but he clamps a hand down on my leg, pinning me in place. He's strong.

'Was it true, that secret you were going to tell them in the cave?' he asks. 'When Harper and Nat tricked you.'

'I don't know,' I say.

'I think you do,' he says gently.

So I look right back at him, relax into his grip. I give in to whatever's going to happen. He must be able to hear my heart now; it's deafening, my pulse going like a series of detonations in my ears. *I know how it's going to feel*, I think vaguely – but what is 'it'?

His eyes hold mine for endless heartbeats. Then Sky pats my arm. 'Thank you for showing me that, Wilder. You should keep writing it.'

He gets up, goes back across the room to his bed. I watch, hypnotised, as he gets under the covers and reaches for the light. The places where he touched me feel cold now, chilly handprints on my flesh.

'Wilder?'

I realise that Sky is asking me something and I shake myself. 'Sure,' I say. 'What?'

'You OK to sleep without the light tonight?'

I nod.

With a click we are plunged into darkness.

'Never,' I whisper into the dark. I wait. 'Sky? Never.'

'Not tonight,' Sky murmurs.

'OK, I'll go again. Never. Ever. Fever.'

'Mmph,' Sky says and turns over. 'Shut up, would you?'

He's quiet after that, I don't know if he's sleeping.

I don't sleep for a long time; I stare into the dark. I replay the scene over and over in my head. I feel the light whispering touch of fear – fear or something else.

Fear. Ear. Near.

I feel like he's been inside me, too.

The next day I'm busy. I'm behind in class and have things to turn in. In the daylight what happened last night seems even more unsettling and I don't know what to feel. I stay late in the library, as late as they'll let me, until they turn the lights out at midnight. I won't admit to myself that I'm avoiding Sky, staying out until I think he'll be asleep.

When I come back to the dorm he's not there. A piece of paper lies on my bed. It's a photocopy of Christy Barham's eulogy, from a column in a tiny local paper. I've never seen it before. It's written by someone who loves her, you can tell. It really brings her to life – I learn that sunflowers were her favourite flower, I read about her closeness with her sisters. I remember her, how kind everyone says she was, how alive she looked that day I saw her, the day Alton Pelletier picked up her Kleenex and put it in his pocket. But even this memory feels helpful, like it's knitting my recollections, my mind back into a whole again, instead of keeping them separate, like Polaroids.

I hold the photocopy to my chest for a moment in relief. Then I slide it carefully into a new plastic sleeve and clip it into the binder safely with the others.

Sky doesn't come back and I drift. I wake to the click of the door as he slips in. It must be late. Has he been avoiding me too?

I listen as he undresses silently in the dark. I think about saying something about the article, about thanking him, but I can't summon any words. He gets into bed but he's not asleep, I can tell. We lie there, listening to one another breathe.

I'm shivering in the quad, waiting for the accommodation office to open to register for vacation residence. I get here early, but I'm not the first. The French girls are here. Some other exchange students, and a couple of shy-looking kids I've never seen before. Everyone who can't get home over the holidays and everyone who doesn't want to. Snow lies in dirty drifts against the stone walls. We all shift from foot to foot, shove hands deep into pockets for warmth.

'I think you should go and see him,' Sky says.

I look up. Sky and I haven't seen each other much for the past couple of weeks. First it was Thanksgiving, and I went back to the empty New York apartment. I spent the holiday watching the parade on TV and eating baloney sandwiches. He went to his mother in Connecticut.

Since our return to campus we have rotated around one another, avoiding long conversations. It has been surprisingly easy, actually. I suppose this is how most people are with their roommates. But I'm lonely; I see how much I've come to rely on him, even in this short time.

'What are you talking about?'

He looks at the queue impatiently, then grabs me by the elbow and tries to pull me out. 'Sky,' I say, standing firm. 'I'm in line, I'll lose my place when they open.'

Sky taps the shoulder of the French girl in front of me. 'Pardon,' he says sweetly. '*Est-ce-que vous pouvez garder sa place en ligne? Pour un instant, seulement.*' He smiles.

She smiles back. 'OK,' she says. Her accent is adorable; I feel like I love her for a second. But when she looks at me the warmth disappears. I get it. I've cost her a lot of sleep.

Sky drags me across the quad, up the west steps and into the hallway leading into commons. It's deserted, breakfast finished an hour ago.

'So I've been thinking about it for a while,' Sky says. 'That you should go and see him in prison.'

'Who?' But I know who.

'Alton.'

'Why?' I feel the world reeling around me.

'To ask him why he did it. Who Nat really was. To *see* him.'

'Why would he tell me that?'

'Maybe he won't,' Sky says. 'But it's the only chance you have. And at least this way you'll know you tried. You could finish that memoir you started. Give yourself an ending. Endings aren't always a bad thing. Endings help you move on.'

'I wouldn't even know how to – how do people contact prisoners? What prison is he in?'

'I don't know, Wilder,' Sky says. 'But there must be a way. What I do know is that you can't go on like this. What you're living is not a life.'

It's on the news later that night. We watch it in the dirty TV den; Sky holds the remote firmly out of reach of the guy who wants to watch a pool tournament. 'Hey, man,' he says, 'just give us a minute, OK?'

The guy goes 'huh' once, then seems to relax into friendliness. He throws his hands up, like *what can you do?* I've noticed that Sky has this effect on people.

When I look back at the screen he is staring back at me – Alton Pelletier. I get a cold shock because he looks just the same, kindly and calm. I don't know what I expected – for his inside to show on the outside, somehow.

'The grieving mother of Christy Barham has implored Pelletier to meet with her, to disclose the identity of the remaining victims or to reveal the location of any other bodies. Pelletier agreed to meet with her, but today, changed his mind and withdrew visiting permission. Mrs Barham was turned away from the prison, head hanging. And Alton Pelletier keeps his silence.' Then the arrest photo comes up again. Mr Pelletier looks at me. His eyes, the kindness they hold.

'He's bored,' Sky murmurs. His eyes are narrowed at the screen. I don't think he's talking to me. 'He's bored. That's why he changed his mind about seeing her.'

'If he's bored, why not see the mother?'

'He wants her to feel his power,' Sky says, absorbed. His eyes are bright and fixed on the TV. 'He offers her hope, makes her come to the terrible decision to visit him – and then after all that, he turns her away at the last minute. Imagines her pleading.' Abruptly he turns to me. 'I think it's worth a shot. I think you should write to him.'

Someone has gummed up the payphone again, and I resignedly take a pencil out of my pocket and scrape it off. At last, when I hear a dial tone, I take the card out of my wallet. I'd forgotten about it until today. The edges are as sharp as the day she gave it to me. If I'd remembered the card I probably would have thrown it away. I went through a stage of tossing everything that reminded me of that time, including all my journals and writing. I was afraid that it would prove difficult to recall events for my memoir, but instead it's been flowing out of me, as if all I ever needed was to open the door (*pry open the lid with a crowbar, the diver's face, vomit floating on the waves*).

Sky hovers beside me. 'OK, Wilder?' He puts a hand on my shoulder. It's the first time he has touched me since that night, and even in the middle of everything else I feel it again, that weird twist of the gut. *Could be fear*, I tell myself. *Could be.*

Maybe she's moved or been promoted, I think. Maybe she's on vacation.

'Hello?' Trooper Harden's voice is the same, too. I hear her take a sip of something, imagine the steaming mug in her hand. She sounds genuinely pleased to hear my voice.

'Heya, Wilder!'

It rushes in with almost painful clarity, the memory of the first time I heard my name said in that accent. The voice that said it. This is almost too much and I have to focus, hard, to get the words out, to explain what I want.

'It isn't a good idea,' she says. 'You know that, right?'

'It's – isn't there some program that organises meetings like this? What do they call it, reconciliation?' Sky mouths the words at me and I repeat them into the receiver. 'Victim-offender dialogues.'

'Not for you,' she says. 'That's for families of the victims.'

'Isn't there any way?'

She takes a deep breath. 'You could write to him,' she says. 'He gets a lot of letters. Might read it, might not. Might answer, might not. Might grant you a visit, might not.'

'OK,' I say. 'Where do I write?'

'I'm not going to do this for you, Wilder,' she says, suddenly decisive. 'You want to get on that merry-go-round – you can. All that information is available if you want it. I don't think you should. I helped search that house after his arrest. I saw what was there. That kind of knowledge buries its way inside you.'

'OK, Trooper,' I say. 'I understand.'

'You can call me Sergeant, now.'

'I'm glad,' I say. 'You deserve it.' On a whim I say, 'What's your first name?'

'Wow,' she says, amused. 'OK, fine. It's Karen.'

'That's – a nice name.'

'It's not, and we both know it. Listen, I'm moving up in the world, to homicide. So I won't be here much longer.' She pauses. 'It took it out of me, that case. I need a change of scene.'

'Where will you go?'

'West. Washington State. The weather's still cool out there, I like that.'

'I wish I could have a change too,' I say. 'I can't leave it behind.'

'You're just a kid,' she says. 'Go be a kid.'

'Too late for that.'

'I hope not. You take care now, Wilder.' And the line is dead. I put the receiver back in the cradle, as gently as if it were a small sleeping animal.

'She won't help,' I say.

'Brave,' Sky says, squeezing my shoulder again.

'Rave,' I answer.

'Cave,' he says quietly. 'Don't worry, we can do it without her. I'll take care of everything. I promise, this will be good for you.'

Sky finds the name of the prison, fills out the visit request form, writes the letter. The whole thing seems to be spiralling further and further from my control, but I let it because I know that Sky is right. I'm not really living, haven't done for some time, not since it happened – and I want to be alive again.

He gives me the letter to read, but I don't want to look at it longer than I have to. I sign at the bottom of the page and Sky takes it away.

I check my mail cubbyhole after breakfast each day but there's nothing. *The truth.* I've been given the faint, pale hope that it might be found. But weeks pass. No reply comes and nothing happens. I realise that I have been counting on an answer, on some kind of resolution. Because it is too late for me to be a kid.

I meet Sky at commons as I do every evening. Darkness falls like a stone; it's the time of year you can feel winter reaching out for you with a cold hand. I'm hungry but I don't want to eat – the smell of meatloaf fills the cafeteria. We woke up to it this morning, drifting up from the kitchen. Smelling my dinner all day tends to put me off it. It doesn't seem to bother Sky. The food here is simple – chilli, mac and cheese, pot roast on Sundays. Most of the students seem happy with it. Rich people like to eat like children. I'd have written that down, once.

Sky digs into his meatloaf, unquestioning. The way it crumbles makes me nauseous. His book lies beside his plate, green pen keeping his place. It looks like the same place it was yesterday. He asks, as he does each evening, 'Any mail today?'

I know he's only trying to help but a hot feeling comes up. 'No there isn't,' I say. 'I wish you'd stop fricking asking.'

'Sorry,' he says, and goes back to *In Search of Lost Time.* He underscores a passage with vivid green ink. He's got another book open beside it, which seems irritating, for some reason. I pick it up. A biography of Proust.

'What's this?' I ask. A red feeling is trickling into me.

'Just doing some background reading alongside my reading,' he says cheerfully. 'I've been thinking about autofiction lately. You know, a kind of fictionalised memoir, a hybrid of a novel and an autobiography. Like this.' He points at *In Search of Lost Time*.

'Why are you thinking about that?' I ask. The red is filling me, it rises up and up.

'For you, Wilder,' he says, surprised. 'So that you can write about what happened.'

'Stop telling me what to do.'

'Someone has to.'

I pick up the copy of *In Search of Lost Time*. Its cover is so stupid, some abstract pretentious design. Sky has marked various passages with little pieces of paper and green ink. There are so many, he must have pored over that book. The red has filled me; it tips over.

'Are you ever going to finish reading that book?' My voice is raised. I'm yelling. Everyone in the cafeteria is looking at me. I don't remember getting up, but I'm on my feet, leaning over Sky, who's looking up at me with alarm. 'Every time I see you you're reading it, but you never get any further in. It's enough to make a person crazy,' I say. 'Constantly making notes, always reading that book – no one has actually read that book, you realise? – it's not going to make you a writer. You know what makes you into a writer? Writing. Why don't you focus on that, instead of asking me the same question over and over!' My fist is clenched. 'You'll use any excuse not to try, so you don't have to fail—'

Sky is on his feet. 'OK,' he says. Then he picks up his book and goes. I'm left standing alone in the cafeteria. All the eyes are on me and I feel terrified. I've pushed away the one person who was really trying to help me.

*

When I come into our room, he's writing, not notes in *In Search of Lost Time* but in a notebook. Lines of green cross the page. 'See?' he says. 'I'm taking your advice.'

'I'm so sorry,' I say to him. 'I can't understand why I did that.' But even I know that sometimes you're yelling at yourself.

'It's OK, Wilder,' he says. 'I hated that book. I only kept going with it because I thought I should. Because I thought it might be useful to you somehow.'

'I know. I'm so sorry.' I pause. 'I guess I've been tense, waiting for a reply. I started to believe in it, you know?'

'We'll just have to find another way to get you a life.' He smiles. 'I'll finish up my notes in the hallway if you want to get some sleep.'

'No.' I say. 'I like the sound.' And I do, it's soothing. I drift off to the scratch of the fountain pen.

I hoped Alton Pelletier could give me peace. Maybe I thought if the story was finally finished, I could be free.

It's not just closure, though. The truth is, I have got into writing it all down – what happened those summers. The act of it has woken the story up again. It's scratching to get out. I need an ending not just for me, but for my book. But there isn't going to be any *deus ex machina*, no dramatic confrontation with a murderer.

'You haven't seen your dad recently,' I say.

Sky looks up. 'What?'

'Your dad. He hasn't been to see you in a while. Did – did your mom find out? Is he OK?'

'He's sick,' Sky says briefly. 'And we had an argument.'

'Oh, sorry to hear that.'

'It's OK,' Sky says. 'We'll make up again, we always do.'

I walk up Pursing Hill through the snowfall, towards the hollow tree stump. Sky's leaning against it, bent intently over something. His hair is a shout of russet. He's not even wearing a coat.

'You must be freezing,' I say.

'Hm?' When he turns to me I see that one eye is ringed with dark plum. There's dried blood under his nose; in the cold it has darkened to purple.

'My god. Who did this?' I ask. 'Sky, are you OK?'

He waves an impatient hand. 'I had a big fight with my dad,' he says.

'I thought you hadn't seen him—'

'I lied,' he says, impatient.

This hurts badly. I take a deep breath. 'You never see him again,' I say, shaking. 'You promise?'

'OK, fine, but—'

'I mean it, Sky.' My voice trembles with anger. 'If someone hurts you like that you don't see them again ev—'

'Wilder, shut up for a second.' Sky takes something out of his pocket, hands it to me. It has a prison postal mark. 'Look. He replied.'

'You're opening my mail?'

'It got mixed up with mine.'

I turn the envelope over and over in my hands. 'Did you read it?'

'Yes.'

'I can't do it, Sky.'

'You have to, Wilder. There are enough secrets in the world. Bad families, bad fathers. Let's light up the truth.'

My heart is filling with lead. I don't want to take the letter. The moment I take it, this will be real.

Snow falls on the envelope, leaving little damp marks. I take it and hunch over, protecting it with my body. Snowflakes settle softly on my back.

His writing is just like Nat's. That's the worst part. I breathe through that.

The next visiting day is Christmas, Alton Pelletier writes. It should be then because he's being moved to a supermax some time in the new year, he doesn't know when. After that, only relatives and his legal counsel can visit.

I fold the letter into my pocket and take Sky's hand. 'Come on, it's cold out here.'

Back in our room I clean his face as gently as I can. When I hurt him he winces but doesn't make a sound, like a child who has been told to be brave.

'You can't go alone,' Sky says.

'I don't know if I'll go at all.' But we both know I will.

'I'll drive,' Sky says. 'I've got the car in the lot, I never use it.'

So we both stay at college. I worry about Sky giving up his Christmas – seeing his mother, going back to that white Palladian mansion in Connecticut that I've seen in pictures, missing out on roaring log fires, on holly and food and carolling.

'Sure, sure, all that good WASPy stuff,' he says cheerfully. 'It will keep until next year. I'd rather be with you.'

I call my mother.

'Hello, monkey,' she says.

'How are you, mother dearest?'

She laughs. 'Getting better all the time. Looking forward to Christmas. Shall I make a turkey or a ham? I'll make those sweet potatoes with marshmallows that you like. So disgusting.'

First, she said she'd be out by Thanksgiving, but that didn't happen. I've spoken to her doctor; she won't be out by Christmas.

'Do you know,' Mom says, 'they won't let us play checkers here? They're afraid we'll swallow the pieces. Would you believe it?'

'You don't play checkers.'

'I know that,' she says, 'but I'd like to have the option.' The medication she's on has made her very talkative. Or maybe it's her condition. She doesn't really sound like herself but it's better than the quiet she sinks into sometimes.

'Looking forward to your visit next week, monkey,' she says. 'We can make holiday plans then.'

'Mom,' I say. 'I have to talk to you about something.'

'Oh, sure.'

'I think – I'm staying here for the holidays. I'm going to visit Alton Pelletier.'

I hear her gum snap. 'Are you insane?' she says crisply.

'I have to do this.' I lean heavily against the scarred wall by the payphone. Someone has carved a line of question marks here. They grow in size. The last one on the end at the right is as big as a hand. Someone else, or maybe the same person, has scribbled the question marks even deeper into the drywall with black ballpoint.

I trace a question mark with a finger. It leaves a faint black stain – it looks like fingerprint ink. I remember the police station in Castine. Maybe it *is* fingerprint ink. Maybe the stain has stayed in me all this time, beneath my skin, only to break the surface now like (*an oil drum*) a dolphin.

'What happened that summer ruined our family,' my mother says. 'Why would you want to go back over it?'

'I have to face it,' I say. 'And I think our family was ruined before that summer.'

146

'I know what this is.' Her breath is fast and erratic. 'You're going to see your dad instead, aren't you? Choosing him over me. No one chooses me.'

'No!' I say, cursing myself. I shouldn't have mentioned Alton. She gets upset.

'Listen,' she says, 'I'm tired. Better get some rest. You take care, monkey, OK?'

'Mom—' I swallow. 'I can't wait to see you next week.'

'Why don't we hold off on that visit, Wilder. I really need my peace and quiet, you know?'

'I want to come—' I say eagerly. But there's a gentle click and she's gone.

It's just an expression, isn't it – heartbreak? But in this moment I actually feel my heart snap inside me like too-taut piano wire.

So that's how I come to spend Christmas with a murderer.

Sky's car turns out to be long and black and shining with headlights that look like big eyes. I don't recognise the logo on the front.

'What is it?'

Sky says a long word in French. 'It's embarrassing,' he says. 'People always look at it, and I'm a terrible driver.'

I hadn't even known Sky had a car and I think how strange that must be, to own something so expensive and beautiful, and never think it worth mentioning.

Sky wasn't lying: he is a really bad driver. The car is a stick shift, and there's a loud grinding noise whenever he changes gear as well as a strong scent of rubber whenever he steps on the clutch.

We drive north, the Appalachians disappear behind us. New

York seems flatter, greyer than even I remember. The winter landscape is bleak as we approach the prison. I feel it as we get nearer the sea and it makes me nauseous.

The prison is a monolith of concrete behind fences and razor wire. It looks so like what I had expected a prison to look like that I'm almost surprised. We come to a halt in the vast parking lot near the gate. White lines stretch out in endless rows. It's nearly empty. Everyone's home, full of holiday turkey and potatoes. I take a deep breath. Sky and I look at one another. 'Shit,' I say, because I can't think what to say.

'Hit,' Sky says.

'It.' The game calms me as it always does. Sometimes I wish I could talk like that always, the structure is so pleasing.

'Here.' He hands me a wad of dollar bills.

'What's this?'

'You can buy stuff from the vending machines. I suggest you get a lot. Treats. He's bored.' He pauses. 'Get your hair out of your face, Wilder.' He tucks my hair, which is getting pretty long I guess, behind my ears. The path of his fingers leave warm traces on my cold skin. 'Clean hair not obstructing the face. Didn't you read the handbook?'

'No,' I say, fear rising up to the brim. What am I doing? Sky softens.

'You'll be fine,' he says. 'Just remember, you can leave. You have all the power.'

The waiting room smells like bleach, like a crime scene.

Each layer deeper that I penetrate they take something from me. My name, at the gate. Then at the next checkpoint someone takes my sweater away – it's beige and looks too much like the colour of the inmates' uniforms. My possessions are stripped from me as I journey inwards towards him. It's like being prepared for sacrifice.

And at last, at the centre is a high-ceilinged room with tall windows. It feels like a museum. A couple of families are seated at the tables. It's quiet like in church.

'Table sixteen,' someone says. I sit down where I'm pointed. I keep my hands on the broad metal table as instructed. A baby stares at me with owlish eyes, over a woman's plaid shoulder.

He's just there, suddenly, unassuming, smaller than I remember. His skin is paler; he's not spending so much time on a boat these days.

'Hi, Mr Pelletier.' My stomach lurches. But what am I supposed to call him? He was my friend's father, and my elder. Now he has become someone else – a number, a person who gets called only by his full name on the TV.

'Hi there, Wilder.'

His voice is the same: dry, characterless. There's something crimson in his hand and my mind is buzzing so hard I can't focus at first; it's red, very red and I think – *blood?* But it's a small square of red felt. He rubs it gently between finger and thumb and yawns.

'Sorry,' he says. 'I didn't sleep last night.' And I recognise the look of the habitual insomniac – all hollowed out behind the eyes. Until Sky and I started rooming together, I had it too.

'Me neither.'

'So, how are you doing, son?' He's relaxed, friendly, like we ran into one another at the store.

'Not bad, thanks,' I say.

'You must have graduated by now. In college?'

'Yes,' I say. 'Near Philadelphia.'

'Inland.'

'I wanted that.'

149

He rubs the little square of felt between his fingers again – sees me looking. 'I just like the feel of it between my fingers,' he says. 'What do you call it, the texture. That's a thing I miss – textures. There's not too many here – metal and cement, plastic – oh, and slop. That's the food. Nothing from the natural world. Wood, water, sand. I took it all for granted, all that time, touching those things. I never knew how much I'd miss it. I go to the supermax next month,' he says. 'They tell me it's only rock outside and concrete inside. Your hands only ever touch two textures. Oh, three including your own skin.'

I watch the red felt in his fingers. I think about some of the things his hands must have touched. 'Did you never think you were going to get caught?'

'We can get into all that later,' he says gently. I flush as if I've been caught out. 'Gum helps me think.'

I jump up, fumble the wad of dollar bills from my pockets. They're damp, somehow. The vending machine has a dent in the side of it, where someone's kicked it. It is chained to the wall. My hands shake so hard I can barely feed the limp bills into the slot. They come out again with a taunting whir. But at last, a jumbo pack of Big Red falls into the well.

'I'm thinking you have questions,' Mr Pelletier says. The scent of cinnamon chewing gum drifts over the visiting room, making me think of girls at school dances. Then I think of oil drums. *Breathe*, I think grimly. *Just breathe. Breath. Wreath. Wrath.*

Alton waits, watching patiently, as if he understands what I'm feeling and sympathises.

'I wanted to ask where he came from,' I say. 'Who was he? Nat.'

'He was my son,' Alton says gently.

'His blood type says he wasn't.'

'Oh, his mother couldn't take care of him,' Alton says. 'Drugs, you know. And I wanted a child.'

150

'Did she – the mother – just give him to you?'

'Now, what could you mean by that?' Alton says, smiling. 'You got a lot of questions. I got questions too.' His fingers rub the felt. Faster. 'Thank you, son,' he says. 'For coming to see me. It's like having a part of him back.'

And I know what he means because it's the same for me. He has brought Nat back. I know they're not actually related – even so I can see my friend in the greying gold of his hair, the warmth of his blue eyes. His laugh has the same hesitant quality as his son's did, like he's just done something he's shy about. The way he says my name. It's so painful and I want it, more of it, all I can get.

'Remember that hole in the cliff with the beer?' Alton says. 'He was so proud, thought it was his secret. I used to raid it all the time when I was short. I even put some bottles back there, once or twice. For fairness. He get mad at you for taking it?'

'Yes,' I say. 'Sometimes. That was you?'

'Ayuh,' he says, and he looks so mischievous and pleased with himself that I snort a laugh before I remember.

'OK,' I say. 'I don't want to talk about him anymore.'

'Sure. How you holding up after everything?'

'I have to carry on. So I just – eat it.'

'Eat it,' he says, smiling. 'That's funny. That's something Nathaniel used to say.'

'I think he meant "suck it up".'

'Even I know that expression,' Alton says. 'Why did he always get it so wrong?'

'I don't know.' I realise that I'm smiling – not at Alton, at the memory, but still – and even worse, he's smiling too. *Remember who this is*, I tell myself. The trouble is that it's so difficult to asso-ciate this slight man with those kind eyes with what happened to the oil-drum women. But then I catch the tiny movement of his fingers, always working on that red, red felt.

'All I want to do is talk about him,' Alton says. He turns that wide, magical stare on me. 'It's hard, being in here, being without my boy.'

'I miss him,' I say. Before I realise, hot tears are making tracks down my face. 'Everything's so messed up.'

'He was good at listening to other people's problems,' Alton says. 'You and he were friends.'

'I just – I have all these things in my head,' I say. 'There's someone I – have feelings for – and I don't know what to do about it. I have these dreams . . .'

'You can talk to me,' Alton says. 'After all's said and done, I'm a father. I'll lend an ear.'

I feel it, his warmth, drawing me in. I could tell him anything. Anything at all. And he'd understand, because he's not a person, really, he's a thing. *It's safe here*, his eyes seem to say. I let the longing in, let it fill me. Just for an instant.

'I'll never tell you anything,' I say, real quiet.

Alton takes a long, slow breath and leans forward. 'Well, that's a shame. But I'll tell you something, Wilder. I'm innocent.'

'What do you—'

'It was all him. My son. I was trying to protect him. I feel like you'll understand that. You're smart.'

'You – you mean he took those pictures of the children?'

'Oh, yes. That too. And he did those terrible things to those poor women.'

'It's not possible. He was too young to have done that to anyone—'

'Yes, he was a boy, just five when he found her in the cave,' Alton says dreamily. 'He was only starting to lose his milk teeth. The first one washed up there, he came across her, but I think that's where he got the idea. And he kept her a couple days so he could practise on them with that knife. I made him that knife, you know. He used to sneak it out all the time. I let him. He kept a boat hook in the *Siren*. Used to brain seals with it. More practice. He practised until he was good and ready – he was a patient boy. When he was twelve he took his first one. The women in the water, he used to call them.' Alton peers at me. I know it's just short-sightedness, but it looks as if he's squinting against the sun. As if the Maine summer follows him everywhere, even here. There's a little snapping sound. He's flicking the nails of his forefinger and index finger against his thumbnail, just like Nat used to do.

'You're lying,' I say.

'You know that I'm not. You've thought about it.' He rubs the felt between his fingers; it almost squeaks with how hard he rubs it.

I understand what Alton is doing, now. He's storing up memories, to sustain him in the concrete. I'm a texture like sand or water. I breathe deep. In, out. I won't let him take me like he took Nat. Instead, I'm going to take Alton, use him for my memoir – my book.

'You've got those wants,' he says softly. 'Those urges.'

'What do you mean, urges?' *How does he know my secret?* I am filled with panic. The closest I've ever come to telling anyone was that day in the cave with Nat and Harper, and even then I never said the words.

'Those wants you told me about, in your letter.'

Now I really have no idea what he means.

A long beep sounds overhead. Around us visitors start to push their chairs back. Neither of us moves a muscle. Alton says, 'I'll write you. You tell me about these urges and I'll tell you about Nathaniel. You can fill his place, be a son to me.'

'No,' I say.

'I'll tell you who he was. Where he was from.'

I know I'm being manipulated. I know it's a trick. But the thought of having an answer pulls at me.

'We're allowed to hug when you leave,' Alton says. His eyes are mild but the challenge lies in the air between us.

I take a deep breath and step in. His arms go around me, tightly. 'Good to see you, son,' he says in my ear, and the words are powerful sweet gusts of Big Red. But under the cinnamon chewing gum Alton smells of nothing – as if he doesn't have a body at all.

It takes a long time to get out of the prison; I have to do it layer by layer just like I went in. The guard who took my beige sweater has no memory of it, and it's nowhere to be found. But at last I'm back out in the parking lot. Sky gets out of the car and starts to come towards me but I wave at him to stay put. I'm dizzy, can't handle a moving target.

I make it to the car OK and lean on the warm hood, surrounded by misty clouds of my panting breath. Sky's hand is on my back. 'That bad, huh?' he says.

'Oh,' I say. 'It was fine.' Then I realise I'm going to throw up, so I do, right there by the car. Sky keeps a hand on my back.

'You're OK,' he says. 'You're OK, Wilder.' When at last I'm all done he asks, 'How about we get in the car so we don't die of exposure out here?'

The heater is blasting, the soft leather seats smell so great and it's so wonderful not to be in prison anymore that I start crying. Sky gives me a pill, baby wipes for my mouth and Kleenex for the tears. He really came prepared.

'He didn't do the murders,' I say. 'Nat. I know that now, at least. They might not be father and son – but they're still father and son, you know?'

'I don't get it, Wilder.'

'Just now Alton told me Nat was a murderer. But he was lying.'

'How do you know?'

'Nat used to do this thing when he lied,' I say. 'He used to flick the nail of his thumb and forefinger together. Alton just did the exact same thing.' The car starts shaking, but then I realise it's me. 'He didn't do it, Sky. Nat didn't hurt those women.'

Sky takes a deep breath. 'That's great. And the Polaroids of the children?'

'He said Nat took them, like everyone thought.'

'Was he lying?'

I pause. 'I don't know,' I say at last. 'No. I think maybe Nat did do that.' There's a peculiar buzzing in me. 'Thank you for making me come, Sky.' I'm so relieved. Years of doubt are lifting from me, because I know I'm right. Though it's a strange, partial vindication: oh, my friend *just* took pictures of sleeping children. Just that. No big deal.

Sky hands me his green fountain pen and a notebook. 'Write it all down,' he says. 'Everything. What he said, how he looked, how it smelled. Everything. Quickly, before you forget.'

So I take the pen from him and we sit there in the desert of the prison parking lot with snow falling all around and I write. At length I slow and stop midsentence. The pen trembles over the paper, a drop of ink falls, makes a perfect emerald circle on the page.

Sky watches me. 'What is it?' he asks.

'I can't write it,' I say. 'It's too fricked up.'

'Don't be afraid of fucked up,' Sky says fiercely. 'Embrace it. Fucked up will save you. Fucked up will set you free.'

155

I take a deep breath. 'In there, he called me son. And just for a second it felt so good.' I don't tell Sky how I almost told Alton Pelletier what I feel about him. I don't tell him about the hug. I keep all that for the story.

The snow starts suddenly outside Albany, a storm of white feathers whirling on the road ahead. Sky drives fast to try to beat it, but it's heavy before we get another ten miles. I feel like it's Alton's will, somehow, clogging our escape.

'We can't go any further in this,' Sky says. 'We have to find somewhere to spend the night.'

We crawl past a motel with a vacancy sign outside, and then another one. 'There's one,' I keep saying, 'you missed it,' but Sky refuses to stop.

'Not that one,' he replies, again and again.

At last, when the road is almost impassable, a sign looms out of the dark. *Oak Lodge Guest House*, it reads.

'Ah,' he says, pleased. 'Here we go.' This place has a drive, not a forecourt. The roof has actual gables and there's a wrought iron storm lantern over the door. No vacancy sign here.

'Sky,' I say in panic. 'I can't afford this.'

'Don't worry about it, Wilder, we're celebrating. Wait here. Keep the car running and pray they have a room.' Sky gets out and strides inside. He's back in under five minutes. 'They have one left,' he says with quiet triumph. 'I think you'll like it.'

Everything in the honeymoon suite is the colour of heavy cream. There is a fireplace hung with fir cones and little lights. I suddenly remember that it's Christmas. I understand why Sky hustled us past reception. The bed is an expanse of satin. The windows have triangular leaded panes, there's a mahogany vanity, a tub with feet, which is something I've only ever seen in movies, and there are chocolates on the pillow.

'Wow,' I say, then, 'I can't afford this. I really mean it.'

'Don't worry about it, and I really mean that. We don't have a choice, anyway. You want to get back out on the road?'

The world through the window is a maelstrom of white.

'Exactly,' Sky says. 'Scotch, I think.'

He orders scotch and steaks. I wait in the bathroom when the guy delivers it. I feel uncomfortable about him knowing that we're sharing this room. Its opulence is suggestive, meant for romance. Everything covered in velvet or linen or cotton, the wood too shining, the bed too soft, too easy to touch, stroke, lie on. Such richness (*such textures*).

Through the door I hear Sky joking with the waiter. I assume he tips him. I stare at the bathtub on its little feet. I think about my friend Nathaniel Pelletier. I wonder if he remembered anything of who he really was, or if sometimes he dreamt about it, the time before – those dreams everyone has sometimes – of being little again. I hope he did. Warm arms holding him, a crib, a blanket, the knowledge of safety.

'You'd better tell me now,' I say to Sky when we're done eating. I'm ready, or as ready as I'll ever be. 'Tell me what you wrote in that letter. The one I signed my name to. He asked me about my urges. At first I thought he meant – what did you say to him?'

'Just – what we agreed,' Sky says. 'You read it.'

'Don't lie to me.' My fists are clenched. 'What are these urges I have, Sky?'

'OK, I added one thing before I mailed it. One sentence at the bottom of the page. It was no big deal.'

'What?' I hold myself in check.

'I told him you felt like doing things like that yourself, sometimes.'

'What?' My heart is in my ears, booming.

'You heard me.'

'Oh my god.' The room swims for a moment. I breathe deeply. 'You had no fricking right to do that, Sky.'

'It worked, didn't it?' Sky is tired and cold and frightened too, his usual calm is deserting him. 'He wouldn't have agreed to your visit if I hadn't. He hasn't allowed anyone else. He needed something special. A connection to you.'

I'm frightened because I felt it, in there opposite Alton. I felt the connection, and it wasn't Sky's doing – not altogether.

'I'll never forgive you,' I say.

'Let's sleep on it?' he says, weary. 'It's been a hell of a day.'

'I'll go ask them for another room,' I say coldly. 'I'll sleep in the car – whatever – but I'm not staying here with you.'

'Please don't.' Sky lifts his head and looks at me. 'Please, Wilder.' He comes and takes my hand. He places it flat on his chest, over his heart. I can feel it, his pulse through my palm, beating into my arm and all through me, his heartbeat.

'Please,' he says again and I realise: *he's scared of losing me.*

'You messed up big time,' I say.

'I know.'

The tip of my little finger grazes the warm skin of his neck, where his top button is undone. I push him away, shove against his heart until he's at arm's length. Not hard, I want to feel it, the muscle and bone of his shoulder under my hand. Sky recoils but then straightens. He leans in closer, and closer. He's taller than me but only slightly, our eyes are almost level.

He reaches and removes my glasses, puts them down gently on the desk. Now he's a blur of cheek, red stubble where he missed a spot shaving, pale skin. His clavicle is an elegant triangle.

'You're staring,' he says.

'You're worth staring at.' What a dumb thing to say. A blush scalds my face.

'So are you.'

'Don't be an asshole.'

'I'm not. These big eyes . . . I've never seen eyes so big.'

'Why was your dad coming out of our room that time, Sky? Why did he hurt you?'

He pauses. 'It's complicated. What do you want from me?'

'An answer.'

'You have all the answers you need, Wilder. It's all here.' His fingers leave hot trails on me, burning pools where they linger. 'Is this what you thought Alton meant by urges?'

My heart, my whole being thrums with his closeness. But I'm stubborn. 'I hate being lied to,' I say.

'It's complicated,' he says. 'Please let's not talk about it. Let's be you and me, alone here. Let's pretend the rest of the world is gone – dead or exploded or something.' His hand, strong and gentle on the back of my neck.

I think I knew how this would end when I saw the room, maybe I knew when we decided to take this trip.

'I've never done this before,' I say.

'With a guy.'

'With anyone.'

'We'll figure it out,' he says, and he's right.

Sometime in the deepest, blackest hours as the snow piles high against the windowpanes, he twists my neck back and pulls my ear to his mouth. 'Do it now,' he says. 'What you always wanted. Pretend I'm Nat.'

I push him away.

'Sky,' I say, 'that's really, really messed up.'

His eyes are dark gold in the low light. He says, 'Fucked up will set you free, remember? Don't be scared, Wilder. It will take the pain away.'

The human heart is deep and dark with many chambers. Things hide down there.

I wake as night breathes into morning. The sky has cleared, the beam of a crescent moon glows on the snowfall outside. The light falls through those old windowpanes onto Sky's face.

He's difficult to describe, physically, because he's always animated. He moves quickly between states and expressions, as though always escaping from one or fleeing another. The only time you can really see what he looks like is when he's asleep.

With that odd colouring he gives the impression of handsomeness but he's not really, his features don't add up. The nose is too big, the mouth a little crooked. Unlike most people he looks older when he sleeps. I can see lines and grooves of care that his restlessness hides when he's awake. The lines are deep for a face so young.

There's just enough light to see, now. Dawn is coming in, turning the dark world pink. I get my binder out of my bag softly. I take Sky's pen from the table and start to write. I put everything down, including what we just did. It's all going to be part of the book. Writers are monsters, really. We eat everything we see.

When it's written I lie back down. I test my mind and feelings gently, like someone putting weight on an injured leg for the first time since it healed. *I'm alive again*, I think. My eyes close. I hadn't realised how heavy the weight was on my heart until it was gone.

A hand wanders through my hair. There's a stinging pain in my scalp. 'Ow!'

Sky's awake, eyes on me. He holds a dark tuft in his fingers.

I clutch the smarting place on my head. 'Sky, did you – did you pull my hair out?'

He grins.

'Is it for the hair doll?'

'No,' he says. 'You're not my enemy, Wilder. I'm going to put this in a box and keep it.'

'You're a strange person.' Neither of us can stop smiling. Through the window the day is gold and blue. I can almost smell it, the cold clear air.

'It's late,' I say. 'They must have ploughed the roads. Should we get going?'

He shrugs. 'I've got nowhere to be.'

'Um.'

'Yes, Wilder?'

'Is this what it's like for everyone?'

'No. Never, actually.' And Sky's dark eyes go big and scared, he reaches for me hard, everything gets hazy, and through the rough sweet ache I think, *oh I see, we really are in trouble.*

Abruptly I push him away. 'Wait, what happens now?'

'You mean this?'

'Well – yeah. With us.'

'I don't know,' he says into my mouth, words warm with his breath. 'I don't know, Wilder, shut up. Please, just . . .' The sunlight pours over us, it seems to come from everywhere and I think, *so here it is at last and I* – but I don't finish the thought.

Love.

When we get back to college, Sky drops me out front. 'I'm starving,' he says. 'You go get us a place for dinner. I'll meet you in commons. Got to put the car in the lot.' His finger grazes the back of my hand gently. The touch runs right through me.

'OK,' I say.

After a minute he says, 'I think you have to get out of the car to do it, Wilder.'

'Sure,' I say. I can feel how stupid my smile is, so wide it almost hurts my face. 'I'm going.'

I go to commons and I save two places. It's early, there's plenty of room. Someone's made a token effort with holiday decorations – there are wreaths and ivy on the walls. I think they're plastic, but it still looks green and glossy. There's a small plastic tree in the corner with lights, paper chains. I feel festive. I look for mistletoe and then feel flushed. A few more students trickle in as I wait.

Sky's taking a while, and I wonder what's keeping him. Maybe there was a problem with the car – a tyre or something? I don't know much about cars. Time passes, and still no Sky. To hell with it, he can catch up when he gets here. I take a plate and load it with food. They have sweet potato with marshmallows.

I'll call my mom later, I think, to wish her happy holidays. And I'll call my dad. Everything will be OK. We can move on. We don't have to be chained to the past anymore. We can all be free.

The hall empties out. They start to put the food away so I quickly grab some turkey and bread for a sandwich and wrap it up in napkins. Sky will just have to make do, it's all I can sneak out of here. He never seems to care what he puts in his mouth anyway. I think about what happened last night and his mouth and suddenly everything feels very hot again. I feel transparent, like anyone who looks at me can see what I'm thinking.

Someone taps me on the shoulder. Time to go, they have to clean up.

I carry the sandwich carefully across the quad and up the stairs. The fire door hits my shin painfully as it swings closed, but I don't care.

The door to our room is slightly ajar. Maybe Sky fell asleep. We didn't sleep much last night.

I push open the door. The room smells strongly of turkey from the nearby kitchen. The bag I took up to the prison is neat and dead centre on my bed. Sky's side of the room is bare. All his stuff is gone. I look in the cubby. The little doll with teeth for eyes is gone. His closet and cubby look dingy, slightly dirty, in that way empty things do.

A folded note lies on his pillow. I seize it and open it with fingers that can't quite seem to grip (*degloved*). All this is becoming slippery as a dream.

The note reads, in ink as green as grass:

Thanks for everything.

A terrible idea is dawning. I hunt through my bag. Panting, I tip the contents out onto the bed. The folder containing all my notes, my writing and my clippings is gone.

I raise my head – are there stealthy sounds on the stairs below? Almost as if someone has been hiding in the showers so they could sneak past the door and down the stairs? As if someone was waiting there, watching, so they could see me one last time.

I hear the fire door click shut downstairs and I run. By the time I get down there no one is in sight. I run across the main quad and out back to the parking lot. There's no sign of Sky or his car. A faint scent of exhaust lingers in the air.

My anger is a ragged red scar in my chest. I'm not sleeping, the dreams are back. I keep the light on at night. The empty bed on the other side of the room gapes like a missing tooth.

Weeks pass, stretching into months. Time is blank.

Someone shakes me by the shoulder. The professor has oatmeal on his tie. There's a slide of a gorgon projected on the screen. It's architecture and the gothic, the class where I first met Sky. For a moment I think I really have slipped back in time and he's about to take me outside, sit me on a bench and teach me a word game. I look around, some feeling soaring in my chest like pain.

The hand shakes my shoulder harder and I look up. The hand belongs to a woman I vaguely recognise from the admissions office. 'If you could come with me, Mr Harlow,' she says, 'the principal would like to see you.'

'What?' I say. 'Why?'

The professor is staring, has stopped his lecture. Everyone else is staring too, the students, all those eyes, it suddenly starts to feel like every eye is a needle in my skin.

'OK,' I say to her. 'Let's go.'

I've never been in the principal's office before. It is panelled in mahogany. The windows are as tall as the ceiling, sunlight plays on the crystal of the chandelier, sends little motes and rainbows scattering across the walls. It's bigger than the room I shared with Sky, it smells like leather; I am sure right away that it never smells like chicken soup or meatloaf in here.

The principal is a woman with hair that looks like it's been cast in metal. She stands up behind her desk, which seems to me to be the size of a bus.

For a second I wonder if I am in love with her, she looks so authoritative. Maybe she can undo this mess.

Someone else stands, too. This man wears a pale suit and has shining russet hair, tamed into strict submission. He looks very like Sky.

'Young man,' he says, 'I understand you roomed with my son. Perhaps you can offer an explanation as to where he might be.'

'No,' I say. 'This is not his dad. It's a trick.'

'It's not a trick,' the man says, cold. 'I am Pierce's father.'

'Pierce?' Then I remember that Sky's real name is Pierce.

A dark crack is opening up inside me. I say to the principal, 'Sky's father has a grey moustache. Not so tall. Kin— I mean, different eyes.' This man has no moustache and does not look kind at all. But he looks very like Sky. The dark crevasse in me grows and widens. I'd known that the kind-eyed man wasn't Sky's dad – since that night I saw him sneaking out of our room. But unwelcome truth is always a cold sharp shock, no matter how prepared you think you are.

Mr Montague peels quails' eggs with his fingers. After that he has a steak which he cuts with a long, shining knife. I try not to watch. Knives like that still make me nervous sometimes. I order a burger which I eat with my hands.

Sky's father asks me questions in a way that suggests no one has ever refused to answer him.

'But maybe he's dead,' I say, feeling almost hopeful.

'He used the credit cards in New York last week,' he tells me.

'Maybe someone stole them and killed him.'

Mr Montague looks at me with a sudden distaste then shakes his head. 'He was always running away when he was young,' he says. He pats his lips with a linen napkin white as snow. 'We had to lock up the silver at night. He kept trying to steal it. Read about someone doing that in a story, I suppose. What was he going to do with sterling silver spoons? Pawn them? He was six. Always hopping from one idea to the next. My son is a disappointment to me, but I love him. He just does whatever rubs off on him. Oh god,' Mr Montague says, 'I don't know what's happening to this country. I thought, *as long as his obsession with this writing thing continues – then at least I know my son is safe.* I wish I knew where he was now.'

'I'm sorry,' I say, feeling a twinge of sympathy.

'He had a bad experience when he was young. It warped him, I'm afraid to say. Perversions.'

I put down my burger. It seems too fleshy, too bloody all of a sudden. My sympathy has evaporated.

'His unhealthy interest in murder developed as his perversion got worse,' Mr Montague says, wiping blood from his chin. 'These unsavoury excitements are all interlinked. He told me he wanted to be called Sky, of all idiocies. We have been Pierces since the Boston Tea Party.' He looks at me, assessing. 'He must have been very excited by you.'

'What?' I feel hot and transparent like blown glass.

'He is always reading about that case – doing research for his novel. I don't understand that kind of book,' Mr Montague says, signalling for the check. 'I like biographies. There's a very good one of Truman which just came out. Why did Pierce want to write, or anyone want to read about, those murders in Maine? The oil-drum women.' Mr Montague leans forward. I smell meat on his breath. 'He keeps working on it, but it never goes anywhere. It's

166

an obsession. We never should have told him what happened to him up there. That's what set it off, of course – the perversion.'

'What happened to him?' My breathing comes faster, I feel black nibbling away at my edges. 'Where?'

'You're an odd fellow,' Mr Montague says, thoughtful. 'Are you odd on the inside, too? Did you lead my son astray, I wonder?'

I'm going to black out if I stay here. I get up from the table and push my way out of the hotel. When I hit the fresh air I break into a run, and I don't stop until I reach the college gates. I don't go in, however, but find myself walking onwards, into the March afternoon.

I go up Pursing Hill to the hollow tree stump, to our place. Sky and I always meet here. Or did. Even months later, I have trouble thinking about him in the past tense. The trees are green, tight catkins are unfurling. Spring will be here soon. I think of his hands on me and snow piling up against leaded panes, sunlight flooding the room. He never existed, Sky, I have to realise that. He was just some rich kid's invention.

Sky knew who I was the whole time. He encouraged me to write it all down, what happened those summers on the Bay, so that he could steal it. I was research.

I know that I will have to write fast. Sky will be finishing his book too. This can be part of the story too. This betrayal. I'll get my ending.

In the following weeks, I try to write – but the words seem to slip away. The order things happened in has become unclear. Even the faces are fading in my memory. Why don't I have any pictures of them? Harper, Nat.

Writer's block isn't being unable to write, I discover – it's being unable to feel. And my body, my mind, my hair and legs, my very fingernails are all taken up with anger.

I stare at the page.

Writing, I think. *Writhing.*

Pursing Hill turns green. There are golden orioles in the trees. Later, they'll move on north I suppose. Maybe up to Maine, to those woods by the sea.

At last, in my empty dorm room, I write to Alton Pelletier. His transfer has been delayed by some kind of red tape, and I've nothing left to lose. *Tell me who he was,* I write. *Nat. I have to know.* Sky did this. He dug deep, uncovered all these longings then left me exposed, an open grave.

He sends back a brief note. *Come next weak. I moov end of Jun.*

It brings back memories almost painful in their intensity. Not great letter writers, either of the Pelletiers.

I spend the last of my textbook money on a train ticket to New York, to the city nearest the prison. I don't know how I'll get there from the station. Take a taxi? Walk? The journey will take twice the time it did in the car with (*don't say his name, don't even think his name*).

I get up on the morning of the visit at 5 a.m. Once more, I haven't really slept. Before I set off, I go to the payphone and call as instructed to confirm my visit.

'The prison is closed to visitors,' a bored voice says.

'But I've booked the visit,' I say stupidly. 'I'm authorised.'

'Not today.'

'Is it rioting?' I ask. 'I've read when you cancel visits it's because of rioting.'

'Are you next of kin?'

I close my eyes, Alton's voice in my ear. *You can fill his place, be a son to me.* 'No,' I say.

'Visit is cancelled, that's all.'

I replace the phone. A soft pad of bright pink gum is stuck to my ear.

I fell for it just like Christy Barham's mother. I picture Alton's gentle smile. I guess I should be grateful that I didn't get all the way to the prison before he changed his mind.

I don't find out until that evening that Alton Pelletier is dead. The news reports it. Alton was set to repair the cracks in the pavement of the yard. He ate handful after handful of wet cement as he worked, without the guards seeing him. When he was sent back to his cell at the end of the day, Alton stuffed his mouth with his bedsheets to muffle his screams as the cement set hard inside him.

I can't know, but I am convinced that this is Alton's last message to me. *Eat it.* And I feel a strange grief.

It's OK, I keep telling myself. *I can still write it.*

But I can't. Everything I put on the page is hieroglyphics. I wonder where Sky is, where my binder is, what Aphrodite is looking out at right now. He took the most important parts of me away when he went.

My mom is no better, so I stay at college over summer break and get a job in a bookstore. Pennsylvania is hot and still, and empty of students the town feels like a place I don't recognise. I long for classes to start again, for people. I drift across the parched quad like a ghost. I have more episodes. The stress even starts to affect my eyesight – I develop a blank, pale spot in the centre of my left field of vision. Stress, I suppose.

'Shall I come visit, son?' My dad's voice on the phone.

He's a loser and a dork and I hate him, of course, but I'm lonely – and he's my family. A flush of love spreads through me and I open my mouth to say *yes, please come, Dad*.

'Edith and I – well, we're not getting on so well,' he goes on. 'Might not be working out.'

'Frick off,' I say and hang up.

The parcel arrives in September, wrapped in brown paper, just before the semester starts. It's ungainly and takes up most of my cubby hole.

I don't wait to get it back to my room – I tear it open.

It's a typed manuscript. *The Sound and the Dagger*, reads the title page. *By Sky Montague*. I snort in disbelief. I flip through with trembling hands. A line jumps out at me.

I don't think people should live by the sea, it reads. *It's too big to understand.*

'No,' I say aloud. 'It's not possible.' He wouldn't, he couldn't.

There is a letter tucked into the pages, written in that vivid green.

Whistler Bay, Maine
1st September 1992

Dear Wilder,

Well, here it is, I finally wrote something, like you said. I shouldn't have tried to make you tell this story when you clearly didn't want to relive those things.

I'm writing this looking at the late summer sun on Whistler Bay. Strange to be back. I haven't been here since it happened – it's beautiful, I'd forgotten.

I wasn't being honest with you, or myself. This is my story, too – you'll see, when you get to page ninety-two.

A publisher has accepted the book, it comes out next year. But I want you to see this final draft, with all my mistakes and corrections. I'm trying to tell the truth these days.

I had to leave quickly Wilder, or I wouldn't have had the courage to go at all.

Go live your life. Be fucked up. Be free. You might not believe this, but—

With all my love,
Sky

Grimly, I turn the cover page and start to read. The manuscript is full of green notes in the margins, crossings out and passages corrected with white-out. *Indecisive*, I think. Always trying to be liked.

I finish *The Sound and the Dagger* in a day. During the first couple of pages I alternate between horror and floods of warm relief. It isn't too well written. I scoff with ashamed glee at each dangling participle. Then every so often I come across a line lifted right from my memoir and my hands clench as if around a throat.

The plot is all too familiar.

The story is told backwards, from the perspective of the hero Skandar. Skandar meets Wiley at college. They become friends.

Wiley reveals his traumatic past to Skandar, and they become lovers. It's kind of sweet, actually. It seems like a coming-of-age story at first. But then the book shifts into the past.

The bullied protagonist Wiley arrives at the summer cottage above a bay named Looking Glass Sound. He befriends two local kids. They sit on a tiny beach eating striper cooked over a fire. Wiley and Nate are both in love with Helen. After a terrible accident in a sea cave, Nate is wounded. His father is arrested for being the serial killer known as the Lifeguard (it's ironic) who abducts women swimmers, tortures and murders them. He stores their bodies in barrels, sunk in the pools of a sea cave.

It's not the thoughtful, truthful memoir I wanted to write. It's horror. It's – schlock. It's obscene. Worst of all, Sky turns Rebecca, a real woman who died, into a kind of Hammer horror ghoul. She's dark and voluptuous and drowns in a long red dress – who goes swimming in a long red dress? There's a bloody wound on her shoulder, from where she was caught in the shark rig the Lifeguard uses to catch swimming women. Her ghost becomes a kind of siren, luring swimmers out into the riptide.

I think of the real Rebecca, the one I've looked at so often in newsprint – blonde, slight, sunlit, leaning against the windowsill, framed by tulips. 'I'm sorry,' I whisper to her.

The other characters don't fare much better. *Helen was slender, with a bright silver streak through her blood-red hair. He could see the age in her young eyes.*

Yuck.

Anton had eyes like the black behind the stars, and hair that lay flat on his head like an oil slick. He carries a boat hook everywhere (it's a red herring).

Nate was whip-thin, brown as tanned leather, with a smile that twisted up at the corner.

Skandar, our hero, is of course tall and self-deprecating. His hair is always tousled, a cloud of auburn.

Then there's Wiley. *Wiley's eyes were so small they seemed to disappear into his face like a mole's. Even in sleep, there was always a suppressed rage about him. Nothing makes a man so angry as knowing that he's part of the wallpaper.*

I shake with anger as I read.

Sky somehow knows things I never told him. He mentions the blood running down into the seawater pooled at the bottom of the boat and turning it crimson. I didn't mention or write that – I'm certain of it. He talks about the shape of Helen's leg, the down on it that *gleamed in the sunlight like fine wire.* I didn't tell him that either. It's like he's been hunting around inside my memories. *Can someone do that?* I think wildly. *Take thoughts right out of your head?*

I wish once more that I could kill him – but kill him a year ago, the day we first met, so I would never have to feel this.

I reach page ninety-two.

The Sound and the Dagger
by Sky Montague

Page 92

'I don't really remember it,' Skandar says. He kicks his sneakers off as they reach the stream. He ties the laces together, slings them round his neck and wades into the fast brown water. Wiley waits patiently on the grassy bank. He hates cold water.

'It was years ago. I was just a little kid.' But Skandar does remember and Wiley knows it.

'Tell me,' he says.

Skandar was excited because he was eleven, and what kid isn't excited to go to the beach for the summer? The house was white and beautiful. The sea was right there below – right there! There were sharks in ocean, he could tell. He was really into sharks.

The holiday was strained at first because his mom and dad were still mad at each other.

It had all started when Sally took him to the store. Sally was NOT his mom, she was the nanny, but she did all the mom stuff like snacks and playing tag and looking under the bed and in closets for monsters. At the store, Sally let him choose his own toy once a week. And the one he chose wasn't good, apparently, not one for boys. But Skandar loved his new doll – she had shiny hair and a string you pulled in her back that made her say, 'I'm pretty!'

The night he bought the pretty toy, Skandar woke to yelling and got out of bed. He followed the voices down the hall. He held his blanket tightly – he had brought it with him for protection. He stood outside the door and listened.

'It's a little girl's doll!' Daddy said. 'Sally can't control him. She's no good. I won't take her on vacation.'

'It was just a goddamn doll, the kid didn't know what he was doing. Kids are not rocket scientists,' Mommy yelled. 'I'm not going without a nanny.'

Mommy was mad because who was going to look after the kid in the middle of goddamn nowhere? She worked hard goddamn it, organising the DAR benefit last month had nearly killed her. Mommy was very loud and Daddy hated that. Usually Mommy being loud was enough to change his mind.

But this time Daddy said, 'Then we'll stay here for the summer,' and Skandar could tell that he meant it. It wasn't just about the doll, he knew that. It was all the other things, the secret things he knew he wasn't supposed to feel. His daddy could see he wasn't right inside and never had been.

Skandar crept back to bed. He thought very carefully about what to do. He wanted Mommy and Daddy to be happy, and he wanted to go on vacation.

So the next day he went to his daddy in his study and said, 'Can I have one more toy this week?'

Daddy looked up from his piles of paper and said sharply, 'You've had your toy this week.'

'I threw that one away,' Skandar said. 'It was a toy for a little kid and for girls. I beat it up to pieces and I threw it in the woods. Now I want an action man. I want an action man with a gun. Sally can take me to the store. Please may I?'

'All right, son,' Daddy said. He patted Skandar on the head. And Skandar played with the action man and the gun for the rest of the week, especially in the evenings after Daddy came home.

So they went on vacation after all and even Sally came after all and she had a little room next to his own room and both rooms had windows that looked out onto the sea. It was great.

Skandar played with his action man on the beach, running up and down, *pow pow*. By the end of the first day he was so tired he nearly fell asleep in his lasagne. Sally put him to bed. He got the pretty doll out from his secret place in his suitcase and slept with her cradled in his arms.

He woke to a flash. *Lightning*, he thought, but there was a person behind the lightning. A hand reached, and the doll was pulled gently from his hand. Skandar saw a figure, the monster behind the lightning. It seemed really tall, and then straight after, he thought it might be a kid, like him. Something shone in its hand – a beam of light, a knife. Skandar felt the cold grip of fear on his guts. He understood right away that this was also him. His other half, the bad stuff inside him coming out. This was Bad Skandar, Shadow Skandar, who wanted to do wrong things. The knife came closer, closer. Something brushed the top of his head. A hand.

Skandar lay frozen in the dark, as Bad Skandar softly stroked his hair.

Skandar closed his eyes and began to scream. When he opened them again the lights were on, Bad Skandar was gone, the curtains were fluttering in the breeze. The open window showed a black square of night. Mommy and Daddy were there. They all looked at the Polaroid which lay on the floor, then back at Skandar. So many eyes. Mommy picked up the Polaroid. It showed Good Skandar sleeping. Something shone at his neck. Her hand covered her mouth, her face was pale like white butter. 'What did he do to you?' she asked. 'What did he do?'

Everything in the bed was wet. Skandar was ashamed; he wasn't a baby, he hadn't wet the bed for years. But the other thing was worse. Daddy was staring and Skandar looked down, following his eyes. He burst into tears, because now Daddy knew he was a liar, and that Bad Skandar was real.

The doll lay on the floor where Bad Skandar had dropped her. Daddy picked her up. 'I'm pretty,' she said in a tinny voice.

They went home the next day and never reported it to the police.

It is years before Skandar understands what really happened that night – when the newspapers start publishing stories about the Dagger Man of Looking Glass Sound.

Wiley kicks off his sandals and wades into the stream to where Skandar stands. His pants are wet to the knees but he doesn't seem to notice. 'I'm sorry,' he says.

'I imagine him sometimes,' Skandar says. 'The Dagger Man. I can't help thinking of him as Bad Skandar, still, out there, alone in the night. I feel sorry for him.'

Wiley's hand comes to rest on Skandar's back. For Skandar the world narrows down to Wiley's palm, warm through the thin cotton.

'It messed me up,' Skandar says.

'It's OK to be messed up,' Wiley says. 'Being messed up sets you free.'

Wiley takes off his glasses and puts them in his breast pocket. His eyes are small but very grey like pinpoints of light. He puts his hand on Skandar's hip, then slides it gently under his t-shirt, up his stomach and chest. His palm comes to rest over Skandar's heart which beats like a drum. All the world stops, they are at its still centre. The stream is gone, everything is gone except Wiley's hand, and his breath soft on Skandar's neck.

Wilder

The Polaroid falls to the floor, loosed from the pages. It's faded now, but I can still make out the features of a sleeping child with messy russet hair. A thin, shining thing hovers by his throat. The shade of the hair, the nose is familiar. The thick lashes on closed lids. It's Sky, of course. I'd know him anywhere.

My heart twists. Sky is so little, in the picture – so easily harmed. I think of them both – Nat and Sky, two messed-up kids in a dark bedroom. This moment, this flash of connection between them before I ever knew either of them existed.

Anger settles back in with its hooked barbs. 'No,' I mutter through clenched teeth. 'That does not give you the right.' I am close to blacking out. But I have to finish reading, I have to know it all.

After his father's arrest, Nate kills himself. It emerges that he had been sneaking into children's bedrooms and taking photographs of them as they slept. He is the Dagger Man of Looking Glass Sound. Back at university Wiley's behaviour is becoming more and more erratic, and his obsession with Skandar more unhinged. So our hero comes to suspect the truth: that Wiley was the Lifeguard all along, and Nate's father was innocent.

Wiley flees from college and Skandar pursues him back to Looking Glass Sound, where they have a confrontation in the cave where the barrel women were found. Wiley attacks Skandar, who kills him in self-defence. The ghost of the first barrel woman, Rebecca, pulls Wiley down into the depths of the ocean. At the end Skandar and Helen realise they're in love. The story ends.

I stand up, unsteady. My breath comes fast, there are bright and dark spots on my vision. I need air. I stumble down the stairs, out into the cool evening. I can hear ravens on the wing above me. The Polaroid is still in my hand, I realise. I throw it as far as I can. It flutters down onto the college lawn.

I wipe my eyes angrily with the back of my sleeve. I take a deep breath. 'Frick you, Pierce,' I shout aloud to the empty quad. I flex my hands, imagine the feel of a throat in them. 'Frick you, frick you!' I yell. Birds scatter like black confetti on the sky.

Right away I go and pick up the Polaroid again, wipe it clean of dew. I have to keep it. Preserve it. Every time I feel my anger dim, I tell myself, I will look at this again. Sky thinks *this* gave him the right to steal my story.

'I should have killed you,' I say aloud. 'It's mine.' Or it was mine. I feel it slipping away from me already. There's no point in trying to write anything now. Sky has emptied me out.

I understand, cool and clear, what I have to do. I'm going to find Sky. I'm going back to Whistler Bay.

Pearl

Pearl is making a tuna sandwich. She plans to drink a glass of milk with it. Simple pleasures. She's happy. Summer's ending and the city feels uncommonly alive. It's a sunny, shining nickel of a New York day.

She sees Harper's number come up on the caller ID display and her heart leaps. *Forgiven,* she thinks. Harper isn't exactly speaking to Pearl – but today seems like a day to believe in things.

She licks tuna from her thumb and answers.

At first, she thinks she's made a mistake because the voice on the other end sounds nothing like Harper. It's cracked, heavy with breath. A ghost's voice. Harper is crying.

'What's the matter?' Pearl asks. 'Oh, Harper, what's wrong?'

When Pearl hears that he is dead, she sits down on the kitchen floor.

In her ear Harper says, 'You did this.'

Pearl realises that the floor is wet. Milk spreads in a cool ghostly pool about her. The carton is broken, nearby. She must have dropped it. She realises with a start that she's still holding the phone and she puts it back on the wall cradle carefully. There's no one on the other end anymore. Harper hung up some time ago. The kitchen smells of tuna fish and so do her hands. Why? Vaguely she remembers the sandwich she was making when she answered the phone. For the rest of her life even the smell of tuna will make her retch.

Pearl thinks about the fact that he is dead. It has been a long time since she felt this kind of pain – since her mother died, in fact. She observes it with detached interest. She wishes she had a notebook and a pen. It's fascinating.

After a certain amount of time she wipes her face – interesting, she hadn't noticed she had been crying – and mops up the milk with paper towel.

'If ever there was a time for witchcraft,' she says to her quiet apartment, 'it's now.' That stuff doesn't work, it never has. Pearl tried it for her mother. She used her pearl, the one she kept from her earring. It didn't work.

But that was more than ten years after she died. Time must make a difference, mustn't it? He's only just gone – freshly dead. She thinks hard and starts to laugh. Of course. She knows where she can always find him – even in death.

Pearl goes to the living room. *The Sound and the Dagger* stares at her from the bookshelf. The cover is unnerving. A boat hook, a night sky over the sea. Blood-red lettering. Somehow that double 'G' in *Dagger* bears an uncomfortable resemblance to a pair of eyes. He's scattered throughout this book. She can use it.

Pearl goes to the cocktail trolley. She takes the knife she uses for cutting lemons and pierces her finger with the tip. It hurts even more than she expects and she dimly recalls some fact about grief exacerbating physical pain. She lets her blood trickle into a wineglass. She pulls the cork out of a random bottle and takes a swig of wine. She swills it around her mouth then spits it into the glass. She's not planning but acting on instinct now, using objects she finds to hand. It's the same kind of hypnotic state she gets into when she's writing.

She knows what she needs next. She takes the doll carefully from the drawer by her bed. Its tooth eyes stare, blank. She takes a couple of precious strands of his hair from the lock she keeps safe. She wraps the letter around it. She takes the chewing gum from the same drawer. For a moment she lets it rest in her mouth. It's cold, hard, holds no memory of his mouth.

In the bathroom, she opens *The Sound and the Dagger*. She finds a part about him and traces the words carefully in blood and wine, with a needle. One line will be enough, she thinks. Pearl puts the book, the doll and the hair in the bath tub and pours over blood and wine. It's thick, viscous, she doesn't like it; there is something alive about the mixture, as though it's gestating. The book's a special advance copy; it's a shame really, but magic has to cost you. She takes the pearl out of her locket. Real magic costs you a lot.

She pushes the pearl into the centre of the doll, like a heart, or a belly button. Then she opens the book so the pages catch better, and strikes a match. At first the pile smokes sullenly, so she squirts on some paint stripper she finds under the sink – magic is like this, it always provides – and then it crackles up, bright and stinking. The hair fizzles with a fecal stench. The bathroom is full of smoke and Pearl's head swims. She thinks, peacefully, *so this is the real magic – this is how I join him.*

She is dimly aware of the cracking of wood and shouting. Someone has broken down the door of her apartment. But the floor grips her like a magnet and she can't move. There are legs and voices all around, kind hands raise her and someone directs white foam at the burning pile in the bathtub.

'Are you crazy, lady?' someone asks, shaking her, before someone else stops them. They're pulling her up, and she sees the bathroom for what it is now: a death chamber with smoke-blackened walls.

As they pull her away Pearl struggles and frees an arm, manages to reach into the smouldering debris in the tub and grab the cracked, blackened pearl from the wreckage. Its surface is charred and rough. It will never be bright again. Neither of them will. There is no such thing as magic or witchcraft; he's dead and will stay dead for ever.

'I love you,' she whispers. But she can already feel it – his absence in the world.

Wilder, Day One

2023

As soon as I hear he's really dead, I get on the train. I don't drive anymore. Emily used to cry over it, my declining eyesight. The truth is, I kind of like it – this gradual blurring, the world fading into white.

Sky went sailing, just struck out to sea and never came home. It was like one of his stories, everyone says. It's like *The Sound and the Dagger*.

He dies in stages – first of all he goes out sailing and doesn't come home. Dark comes and he's still gone. The next day, the coastguard is called out, they comb the shore. The hospitals are checked. On the fourth day, his boat is found washed up on a sandbank. On the fifth day, a severed finger is caught in a net by a trawler north of the point. It's wearing Sky's ring. It has his fingerprint. He's presumed dead. Rescuers give up the search.

At dusk they announce it on the satellite news channels – Sky Montague is dead. Only then do I let myself believe it.

Lost at sea. A romantic end; he would have appreciated it. I would have preferred he'd died of something involving a rash. I imagine it – the sea all around him, navy-blue and cold, clutching him tighter, pulling him deeper and deeper into its folds. I wonder if parts of him are keeping her company, the last, lost oil-drum woman, where she lies on the ocean floor.

Maybe it suits him after all – that death.

The Sound, Sky's boat was called. He could never get away from that first book.

I buy a can of beer from the automated vending machine when it comes trundling down the aisle. There's not much left on the credit card I suspect – but I'm celebrating, after all.

The manuscript of *The Sound and the Dagger* sits on the seat beside me, tied up with string and carefully enclosed in Saran wrap. His letter is on top, encased in a plastic sleeve. Each time the train rounds a bend I hear the book shift on the seat, as if it's whispering to itself.

I kept it, of course I did. I make myself read it sometimes to keep the fires fresh. The hurt. You have to coax anger along, otherwise after a certain time it dies.

I have a published copy of *The Sound and the Dagger* in my briefcase, too. I might need it for reference. But it's the manuscript that grips me. All those frantic green corrections, the little crusted islands of white-out, hiding Sky's first, corrected thoughts. Sometimes I think about scraping them off to see what lies beneath.

He wrote other books after *The Sound and the Dagger*. I think people only bought them because they loved that first damn book so much. He got the keys to the kingdom because of that book. He conned everyone into thinking he was a writer, when all he was, was a thief. I find my hands tightening into fists.

'Fuck you, *Pierce*.'

A woman across the aisle looks at me in alarm and I realise I'm muttering the words aloud. A beam of rose-coloured light passes though the carriage, through the woman, surrounding her head with a holy corona, all the shades of a summer dawn.

I'm finally finishing that journey I started thirty-one years ago. I'm going to Whistler Bay to kill Sky. I didn't do it back then of course. I got as far as New York City before I lost my nerve. I got off the train and headed back to Philadelphia. Part of me has always been glad I did. Another part hates myself for my cowardice.

With the new maglev rail, the journey takes half the time it did when I was seventeen. But it's the same: train to Portland, a bus to Castine and a cab out here.

'Nice to see you again,' the cab driver says, which adds to the unreality of it all. He's no more than twenty, must be mistaking me for someone else. I see a soap playing on a little screen set into the dash. Was he talking to the TV? This must be a lonely job.

I expect it to be different somehow – the hill less green, the house less neat and perfect. But Whistler Cottage looks just the same, white like a gull perched up there. I'm the one who's different.

I get out of the cab down in the road. There's the spot, right there, where I found the Polaroid of the Abbott girl.

I try to notice my feelings as I climb the hill (that's more difficult than it was, there's a difference right there). I notice that I feel sweaty and maybe hungry. Big moments are like that sometimes. You wait for the burst of feeling but actually you just kind of want a snack.

In the kitchen, I lean against the wall and breathe.

'Hello again.' I feel my sixteen-year-old self stirring. Time travel. Dusk is falling but I don't turn on a light. Through the window the sun sinks, a copper ball on the sea. Exhaustion creeps up my limbs. It's been a long day and I head for the bedroom, feeling my way along the walls with fingertips. I need to get used to the house.

I could sleep in the master, I suppose, but I don't want to. That's my parents' room. They have both been dead for years, but they still follow me almost everywhere. Or that's what it feels like.

The room is smaller than I remember. There's a soft blue blanket folded at the foot of the single bed. I open the porthole. The restrictors my father put on all those years ago are long gone. I breathe the night air and wait. The sea whispers, faint. It sounds like pages shuffling. A seal barks. I lick a finger and test the breeze. The wind is in the east.

A moment later it comes, mournful and high. The stones are singing and I feel it, at last, that I'm home. I listen for a time, despite my tiredness. I think, *if heartbreak had a sound, it would be just like this.* I imagine what the stones might be saying about me – Wilder Harlow, come back to Whistler Cottage thirty-three years later and just as many pounds heavier, almost blind, to write this book. This time I won't fail.

In the night I wake to a sound like scratching. I close the porthole but the sound continues. I know it's just a branch on a windowpane somewhere down the side of the house – but it sounds like a pen, writing on paper. I recall that first night Sky moved into my dorm room, when I had the nightmare. How he comforted me, kept the light on so I wouldn't be afraid. I fell asleep to the sound of his pen scratching across the page. For a moment there's a beat of warmth in me.

But what was he writing? Skandar's story probably. My warmth evaporates. I imagine that vivid green ink scrawling all over the cottage, the bay, the sky, like marker pen on transparency. Him, marking my stuff. My house, my past, my place. Me.

A long chorus line of small, elven figures dances across the dark before me. They doff their scarlet caps in unison. Their bright eyes flash.

It's called Charles Bonnet syndrome and it often accompanies macular degeneration. That pale spot that developed on my vision during college has been spreading for years. Now the centre is almost entirely white and gone. At the moment I can still see fairly well on the peripheries. The fancy Manhattan doctor Emily took me to told me to prepare myself for a long, slow descent into blindness.

What no one expected were the visions.

The first time I had one, Emily and I were in a restaurant. I saw a wisteria plant growing up the waiter. It captured his waist in its twisting grey branches, spread its delicate purple blossoms all over his head.

The fancy Manhattan doctor thinks that the only thing that prevents this from happening to everyone is the brain being forced to process sight all the time. When there's no more work to do, it goes rogue.

'Try and see this as your mind playing, being free, now that it's not so busy with sight.'

And I did for a second, I really did try to think of my coming blindness as freedom, as an extra ability. Then I felt like kicking him in the nuts.

Anyway I've gotten somewhat used to it. The visions don't frighten me anymore. I can usually tell what's real and what isn't.

In the helpful light of morning I do a quick inventory. I have the credit card I took from Emily's wallet and some cash. Not much. It will be enough.

The cottage is decorated in a way I don't recognise. Who chose all this stuff? The bright rag rugs, the white cotton, the rattan furniture. Everything neat and clean. I can't associate it with the grumpy man I speak to on the phone at the rental agency.

Sometimes he mentions 'a girl from town who comes in to help', so I guess she picked all this. I like it.

Uncle Vernon's terrible Polaroids are gone, disappeared somewhere over the years. I kind of miss them. The refrigerator's the new kind with the voice controls and the store cupboards are stocked. Even the instant macaroni and cheese I used to like is here. As a teenager I ate it by the bucket. I feel like someone's looking after me. Like maybe Whistler Bay is glad I'm back.

OK. Begin. Time to really kill him.

I get out my old Remington. *Laptops are for taxes and satmails*, I tell myself. *Typewriters are for writing.* The truth is that it's difficult for me to see the screen on a laptop. Typescript on a white page is easier.

I pull my desk out under the old sugar maple. It has grown so tall – it's the only thing around here that looks bigger than it used to. Thirty-three years will grow and shrink you in unexpected ways. I make instant coffee in a pan, on the stove, add milk and take it outside. The coffee's too hot and I burn my lips. Overhead, the leaves whisper.

I couldn't come back here after *The Sound and the Dagger* was published. Not after Sky started renting the big house each summer. The one Harper's parents used to own. What an imagination he had, everyone says so. What a book it was. Even the families of the oil-drum women felt he really captured the atmosphere of the place. The feeling. Their grief.

I still remember how I felt when I first saw a photograph of Sky, here – standing on Main Street in Castine, in front of the place the fishmonger used to be. Christy Barham's old store. It's a VR café now. The kids love them, I hear. I don't get it. Who needs virtual reality when you have books?

Anyway, I was at the dentist, I opened a magazine and there he was, staring at me, hair tousled, russet. It was the summer the book came out. That was a bad one – hot in Pennsylvania but also burning hot inside me, like there were handfuls of coal in my stomach. That day I had an episode in my class on Faulkner. It was, as it turns out, me who lay dying. On the floor. Of the classroom. Bad joke, never mind.

After that Sky came up to the bay every summer. He became famous for it. People used to come here from all over the world, hoping to run into him.

I've had years to think about my time with Sky. There's not a moment I haven't pored over and analysed. And I know why he read *In Search of Lost Time* obsessively throughout the semester, alongside that biography of Proust. He was working out the mechanics of it – how to blend my writing, my truth with his egotistical schlock.

No one knows the truth but they will soon. I have to be smart about this. You can't libel dead people, of course, but you also can't be too careful. I want it published, and widely. Also, even if it can't bother me, I don't want people to think I'm petty. Also some of the stuff that happened might be difficult for Emily to take.

Autofiction indeed.

I stare at the great white expanse of page. I realise that I don't want to start. *Don't go there*, as my students say.

Snow on windowpanes, his touch, sunlight everywhere. *Fucked up will set you free.* I've nailed the first part. Soon, with any luck, I'll be free.

It's not working. I can see it all, glowing in my mind like stained glass. Why can't I write it?

The maple tree whispers. A neon-yellow cloud of songbirds burst from the sea. They drag bright golden script behind them – beautiful, flowing calligraphy. *Wilder, Wilder, Wilder* it says over and over. I close my eyes and count like the doctor showed me. I take deep breaths. When I open my eyes again they're gone.

Even the birds I hallucinate are writing. Why can't I?

I start up, with the sense of someone having just left or maybe touched me gently before running away. Is the gate swaying in the wind? Is there a scent, some acrid tang in the air?

There's a breeze up so when the sound comes again it's still faint enough to be imagination. My first thought is *the stones?* I test the wind with a licked finger, but it's blowing from the south. The next time it comes I'm sure – it's a human voice, calling from the cove below. And on the third I can even make out the words.

'Help, can someone help me?'

I go to the edge as quickly as I can, shade my eyes and stare at the glittering water below. I can just about see a black shape

– a head perhaps, bobbing. It dips beneath the gleaming skin of water, and then reappears. 'Please,' she shouts. 'Help!'

The ground gives with a squelch as I hurry out of the gate. Sand and shale scatter in my wake as I go down the narrow path to the sea. When I reach the little beach I see her more clearly, out at the mouth of the bay where the grey cliffs stop and it turns to open water. Pale face framed by dark hair, slick on her head.

The woman waves with a frantic arm as she disappears beneath the surface once more. I kick my shoes off in the sand and plunge fully dressed into the water. She shouts something indistinct. I think she's getting tired.

'I'm coming!' I yell.

I gasp as the freezing sea reaches my heart. I strike out in a crawl, wheezing with the deathly cold. The waves slap my face, my mouth is filled with frigid salt water. She must have a cramp. Or maybe her leg is caught in something beneath the surface? Old fishing net or something similar. That happened to a child just down the coast a few summers ago; I read about it. I see that she's right next to a pale blue buoy; maybe she's tangled in its rope.

I can make out her features now. A heart-shaped face, full, beautiful lips. She's wearing something dark, not a swimsuit, I don't think. Her shoulders are sharp and shapely through translucent dark linen.

The dress slips off her shoulder and for a horrified moment I think she's wounded. But then I see she has a large birthmark, roughly the shape of an apple with one bite taken out of it, spreading dark over one shoulder.

She gasps and spits a jet of water. The dress isn't black, I see, but blue, darker with the water. It billows and floats about her. Her skirts balloon on the waves. So she went in the water fully clothed. That's not a good sign. People don't generally get in the sea in long dresses when everything is going well. But maybe she fell off a cliff or a boat or—

A roller dashes me directly in the face. I cough and sink. For a moment I drop below the cold green horizon. Water rushes by my ears, into my nostrils. I kick up and break the surface, gasping.

She's gone. I can't see her anywhere. She must have grown tired. I've got to be quick. I redouble my efforts, muscles burning with the unexpected strain. When I reach the blue buoy I take a deep breath and dip beneath the surface, peering for a glimpse of fluttering blue linen. There's nothing but clear, still sea.

I'm no longer out of my depth, here. The middle of the bay is deeper than the narrow mouth, which is protected by an under-water sandbank. So when I sink my feet into the soft bottom, the water only reaches my waist. Even if she's much shorter than me, she should have been able to stand here comfortably. Where is she? Frantic, I plunge down again and again, peering in every direction. There's good visibility for some distance. The current isn't strong; I should be able to see her, or at least that billowing blue dress, even at a distance, even beneath the water.

Fear is washing through me, colder than the sea. There must be a riptide somewhere; it caught her, pulled her under, out into the open ocean.

I flail back to the shore and stumble up the path barefoot. From the clifftop, I can see the buoy bobbing on the ocean. No waving arm, no blue-clad form floating face down. She is simply gone – not drowned, because where is the body? – but vanished. I run inside, grab my cellphone and dial 911. The operator is soothing but seems to me unhurried so my voice rises higher and higher in frustration.

'Sir?' she says. 'I need you to breathe?'

It feels like forever, but actually someone is here within the hour.

The coastguard shouts as he rounds the headland in a boat with an outboard motor. I think I expected something more official. As the sun sinks lower he combs the cove and the open sea beyond, but finds nothing. He comes ashore as darkness takes the bay. He's older, with that skin you see round here, cured brown by being on the sea.

I wonder if he was on that boat that day, the day the oil-drum women were found.

'Are you sure it was a person?' he asks. 'Could it have been a plastic bag floating on the surface? The water plays tricks on the eyes.'

'I'm sure,' I say. 'She was calling for help – I saw and heard her quite clearly.'

'Well,' he says. 'The only access way to this cove is to come past your cottage up there, right?'

'Yes.'

'She would have to have come straight past you.'

'That – yes, that's correct.'

'Unless she fell overboard from a boat. And nothing of that nature has been reported.'

'All right,' I say, irritable. I recognise what he's doing; I do it to my worst Great American Lit students all the time – make them state the facts out loud, logic themselves out of their own bad assertions.

'There's always one or two called in each year,' he says. 'Mermaids, sirens. People want to believe those things.'

'It's got a soul of its own, this place,' I say.

'That it does,' he agrees, looking at me with a flicker of interest.

'Were you here when the oil-drum women were found?' I ask.

His expression goes cold. 'You make up that story about a woman drowning so you could call me out, talk to me about that? You got a lot of nerve.'

195

'No,' I say, horrified. 'Of course not!'

'We get your kind round here all the time. Be aware that you can be charged for making a false report and wasting coastguard resources.' I wonder if this is true.

'She was *there*,' I say. 'I saw her and heard her.'

'You take care,' he says in a tone that says he hopes I don't.

After he leaves I watch the moon on the cove for a time, before the night chill drives me indoors, shivering. I'm really upset. I didn't hallucinate her, I know that.

My condition is strictly a visual one. You don't hear or feel anything, the doctor was very clear on that.

And I heard her voice. *Help.* I always know what's real and what isn't, I tell myself.

The thought that pokes at my mind, like a tongue at a bad tooth is – *I know her somehow, that woman.* I hope she's not dead.

In the kitchen, in the warmth of the range, I take off my wet clothes wearily. I mustn't ruin them, I only brought a couple things with me. Emily is the one with the money. My heart gives a sad little dip. Divorce is such a sundering. Plus, expensive. I can save her that.

After lots of searching and opening and closing of cupboards and once, accidentally shutting myself into the closet under the stairs, I find a wooden rack. I spread the wet clothes over it and put it in front of the stove to dry. Even with the terrible day I've had, I feel a little pleased with myself for having solved this domestic problem.

I gasp myself out of a shallow sleep, fighting the sheets, trying to dispel the dream of being smothered in wet blue linen. I am flooded with that same sense of recognition which visited me earlier tonight – about her, yes, but more – the whole scene is like something I've seen or dreamed: the dress billowing in the cold sea, her cry for help, my cold rescue attempt. I stare into the dark, my heart drumming in my chest. Who was she? Where did she go? And how do I know her? It eats at me until dawn puts pale fingers through the shutters and it's time to start the ghastly business of the day all over again.

A pattern of dashes and diamonds rolls black over the dawn sky.

My pants, underwear and shirt have dried into solid crisp shapes, which still hold the form of the rack after I lift them off. I think they are still wearable. The belt is ruined. The wet leather has shrunk and hardened to the consistency of rock.

I call Emily.

'Yes, Wilder, what is it?' She sounds like she's in a restaurant or some busy place, which is strange: she hates to go out before noon. Or maybe it was me who hated it. That's marriage – you grow into one another like that.

I say without thinking, 'Hello, darling.'

An awful silence falls, a deep plunge of horror and regret. Someone has to break it, so I do. 'I wanted to ask you something.' At least my voice sounds relatively normal, no sign of the hideousness inside me. 'I had a strange exchange with a girl in Castine the other day; she seemed to know me, but I couldn't place her.

I was wondering if she was a girl from the city, maybe? Or from around here and maybe we met her in the city . . .'

Emily takes a breath. 'Describe.' That was a bad moment, but she could never resist gossip.

'Mid-twenties, dark hair, attractive, large birthmark on her shoulder.'

'We don't know anyone like that.' She's eating something as we talk, I can hear it – there's a fullness, a wetness around her words.

'She was wearing a blue dress,' I say. 'She looked kind of like something out of an old Italian movie.'

'Rings no bells,' she says.

'Well thanks for your time,' I say frostily. 'I won't keep you from your lunch any longer.' Though it's barely ten o'clock.

'It sounds like something out of that book you hate.' She takes another bite of whatever it is.

'Emily—' I had thought I was annoyed with her, but it's so easy to mistake one feeling for another. My chest feels spongy, soft with longing, 'Can I come home?'

She clears her throat, that sound I know so well. It has nothing to do with actual throat clearing. It means she's nervous. *Oh no. Ask me anything but that.*

'Where were you that weekend I was in the Hamptons?' she asks.

'We've been through all this.'

'You're still lying.' I feel her withdrawal, cold like an open window in winter.

'It's not a lie!' I'm shouting, I realise.

'Wilder, you need to think about your condition. You need to make preparations.'

'These are my preparations. Writing a book.'

'I can't look after you if you won't look after yourself.' The words have the crack of tears in them. 'I don't think we should speak for a while.'

'Fine.' I hang up before she can reply. I feel so mad I have to walk around the little square of garden three times before I can breathe evenly again. But it's welcome, the hot red rush.

The thing about anger is, you mustn't let it drop or you might find out how you really feel.

As I sit down to work it arrives, diamond-sharp and perfect – the title. The book will be called *The Sound Revisited*.

Oh *dear*. What an awful – what a truly *terrible* – name for a book. It's amazing how good bad ideas can seem in the night. The blinding shaft of light that turns out to be nothing but a mirror-trick.

I try to write. Again, no good. Every so often I cast my eye down at the bay, expecting to see a dash of blue in the water, linen fluttering and trailing like a sea creature. I start at the wind in the trees, on my skin. But all is quiet and the bay remains clear and shining.

In the afternoon, I have a visitor.

I'm staring hard at the sentence I've just written. I've been staring so long it looks like cuneiform.

I look up and she's there, leaning over the white gate, smiling at me. A woman – a reassuringly solid one, this time. She must be cold; there's a bite in the breeze but she wears a voluminous cotton blouse, baggy pants of some rough fabric and a straw sunhat. She's weather-beaten, which speaks of life round here, but the accent doesn't.

'Wilder Harlow.'

'Yes? How can I help you?' I'm so glad to speak to someone, anyone, to escape from staring at that one line of typescript.

The woman looks at me for a second and then says, 'Everything OK with the cottage? To your liking?' She's British. There will be a story there, no doubt. Maybe I'll ask her in for a cup of stove coffee. There's something I like about her.

'Oh, yes!' I say. 'Everything is great in the cottage, thank you.' I realise that this must be the girl from town who 'comes in to help.'

'I stocked the kitchen with your favourite things. I even found some of that disgusting instant macaroni and cheese you used to like.' She sighs. 'That was a million years ago. I imagine you don't like it anymore.'

'I do still like it,' I say. 'Some things never ever change and one of those is macaroni and cheese. But you—' A terrible suspicion is dawning. She takes off her hat, and her hair is grey, but there's something about the shape of her head, and then I see that the grey is streaked with red.

'Oh my god. Harper?'

She smiles.

I go to the fence, give her a pat on the shoulder and an awkward kiss on the cheek. Her face is still broad, her wide gaze that of a child. But she's missing that air of cunning, of assurance that enveloped her when she was younger. Age strips us of our certainties, I suppose.

She takes my face and turns it this way and that. It's a weird thing for someone to do, who is to all intents and purposes a stranger. But it doesn't feel weird. I can't stop looking at her either, tracing the lines of her old self in her adult face.

'I'm so sorry,' I say. 'I don't see so well.'

'Well, you've not changed at all,' she says, which I know to be untrue, but she has the grace to sound sincere.

'Yes, it's a pity.'

She starts to laugh then stops abruptly, watching me. 'Do you have everything you need? They only told me you were coming at the last minute, I had to stock the cupboards quickly.'

'Why were you stocking my cupboards?'

'I help people out with things round here – cleaning, cooking, shopping. Taking care of the summer houses in the winter, and so on. It's easy enough, mindless.'

I feel the sting of awkwardness. 'But you – what happened?'

'To all the money, you mean?' She smiles. 'My family and I – we had some differences of opinion. They don't speak to me anymore. And I don't want to speak to them.' She sees my look. 'Those were hard years, after it all happened, Wilder. I fell back into some bad habits. And picked up some new ones. They decided they'd had enough. I can't blame them, really. I was pretty vile.'

'Where are you living?'

'Down on the water, up from Castine.'

'Near—'

'I couldn't afford much. It's the old Pelletier place. Or it was. It's mine now.'

Horror is all through me. 'Harper, why there?'

'Don't, Wilder,' she says, quiet and firm. 'It's the right place for me. It reminds me of him. Besides, I've made it nice.'

There's something extra upper class, something brittle about her Britishness, now. I've observed this in some of them who settle in the US. Their accents become more pronounced, their speech becomes more and more liberally peppered with those quaint phrases, as if they're afraid their identity will be fatally diluted by contact with us.

'I thought I'd never see you again,' I say. And at the same time she says 'So, I've come to call.' We're both awkward and hectic, we can't get the cadence of conversation going.

'No, no change in you whatsoever.' Harper unlatches the gate, uninvited, and comes into the garden. She leaps up into the arms of the maple and sits in the crook of the tree. The leafshadow chases across her face. She hasn't really changed at all, I realise.

'Come on in,' I say. 'Have a seat. Stay a while.'

She grins and just for an instant I am quite in love with her again.

'Why are we back here, both of us?' I ask. 'Why are we such gluttons for punishment?'

'Maybe everything we do after the age of sixteen is just a kind of rehash.'

Silence falls between us. There is too much to talk about.

Harper reaches out her foot and touches me lightly on the knee with her toe. 'Welcome back, you old git.'

'Thank you.' I am oddly moved.

'I've read one of his books,' Harper says. 'Not *that* one, another one. What was it called? *The Wallaby?*' I feel a punch of resentment. Sky's everywhere, it seems.

'*The Platypus*,' I said. 'I don't really read horror. Not my thing.'

'The one about the man who accidentally kills everyone he loves. I thought, "this is a lonely person". Did he mean to show how lonely he was – in the book?'

'Hey,' I say to change the subject. 'Do kids still come out here to swim?'

'No, I mean, I don't think so. There are far better beaches on the other side of town. Didn't you know him? Sky Montague?'

'We were at the same college, at around the same time, many years ago. I wouldn't say I knew him.'

'It must be strange – someone you went to college with, getting so famous.'

'As I said, I really didn't know him.'

'We saw him round here sometimes. Our local celebrity. No one seems to have spoken to him properly though. Seems like the more famous you are, the fewer friends you have.'

'By that logic, I must have thousands of friends.'

'Yes, you're swimming in them.' Harper looks around. 'You're alone, Wilder? No wife or children?'

'No.'

'Autumn's well underway. Winter comes on fast in these parts.' She pauses, watching, but I don't answer. 'If you're planning to stay that long you might want to think about putting the storm shutters up again, insulating the pipes, getting some tins in for power cuts and so on.'

I don't take the bait. 'Thanks for the advice.'

'Well, home for tea, I suppose. I'm off, you old plonker.'

'See you later, you old, old—' But I find that I am bent double, gasping. The world becomes vague and I fall to my hands and knees. The ground seems spongy, too soft for support and I think, *this isn't real, none of it is, it's not right that such pain can be real.*

'All right. Come here. You're all right.' She sits me up gently; her understanding is more than I can bear. The fist in my chest squeezes ever tighter. I touch a hand to my cheek – it comes away wet. I'm crying, it seems. This is terrible – what is happening? Harper comes up close, far too close. The concern on her face is appalling.

I realise that I haven't been touched by another living being in days – not since it happened. That's a wonderful thing about marriage – the casual, day-to-day intimacy, those little glancing moments of closeness. Fingers grazing as I hand Emily a dish, wet with suds. A kiss planted on the top of my head as I squint over an exam paper. Brushing past one another in the narrow hallway as we hurry in opposite directions. One becomes so quickly accustomed to it – the thousand touches that make up a day.

'What's wrong, Wilder?'

'I don't know how to start my book,' I say. 'And I think I saw a ghost.' I watch in fascination as a bright green frog leaps gracefully from her shoulder.

'Wilder,' she says. 'You – don't seem too well.'

'I didn't imagine it.'

'Ghosts don't exist,' she says gently. 'They're just your mind telling you things you don't want to know.'

Her words land like tumblers falling into place. I stare at her. 'You're a genius, Harper.'

She makes a sound of disgust.

I hardly hear her leave; I'm bent over the typewriter. The keys fly. That's it.

Autofiction. *Tell all the truth but tell it slant.* That's what my unconscious mind was trying to tell me when it showed me the drowning woman. It was a kind of waking dream, perhaps. Or maybe (and I would never admit this to the coastguard) I did mistake some floating debris for her . . .

The reason she seemed so familiar, the woman, is that she looked a little like Sky. Different colouring, but even so, there was something about the nose . . . anyway, here's the thing.

The book isn't about Sky, it's about *Skye*. A woman. It unlocks everything and resolves all those pesky issues of libel. It solves the other problem, too, which I've been worrying over – how to write *around* those certain aspects of what happened between us. They don't belong in this book, which is all about the theft.

You know, I can see her – Skye. I can even hear her voice. It's as if she's been waiting down in the dark all this time – for me to bring her up, into the light.

How about simply *Skye*? I kind of like that. I'll set it in 1991 – exactly as it happened.

Skye

She gets her chance the first day in class. The room has that particular smell of new textbooks and marker pen. The professor has oatmeal on his tie and an air of despair.

Skye sees him right away. In her head, he's just *him*. He's not a person, doesn't get a name. He's just a force she's chasing, a long-sought destination.

She doesn't sit right by him, of course not. She doesn't approach. She's not an idiot. She sits in the row behind. She watches the back of his neck. It's an overlooked area, the back of the neck. It is very expressive. His is no different.

He is very pale, and the flush that steals over it is revealing. He flushes a lot. Not from embarrassment, she realises, but from tension, a particular kind – the effort of keeping things together. Skye recognises that.

The professor puts a transparency on the projector, an arched window with stained glass the colour of jewels. A unicorn, wings, a sword. The dark classroom becomes a cave with a mouth of vivid

206

light. No sooner has Skye had this thought than she draws in her breath and looks at him.

She is right, he has had the thought too. In the dim she can see his head is bowed, neck thrust forward like a vulture's. His breath is heavy, like someone just falling asleep, but that's not what's happening. He gets up, arms outstretched like a blind person. He seems drunk, can't get out of the raked seating of the lecture hall. He pushes hard past a girl who cries out – not from hurt, but surprise. He makes an anguished noise and shoves harder past legs, hands groping for purchase on the desk, sending books and pens flying.

Skye gets up quickly. The light flares all around; the professor has turned it on. 'Young man,' he says to Wilder. 'Please sit back down.'

Wilder waves his hand and then covers his mouth with it. Skye realises what is about to happen, and slips out of her seat. In an instant she is by his side, holding his elbow.

'I know him from home,' she says. 'It's a panic attack. I'll take him outside. He'll be fine in a little while.'

She manages to get him to a bench in the sunshine on the other side of the quad. She can hear the river rushing somewhere behind them.

In the end he doesn't throw up. He leans back, turns his face to the sun. He seems exhausted.

It's strange being near him, this person she has thought so much about. He looks alien in photographs – with those pale eyes, barely grey or blue, almost the colour of his white skin, made whiter by the contrast of very dark hair. In photographs those protruding eyes look menacing. In person he just looks young. Somewhat fragile. He opens his mouth, gasps. She sees he has gum in there. She realises he might choke so she hooks it out quickly with a finger. It's bright pink. She sits there with it on her finger, still warm. After a moment's thought she puts it in her mouth. For a moment it tastes of him, clean and slightly alkaline. Then it's just a piece of gum. She tears a piece of paper from her notebook and wraps it up, puts it in her pocket.

When she looks back at him he's watching her.

'Hey,' she says. 'You OK?'

'You again,' he says. 'We met on the steps outside the dorm the day we got here. You were with your dad.'

She nods. 'That's right.'

'You didn't help.'

'No, I guess I'm not very helpful,' she says.

'You've been helpful to me,' he says, awkwardly. 'Thanks.' After a moment he says, 'I'm Wilder,' and offers a hand to shake.

She takes it. 'Like Thornton Wilder?'

'Yes.'

'I'm Skye.'

'It suits you,' he says, and smiles. 'You have very shiny hair, like a horse's hide.'

'Thank you.' She smiles back, the widest and sunniest of smiles, one that comes right up from the depths of her. *Oh no*, she thinks, torn between exhilaration and horror.

She says to Elodie, '*Je peux payer*.' Elodie nods briefly. They haggle a little but it's a deal easily done. She moves her stuff into Elodie's single room. She can feel his presence through the wall.

It's located in what the more affluent freshmen call the orphanage – this is the wing where they put the scholarship and exchange students. It overlooks the kitchens and everything smells like meatloaf. No one parties hard in the orphanage – these students are here to work. The rooms are small, cramped; there's only room for one bed in most of them.

Skye's allocated room is way better, on the front quad. She shares with a hockey-playing girl who eats boiled eggs in bed but the room is warm and good and smells like beeswax and cleanliness so on top of the hundred dollars Skye gives her, she doesn't think Elodie is getting a bad deal in the trade.

Sometimes as Skye lies here at night she can feel him through the wall, breathing, those big lantern eyes lidded in sleep. She knows he doesn't lock his door at night. She knows the sound of his lock, a stiff sludgy click. She has memorised it, along with all his sounds.

She runs through when she hears it, the dream. He's sweating, eyes open and staring, not seeing this world. He doesn't seem surprised, or even aware of a strange girl in his room.

She puts an arm around him the way one would a child. She feels it as he slowly returns to his body.

'I need this,' he says and reaches into his bedside cubby. It's a binder with a picture of Aphrodite on it. Inside are newspaper clippings, each one encased in plastic.

Skye's breath seizes in her throat. She knows each one, could recite each article from memory. She doesn't say anything.

He stares at the clippings. 'I expect you think I'm a weirdo, reading about murders after I have a nightmare.'

'No more than me,' she says honestly. 'When I can't sleep I plan my suicide.'

'Really?'

'Really.'

'What did you go for?'

'Drowning,' she says. 'It's pretty painless.'

'What about hemlock?' he asks. 'Totally pain-free. And it grows

209

everywhere. It looks kind of like a carrot.' After a pause he says, 'I didn't know you were next door. That's a weird coincidence.'

She shrugs. 'Sometimes the universe moves in your favour,' she says. 'Just once in a while.'

Their smile holds, the warm feeling dips and grows. He looks down, suddenly abashed. 'I'm OK now,' he says. 'You can go.'

'I can hang out a little,' Skye replies. 'What's that?' She reaches out. Behind the clippings at the back of the binder there are lined pages. Typing, not newsprint.

He flushes and she feels the sudden lurch of intimacy. 'I'm writing something.'

He covers the pages quickly with newsprint. She knows she has to read whatever this is. On the one exposed corner she reads: . . . *is hauled from the deep. The divers lug it up* . . . The top of the *l* key is missing. It looks like an *i*.

He looks at her for a moment. Then he slowly pulls the pages from the binder and hands them to her.

Her heart beats fast – how can it be this easy?

'This is why I have the dreams,' he says, shy. 'You've been kind, you deserve to know why you're getting woken up all the time. If you want to.'

The Dagger Man of Whistler Bay, the title page says. *By Wilder Harlow.*

She reads like someone starving, keeping her face neutral. By the time she's finished, dawn is coming in over the kitchen and she can smell sausage.

'Thank you,' she says to Wilder. She kisses him once on the cheek. He starts but permits it.

She goes back to her room and gets out her pen, fills it with her favourite grass-green ink. She writes it all down quickly before she forgets any detail of what he wrote. But not just that – what he said, what she said back, the shape his knee made, crooked beneath the sheet, the particular sheen of sweat on his brow, carried from the dream back into the waking world. How he didn't flinch or react to her physical presence at all, even when she sat on the bed and leaned close to test him. To breathe him.

Being right next door to him is good; the walls are so thin they feel at times like porous skin. But it goes both ways. He can hear her too and she needs privacy. She needs company at night sometimes.

She has learned to do her crying elsewhere, in measured bursts. That's private, too. Sometimes she sits in coffee shops with her Walkman, earphones in. Then she cries. People don't question it so much if there's something playing in her ears. But what they don't realise is that she's not sad, all that was burnt out of her long ago – she's gone. What they're looking at is the charred case for her rage.

If he's next door she becomes alive, a trembling mast, every fibre alert for his movements, his coughing. His dreams. Observing someone so closely – it's very like being in love. No wonder she gets the two confused, she tells herself.

It's just transference. Wilder is the gateway. It's not him she really wants to be around. This is stray love, orphaned love, vagrant love looking for a home – for its belonging place. She knows all this.

But she finds herself thinking of his hands all the same – and laughing a little in the middle of a test, when she thinks of how he can't bring himself to say the word *fuck*.

'I've been thinking about you,' she says the next day. She hears him catch his breath. They're lying on her bed with their legs propped up against the wall. Her feet rest on a Pearl Jam poster, right on Eddie Vedder's face.

'What were you thinking?'

'You could try sleeping somewhere else,' she says. 'If you have enough nightmares in a room they kind of sink into the walls. Try different places.'

'Like where?'

'There's this storage room for old props,' she says. 'Try sleeping somewhere like that.'

When she sees him the next morning he's letting himself into his room, shadowy eyes haunted.

'The security guard nearly caught me in that old shed this morning,' he says, almost mad at her, and she can't stop laughing.

'I didn't think you'd actually do it,' she says.

'Oh, frick you. I need a shower.'

'Did it work, though?'

'I didn't have any dreams,' he says reluctantly.

So she can make him do it again.

She's got a lot of material, but she needs more, she tells herself. She doesn't know what that *more* is, until they see the news item on the big TV in the common room. Alton Pelletier is refusing to see visitors. He won't see Christy Barham's mother. And here, she realises, is the perfect end to her book.

'I think he would see you,' she says to Wilder. He is even paler than usual; he's holding back a panic attack.

She looks at him carefully, sees how close he is to the edge.

So she decides not to push it, not just yet. Not like this. At some point, she couldn't identify it, he has transformed from *him* into Wilder.

In her room Skye stretches lazily and listens to Wilder clattering next door. Undressing, getting ready for the trek to the spider-ridden showers. Her bed still holds the warm contours of her most recent visitor. She found him at last call in a bar in town the night before, didn't need his name. She took his credit card from his pants pocket on a whim, but she knows she can't use it. Too easily traced back to her. So it's the hunt today.

She picks a café on the other side of town. It's in a bookstore, which is good – those kinds of people tend to be absentminded. Easily lost to the world.

In the store she spends a moment drawing her hands along the spines in her favourite section. The covers are dark, on these shelves. The titles shine out like neon lights. These books tell the truth about life. The horror.

Skye has spent everything she has on the plan so she has to supplement her funds. And she has to be strategic. Never steal from students, never near the college. Cash where possible. She sees him across the room. Big, mid-forties, the pouched face of someone who drinks their feelings.

She drops her notebook at his feet as she passes. 'Oh, sorry,' she says. 'I'm such a klutz.'

Skye manages to walk fairly normally across the quad, holding a pile of books in front of her face. Getting to her room is a relief.

After that she sits and waits. Not long now. Wilder always comes by after his English Lit class.

He knocks and opens the door all in one instant. They've got a familiar way between them now. Skye would know it was Wilder without looking up, even if she wasn't expecting him. She can smell him the way wild animals smell prey.

She feels the shock run through him when he sees her face. The rusted trail of blood down her philtrum, the lush velvet of the bruise around her eye.

She'll hold it inside her forever, the feel of the brick against her back, the smell of the dumpster, the sound of traffic fifty feet away, in another world. The expression on the guy's face, the almost comical surprise when she asked him to hit her. He was reluctant at first. 'Honestly,' she said. 'You'd be doing me a favour. It's for a science project.' Who would believe such a thing? She picked well; she sensed it in him.

The moment, the flicker in his face, when he realised he enjoyed it.

She wasn't sure he would stop so in the end she ran, spatters of blood flying from her nose behind her. She's not even sure he ran after her. It was a valuable lesson. Power turns on a dime, can be exchanged or lost in an instant. She will be more careful in future.

But when he finds his credit card is gone he won't report her. There is that.

'Who did this to you?' Wilder says again. She realises, in surprise, that he is close to tears.

'I had a fight with my dad,' she whispers into his ear.

Wilder's horror, his indrawn breath, sends shivers of excitement down her. His arms are warm and good. She puts her cheek against his even though it hurts. Just for this moment, she allows herself to feel this, and nothing more.

*

He cleans her face tenderly but clumsily. The wet cloth stings on her bruises.

'You must never see him again,' he says. Skye has persuaded him, just, out of reporting it to the police.

'I think you should write to him,' she says. The lamplight is low. Despite the Advil her wounds pulse in her, aching. With him so close, with such attention to her physical being, she's getting mixed up. It's almost like that other feeling, that low level hum, that need.

'Write to who?'

'Alton Pelletier.'

His being goes still. 'Why would you say that?'

Careful, she thinks. *Tread carefully.* This afternoon's experience has left her wary. Of course Wilder won't hit her. Of course he would never. But things turn on a dime, don't they?

'Men who hurt people shouldn't get away with it,' she says, fierce. 'I'm too much of a coward to even hold my dad to account. But Alton ... you could ask him who they are. The women they haven't identified. You could make him confront himself. Hold him to account.'

'He wouldn't tell me any of that,' Wilder says. The cloth he's holding is stained with her blood.

'But he might.'

'Just leave it, Skye,' he says, because he knows she's right. Somehow, they both know. Alton will see Wilder. If he asks the right way.

[ ]

Hello
Hell
Help

Wilder, Day Four

Skandar reached his hand out to the woman. Her dress billowed about her in the water. 'Reach for me,' he said urgently. 'Reach for my hand.' The woman opened her mouth as if to scream. Her throat opened wider and wider. He saw, too late, that in her mouth was a tiny, lit-up scene – a family picnicking on a beach.

'Who are you?' he asked, desperate.

'Rebecca,' came the answer. Her voice was the grinding of metal on stone.

The Sound and the Dagger, by Sky Montague

I'm up with the dawn – I fetch the typewriter, pull the table outside under the maple, facing the bay. It's been an excellent, excellent couple of days, and I feel this will be another one. I admit, it's turning into more of a novel than I had anticipated. She seems to be running away with the story, Skye.

I always had this feeling, this knowledge that after Sky died, I would be able to write again. I hoped, I prayed it would be true, and it is.

I love typing on the Remington, love the sound of it, the rattle and clack as thoughts make their way through my fingertips and become fixed on the page. I know I should get it fixed but I like the broken *l*. It's been that way for so long, it feels like part of my personality now.

I'll do it as soon as it's finished. How, though? The oven range is the kind that's always on. Even if I knew how to turn it off, it's not gas. So that's out of the question – no Sylvia Plath for me.

I've measured the drop from the most robust branch of the maple tree – I don't think it's high enough. Besides, I don't know how to tie those noose doodads you always see in the movies. I can't stand knives and blades and blood and that kind of thing so strike that from the list. Suffocation? Duct tape, a plastic bag over the head? I don't trust myself not to change my mind.

The obvious answer is out there through the window, lapping at the cliffs below, of course. The sea. But ever since I saw the woman I've known it won't be the sea. What if, after I load my pockets with stones and wade into the deep, I open my eyes, and come face to face with her? Blue linen billowing about her face, arms reaching for me. What if I'm wrong and she is a ghost? What if I die but she keeps me here, trapped forever in her arms, listening to the whistling of the bay? Odd how some things are more frightening than even the prospect of death. So no Virginia Woolf, either.

It will be pills, I suppose. I have Emily's prescription, grabbed as I was leaving the apartment. The box has a reassuring number of warnings on it. I'll get some vodka, too, to help things along. And perhaps I'll sit in a full bathtub? I don't know, it all sounds so stressful.

I won't leave a note – I'll call Emily just before I do it and give her my instructions. Maybe I'll get the answering machine – that would be best, really.

'Our time has run out, Wilder,' Emily said. As though time were milk in the refrigerator and we needed to go to the store. I knew she meant it; she never calls me Wilder, but Will. That never sat right to me – the name always felt like a kind of disguise. It has been stripped from me now; she hasn't called me Will since we parted. It sounds cold in her voice – *Wilder*.

These days *Wilder* makes me think of an oldish man in a bow tie – then I catch a glimpse of the bow tie at my neck, feel the beginnings of a paunch and realise with a dull thud, *but that's me. That's what I am.*

Why don't they make recordings of someone breathing? I miss the sound in the night. There can be comfort in a disguise. Being who you are can be lonely.

This evening is cool. The little kerchief of lawn is covered in red leaves. I rake them and make a small bonfire on the cliff, away from the maple's spreading limbs. Smoke climbs into the dusk in a spire. Like a signal, out to sea.

There's a shout from down in the bay. I run to the cliffside and peer over. Two kids kayak past the cove in neon lifejackets. They're laughing. Is there something behind them? A dark head perhaps, bobbing in the water? I strain and lean forward and for a terrible second I lose my balance. The long rock fall pulls at me.

I gasp and grab clumps of turf, steady myself. I nearly went over. *That would be a way to do it,* I think. But how certain could I be that I would die? I imagine lying at the foot of the cliff, maimed and broken, until I die of exposure or someone finds me.

No.

Dinner is macaroni and cheese, very delicious, though there is a little purple fire burning in the middle of the plate.

Afterwards I sit with the green fountain pen and paper. I practise all night, using his writing in the manuscript for comparison. The pile of paper is growing at my elbow. The ink is as green as grass, as green as wickedness.

It's kind of, how would you put it, character work. Actors do the same thing. I find it helps me get into his mindset, remembering things Sky said, writing them down with the kind of pen he used, imitating his penmanship as closely as possible. It brings stuff back. Odd little moments. Notes from the dead to the living.

Fucked up will set you free, says one. I pick up another note. *Getting close now*, it says. The next one just says, *I'm here*.

'No you're not,' I say aloud. 'You're nowhere. Dead. Gone.'

I leaf through the MS of *The Sound and the Dagger*. Every time the past comes up to tap me on the shoulder, and I risk feeling anything but rage, I read the descriptions of Wiley.

Even in sleep, there was always a suppressed rage about him. Nothing makes a man so angry as knowing that he's part of the wallpaper.

I replace the page with a shaking hand. No matter how many years pass, those words will always be a wound to the heart. Did he really think of me that way?

'I'm not part of the wallpaper,' I say aloud. My voice is startlingly loud in the quiet kitchen and I realise how long I've been alone.

Something flutters from the table. One of my green notes.

I'm sorry, Wilder.

This one is particularly well done. I've really captured his handwriting, the wild scrawl. But of course this is the impossible note – it says what Sky would never write. He was never sorry for what he did.

Wilder, Day Five

Helen wore the pain of the past on her like an extra skin. Her hair was red as an alarm.

The Sound and the Dagger, by Sky Montague

I come to, realising I can't see the page in front of me anymore. I don't know what time it is but dark is almost here. My fingers are numb with cold.

Have I made myself too likeable? But Sky must have liked something in me. Surely I have to start there. Am I making Skye too unlikable? That also needs thinking on. People forgive male characters for that – everyone loves an antihero. Less so with women, I've noticed.

I grab a coat and go into the garden. The moon is a silver dime, the sea shines black and white and broken under its beams. But clouds are gathering close in the distance. The air is icy. I feel the past around me.

As I get older I see more and more how fluid a thing time is. There are so many ways to slip in and out of it. The wonder is that we ever stick in the now.

You can't write someone you can't feel for. Telling the story from her point of view makes it, oddly, mine. I have to know her. Sky's voice is in my mind, clear through the years. *Reading that was like being inside you.* The air smelled of snow that night too.

I stop. A voice calls from down in the bay.

'Help,' she calls. 'Help!'

I grab a flashlight, run down and shine it onto the water of the cove. It's still and black as oil (*oil drums*). 'Help!' the voice calls faintly. But there's no one there.

I run inside and slam the door.

Ghost
Host
Most

Taking the word apart makes me feel a little better. Because of course she wasn't a ghost. She was a manifestation of my creative self.

A little nagging voice in my depths.

So why does she need help?

Problems this morning. The typewriter ribbon is beginning to run out. I can tell because when it gets worn the ink fades from black through all the colours of the spectrum. Right now it's a kind of deep green. I know from experience that it will turn blue, then grey, then fade altogether.

I swear I brought a replacement with me from New York but I

can't find it anywhere. I turn my drawers and briefcase inside out. But there isn't one. How irritating.

I give up on the hunt for the typewriter ribbon and take a notebook outside. The pages whip cheerfully in the wind.

My writer's block has lasted thirty-two years. I've tried, believe me. I've written many, many failed books. Failed or not, each book has a different nature and they like you to respect that, as you write them. You can't hustle a slow, deliberate book for instance, and you have to write that jaunty little comedy in a sidewalk café. In that respect Skye's character is perplexing. It requires me to see everything backwards, as if the camera had turned around to shoot the scene from another angle. The book is a mirror and I am stepping through the looking glass.

Even half asleep I recognise the sound. I think, *oh, they do make recordings of breathing after all. I am loved. Being loved tells me who I am.* I struggle towards consciousness, fighting off the black slumber that holds me. *That's not a recording.* I feel it, the warmth of a body at my back, one arm flung over me. A sleepy hand strokes my chest. I'm filled with a joy so sharp it makes me gasp. The hand trails up over my arm, my shoulder and taps me twice, as if to say, *follow me. Wait,* I think, *wait, I'm coming.*

Moonlight reflects on the snow outside. I'm filled with new feeling, the world is new.

I turn to face him, to pursue. The porthole casts a pale circle on the bed, a spotlight. His back is so familiar, that russet head. I pull his shoulder and turn him to me. Beneath the sleek hair there is no face, just a green S.

I wake shuddering. It hurts to pull myself away from that old grief, away from the memory of snow on windowpanes. None of that stuff is going into the book, of course. It's really not the story. The story of *Skye* is the theft.

Anyway that's often what writing is, isn't it? What you leave out.

In a way, I'm sorry he took the matter out of my hands because I meant to kill him one day – Sky. At least, I think I did. I used to fantasize about it. I would plot his end, the way I plan my own now.

I plan every detail. It goes, as they say, a little something like this.

I wait until Emily's out of town. She loves the Hamptons at this time of year, says it's less vulgar than at high summer when just anyone goes.

I take the train to Portland, the bus to Castine and then a taxi out to the cottage. The taxi is the risky part, but surely with the glut of visitors I won't stand out too much. The cottage is vacant, I've made sure of that. I feel a rush of homecoming, as I climb the hill and see the cottage perched on the hill above me, a white gull.

The catch is loose on the porthole window on the seaward side. The rental agency is always complaining about it. I open the window and slip inside. I don't do it with the grace I once did – perhaps I even stick a little, around the middle. But a few heaves and I'm through. The house greets me with dim silence.

I know Sky's habits, I've read about them often enough. He talks endlessly to journalists about his 'process'.

Every morning in the dawn he takes a walk from Harper's house (that will always be how I think of it, no matter how often he stays there) along the coastal path, which leads past Whistler Cottage. I wait.

When the time comes I go out to the maple tree, watch as

ribbons of mist melt into silver above the sea. I'll know him when he approaches, even with my sight failing. There are some things that fix forever inside you. His tread, the way he breathes. I can feel him like a storm coming.

A figure approaches, dark on the mist.

I step out from behind the tree and smile. He hesitates, and then recognition spreads all through him. He stops short and neither of us speaks for a moment. What will happen?

'You got old,' he says.

'So did you,' I say, though I can't really see him in detail. I can make out the silver streaks through his russet hair.

'I missed you,' I say quietly.

'I—' he says, at a loss for words, for once. 'I . . .'

I go to him slowly. I take his head in my hands and kiss his crooked mouth. His breath is soft on my cheek. Our lips part and I gently, softly pass the hemlock, the thinnest, merest sliver of it, into his warm mouth with my tongue.

We walk on together for half a mile or so before we both begin to stagger. Sky grabs my arm. I feel the surprise all through his body, feel it turn to fear.

Of course, this is idle thought. I couldn't write my book if I were dead.

I drift gently into sleep, thinking of other ways I would have done it.

Ayuh, says a voice. A dark figure stands in the corner of the room. His eyes are large and black. In his hand, there shines a boat hook. He takes one step forward into the stormlight. *You from away?*

Water drips from his rubber coat, his boots, pools on the floor. Fish blood trails down his jacket, a spray of brains.

I turn the light on, gasping. I feel the blackness threaten to take me, in a way it hasn't, not for many years. *Breathe*, I tell myself. *Breathe*. It had Alton's words in its mouth, but it wasn't him. The eyes were different – pitch black where they should be blue. And he never wore that wet weather gear that I saw.

Even so, it runs through my mind. *Maybe he's not dead.*

So I check it on the satellite news archives on my phone, tapping the keys with shaky hands, waiting anxiously for the results to load. There it is, in black and white. He killed himself by swallowing cement. The virtual news archive is a wonderful thing. *Eat it*, I whisper to myself, staring at the lit square of the screen, where the cursor pulses. I should feel better but I'm still shaking.

I go down to the kitchen and I take up a heavy cast-iron skillet. I haven't done this in years. Living with someone prevents you, in general. But it always used to calm me down.

I raise the skillet and take aim. Then I slam it into my leg. Yes, that's it. I do it again and again. Crack. The flesh smarts, reddens, then numbs. My legs sing with pain; I hit myself harder. I can hear my own panting, hear the blows on flesh, but it seems far away. I do it and do it and do it, until all the world sings and I am the only thing that exists, right at the centre of everything.

There will be bruises tomorrow. But there's a still place at my centre now. I feel clear.

It wasn't Alton, I tell myself again, and this time I believe it. He carried a boat hook, sure. But the face was different. The voice was wrong. His eyes, especially, belonged on a different man. They weren't warm blue in a leathery face. Those black eyes, that white face – they were those of a stranger. He looked a little like

Sky too, I realise. No surprise there; Sky is rarely far from my thoughts these days.

It was just my mind, making pictures on the dark. Old fears, reaching long fingers up from the pit of the past. Did I really expect that there would be no consequences, when I decided to open the coffin of the past and poke at its corpse?

Ooh. Good line.

I go to the typewriter. The keys fly, deafening, hypnotic. The world vanishes.

Skye

When Wilder wakes up on a Sunday morning, he usually knocks on Skye's wall to rouse her. Then they take a walk together – a long one that helps fill the short winter day.

Skye is up early, transcribing her notes. She writes all her observations down in shorthand with her green pen, while Wilder's not looking. Normally she writes in her copy of *In Search of Lost Time* – it looks like she's making notes on her reading. If she doesn't have that with her any surface will do – her takeaway coffee cup, her bus ticket. Once she untucked her shirttail to scribble *sexually ambivalent* on it, then tucked it in quickly when he turned around. When she gets back to her room she adds it all to her big file.

Alton's letter is open on the bed beside her. Skye developed the habit of going through Wilder's mail early on – this morning it paid off. She knew what it was right away: it's stamped with the name of the prison, the sender's name on the back in black and white.

Dear Wilder,
It was a pleasure to get your male. Of course I remmember you.

First thank you for being strait with me. Second do not be ashamed of your urges. If they are your true feelings then you are just being honust with yourself. What is normal anyway? You are and always have been a good frend to my son and I know he was fond of you.

I wuld be OK for you to visit if it is soon. they say they move me next month an I dont think there will be receeving visiters at the new place. We can go over old times. I would be happy to answer your questins if I can. I feel like if you are being honest with yourself like this, then it makes me think I can do the same. We can continue to write after I am moved. We will get to know each other more.

Thank you for your kind words about Nathaniel. I mist my son very much these last months. You know they dint even let me see him before died.

Yrs
A. Pelletier

Skye holds the letter with her fingertips. In the corner, the writing paper has a little cowboy on a rearing horse. She feels like it will burn her or poison her. She's sorry she made Wilder write. She doesn't need to put him through this, she has what she needs. She's going to destroy the letter, but first, she's going to copy it out, word for word.

She puts the letter in the drawer in her bedside table, beside the doll of human, copper hair. Teeth for eyes. Her own baby teeth, actually. A single, unset pearl for a navel.

She starts at the sharp rat-a-tat-tat of knuckles on the thin room divider. She doesn't answer; lets him wait. After a minute he knocks again. Again, she draws out the pause. Then she knocks back.

They open their doors at almost the same moment, like in one of those British farces. His scarf covers the lower half of his face, making his eyes look even larger and less human than usual.

They've established a regular route around the top of Pursing Hill. It's bleak in winter, the trees bare, the crows cawing their ragged secrets to one another. Skye prefers this to a beautiful landscape, to sunshine. This kind of weather doesn't demand happiness from her. It's relaxing.

When they reach the fork in the path and she starts along their usual route, he touches her elbow. 'Let's go the other way today,' he says.

'Why?'

'I want to show you something.' Briefly, hysterically, she wonders if he's going to kill her. She often wonders this about people. More often than she should, she guesses. It's a side effect of spending all your time thinking about murder.

Each bramble and branch carries a fine burden of snow. Glossy ice frames the leaves. Even with the grim steel bowl of sky overhead, it's beautiful.

Wilder bends double every now and again, peering into the undergrowth.

'What are you looking for?'

'You'll see,' he says. He's excited, she can feel it coming off him in waves. His pale skin has rare colour, flushed to the shade of pale peony. He looks almost living, for once. She resists the urge to touch his cheek.

He shouts with happiness, crouching over a thicket of thorns. She can see there's something coming out of the ground there, a frilly, lacy fall of startling green.

'What is it?'

'The day we met you said that when you were scared in the night, what made you feel safe was imagining killing yourself.'

'Right.'

'By drowning.'

'Wilder—'

'I told you I had a better idea. Look,' he says and takes something from his pocket. It's a page ripped from an encyclopaedia.

'You can't do that,' she says, amused. 'They're library books – for everyone, you know?'

He points to the picture, and to the little fall of green. 'This is the same plant, right?'

'It could be.'

'It is,' he says triumphant. 'It's hemlock. It matches the picture. If we pull it up, it'll look just like this. A white carrot. Now you always know it's here.'

'Why would you show me this?'

'No one can stop you doing it,' he says. 'If you really want to. But I thought, maybe – if you know where the plant is, you'd always have the plan ready. You could always feel safe.'

It makes an odd kind of sense. She stares at the green fronds in their ice casket. Absentmindedly, she reaches to touch it.

He makes an alarmed sound. But her fingers stop short of the ice. Would it be enough to kill her, this casual contact? She doesn't know.

'It's my present to you,' Wilder says.

'It's the weirdest gift I've ever heard of.'

'Do you like it?'

'I like it.' She's overwhelmed. It's horrible and perfect.

She steps forward – slowly so as not to startle either of them – and puts her arms around him. After a second, his close about her. It's strange being so close to someone; they stop being a person and become a series of impressions. Breath on her cheek, the faint smell of peppermint from his toothpaste, warm skin grazed with stubble. The blurry pink curve of an ear. A heart, beating through cloth.

'I wrote to him,' Wilder says into her ear. She's kind of drunk on his breath. 'Alton. I asked to go see him.' She knows that this is Wilder's real gift to her. Of course, she already knows he's done it, but she is moved.

Wilder is just a character, she reminds herself. Just part of a book. But she tightens her arms around him anyway. She wants to give him something back but can't think what.

Then it comes to her, the thought, spined and exciting. She could show him her story.

'Let's get inside,' she says. 'I want to show you something.' It comes out breathy, suggestive, and he looks startled. She laughs. 'I mean – not like that. Let's go.'

She's going to take the risk of showing him this part of herself.

Skye offers the pages shyly. She tries for indifference but she doesn't know how well she pulls it off. She has been working on this for days, feverish, crouched over the keyboard.

'It's called *Pearl*,' she says. 'I'm working on a series of stories about murder.'

He takes the pages with a big smile. 'Oh, wow. I didn't know you wrote stories, Skye.'

'I mean, a little . . .' She hates herself for the hesitation in her voice.

'Do you want me to stay here while I read it?'

She can't decide which is worse, him reading it here in front of her or somewhere else, feeling something she can't see.

'Might as well stay,' she says. 'I've got studying to do anyway.'

She stares at the physics textbook. Every fibre of her is attuned to the scratch and turn of the page. It's seven printed pages and she counts as he finishes each one. When the last one turns, she waits for him to say something. She stares unblinking at the graph before her, eyes watering. Still she waits.

At last, she has to look up. He's smiling but something is wrong. Badly, badly wrong. He doesn't look transported, thoughtful, like he's just been on the journey she laid out so carefully. He looks – and this is interesting, because she has never seen this expression on his face before, and she makes a point of noting all his expressions – he looks embarrassed.

'So,' she says lightly. 'What did you think?'

'It's really evocative,' he says. 'You've got a really good use of language.'

'Right,' she says, the crevasse opening wider and wider before her. 'Listen, be honest, I can take it. It's helpful to know if something's not working.'

'It's so bleak,' he says. 'So – dark.'

'That's kind of the point.' Her smile is a wooden board nailed to her face; it's cement.

'Writing about that stuff – you know, murder and so on – you have to try and not sensationalise it.'

'It's life and death,' she says. 'Those are sensational things.'

'Maybe it's just a matter of practice,' he says, and the dark crevasse swallows her whole. She sees that he thinks he owns it, what happened at Whistler Bay. He thinks it's something that happened to him.

'One day I'll write about you.' She's going for a playful tone but she hears the glassy, hectic edge in her voice.

Wilder looks nervous. 'What?'

She realises that this was an unwise thing to say. Truth is leaking out of her. Too late to take the words back.

'Writing is power,' she says. 'Big magic. It's a way of keeping someone alive forever.'

'Why would someone want to live forever in a book?'

'Maybe they don't. Maybe the writer keeps them prisoner.' She leans in, puts her lips to his ear. 'You can trap someone in a book, their soul – make a prison of words. A cage.' It's something she vaguely remembers from somewhere. Something about trapping a soul in an object.

'Wow, Skye,' he says, nervous. 'Every time I think you can't get any creepier . . .'

'Nearly time for commons,' she says. 'Let's go. Maybe there'll be meatloaf again. Yum.'

'Skye,' he says. 'Hey, I'm sorry. Don't be upset.'

'Why would I be upset?' she asks. He opens his mouth but she suddenly can't handle whatever's about to come out of it.

He calls after her as she heads down the hall, asking her to wait, but she doesn't turn. She wants him to feel the distance between them, the indifference of her back.

He finds her later in the rec room. All the sports guys are squabbling over the remote, everyone wanting different things. Basketball, baseball. She catches an eye, smiles a little. The guy smiles back, then topples over as his buddy tackles him, tall as a felled tree. She'll find him later tonight. Maybe.

'Skye,' Wilder says. She starts. How long has he been there? 'I'm sorry.'

'For what?' she says, smiling.

'You left in such a hurry . . . I thought maybe you were upset.'

'Nah,' she says. 'I just really wanted to catch the beginning of this – she squints at the TV – 'inning? First half? Rally?'

He smiles back, relieved that she's decided to make a joke of it. 'Dramatic stuff. But I really am sorry if I said something to – you know, upset you.'

And she thinks, *you will be.*

She seals Alton Pelletier's letter with Elmer's glue and slips it back into his mail slot early the next morning. She practises her face for when he shows it to her. She was being dumb, before, trying to spare him. She needs to see this through. The effect on him is irrelevant.

Even so, she sees it when they meet for noon commons. His face is like paper; as if someone has placed a very thin Wilder-mask on top of an open wound.

He jumps and drops his fork. Peas spill all over the table, grey-green. A girl with a ponytail makes a point of shifting her chair further away from them. Though that might not be about the peas.

'You OK?' Skye asks.

'Sure,' he says. 'Just jumpy I guess. Maybe there'll be thunder later.'

She nods and says nothing. She feels a mean little razor-slice of pleasure. *Pretty sensational stuff, isn't it, Wilder? After all.*

*

He tells her through the wall, as though he can't bear to look at her – as though looking into her face will make it real.

'Night, Skye,' he says.

'Night, Wilder.'

'Skye? He wrote back,' says his muffled voice. There is a long pause. 'I don't think I can do this.'

236

'You can,' she says. 'I'll be with you every step of the way. I'll even drive.' She wonders if she's still mad at him, whether she even was, really. She strokes the wall gently with her fingertips. Her feelings are getting all tangled up in the pretence. Surely it was all an act, to make him feel guilty. His opinion on her writing doesn't mean anything to her.

The prison is vast, though not as big as the parking lot which stretches out like the great plains in the falling snow.

'I can't do it,' Wilder says, and he does look like he's going to throw up. She doesn't try to persuade him. She takes him tentatively in her arms. They've started doing that more and more in recent weeks.

'Give me your loose change,' she says. 'Your keys, wallet. They'll stop you otherwise. Just take your ID. And – wait' – she reaches in back – 'you'll have to change that sweater. Your one's tan, they don't let visitors wear beige or orange.'

'Why not?'

'It's too close to the colours of the inmates' uniforms. They might mistake you for someone who belongs there, and never let you out.' She smiles but immediately sees she's made a mistake. His skin turns a pale green.

'You have to do this for Nat,' she says. 'Remember? It's the last chance to find out the truth.'

He nods. She doesn't say that name too often, knows how powerful an effect it has on him. But they are in the endgame, now.

Skye stares at the prison through the windshield. He's in there. Odd to think it.

She called the inn from the payphone before they left, to confirm her reservation. It's on the route back to college, and she picked it because it's romantic, because she wants to make it special, and because they were the only ones who had a room available on Christmas Day. It's starting to snow. She hopes they'll make it to the inn – and part of her hopes they won't. She's strangely frightened of what she plans to do.

Wilder is a tiny figure in the distance; he grows larger slowly through the whirling snow. She gets out and runs to meet him. He leans on her all the way back to the car, pausing once to throw up. His vomit disappears, sinks into the white.

In the warm, she makes him write it all down. She has pen and paper waiting for exactly this. The snow is falling thicker, thicker. *Just write*, she wants to scream; she knows they're running out of time, soon the road as far as the inn will be impassable. But she needs him to get it down while it's all fresh in his memory. So she keeps an iron hand on her feelings, doesn't hurry him, doesn't let him see her panic at every hesitation, every pause of the nib on the page.

They drive into snowfall almost as solid as a wall. He keeps suggesting that they stop at motels they pass. It would be the sensible thing to do.

'No,' she says again and again, 'not that one, not that one.' The car has chains on the tyres but even so she knows she's cutting it dangerously close. She can barely see the road through the snow, falling like a rain of ash.

But at last, with a feeling inside like a shout, she sees the inn ahead.

'I can't afford this,' Wilder says over and over, and she thinks, *god, how many times can my heart break?* But there are no more choices left, now.

'It's OK,' she tells him. 'Stay in the car while I see if they have room.'

The honeymoon suite is just as opulent and ridiculous as the photographs in the brochure promised. The bath has feet. She knows they need to be taken outside themselves, given scenery.

They also need booze. Whiskey and steak together make a heady, rich haze in her head.

'You put something else in the letter,' he says. He's mad but she knows where this is going, it's the helpless snapping of the trapped animal.

So she tells him. He backs away from her, eyes impossibly wide.

'I'll take the couch,' Wilder says, and she puts her hand over his heart. It beats hard under her palm.

'Please don't,' she says, making her eyes soft. Genuine vulnerability is a luxury she can't afford but she knows how to perform it. Enjoys it. Sometimes, like now, she even feels a flutter of the real thing. She flings her arms around him and taps his shoulder, like someone saying *follow me*. And Wilder does. They figure it out gradually. She thinks maybe he hasn't been with a woman before.

'Pretend I'm him,' she whispers into his ear. 'Pretend I'm Nathaniel Pelletier.'

Skye pretends, too. She pretends to be her real self, the person she was before all this.

Skye stays awake, watches him in the glow of the moon, reflected on the crystalline snow.

When he stirs she quickly arranges herself on the pillow, her own hair spread, to give him the pleasure of watching her sleep.

She probably won't have any room in her life for romance or anything after this, so she wants to enjoy it while she can. He watches her, she can feel it.

As dawn comes in pink she can hear the scratch of the pen on paper. *Yes,* she thinks, full of joy, *that's right, that's it, write it all down for me.*

At length, when day has come in full, she leans over and yanks out a pinch of his hair. Wilder yells and she grins at him.

Later Skye wraps the soft inky black lock tightly in a piece of paper and puts it at the bottom of her makeup bag. She allows herself this one indulgence. Something to remember him by.

The drive back to college is quiet. Sometimes, she thinks, you can actually feel happiness taking up space, almost see it. Like a balloon hanging in the air.

'Go get us a place in commons,' she says and he goes quickly, glad to do something for her.

She waits until he's fully out of sight. She tucks his wallet into his backpack with all his overnight stuff. She takes out his folder, the one with Aphrodite coming out of the waves. She can feel the words pulsing in it. She's desperate to open it, to go through it, but she resists. She puts the folder carefully into the back seat behind her. Skye was going to let him keep it – she knows most of it off by heart. But she has decided not to. It belongs to her, not Wilder. She has earned it.

I'll write it the way I want, she thinks, fierce. Like a wound in the chest.

Then she leans over and opens the passenger door. She puts

Wilder's backpack out carefully onto the curb. It will probably be OK there until he comes looking for her – the college is full of rich kids, after all – and people are mostly honest.

[ ]

Won't
Don't

Moss
Muss
Must
Rust
Trust

Herd
Her

Donut
Don't

Dust
Rust
Trust

Hem
Them

Whelp
Help

Held
Help

Heap
Help

Wilder, Days Six through Ten

Nate wore his ragged clothes with style. He gave the impression of being made of natural things – wood and sand worn smooth by the tide.

The Sound and the Dagger, by Sky Montague

I wake to the sound of breath. No hand caressing me, this time. Instead I have the sense that I am being pummelled and stretched, pulled by firm hands into agonising, geometrical shapes. I scream but no voice comes from my throat. Instead, an infernal scratching – horrible, like rats' claws on stone, like bone grinding, like the creak of a bough before it breaks. Or like a pen scratching on paper.

I hit the floor with a crack.

In the morning I have a bruise all down one side, purpling and fresh as thunderclouds. Some of it is yellowing and greenish, as though already healing. There's something horrible about that and I pull my shirt down, wincing.

The yellowish green parts of the bruise have a distinctive shape. Almost like the double curve of a snake.

So today I type one-handed, nursing my aching arm. I punch out a letter at a time, peering at the keyboard askance, as though afraid to look directly at it. There's a kind of familiarity to it, this expression, and I wonder why – then I realise. It's Sky's expression. It's how he used to look when he was concentrating.

I'm wearing him like a skin.

I went to see the movie of *The Sound and the Dagger* they made, oh, years later. Of course I did – who could resist? They mixed up the timeframes – it all happened in college in the film. It lost some of the youthful naivete of the story, but it lent it some depth and complexity. I watched as handsome Skandar went to the cave alongside Wiley, Helen and Nate. Somehow the fact that there were four kids in the boat, not three, made me maddest. It hammered home how he had added himself in.

The actor who played Wiley looked just like me at that age. And the actor who played Skandar looked exactly like Sky. Memory and film have merged together over the years. The mind is faithless. So now when I recall that summer all that I can see before my mind's eye is the movie – Helen, Nate, Skandar and Wiley in that boat, on the bright sea. He has even taken my memory.

How could I have forgotten Sky showing me his short story? Maybe I wanted to gloss over it, because he was so offended. I hated it when we fought. But of course things escalated after that. He realised I was a better writer – that he had to move fast.

Strange how memory is flooding back now. I've unlocked the

past. It's all falling into place. It's like being a detective, hunting through a mystery. Of course, you only need a detective when there's been a crime. The murder of my life, I guess. My career.

Reading back today's pages, something else starts tugging at my memory – but I can't grasp it. Something about the hemlock being shaped like a carrot? For some reason I keep seeing Harper's face. It'll come to me.

I'm getting a sweater from the closet when I see it, a white edge, sticking out through a crack in the boards at the back. I can see half a cursive letter, written in that snake-green ink. I know what it is, of course, or at least I have a terrible feeling.

'Come on,' I mutter, fingertips scrabbling and pinching at the paper. 'Come on.'

I get the toolbox and lever the back of the closet open with a crowbar. The wood yawns, gives and breaks. I wipe the sweat from my brow.

The note reads, *Missing you, missing y.*

The y trails off in a long tail, as though the writer was inter- rupted. Ink bright green as grass. It looks wet. 'Sky?' I whisper, even though it's not him. It can't be.

'Enough,' I say aloud.

I see something lying in a shadowed corner. White, green ink. I pick the note up with shaking hands.

Miss you badly today. S.

The end of the slip of paper looks singed, burnt, which for some reason is terrifying. It's as if the note is telling me what to do with it.

I set a match to the notes, watch as the writing disappears, goes up into flame. Ash whirls out into the air, over the sea, and is gone.

'You can't get me,' I whisper out loud. 'You're not here, Sky. You're dead.'

I regret it immediately because now that they're gone, I have an awful creeping doubt that they ever existed. I know that I've been getting too close to him, going inside him. Am I maybe becoming him?

Shivering, with the bedclothes pulled up to my neck, I wait for sleep. It's dark outside the window. At least I think it is. Comets of green fire stroke across the horizon.

It's bright today and very cold but I don't want to be in the cottage. I put on my hat and muffler, two pairs of socks and the boots Emily got me for hiking in the Catskills. I drag the desk outside.

The morning goes well and I eat lunch outside too, the last box of mac and cheese. Is this my last mac and cheese ever? I'll tidy the cottage before I do it. I don't want people to think I was losing my mind. I need them to take the book seriously.

I check my faculty satmail too – if I don't, they might get concerned. A colleague might send a police officer to do a, what's it called, a welfare check. I know this, because Emily did it once, when she was in Cabo and I didn't answer the phone for a couple of days.

Footsteps break up my thoughts. Harper comes into view, heavily laden. A bucket, cloths, scrubbing brushes, cleaning products.

I smile and wave and then take in her burden with a terrible lurch of embarrassment. 'The cottage doesn't need cleaning,' I say. I can't let her in there.

'Wilder,' she says. 'I haven't come to scrub your bloody floors, OK?'

'Where are you going?' I indicate her load.

'Doing public service. Want to help?'

I want company, so I nod.

The wind roars as we go down the cliff path together, then once we're down in the arms of the bay it falls still. The stones aren't singing today, thank goodness. Though is there the odd faint note over the quiet rippling water? I close my eyes and breathe.

We pick our way over the pebble spits that reach out across the cove. 'Here,' Harper says.

I don't see it until I turn back, landwards. On the cliff something drips, green. In shaking, sloppy letters, the cliff walls spell out one word in green paint. *Murderer.* I feel sick and faint for a moment. 'Who could have done this?' I ask Harper. 'Did they come up the path – no, it must have been by boat.'

From the land the message is invisible, hidden from sight on the sea-facing cliff wall below. If you were passing in a boat however, you would see the word *Murderer* written in brilliant green on the cliff. Directly above it, you would see the sugar maple and my desk where I sit each day to write. *Murderer.* A warning for only those on the ocean, who will know to look for it.

'Is that a joke?'

She looks at me. 'What's funny? It's just some local kid's tag.'

'Why would they choose that?'

'Maybe they think it sounds tough? Cool?'

'It's for me,' I say. 'It's a message.'

'I don't think it is, Wilder.'

'Who then? You?'

She ruffles my hair, absent. 'You've got to run a comb through this. It's frizzy as a carrot top.'

I suddenly feel cold. *Carrot.* The memory's been tugging at me since I wrote about the day I found the hemlock on Pursing Hill . . . I showed it to Sky. But who was it, who first showed *me* hemlock?

'Harper,' I say. 'Have you been leaving little notes in my house? Little notes written in green ink? You were always one for games.'

She says, tight, 'I have no idea what you're talking about.'

'What really happened to Nat, Harper?'

'He's dead, Wilder, as you well know.'

'You had a paper bag with you that day I saw you outside urgent care – it had something in it wrapped in aluminium foil. A thing you took to Nat. What was it?'

'I don't know, Wilder. A joint? A snack? Nothing important. Why would you bring this up now? That was all years ago.'

I gesture at the cliff. 'Maybe this is about you, not me.'

'Maybe what is about me?' Harper says. She sounds puzzled. 'Wilder, it's just some kids messing around.'

'Maybe you've learned it's best to keep your enemies close. So they don't start to figure out what you really are.'

Harper smiles at me. Her smile is too big. It grows long enough to wrap around her head, almost, and she has so many teeth, I see that now, how could I not have seen it before? How wide that slash of a smile is – too broad and toothy to be human.

I stumble up the cliff path, blinded by panic. I can't hear whether I am pursued or not, over the clatter and my panting – I don't turn to look.

I'm shaking, though I feel better with the cottage door shut behind me. I remember again the carrot-shaped object that Harper took into the Castine urgent care centre, when she went to see Nat all those years ago – just before he died of sudden heart failure.

249

I imagine villagers with pitchforks. *Heart failure*, they would say. Like Nat. *The sea got him*, they would say. Like Sky.

I take up *The Sound and the Dagger*, flipping the pages with trembling hands. I find it quickly. Sky did use the scene where I spray-painted *THE DAGGER MAN WAS HERE* on the cliff. But he transformed it. In the book, local kids congregate on the beach below Wiley's house. They don't believe Anton is responsible for the murders. They know better. They spray, on the cliff below, the word: *Murderer*. A secret message that can only be read from the sea.

I look cautiously out of the door, and then peer over the cliff. Harper's gone, somehow, though I didn't hear her pass on the path.

I go down to the beach. The cliff wall gleams, freshly scrubbed. I smell detergent. But there are still traces of green paint on the rock. My sleep is uneasy, filled with the sound of the front door blowing open, as it sometimes does. But every time I get up, it's locked.

Disaster, this morning. There's no more coffee in the can.

Maybe there's a secret stash. Emily always does this – hides stores of nice or necessary things like chocolate or toilet paper – so that when we think we've run out we have the joy of realising there's actually more. I miss her.

I hunt through the shelves. None to be found. Right. I'll have to get to the store somehow. I can go without food and sleep, I can live without love if I must, but I cannot carry on without coffee.

*

I walk to the main road and stick my thumb out. There's a wind up, I wish I'd brought a warmer jacket. Cars roar by. No one seems likely to stop. Who can blame them? No one hitchhikes anymore and who's going to pick up a dishevelled middle-aged man with odd protruding eyes? I accept defeat and take out my cellphone to call a cab.

Behind me, a car pulls over onto the verge and comes to a halt. 'Wilder Harlow,' calls a voice. The passenger is a neat-looking elderly woman. Even my peripheral vision is slightly fuzzy today; lack of sleep I guess.

'You don't recognise me, huh.' The voice is familiar. Voices don't change the way faces do. Voices come from inside us, and the inside never changes as much as the outside.

'Hi, Trooper Karen.' I'm actually really happy to see her.

'It's detective, now,' she says. 'Or was. Now it's just Karen. Jump in.'

'Oh,' I say. 'I don't know . . .'

'Come on,' she says, 'it's perfectly safe.'

I climb nervously into the back seat beside her. She pushes the start button and the car moves away smoothly.

I try not to look forward, where there should be a steering wheel, dashboard, driver's seat. I'll never get used to driverless cars.

Karen Harden smiles and pats my hand. 'It's been a minute.'

'You came back to Castine,' I say.

'Oh yes. Once you're from here, you're from here.' The fall land rushes by.

'Are you with the police, here?'

'I'm retired. It's good to do nothing, you know?'

'No,' I say, honestly. 'I don't know.'

'What you doing back here?'

251

'I'm writing a book,' I say.

'Lots of writers come out here these days,' she says, nodding. 'Terrible thing that happened to that poor man. You know, I would have asked more questions about that death.'

'We've got vandals out by the cove,' I say, to change the subject. 'Kids.'

'I saw. It made the paper.'

'Did you know him?' I ask suddenly, without meaning to. 'Sky Montague. What was he like?' For some reason I want to know what kind of man he became.

Trooper Harden purses her lips, thinking.

'Distant,' she says eventually. 'Kind, though. Always had a word for people who wanted to say hello. They came a long way, some of them. I thought he was sad.'

Castine is bustling; I realise it's a Saturday. Karen Harden drops me outside the general store. This has changed since my day. What used to be a small family-run business is a branch of a big chain, now. The green lettering above the storefront gleams in the fall sunlight. It's made to look like handwriting.

'You OK?'

'Sure,' I say quickly, tearing my eyes off the green sign. 'Thanks for the ride. It was good to see you.' I slam the car door and hurry away.

Inside the store I pick up a pound of coffee and then I go to the news stand. It's not on the front page of the local, but it's on page five. A picture, must have been taken from a boat.

There's the cottage, the bay. I can even see my writing desk under the maple tree if I squint. A tiny splotch. Underneath, the cliff is spray-painted. I peer closer. The childlike letters are orange, not green. They read: *Mickey222*

I check the date of the paper. There's no mistake: it's today's.

I buy the paper and go out onto Main Street. I keep looking at it in the daylight to see if the headline changes. It doesn't. The Saturday crowds mill around me. Someone jostles my elbow.

'Watch it,' I say – perhaps too sharply – I turn and catch a flash of blood-red hair. Harper. It's her. I'd know her anywhere, that upright back, her walk, as though she'd walk right through anyone who gets in her way.

'Harper!' I yell. But she's gone, hidden behind a family on the sidewalk, father harried-looking, dragging two kids by the hands. The dad gives me a dubious look as I hurry past.

I run up the street, ducking and dodging people. At last, I think I see a glimpse of red turning a corner into a narrow back street, just by the old fishmonger. By the time I get there, there's no sign of Harper. I put my hands on my knees and pant, a shooting pain rushing up my arm. Careful, I think. Got to finish the book first.

I use precious minutes on my cellphone plan to call a cab to take me back to Whistler Bay. It only occurs to me as I wait under the green store sign for it to arrive, sweating, that Harper must have dyed her hair back to its original colour. The other day her hair was mostly grey.

The storm wakes me. Lightning judders in the sky outside, the glare so bright, everything in the bedroom in black and white. Beside me, soft breathing. I reach out for the breath, longing. *Oh, let me undo it. Be here. Be you. That hand, stroking my chest.*

She's standing beside the bed, the woman from the sea. Water pours from her hair and clothes. The blue of her dress is dark as wine in the electric light, but I can see the birthmark on her bared shoulder.

'Who are you?' I whisper.

Her mouth opens and water pours forth in a long straight stream, shining in the flickering light. It looks as if a knife is being thrust down her throat. She is choking and screaming through the water, but still it comes, hitting the bedclothes and the floor with a blow, the strength of a fire hose, spraying a fine mist of droplets on impact. Above her rictus mouth, her eyes implore me. *Help*, I hear in my mind, clear as a bell.

I fall to the floor. Moisture seeps into the sheets twisted about my ankles. My face comes away from the boards wet. The floor is dotted with gleaming pools. I lick my lips and taste salt.

Help, she says in my ear. The odour strengthens. Wet linen and salt water and the slightest note of rot. On the floor something glistens. A wet, sandy footprint. Slowly, I look up.

There she is above me, stretching out flat across the ceiling.

Help, she says, and something drips onto my shoulder.

'Who are you?' I say again. I hear the tears in my voice but inside I'm echoing with fear.

She raises a finger. I can see it's bent at an angle, as if it's been broken. She starts to trace letters on the air. They shine green and luminous, like light through clear water.

Rebecca, she writes with her maimed finger; the word shimmers like a sunlit sea.

I think of the young, blonde, sporty woman from that long-ago picture in the paper. I take out my phone and search the satellite newspaper archive. The picture comes up quickly. There she is, Rebecca Boone. I breathe a sigh of relief. I was right. Whatever this is, it's not her – nothing like the thoughtful, young woman leaning against the windowsill.

'You're lying!' I say. 'You're not her.'

The thing hovers above me.

'Maybe you're looking for someone else?' I say. 'Your family? I'm definitely not the right person.' Do ghosts do that? Dial and get the wrong number, as it were? 'Who are you?'

She points again to the name, *Rebecca*.

Oh god, I'm lying on the wet floor arguing with – what?

Run, I think, *just get out of here.* My legs won't obey me at first; I crawl with her at my back, towards the front door. If I can just get to the air, the light—

Something white lies on the doormat. I unfold the note with trembling hands.

Don't hate me, Wilder.

S

The vile, snake-green ink seems to gleam.

A sudden twinge of pain comes in my side, and I double over.

I pull up my shirt, wincing. The thin line of bruised flesh is deep yellow, healing to a murky green. I look from the note, to my side, and back again. The bruise is now shaped like a calligraphy S, the same shape as Sky's initial, on the page.

My stomach drops down into my bowels, and I think for a moment I am actually going to empty them right here and now, into my pyjamas. I scream.

When at last I run out of breath, she's gone. I look around the room wildly, open drawers and look under the bed, but the dead woman is nowhere to be seen.

I have a terrible idea. I need to test it.

I hunt in my briefcase for my published first edition of *The Sound and the Dagger*. I read this version years ago but it doesn't seem real to me, the way the manuscript does.

Fingers trembling, I flip to the description of Rebecca.

He was halfway out to the drowning woman and Skandar could make out her features now. A ragged, chalk-white face. She wore something blue, though not a swimsuit. Her shoulder blades were sharp and starving though translucent blue linen. A birthmark spread over one shoulder. The girl seemed like she was breathing too fast, and he worried she might exhaust herself. She looked half-dead already. There was a scent of rot in the air.

'What's your name?' He had heard that being called by your name in times of stress was calming. You remembered yourself.

'Rebecca,' she answered faintly in a cracked voice like pepper being ground. It was the most frightening sound he had ever heard. No human voice should sound like that.

I've read the other description so many times, in Sky's first draft, I forgot he changed this description for publication. It's the dress that fooled me – Rebecca's dress in the manuscript of *The Sound and the Dagger* is red. The thing I see is dressed in blue. And she has a birthmark on her shoulder, not a wound.

For some reason my hands expect the manuscript of *The Sound and the Dagger* to be soft, mouldy and rotten. But it's dry to the touch, just a pile of papers.

I flip through them at the kitchen table – I find myself swatting with my right hand at an area behind me, as I used to when I could feel Emily trying to read over my shoulder. I turn and stare at the kitchen. Empty. Or at least it looks empty. I turn the pages with trembling hands. Here.

He was halfway out to the drowning woman and Wiley could make out her features now. A heart-shaped face, full, beautiful lips.

She wore something red, voluminous, that spread about her like a bell in the water. Her shoulders were sharp and shapely though translucent linen. The cloth slipped, and he saw she had a wound on her shoulder, red and bloody like a bite from an apple. The girl was breathing too fast, and he worried she might exhaust herself.

'What's your name?' he called. He had heard that being called by your name in times of stress was calming. You remembered yourself.

'Rebecca,' she answered faintly.

But the description didn't always read like this. The page is covered with rough patches of white-out.

I wonder, I wonder, I wonder. I get a sharp knife from the drawer. Delicately, gently, I scrape away at the white-out. Soon the table is covered with little dusty white flakes. I can't believe we used to write like this – so painstakingly. After a few minutes I have completed my excavation. I carefully blow the last particles of white powder from the page. There. Just as I thought.

Rebecca's red dress was originally blue in the manuscript he sent me, just like the published version. Sky was always one for changing his mind.

I dab quickly at the manuscript page with white-out, blowing on it impatiently to speed the process. At long last, it's dry. I scribble over the description of her dress, replacing blue with red again, returning the birthmark to a wound.

I need her to come back, to test my theory. I wait, hair rising in quills on the back of my neck. Every shadowed corner of the kitchen seems to hold eyes.

The smell comes first. A taint of rot on the air. My heart slows, begins to beat cold and sludgy in my chest. Even though I'm waiting for her, even though this time I want her to come.

She's here, skirts dripping. I avert my gaze, looking without looking. Rebecca moves rapidly to and fro, shivering in and out of existence. I can see, even in the corner of my eye, that her dress has changed to a deep, dripping red. I can smell the blood from the wound on her shoulder.

I scratch at the white-out again and watch her from the corner of my eye.

A dark stain creeps up the hem of Rebecca's skirt. She opens her mouth in a silent rictus. I can't hear her but I can tell she's screaming. The hem of her dress changes to a deep blue, the colour of the ocean. Her blood dries and flattens into a birthmark on her shoulder.

The blue creeps up her skirts, to her waist. When it reaches the place where her heart would be, she puts her hand protectively over the place. Slowly, inch by inch, the blue bleeds up her red dress. She cries in silence. She reaches out a hand, imploring me to stop. It's not an easy thing, being rewritten. But you can always play around with a first draft.

I'm not being haunted by a ghost – I'm being haunted by a book. More specifically, by the characters from *The Sound and the Dagger*.

That's why only I could see the word *Murderer* in green on the cliff face. Why Harper looked so young, when I saw her from a distance in Castine. It wasn't Harper. It was Helen.

A high giggle escapes me, rolls out and out. I laugh and laugh and I can't seem to stop, even though it aches and I can't breathe and my eyes water. The world has gone insane, or maybe I have. I don't know which answer is worse. Another possibility, of course, is that I am already dead. A ghost, in some kind of fever dream of an afterlife. Oh god – please don't let me be dead.

[   ]

'It will work this time,' Grace says. 'Because you'll use me.'

'Sit down and be quiet.' She is too eager to give me her blood. The knife opens a crevice of red in her skin.

'Careful,' I snap. 'I don't want to call an ambulance.'

I take the bowl. It's stainless steel where it should be silver, but I'll make do. This will be the last time. The last chance.

Her blood hits the bowl with a patter like rain.

I pierce my finger with a sharp knife, wincing. I've done this a hundred times, but habit doesn't dull pain. *It will work this time*, I tell myself. It will. It has to.

I let my blood join hers in the bottom of the bowl. There is a light *plink* as the drops fall. I mix in the wine and seawater. In the past I used water from the bay. I knew it wasn't good enough. So this time, I made myself go there. It remembers, that water.

The stone ceiling was alive, reflecting the endless patterns of light. The pools spread out in the black, a dark mirror-land. I felt like they were there – all of them – watching from their rusted drums. Then I shook myself. They were gone, long gone. *Get it and go*, I told myself.

The touch of the water was cold as death. I scooped it up in a plastic bottle – not very magical but it got the job done.

Somewhere near the back, something stirred. I knew I was imagining things but I ran for the water, swam for the light, before I could be forced to know.

I'm nervous. This is big magic. I've never done anything this big before. And it's been so long.

I take the hair and drop it into the bowl. I'm breathing harder than I should be. The surface of the mixture swirls unpleasantly with each breath.

'Come into this ink,' I ask. 'Be bound by it.' Nothing happens, but often you don't know if magic is working until later.

But of course it won't work. None of this stuff really works, I know that, deep down. It's just a way of putting a tiny drop of your will into the great black ocean of the universe. Sometimes it's just too hard to lose what you love.

'Keep him. Bind him.'

The tears are here before I know they're coming, spilling almost painfully down my cheeks. I lean forward and let them drip down my face, off my chin and into the spell. Real tears are big magic too. You can't plan for them, in witchcraft. They either happen or they don't.

I grind the singed and blackened pearl to dust with a pestle and mortar. I add it to the mixture. Now, it's time.

I pick up the bowl, stomach already churning. The scent of wine rises, but there's an edge to it, a bloody salty undertone which makes my stomach heave.

I turn my head away, take a deep breath and hold it. I drink from the bowl. It tastes fleshy and human on my tongue. I immediately run for the bathroom. Blood and wine mingle uneasily in my throat, my tongue seems coated with it. I half spit, half heave into the toilet bowl. I don't think I have to swallow it for this to work, do I? Anyway I just can't.

With the rest of the liquid, I trace the first words of the book carefully with a needle. There. It's begun in blood. This book isn't finished yet. I think that's the key.

But nothing's happening. Surely there should be some sign? I flip through the printout sadly.

He won't be back. I'll never see either of them again.

And there it is.

```
Hello
Hell
Help
```

'Hello,' I whisper.

'Did it work?' She takes my hand and love stirs in me, strange and painful.

'Thank you,' I say to her.

'I'm yours,' she says. 'All I want is to be near you. Have I earned that?'

'Yes.' I'm crying. It has been so many years since I've let myself feel this – opened these dark places to the daylight. It's painful.

I look again at the words on the page. I still can't believe it.

'It worked.'

And now I open my mouth and let out a scream, so all the dead can hear – we'll be together again at last.

Wilder, Day Eleven

I don't remember writing that section with the witchcraft. I must have been playing around with that idea Sky put in my head all that time ago, about trapping people in a book.

I must have been.

Great start this morning because I think she's gone – a wonderful moment. I check the corners of my bedroom, the ceiling. I get out of bed, looking for the icy wet footprints she leaves in her wake. But the floor is bare.

Hope rises. Maybe she's gone for good. Maybe she got bored, found somewhere else to be or died. Can whatever she is die?

But when I open the bedroom door she's there in the hallway, waiting, floating, blue dress billowing. I think her face is getting whiter and more decayed each time I see her – lips a deeper blue. This morning something has been nibbling at her ear. There's a ragged place where the left lobe should be. Has that always been there?

She follows close behind as I go to the bathroom. I don't turn around. I have a theory that she gets more detailed the more I look at her. Little things, like the mother-of-pearl buttons on her cuffs, which weren't there yesterday. She doesn't follow me into the shower. She waits politely outside the door.

In the kitchen I edge around Rebecca carefully to get to the kettle. It's not good to touch her. Not good at all. I won't make that mistake twice. My body goes cold when I think about it.

You're not supposed to be able to touch them, hear them, smell them – Charles Bonnet hallucinations. But of course, even doctors make mistakes.

Something falls around me in drifts. The ashes of my life. No, snow. It's snowing. I become aware that someone is shaking me and I get ready to scream. Can she touch me now, Rebecca?

'Hey,' says Harper's voice. 'Come inside.'

Even if she is a murderer, I am so happy to see a person. I cling to Harper as we go inside.

'I can tell that it's all going to sound insane,' I say. The coffee steams in my hands.

And I'm right, it does. Harper gives me that look I give my undergrads when they lie clumsily to get an extension on their term paper. There's pity in it. 'You're saying a character from a book is haunting you.'

'From Sky's book,' I say, desperate. 'Not just her, either. Look.' I go to the cutlery drawer. I've started keeping the notes I find around the house. I've grown to dread that vivid green. 'Look. It's his handwriting! They're everywhere! I'm getting notes from a dead man! Explain that.'

'They don't look very threatening,' she says. *'Happy reading?'*

'It's cruel,' I say. 'That's what it is.'

'You've been under a lot of strain,' Harper says. 'I don't think being alone out here is good for you.'

'I didn't imagine it,' I whisper, once again quite close to tears. 'Look.' I pull my shirt up. The S-shaped bruise hurts, bad as ever. 'This bruise won't fade – it turned that awful green, and now it just stays that way.'

'Wilder, it's a bruise.'

'The shape of it! It's an S.' I hold out a note. My hand shakes. 'It's the exact same shape. His writing. His signature. He's *here. He signed me.'*

She says, gently, 'You were flinging about some pretty wild accusations the other day, Wilder. Are you OK?'

'I don't know,' I say. 'I'm seeing things. Or I'm not. I don't know!'

'They used to call it a nervous breakdown,' she says. 'I like that better than any of those scientific terms. Because that's what it feels like, doesn't it? Like everything in you is broken.'

I can't believe Harper's right. Because her being right would mean I have truly let go.

'And the notes?'

'Maybe you wrote them and forgot,' she says. 'Maybe you brought old notes with you and have repressed it. Maybe someone's messing with you. I don't know, but I'm a logical woman and I do know there's a logical explanation for everything.'

'Everything? Even your hair being red again?'

'You saw a girl with red hair,' she says gently. 'Your mind filled in the rest. We see what we want, Wilder.' She kisses me on the cheek. 'You call me if you need anything, OK?'

I follow her to the door. Snow falls on Harper's red and silver hair, swirls around her face, and I think, *how beautiful she is.* Her hair is caught by the wind. In that moment it looks like red skirts billowing in water and I almost scream.

I stride about the garden vigorously in the building wind, with fine, freezing rain misting my face. Clouds are boiling in the distance. 'Come out, show yourself!' I yell at the sky. I yell it again and again, until my throat is hoarse and dry from that stormy air.

A herd of deer graze peacefully on the surface of the bay. Their eyes are deep red. Heavy stripes of indigo race across the sky.

And I'm forced to ask myself, was Harper really here at all?

Wilder, Day Twelve

Skandar froze in horror as he bent to pick up the thing that lay on the doormat. It was an aging Polaroid photograph of a child asleep. Skandar reached for his younger self. A small hand rested gently against his cheek.

Only one person could have put it through the mail slot. The person he gave it to, all those years ago.

'Wiley,' he whispered.

He felt the breath then, on the back of his neck.

The Sound and the Dagger, by Sky Montague

My head pulses gently where it rests on cold metal. I feel Rebecca's dead gaze move over me and I hold my breath. But today she must have other business, because she moves on. I feel her recede, go elsewhere.

It's so cold. My teeth are actually chattering. The light is grey and low, clouded. Below, the bay is cool steel. The sun is going down, or maybe coming up?

When I sit up, the typewriter keys spring up with a cheerful click. They have left imprints on my cheek, neat rows of square red recesses, as though I am now ready for the placement of fingers. I unspool the pages with trembling hands.

I don't remember writing this. Magic seems to be making its way into this book. Or maybe it started with magic, because there is a worse possibility than all of this. I'm not being haunted by a book. I'm *in* a book.

'You can trap someone in a book, their soul – make a prison of words. A cage,' Sky said that long-ago day. It seems outlandish, farcical. But what if he found a way to do it?

A soft sound at the kitchen door and my heart stops. But it's just the mail.

When I glance at what lies on the doormat, I freeze, quite literally; my body grows icy cold. I don't think those are letters.

I go close, even though I don't want to. I have to, because I am in a plot, aren't I? I have to do what the writer wants, and no writer wants me to turn away, to never look at these terrible things.

My face is peaceful on the pillow, one hand curled under my cheek, skin pale as a corpse in the glare of the flash. It's horrible.

My fingers tremble as I reach for them. But I stop short, I don't touch. Because if I touch, and these are real, I'll know this is really happening.

Footsteps on the path outside. Someone running away. I look out of the window. I just glimpse the back of a shaggy head of hair. It looks like a teenage boy, tall and whip-thin.

I throw open the door and yell after him. 'What?' The air seems to vibrate with danger. 'What do you want?' But there's nothing but the faint mineral tang of the sea.

Sky is here. He's all around me. Because they're all just part of him, aren't they? The ghosts never existed until he wrote them. Nothing is real here, except *The Sound and the Dagger*.

Her breath is rotten on the back of my neck, stinking of death and the endless sea. 'Leave me alone,' I whisper.

Behind me I hear a sound like the belly of a snake on the earth. Or like the scratch of pen on paper. I close my eyes. 'Please,' I whisper, 'please leave me alone.'

I start and choke. Coughing, I put my finger into my mouth. The paper is moist, sodden. I manage to unfold it with careful fingertips.

The green ink is wet, the words blurred, as if they're out of focus. But I can read them, all right.

Burn
Urn
Turn
Tarn
Earn
Earl
Pearl

Pearl

They pull Pearl out of Home Ec to tell her. After ten years, Pearl's mother has come home. Not drowned after all – that would have been better. They have made an arrest.

They take Pearl to the principal's office – Pearl has been there in the past but it seems different now. They are acting like they're the ones in trouble. The counsellor is there and the nurse. Pearl wonders if they think she's going to attack them.

'She doesn't seem to be taking it in,' the principal says to the nurse.

'Shock,' said the nurse. 'I'll take her pulse.' The nurse's hands are a little damp, as if from nerves.

Pearl thinks of Rebecca lying in a cave all those years, alone, under the water. They were right, she isn't taking it in. Weirdly, it's the Polaroids she can't stop thinking about, the ones of the sleeping children. She hopes those little kids are OK. She wonders if it made its way into their dreams, somehow – the click, the flash. The nightlight shining soft on closed eyelids.

The principal's voice sounds distant, as if underwater. 'Your father will come and collect you as soon as he can. Thursday.' She's wearing the blush-coloured twinset and pearls today. Sometimes she wears a smart pantsuit. There's something in her eyes on those days, a little secret smile, maybe. Pearl can tell she feels daring on pantsuit days.

The bell screams its warning and she jumps.

'You had better get back to Home Ec,' says the principal. 'Your classes will keep you from thinking too much.'

She hears the words just fine, but the underwater thing is getting worse. The office shivers and ripples. The sound of wind rises in Pearl's head. Or is it waves beating against a cave wall?

This all happens on Monday, she thinks, but it might have been Tuesday. Afterwards it bothers her that she can never be completely sure.

Around Pearl, girls are sewing, darning. They are all supposed to be homemakers by the time they leave school.

Muriel slips her hand into the waistband of Pearl's skirt. There's a little puppy fat there. Muriel pinches hard with strong fingers. Pearl's eyes water.

'Don't cry,' she said softly. 'You'll get in trouble.' This is a genuine warning. Crying is regarded as showing off. Pearl gets that the way Muriel acts towards her isn't personal. It's the way it is.

'What did the principal want?'

'My uncle died,' Pearl says at random. The truth is precious, not everyone deserves it.

Muriel leaves her alone for the rest of the period. An uncle is distant enough. Everyone has an uncle. The discovery of Pearl's mother's body, stored by a serial killer in an oil drum, probably would have made Muriel feel uncomfortable. People are unpredictable when they're uncomfortable.

That night Pearl tries to summon the mountaintop, her mother, waits for her voice, her warm hands on her head. Tonight, surely, of all nights, she will come. *I'm trying to be cool, Mama,* she thinks. *Cool as a drink of water.*

Her mother doesn't come.

There are whole chunks of memory missing around here, for Pearl. The funeral, the weeks after, the return to school. They're not faint or repressed or anything. They're just gone.

Nothing, really, for months – until the day the new girl arrives at Fairview.

Pearl can already tell there's something different when she gets to history class. There's a warmth in the air. A brightness. And there's someone sitting in the usually empty seat beside Pearl's. The girl has a round childlike face with innocent eyes, red hair like a shout.

Pearl knows her name, of course she does. She has seen her picture in the paper. She feels everything rearrange – the classroom, her organs, the world.

'Hello,' Harper says. Of course, she doesn't know who Pearl is. Pearl's picture wasn't published in the newspaper.

If you summer in all the same places, and send your kids to all the same schools, then yes, of course sooner or later they are going to bump into one another – Pearl and the girl who helped find her mother's body.

Pearl opens her mouth to speak. She doesn't know what she's going to say.

Harper plays with her Fairview pin, turning it nervously in her fingers.

Muriel beats her to it. 'Don't pay any attention to Moony Boony,' she says to the new girl. Moony Boony is what Muriel calls Pearl, on account of her last name being Boone. 'Her uncle died months ago. She's still being weird about it. I'm Muriel.'

'Harper,' says the new girl.

Muriel reaches out. 'Let me help you with that pin.'

Pearl thinks about warning the new girl, but it's too late. The pin sinks into the ball of Harper's thumb. The girl's lips part silently but she doesn't make a sound.

Muriel nods approvingly and turns away. The history lesson begins.

Pearl watches the new girl take the pin from her thumb. The silver needle is crimson and shining. She senses Pearl's eyes on her and looks up. Looking Pearl right in the eye, she puts the sharp bloodied end between her lips and sucks, leaving the pin shining and silver and clean. She fastens it neatly to the lapel of her blazer.

'Ew,' Pearl whispers, fascinated. 'You drank your own blood.'

Harper checks the front of the classroom. The teacher is frowning at the blackboard.

She leans in close to Pearl. 'Don't let your blood fall just anywhere,' she whispers in her ear. 'With each drop, you leave a part of yourself there. Who's the giraffe?'

'Muriel,' Pearl whispers, exhilarated. Muriel hurt her but Harper doesn't care. She's found a way to keep her power. She can breathe again, in the new girl's presence.

'Come for a walk after classes?' she asks. Pearl's heart races until the new girl nods.

*

The rain falls in dull sheets around the bleachers, hammering on the metal like applause. A spider runs up a gossamer rope. It's his place, down here, it's not for human girls – but that's OK, Pearl hasn't felt like a human girl in some time. Harper hands her a bottle from her satchel.

The burning swallow tells Pearl she's alive.

'What?' Harper says. 'Are you sad about your uncle?'

'I have to tell you something,' Pearl says.

Harper's eyes get bigger and bigger as Pearl talks, and she puts her head in her hands as though Pearl's story has physical weight, as though it is filling her skull with lead.

'Bloody hell.' Harper touches Pearl's shoulder, just once, and Pearl wonders how she knows how badly Pearl wants to be touched right now – but that a hug is smothering.

'In future,' Harper says, 'if you want them to leave you alone, tell them your dog died. People really care about that.'

Harper got it from a book originally, the magic. It was given to her when she was a kid, so it's a book for kids. The book has a badly drawn cauldron on the cover and a woman with long hair floating on the wind, with a sprig of something in her hand. There's a lot of stuff about balance and the earth and Gaia. Harper doesn't care about that. She's interested in the good stuff that makes people fall in love with you or rot their living flesh or change the colour of their eyes, maybe.

There isn't enough of that in it. Pearl and Harper abandon the book.

You have to invent witchcraft in the moment, they discover.

273

There's no such thing as an actual spell. Nothing ever works twice. They can tell they're doing it right when the world goes all blue at the edges and sound drops away, and it's just them, and whatever they're focusing on. A bloody slip of paper, a piece of bark to which they've whispered a wish. Blood, mixed with the dirt from a girl's shoe, to make her get her period in front of everyone on the soccer field. Names written on a piece of paper with a date on it. Something bad will happen on that date, to that person. They don't specify what. That's up to the universe.

Pearl grits her teeth and picks up a fine strand of Muriel's hair. All around her, in the dark, sleeping girls breathe.

The scissors make a quiet crunch as they close. It's so loud in the dark. But Muriel sleeps on.

Harper takes Pearl's hand and leads her silently. They glide like ghosts down the rows. Someone turns over and groans and they stop in terror, arrested like statues with joined hands. But no one wakes. Pearl feels the power of it. They could do anything to the sleeping girls, anything – to their necks and ears and vulnerable eyes.

They sneak out the loose window on the ground floor – the catch doesn't sit flush to the frame, Harper noticed this her first day. Pearl would never have thought of looking for such a thing. 'Years of experience,' Harper says cheerfully. 'That's partly what magic is – knowing what to look for.'

The night air is silky on their faces and they run, hearts pounding, through the rain to their spot under the bleachers which will, they figure, hide the flame from anyone looking out into the dark.

They burn the hair in a silver bowl (trash can lid) under a full moon (probably, though it's hidden behind the evening drizzle). They ask for her to be expelled.

Nothing happens to Muriel, but she has a small cropped place on her head the next day. She keeps touching it, puzzled.

Harper is friends with the man who works at the gas station a mile away. She walks there most days. Walks are allowed, they're healthy for young ladies. It's only later that Pearl wonders what kind of friendship there can be between a seventeen-year-old girl and a middle-aged man. Harper always comes back with sweet-sour breath.

Sometimes Pearl sees Harper doing her own private magic. She whispers to a flower or a bird or a cloud. 'Tell her I love her,' Harper whispers. Pearl knows who Harper's talking to. Nathaniel Pelletier died before he knew.

It's sad, but it was sensible, Pearl thinks. What person in the world would have let a teenager carry that baby to term?

'Do you think he blames me for not keeping her?' Harper says sometimes, staring wide at Pearl. 'Do you think he knows now? Do you think he's with her?'

Pearl shivers at the thought of Nathaniel Pelletier looming above them somewhere in the sky, with a crying ghost baby in his arms.

'I was getting better before it all happened,' Harper says. 'Now it's too late for me. I've gone too far into the dark.' She picks up a moth whose wings are sodden and gently places it high on a strut of the bleachers so its wings can dry.

'That's not true,' Pearl says. 'We have plans.' She squeezes Harper's hand. They do have plans. They're both going to be famous artists or writers or painters. They do spells for it with moss and bird bones, burning the hair off their arms with a thrilling sizzle.

'Success,' Harper whispers.

'Success,' Pearl whispers back. 'We can do anything we want.'

'I'm going to be a film star like Grace Kelly then,' Harper says, batting her eyelids. 'Grace Kelly doesn't do all the stupid things I do. I'm going to be in the cinema.' She sighs. 'I love her.'

'Movies are so weird though,' Pearl says. They have recently shared a small yellow pill Pearl found while going through Muriel's purse, which she does on a regular basis. It's starting to kick in. 'They're traps, for moments in time.' The edges of the world pulse pleasantly.

'You can make a trap out of anything; a painting, or a word,' Harper says. Her head droops like a wilting flower. 'You can send a soul out into a star, imprison it on the head of a pin.' Her consonants jostle softly against one another. 'Anything can be a prison.'

Pearl nods, she knows what Harper means. Prisons are all around, if you choose to look. Out on the dark hockey field some small animal moves. The last of the rain falls in silver knitting needles through the night.

'Where does it come from?' Pearl whispers, as everything pulses blue around the edges. 'Magic.'

'From everything,' Harper says sadly.

They are nearly caught coming back into the dormitory. Pearl has trouble getting Harper back in the window. Harper has lost control of her limbs and she's angry. She hits Pearl in the face, leaving a red welt. Pearl gets Harper to the bathroom in time, before she throws up. After this Harper goes to bed, docile. Pearl cleans the bathroom. The streaked tile is red as murder; the smell follows her, clings to her hair. But it's all done in time for morning bell.

Harper sleeps through her classes the next day and gets grounded. No more walks to the gas station. But they can't prove anything which is good. Girls are expelled for that kind of thing. Pearl is worried about Harper. Harper arrived late in the year and missed a lot of school – she isn't keeping up in class.

Harper apologises to Pearl a hundred times. 'I'm so sorry,' she keeps saying. 'I won't do that anymore.'

'It's OK,' Pearl says. 'It's OK.' She strokes Harper's hair.

'I'll make it up to you,' Harper says. 'I'll do anything.'

'Tell me about it,' Pearl says. 'The cave.'

She feels Harper go cold in her arms. 'I can't do that,' she whispers. 'Please, don't make me.'

'It's the only thing I want,' Pearl says. She feels a cold hard place in her being exposed. She didn't know she could be this person.

Harper and Pearl sit under the bleachers. There are more spiders here now, it's their season; they hang like bombs about to drop. She and Harper are witches, Pearl reminds herself, so spiders are their friends. Out on the field, the lacrosse team slop and slide through puddles, mud. It seems to rain all the time at Fairview.

'What's it like?' Pearl asks. 'Look, smell.'

Harper thinks carefully. It makes Pearl love her – that she is answering with such care, even though Pearl is making her. 'It's behind a rock,' she says. 'That looks like an obelisk. A narrow channel leads to it. Inside it's kind of beautiful. Water playing on the ceiling and so on. At low tide it's a cave with places to sit. I used to just go there to think. With – Nat. It smelled like a tin can, but clean, you know. Not bad. At high tide it's like an underground lake.'

'Do you still miss him – Nathaniel?' A worm is writhing, pink at her feet. Pearl knows that normal girls would be afraid. They'd jump up and make expressions of disgust. But that's why she and

Harper like it down here. They don't have to pretend to be normal.

'I miss him,' Harper says. She stares at the worm. 'But I'm afraid of my memories. They're scary.'

Pearl feels sick and she realises, looking at Harper's pale face, that Harper does too. It costs Harper every time she relives this, Pearl knows. But she can't stop asking, either.

'Tell me about the other one,' Pearl says.

'Wilder. He tagged along after us and we let him. He was a sweet kid, I guess – weird though. Big bug eyes. Grey or blue I think, hard to tell, they were just so – pale. Too much going on inside them – like they were blank and busy at the same time. He had this . . . this want in him. For what, I don't know, but it was frightening – strong. I don't think he even knew what it was he wanted.' Harper shivers. 'If I had to pick the one who did stuff like – what happened – it wouldn't have been Nat. It would have been Wilder.'

Pearl nods. He haunts her like a light in the corner of her eye, this person, Wilder, like a light that goes out as soon as she looks at it.

'Tell me about the last day in the cave.'

'Pearl,' Harper says. 'I don't want to. Please, no more.'

Pearl takes a soda bottle out of her coat pocket. She walked to the gas station yesterday and had a good talk to the man there. 'Here,' she says to Harper.

Harper takes it, and Pearl hates that she's seen that moment in her friend's face just now – she stopped being a person, for a second.

'You started out in god weather,' Pearl says.

'We picked Wilder up just after dawn,' Harper's voice is steadier now. She holds the soda bottle tightly.

Pearl knows that if she fills in enough details, if she knows enough, then finally she will understand, she will be healed. She'll

278

hear her mother's voice in her head again, the way she used to. Back when she had just drowned, out at sea, and had not suffered those unspeakable things in the dark, before her death.

'I want to kill him,' Pearl says, when Harper's done.

'I know you do.' Harper knows that Pearl means Alton Pelletier.

'Let's do it,' Pearl says. 'We can do it with the blood.' Excitement floods her, hot and itchy. It's the kind of excitement that will eat her up, she knows that. It's not good for her.

'What do you mean?'

'Kill him.'

'Pearl . . .'

'We'll use magic,' she says. 'You were there in the cave, you swam over her bones. And I'm of her blood too. So we're all connected.'

Harper's hand is kind on Pearl's shoulder. She knows what Pearl wants to say, but can't. Words are very powerful in themselves, and if she says it, puts it into the world with her breath, the idea will be there and Pearl will have to deal with it.

Maybe if we kill him she'll come back.

It's impossible, of course, and Pearl can't handle facing that, the impossibility. So she doesn't say it.

As they creep out from under the bleachers Pearl steps on the worm, grinds it beneath her heel. *It's kinder this way*, she tells it silently.

*

In the following days, she can't stop looking at Harper's pale skin, thinking of the blood that runs under it, and the blood that runs under her own.

She knows, of course she does, that it's just nonsense, a game. A

279

way of protecting her mind from sadness and fear. But at the same time she knows that it isn't.

Harper cuts herself with a scalpel dissecting a frog. She throws the Band-Aid into the trash after biology. Pearl stares at it, thinking of the spell she would invent, which will link her with her mother, using her blood.

Pearl looks up and sees Harper watching. She knows Pearl is thinking of taking the Band-Aid out of the trash. She understands Pearl really well. People always think she talks too much, but Pearl knows why she does that, the incessant stream of words. She does it because she notices too much, and it's too much for her to take, all these things she sees. Sometimes she has to shut it all out with talk or gas-station wine.

Pearl knows, if there were such a thing as a witch in the real world, it would be Harper.

'Don't, Pearl,' she says. 'Let it go.'

'Let's go out tonight,' Pearl says. They're walking from Biology to Chem. The halls stink of mud and wet leather. 'Let's take some of Muriel's toenail. I bet I can do it without waking her up.'

'Not tonight, Pearl.'

'I took a walk to the gas station yesterday,' Pearl says.

'No!' Harper says. She almost yells it and a couple of girls look back at them. She lowers her voice. 'Not tonight, maybe never.'

Pearl starts to shake. 'What does it look like, Harper, the cave?'

'I meant it, Pearl.'

She looks at Harper, stunned. The sound of roaring waves almost drown her voice.

'I won't do that anymore,' Harper says. 'It's not good for you –
and it's not good for me.'

'But I need it,' Pearl said. 'I need you to tell me—'

'We both have to move on. Get a life.'

Pearl scratches at Harper's face. Harper grabs her wrist in a
strong grip. 'I'm sorry,' she says, and she sounds it.

Pearl shrugs. 'You're right,' she says. 'Sorry. Went kind of crazy
there for a second.'

Harper hugs her and Pearl hugs her back. Pearl knows her
really well, too. She knows how deep she has to hide the feelings,
so Harper won't see them.

Once or twice, some nights, it seemed like Harper half woke as
Pearl stood over her. Pearl held her breath and was still, and soon
enough Harper turned over and Pearl thought she had fallen back
to sleep. But she wonders now if she really did.

No one knows who tips off the principal but during the search they
find wine under Harper's pillow.

Harper stands there for a second, looking at the bottle. Then
she looks up at Pearl, and her smile is sad, not angry.

Harper's parents come for her the next day. No one is allowed to
say goodbye. Pearl watches from an upstairs window as Harper
gets into the car, pale, looking somehow half her usual size. Pearl
wonders what will happen to Harper. Where will she go? Who will
she become?

She pulls the doll out of her pocket. It's made mostly of her
braided hair, dull brown. But the coppery red strands from Harper's
head give it a metallic appearance in places. She took it slowly,

hair by hair, over many nights as she slept. Pearl got the idea from what they did to Muriel.

The little blank, braided face stares up at her. The doll seems to absorb all the light, a patch of dark in the bright day. There's a narrow swipe of rust across the doll's face, where Pearl wiped Harper's blood, from where she scratched her.

'I don't need you anymore anyway,' she whispers as Harper's car draws away with a crunch on the gravel. But she knows it's a lie. She needs Harper more than anything.

Pearl doesn't know, even now, whether she really once thought she could kill a man or raise her mother from the dead with a doll of hair. She isn't sure what she thinks now. Panic rises. Who is she without Harper? She's alone, alone, all all alone.

Pearl breathes deeply. *Cool*, she thinks. *Be cool as a drink of water.*

When she opens her eyes she knows what she's going to do. Maybe she has always known. It might take some time. It might take years. But she'll get it done.

Wilder, the Last Day

Rebecca hums, darkens and fades in the corner. I've stopped changing her in the text – at first I did it for fun, but it stopped being fun. She suffers when I do it. It's cruel, I see that now.

She's rotting badly; ribbons of flesh are loosening from her face, floating free on the unseen tide. It feels good to have given her a story. It feels like justice somehow. I've found reasons for all the things that are happening to me. I snort a little amused snort to myself because *Skye* makes way more sense than what's happening in real life.

I reread *Skye* as the sun rises. It's not too long – more a novella than a novel. I can't tell whether it's any good or not, it just is. Some of it I don't recall writing.

Time to finish my story, too.

I box up my typewriter. I put *Skye* beside it, with a brief note. No explanations, just instructions. I asked Harper to come over for lunch.

She'll find the note. I hate to do this to her but there's no one else.

So Sky found a way to trap me in the book. It's obvious to me now. I've seen Helen, on the streets of Castine. Rebecca follows me faithfully. Even Anton has paid me a visit. Skandar strokes my chest at night. Nate put Polaroids through my mail slot.

The cast of *The Sound and the Dagger* is all around me and there's only one character missing. Where's Wiley? There's no Wiley, because it's me. I'm in the book.

I put on a coat. It's due to snow later. Then I take it off again. It's a nice coat; Emily bought it for me. I don't want to spoil it. Someone might want it after.

I make my way behind the cottage, up the hill to the meadow. The air warms as I go. The meadow is covered in wildflowers. There are birds on the wing. Spring has crept in close without my noticing. But that can't be right, it's far too early. The birds are summer birds, chickadees, cuckoos, goldfinches. The meadow is covered in nodding grass, starred with daisies and black-eyed Susan. The copse of beech trees is in full leaf. The ground beneath them is carpeted with violets, yellow and purple.

It isn't spring, it's summer, a blue and gold summer. I walk through the weather of *The Sound and the Dagger*. The bay below is a different shape, the beach wider. Seals luxuriate on warm rock. It's not Whistler Bay. It's Looking Glass Sound.

Sky's original manuscript is under my arm.

Rebecca drifts behind me, blue skirts making no impression on the young grass. In the sunlight her suppurating flesh is a horror. Her eyes are blank as pearls. Maybe I can give her some peace. I mean to try. She may not be real, but she can feel pain, all right.

Should that fact have some kind of meaning – tell me something about life? Perhaps it should, but I don't know what.

Ahead of me, he's walking – Nate. Thin brown legs brushed by long grass. Denim cutoffs worn to a softness so thin that you can almost see his shorts under. One hand trails beside him, stroking the switchgrass.

I bend to breathe it, the warm earth. A daisy nods at my fingertips. I see that something is wrong with my hands. They're smooth – the knuckles don't have those maddening, fine tufts of hair that seemed to appear as if by magic on my forty-fifth birthday. No age spots, the nailbeds are pink. Young.

I put my hands to my face then my stomach. I'm thinner; I can feel the firmness of stomach muscles, ribs, cheekbones. My hair is thick, the forelock that hangs over my brow is silken, dark as pitch.

I see it up ahead, the treeline, the branches shushing and murmuring in the summer breeze. A wood pigeon calls, a cuckoo. It's warm, so warm I feel like I could just lie down here in the sunshine and fall asleep. In a way that's what I'm going to do.

In the trees, the light filters through all strange, a summer green. First, I clear a space in the grass and gather sticks for kindling. I brought lighter fuel and pretty soon the fire is crackling merrily. I put the manuscript of *The Sound and the Dagger* on the fire. The pages catch and curl, then roar up in a gout of flame.

Nate, Skandar, Anton and Helen stand in a circle, watching me. Their eyes are hollow places. Rebecca hovers, her mouth opens wide. Even though it's silent, I can tell it's a scream.

'I'm sorry,' I whisper. 'Just a couple moments longer.'

Her jaw extends lower and lower; her mouth is a long black place, a doorway opening. When I look I see there's a tiny lit-up scene inside her mouth – a family, picnicking on the beach. A mother, a father, a little girl.

'Did you eat them?' I ask her, 'Oh, god, please don't eat me.' Her hands reach rotten for my neck. Her white eyes stare.

The book is almost gone. I kick the crackling red pyre. *The Sound and the Dagger* flies apart and as it does, the book ghosts explode in a shower of red sparks. There's a smell like bad meat cooking. Rebecca goes last. As she burns, her hair goes blonde and curly. She seems to get smaller, slighter, more athletic. She has revealed herself at last. It's difficult to read her expression in the moment before she disappears, but I hope it's relief.

Soon the book is no more than a storm of ash, floating on the wind. I pick a posy of wild tulips in her honour and lay them on the remaining ashes. A crimson poppy nods among the grass. A squirrel chatters overhead, racing from branch to branch. There's so much growing life.

The other thing grows here, too. I find it again without too much difficulty, even with my eyesight – it's like it wants to be found. Green fronds. I start to pull my sleeve down over my hand, to grasp the stem, and then stop. What would be the point of that?

This is the right ending. I've finished the story, I've burned the past. There's nothing left for me. I'm an aging failure. Sooner or later, I'll go blind.

Still, I hesitate for a moment.

The weekend Emily was in the Hamptons I went on the satweb to find, what do you call it these days, a date. And I waited, and waited, and the guy didn't even show. But she came home early – I wasn't there, like I said I was.

Emily knows me really – I think she's always known. The funny thing is, she might have listened, if I'd talked to her about everything. About Sky and desire and all those things that float in our darkness, like lights on the water. Too late now. It's all too late.

I take the hemlock in a firm grasp. The stalk is spongy, it gives at the pressure of my grip and the sap comes away sticky on my hand. I pull it right out of the ground. The root is like misshapen fingers. It looks evil. I don't even shake it free of dirt. There's no point in that, either. I close my eyes and bite. It tastes sharp and fresh, not like poison at all.

I wait. The sun rises higher over the sea. Nothing happens. I shove more hemlock into my mouth, chewing furiously, trying not to gag on the dirt. My suspicion turns to certainty. I start laughing, around mouthfuls of wild carrot.

I spit out the last soily mouthful and get up. This isn't my ending, apparently.

A sound on the wind. I turn my head sharply.

'Are you there?' I whisper. 'Rebecca?' But she burned up – there is only the wind.

Help, comes the voice.

'What do you want from me?' I shout.

'Here,' comes the voice. 'Help. I'm in here.' Slowly, I turn my head. It can't be. But it is. The cliff is calling. It's coming from the hole in the cliff that Nat kept his beers in.

I go to the hole. 'You're not real,' I tell it. 'You're not talking.'

'Please, give me your hand,' the hole says to me. 'Please.'

I don't want to but I do, just to prove to myself that I'm right and this is all some kind of dream. Maybe his ghost left me a beer, I think, hysterical. I wait to feel the smooth shape of a glass bottle.

'I'm in so much pain,' moans the hill.

'Nat?' But it's not his voice. Darkness creeps up my arm like ink. I remember this feeling, that the hole is a mouth preparing to close on me. Further, further, I insert myself into the rock, the land. I think of snakes and spiders and rats, and all the things that live in holes. I gasp and brace myself, preparing to feel fur, the smooth scales sliding past my fingers. But there's only rough rock.

Maybe the hemlock worked after all. Maybe I'm dead. How would I know? I am up to my shoulder, buried in the cliff.

A hand closes around mine. Fingers grip like a vice. The earth has hands. I gasp and struggle.

Help, says Rebecca from inside the earth.

Even though I don't want to, I bend and look into the rocky passage.

Fingers grip mine, dark with dirt and blood. I can see crescents of nail, black with earth. From the back, a gleam in the darkness. An eye blinks. I am in a dream. The meadow is looking at me with its shining eye.

I scream then, a raw sound that comes from the very pit of me. It fills the air with jagged noise.

'You found me,' the voice says again, and it's not Rebecca. Not a woman at all.

I stop, weak.

'Sky?' No sound to the hallucinations, I tell myself again. There is supposed to be *no sound*.

So I have finally gone mad. This is it.

'Wilder? Oh, Wilder, it's you.'

It takes a day for the rescue crew, working with pickaxes and drills, to widen the hole in the cliff and drag Sky out. He is thin

288

almost beyond recognition. His left hand is wrapped in muddy, dirty fabric. He can't stop shaking and sticking his tongue out, as if he's still trying to lick the runoff from the stream which trickles down the cave walls.

Nat's hidey hole leads down, down into the bowels of the hill. At the bottom is a chamber. There's a narrow underwater entrance from the cove, which was closed by a rockfall. In it is a metal barrel, surface rough with time. She has been found at last – the missing oil-drum woman.

They identify her by her fingerprints. It's Arlene Pelletier, Nat's mother. She never left Whistler Bay, after all.

'I kept going towards the light,' Sky says.

His room is quiet, there's only the soft whir of machines. I don't know what they all do. There's intermittent gentle beeping. Behind the door comes the muted sounds of a hospital at night.

Sky couldn't feed himself at first, but he got his nasogastric tube out yesterday and he opens a tub of apple sauce. The noises of enjoyment he makes while eating it are almost obscene.

'You want me to leave you alone with that?' I ask.

He looks frightened. 'No,' he says, 'please don't leave me alone.' I'm sorry right away that I teased. He's still pale, almost as pale as his white-bandaged stump. They couldn't save the hand. What was left of it.

'I didn't mean it,' I say, touching his remaining hand. 'And you don't have to talk about it if you don't want to.'

'I want to, Wilder. It's wonderful to have someone to talk to. To have you here. Mmm.' He makes an appreciative noise and sticks his tongue into the applesauce pot.

'Almost three weeks with nothing but crabs,' he says. 'Have you ever eaten a live crab in its shell, Wilder? It's horrible.' His voice is still hoarse. He spent days yelling, calling for help beneath the hill.

'But I could always see it up on the scree – that little square of light. I crawled as far as I could each day. Sometimes that was only an inch. Never seemed to get closer, so sometimes I thought I was imagining it, the daylight. But at night I could see stars too and I thought, well, I could be dreaming the day, but not both – sunlight and starlight. I don't know why I was so convinced of that, it doesn't make much sense. You narrow down, when you're trapped in the dark like that. You reduce everything to a couple of certainties.'

He found the cave when he was anchoring his boat in Whistler Bay one night.

'What were you doing there in the dark? Or,' I pause. 'At all?'

'Well,' he says, looking sheepish. 'Sometimes, when I'm up here, I go to the cottage at night. If it's empty, I let myself in. The latch on that porthole window is really loose. You should get that fixed.'

'Good to know,' I say dryly. 'Why?'

'I leave you notes,' he says, suddenly shy. 'Just in case you ever come back here. Not long ones, just a word or two. I hide them around the cottage.'

'Like behind skirting boards and the backs of drawers?'

'Yes.'

'That,' I say, 'is as creepy as hell.'

He smiles. 'It sounds it, now I say it out loud . . . I've been going through a hard time, these last couple years. Been thinking about things I could have done differently.' He pauses. 'And I thought it was romantic. At the time.' We look at one another.

'So you were in the cove—'

'Right,' he says hurriedly. 'The anchor was stuck on something so I jumped in to get it, and there it was, this little dark hole, a cave – I could see the rim of the opening, just above the surface.'

'It doesn't make sense,' I say. 'How could we not have known? How could we not have seen it?'

'The tides have changed in the last thirty-three years. The sea levels are different. Anyway, I swam in. And I found her, the oil drum, wedged in the rock. I tried to get her out and that's what did it. When I moved her, the rockfall came. It was so loud, everything was crashing around me, I thought I was going to die. When it was quiet again I was surprised to find myself alive. Later I started to wish I wasn't.

'I took a pretty good blow to the head. When I woke up, my hand was buried under these sharp rocks, up to the wrist. I was in so much pain. I couldn't see, but I could tell I'd lost a finger. It felt like it was on fire. I could smell blood.

'When the tide came in it half-filled the cave. The water rose as high as my chest. The next day it was higher, nearly up to my shoulders. I knew if I stayed there too long, I'd drown. I had to get free. The knife was in my belt. I'd brought it with me, in case I needed to cut the anchor loose.' He stops, swallows. 'Still, it took me three days to get up the resolve to cut it off,' he says. 'My hand.

'I made a tourniquet out of everything I could tear off my clothes. Managed to get my belt off. It took longer than I thought it would. I couldn't do much at one time. Had to saw through in stages. But I was getting weaker and weaker, and I couldn't – get through the bone.'

I feel lightheaded. 'How did you—'

'I remembered that dream you used to have. In the end I just – pulled, and the skin came off like a glove.'

'Oh my god,' I say, heat rising in my throat. *Degloved.*

'It saved my life,' he says. 'It was interesting, in a way, looking at my hand without any flesh. I wrapped it up in what was left of my shirt but I knew I'd never see it again, one way or the other. I wonder if the rest of my hand is still down there – I wonder if the crabs are eating me, now?'

'How can you smile?' I say, shivering. I picture a bloody glove of flesh, trapped in the rock.

'I'm happy,' he says, surprised. 'I'm alive when I was sure I'd die. And you're here. I've always hoped I would see you again.' He touches my hand lightly with his good one. 'I could hear your voice, Wilder. I thought I was dreaming – thought it was death coming for me. I called out to you. Again, and again.'

'I heard you calling for help. I thought you were a ghost.'

'Host,' he says.

'Lost,' I say.

Sky bows his head. His messy russet hair is streaked with grey. 'Everything got so messed up between us,' he says.

'Yes, totally fucked up.'

'Don't you mean fricked up, Wilder?' He raises his head and looks at me with the trace of a smile.

'No,' I say. 'I don't.'

'What I don't understand,' he says, 'is what you were doing there. I'd only just crawled within reach of the hole. If you'd been any later I think I might have been dead. I was so nearly dead as it was. How did you get there just then?'

'I don't know,' I say. 'But somehow your book led me there. I can't explain it. *The Sound and the Dagger* brought me to you.'

'That's . . . nonsense, Wilder.'

'Maybe nonsense is all we have left.'

The doctors and nurses all fall in love with Sky. Even twenty pounds underweight, his skull cadaverous, his smile is as warm as ever.

'He's such a fascinating man. You two must have such interesting conversations,' a nurse says to me, breathless.

'Oh, I'm sure we will,' I say dryly, looking at Sky.

Somehow, there is no question that he will come to Whistler Cottage when he's released from hospital.

I wake with his arm flung over me, his warmth at my back. I yawn and prepare myself to face the morning chill. It's still dark out. The winter is a hard one. Snow falls, and a couple of times the power has gone out for an hour or so.

Sky makes a complaining sound and taps my shoulder, like, *be quiet.*

'Sh,' I say. 'No need for you to get up yet.' We took to sharing a bed for warmth, after the heating cut out one night.

Sky's a lot better but he's still weak. I cut up his food, I help him dress and brush his hair for him.

'We could go somewhere else,' I say when I bring him oatmeal. 'South. California. Wouldn't that be better?' The light is coming in over the sea.

'I hate California.'

'Oh,' I say. 'Well, I'm sure California started it.' He's been touchy, these last few days.

I have his arm halfway into a cardigan when he stops me, impatient. 'I'm not going to apologise to you for what happened back then,' he says. 'You know that.'

'Oh,' I say. 'I do know. Believe me, I know the kind of monster you are.'

'It didn't belong to anyone, that story. It was as much mine as yours.'

'Whatever you need to tell yourself,' I say. I draw the sleeve very gently up his maimed arm. He is healing well but he still feels pain there, in the missing hand. 'Do you remember that first architecture class?' I ask, absent. 'You—'

'I gave you my coat,' he says.

'It was so warm,' I say. 'From you. It was like being inside your skin.' And suddenly we're aware: of the sea murmuring outside, of the maple with its shushing leaves, and most of all we're conscious of space and time and skin, our bodies, my hands on him.

'The thing is,' I say. 'You did cure me, in a way. I never had a panic attack again after that book was published. I was too angry.'

'There's a package for you in the bottom drawer of the dresser,' he says. 'I had it sent over.'

She's unchanged by time, a little faded maybe but I still recognise her – Aphrodite, coming out of the waves. The pages are crisp, the typescript greenish with age. It's strange to hold it in my hands again. *The Dagger Man of Whistler Bay*.

'You kept it.'

'Of course.'

'I've been trying again,' I say. 'Writing.'

'I need to know you're not going to try that other thing again, Wilder – that stunt with the hemlock. Can you promise me that?'

'You're only alive because I tried to do that. Imagine if I hadn't been there.'

'I need to know.'

I look at his face, obscured by bright blue worms, writhing. The white patch is spreading fast over my vision.

'I'll be blind soon,' I say bitterly.

'There are worse things than blind. Promise me.' His hand is warm on my cheek.

*

294

I see the visions for a couple months longer – little parades of elf men marching up the lampshades. Beautiful bright fronds waving in the air, like live corals in the tide. Nothing from the past, though. That part seems to be done.

Winter comes. In Castine they say that the Pelletier place stands empty, now – Harper is gone, no one seems to know where. I'm glad. It feels like some spell has been broken, releasing her from this place. Perhaps we can all move on, now.

My sight deteriorates sharply. Darkness begins to fall. As soon as Sky can move around, he has to start looking after me.

I feel the spring come in, rather than see it. It's late afternoon, too warm in the kitchen because the oven has been on. Sky opens the door, even though it's bitter-bright. I smell cold spring tides, the waking of the land. There's a tractor working in a field somewhere. A blackbird sings in the woods behind. Sky is writing something. I hear the scratch of his pen. It makes me think of a warm horse barn at night. The timer goes and he gets up. The oven opens, there's a brief faint pulse of heat.

'Scoot your chair in,' he says. 'Dinner's here.' I move carefully – I'm still getting used to the dark. I think, *ordinary things are wonderful.*

'Salmon is at twelve o'clock,' Sky says. 'Peas are at nine. Potatoes are kind of three to six. Do you want watercress sauce? This is an old family recipe.' I don't tell him I heard him open the carton. I let him lie to me about little things, sometimes. I know he needs it.

Sky describes where the food is on the plate, so I know what I'm eating. In return I cut his potatoes up for him. He hasn't had his prosthetic hand fitted yet. We like to eat early, before the light goes, because I can still kind of see the sunset if it's red enough, and besides, that's what we prefer – so who cares that it's the time when old people sit down to eat?

I almost manage to stifle the stray thoughts that scratch at me in the night, while Sky sleeps beside me. Nat and Sky both lost a hand. It's symmetrical. Neat. Almost like someone's written it.

I think about our three names, us kids, as we were. 'Wilder,' I whisper to myself sometimes. 'Nathaniel, Harper.' We're all named after writers. It's too much of a coincidence. *Harper. Wilder Harlow.* The names chime together. The kind of thing that would never happen in real life but it might happen in a book.

I take a deep breath. Such thoughts lead nowhere. I have to start trusting sometime. This. Him. Just because I can't see him doesn't mean he's not there.

'Can you, Wilder?' Sky says, breaking into my thoughts. I can tell he's struggling with the sauce and I find the bowl with careful hands and spoon it over his salmon. The scent rises, creamy. Scent has become a tapestry for me. There's so much more of it than I'd ever thought, when I had my sight. It's a book in itself.

'We're a fine pair, aren't we?' Sky says, cheerful.

'I don't think I ever got over it,' I say, suddenly putting down the bowl of sauce with a crack. 'I never got over you leaving.'

There's a long silence. One terrible thing about being almost blind is that you can't scan people's faces. You have to learn to read silences, to breathe the feelings coming off people's skin. But I can't read this one. I don't know what he's thinking.

'I miss you,' I say. 'I have done ever since. The missing, it's worse than pain. It lives inside me, it eats me like a parasite. I won't be able to bear it if you leave again.'

'I have an idea,' he says, at last. 'If we both stay in the same place, we won't miss one another. What do you think?'

There's a crash that shakes me, goes right into my gut.

'That damn door,' Sky says. I hear him get up and close it, but it breaks free again and hits the wall with a crack.

The wind roars in, pushing like a bully, tearing at my hair and clothes and all the doors in the house slam and the windows are rattling hard in their frames. Sky's hand finds mine, he flings his good warm arm around me. We are breathless, clinging to one another.

The wind whistles through the house, lifting objects in its path. Is everything floating? I picture it, furniture and beds and tables and chairs and us, all being sucked out of the door, flung out over the wide terrible sea, dropped into the deep, lost forever. 'Am I blowing away?' I ask Sky. 'Is the house still here?'

Sky holds me tighter. 'It's the wind,' he says. 'Just the wind, darling.'

And with his words I feel the ground beneath my feet again, and I can smell that blue-green mineral tang in the air. I take his earlobe gently between my teeth and tug. There will be snow before nightfall.

The End
Whistler Bay, Maine, 2011

Pearl

2011

Pearl Boone finishes writing the book as first light spreads over the sea. The words pulse on the screen in front of her.

Whistler Bay, Maine, 2011

Her head aches, she feels scared and sick. First draft done. It's not finished, but it's there.

It's bold, it experiments with form, it's metafiction. All that crap the critics like. It sold well, *The Sound and the Dagger*, but no one really respected it. They'll respect this, she hopes. Then she thinks – *why, after all these years, do I care?*

Through the window, the sea is steel grey, lashing white. It's cold out there; all she wants to do is curl up in front of the TV. But she can't, she has a promise to keep. She goes there every time she finishes a book.

She puts on boots, a sweater, a jacket. The wind blasts her face. Castine is quiet, cold, asleep for the winter. She can't stand the sight of so many boarded-up storefronts. They remind her of death, some-how. Pearl strikes out along the rocky shore, spirits rising. She'll be a different person now she's put it all down on the page, she's sure. She'll be free. But then, she feels that every time she finishes.

It's just ten minutes' walk from town but it could be another world. The tarry beach, littered with tide debris. Empty plastic bottles, the odd shoe, fragments of net. And the old house itself, hunched on the shingle, as though keeping a secret.

Layers of paint peel to show the bare wood silvered grey with time. There's an empty KFC bucket hung on the gatepost. The one remaining pane of glass winks in the early sun like a gleaming eye.

Sun, she thinks. *Sin*. That old game her dad made her play when she came in drunk. *She was here*, she thinks, as she always does. It's a sacred place for that reason. She died here, they think. Rebecca Boone. Pearl doesn't go into the hows of that, lets her mind cover it with merciful velvet black. But she feels the power of the house. It's the last place her mother was alive, and so Pearl is connected to her here.

She tests herself but she knows her limits, these days. She never goes in. People do, all the time. Kids keep breaking into the house looking for ghosts – as kids have done since there were first kids. Nor does she go out back to the seaward side, down to the little pier where the boat used to dock.

Pearl has been on to the town council, time and again, to tear the place down, but it keeps getting snarled up in zoning and red tape. They don't admit it, but the house is a tourist attraction. Pearl can see them from the boat sometimes in the summers, walking in a long line, single file along the narrow beach at high tide, to see the place where women were killed. The shingles on the roof are all gone. People take them. The roof is ribbed and bare like the skeleton of a whale.

Sometimes Pearl imagines them, these shingles, sitting on mantlepieces or bedside tables or stored in shoeboxes in teenagers' bedrooms. Do people like sleeping in the same room as a roof shingle that once absorbed the sound of women dying? The council filled the cellar with earth. At least they did that.

Pearl turns to start the trek back to her car, and then she stops dead. There's a sound on the air, it's unmistakeable. Weeping. *Don't be coming from in there*, she thinks. *Anywhere but there*. But she understands right away with a heavy sinking that there's a child crying in the old Pelletier place.

The tearful moan comes again, from inside the house. Maybe it's not a child, but an adult. *Maybe they came here to be upset in private*, Pearl tells herself. Maybe Pearl is actually bothering them and she should just go—

'Are you OK?' Pearl calls.

'My foot is stuck,' a small voice replies.

Shit, she thinks. 'OK, keep still. Don't move. I'm coming in.'

The doorway is still standing but Pearl doesn't like the look of it. There's something creepy about opening a door to a place that's open to the sky. She steps through a hole in the wall.

'Where are you?' But she sees the leg dangling from the ceiling, bloody. The girl was exploring upstairs and stepped on a rotten place. The boards parted like butter left out all night.

'Coming,' she says, suddenly finding it difficult to breathe.

The stairs are OK; someone has laid new boards over the old rotting ones, hammered them into the joists. *Sure, great*, Pearl thinks. Make it easier to access this death trap.

The door to what was once Nathaniel's bedroom has come off its hinges. It leans against the wall. She's in there, sitting back on her haunches. One leg is plunged into the hole in the rotted board. There's blood on the old wood and everything swims around Pearl for a second. *More blood,* she thinks. *The house feeds on it.*

'I fell through,' the girl says unnecessarily. She's got a fierce chin, copper hair. Her eyes are wide with fear.

'I see that. Does it hurt?'

'A little.' She winces as she says it. A fresh thread of blood runs damson-dark across the boards.

'I'm going to help you,' Pearl says calmly. 'But I need to get some stuff from my car. Can you hold on? Don't move while I'm gone. Stay completely still. Can you do that?'

'I think so,' the girl says. Her pupils are dilated, black suns. She's in shock.

Pearl runs back along the beach, heart hot in her throat. She could see the white of bone amidst the crimson mess of the girl's leg. She calls 911 as soon as she hits cellphone reception. They'll be out as soon as they can. It might be an hour; it's treefall season, the roads are bad.

She grabs the hacksaw from her trunk. Everyone keeps one of these handy this time of year – fallen branches block the roads sometimes. She takes a blanket from the back seat and opens the little first aid kit she keeps behind the spare wheel. Looking at the contents, she feels the give of fear. A roll of gauze, antiseptic, ointment for insect bites. She thinks of the open mouth of flesh in the girl's leg. It's a kit for nicks and scrapes, not wounds where the bone peeks out like a shy smile.

'We'll work with what we've got,' she says aloud to herself.

She must run pretty fast back across the shore; she doesn't remember doing it but suddenly she's there, blinking in front of the ruined house.

She climbs the stairs carefully, looks at the girl trapped in the floor, at the ragged splintered gap. She doesn't step across the threshold into the bedroom for now. No use both of them going down.

Pearl thinks. She examines the door, which leans against the wall. Unlike the floor, it seems sound. She lays it gently down on the floor, over the rotted boards. If she crawls out onto it and reaches out her arms, she should be able to touch the girl.

'I'm going to slide you this saw,' Pearl says, 'can you grab it? Reach with your arm, don't shift your weight. Try not to move your leg.'

'OK.'

'Then I'll crawl over to you.'

The girl grabs the handsaw by the blade as it whistles past her. One of its sharp teeth pierces her finger. A drop of blood rises. A princess in a fairytale. It seems so insignificant compared to the gaping wound in her leg – but all wounds are significant, aren't they? Pearl feels her thoughts getting wild, panic is sending up its little red tendrils.

No, she thinks. *Be cool. Be a drink of water.*

She takes a deep breath and lowers herself onto her belly. Down here she can smell the Pelletier place. She's kissing distance from its bones, its body.

Pearl crawls slowly across the door. Her sweater rides up and she feels the sand and dust scrape her flesh, feels the filth of the place touch her. *Doesn't matter*, she thinks again. It's kind of her mantra. *Doesn't matter, doesn't matter.*

The boards creak beneath her and she catches her breath, feels the fall, sees her death. But the boards stay sound.

When she gets to the girl she sits up very slowly, one movement at a time. Pushes up onto her hands. Turns over. Lowers herself into a sitting position. When she's done it and she and the girl are face to face they smile at each other, goofy with accomplishment. The girl reaches out and squeezes Pearl's hand briefly.

'OK,' Pearl says, 'Here goes.' The saw bites and drags in the old, splintering wood, which is riddled with soft spots. It releases the scent of rot as she cuts. The texture is that of something dead that's been lying out.

'Ow,' Pearl sucks her finger.

'Are you OK?' The girl looks terrified. Pearl can understand that. A drop or two of her blood falls, marks the girl's faded, filthy jeans and she sees the girl losing her colour, sees the white creeping into her face.

'I'm Pearl. What's your name?' she asks.

'Gracie.'

'That's a nice name,' Pearl says.

'I'm going to change it.'

'Why?'

'My mom gave it to me.' Gracie wriggles her nose, uncomfortable. 'She didn't want me, so why should I be who she wanted?'

'Mine was murdered,' Pearl hears herself say.

They both kind of take that in for a moment.

'I changed my name from Pearl to Skye while I was in college,' Pearl says.

'It's a nice name, Pearl.'

'I guess.'

'Why'd you change it?'

'I was feeling pretentious that day. Maybe I was tired of being me. I changed it back later.'

'You write the books,' Gracie says. 'I know you.'

'Yes.'

Gracie's face contracts with pain. The anaesthesia of shock is wearing off.

'My best book was my first book,' Pearl says quickly. 'I think they've all been crappy since then.'

Gracie smirks, the way young people do when grownups try and be cool by swearing in front of them.

'It was about what happened here,' Pearl says. 'This town. This place. Or at least, Whistler Bay, up the coast. But I changed the name. I called it Looking Glass Sound in the book. It was about the murders.'

'I know,' Gracie says. 'I've read it. I've read everything about them.'

'Of course you have,' Pearl says. She knows Gracie is young, tries not to let the anger rise in her. Why must people come here like this? To stare, to imagine the suffering. It's like they're feeding the house, keeping it alive. But then isn't that what she's doing herself, in a way?

'Where you from, Gracie?'

'All over,' Gracie says, and Pearl feels the heaviness behind the words. She sees the signs. Hands clean but nails dirty, a collar of grime at her neck. It's a quick gas station wash, one where you act fast and don't take off any clothes. Her t-shirt is three sizes too big. The one foot Pearl can see is shod in a dirty sneaker, the disintegrating sole bound onto the shoe with duct tape. Homeless, probably. Definitely poor. Pearl's anger dies down as quickly as it flared.

'How old are you, Gracie?'

'Nineteen.'

Pearl's heart gives a tug. It's so young.

'All done,' Pearl says. She has cut a circle around Gracie's leg with the hacksaw. She hopes this is the right thing to do. If she can lift the leg out within its tight corona of boards, maybe they can get out of there without hurting her too much.

'Like a cookie cutter,' Gracie says, looking at Pearl's handi-work. Her eyelids flicker and her head dips for a second as if she's sleepy. Pearl doesn't like that.

'Just like a cookie cutter,' she replies. She sticks a metal ruler in at various points around the circle and gently, gently as she can, applies pressure, lifting. She hears dust and detritus falling to the kitchen floor downstairs. Gracie moans and winces.

'I'll stop,' says Pearl, suddenly terrified. 'This was a bad idea.'

Just then a piece of floor falls away, and Gracie and Pearl are looking down into the kitchen through a jagged hole. Gracie lifts her leg tentatively. Her ankle is still encased in a collar of wood, but she is free.

Pearl slips her arms under Gracie's and slides herself backwards inch by inch across the door, pulling Gracie with her. She can feel the girl's ribs working as she breathes. She can tell that she's trying not to panic.

Once they reach the door of the bedroom and are back on fairly solid footing, they just sit for a second. Pearl feels almost euphoric. 'We did it,' she says, wild.

Gracie sinks back against her, as if relaxing. Pearl realises that she has passed out.

From below comes the sound of running footsteps. Voices call from the beach. Help is here.

The little emergency room in Castine is quiet. Night is falling. Pearl sits on the uncomfortable orange seats and waits.

They close the wound in Gracie's leg with a flap of skin. Otherwise, if left exposed the bone would become dry and brittle. To Pearl it seems so strange and logical – that the best way of treating damage is to cover it up.

Gracie has no insurance. They treat her, but she can't stay.

'You can come home with me,' Pearl hears herself say. She's startled. It's the last thing she wants, she tells herself. 'Just one night.'

*

The stones are whistling below as they reach the cottage. The sugar maple is crimson in the fading light.

Pearl bought the cottage off Wilder's mom after his death but she doesn't come here much. She came this year, to write the book. Harper still lives on the bay, in her white house that looks like crème pâtissière. Pearl feels a moment of guilt that she made her Harper character live in the old Pelletier place.

Pearl and Harper don't speak, haven't since the day, all those years ago, that she heard about Wilder.

'What's that sound?' Gracie says. She's a slip of white in the dusk. She's using old wooden crutches, which were all the hospital was willing to part with.

'It's just a trick of the wind,' Pearl says. 'Don't worry.' She can't tell if Gracie is worried or not. The girl has a still surface. Pearl recognises that. It's a way of protecting yourself from others – of hiding the deep warm things that are happening inside.

Gracie is almost asleep but Pearl warms soup from a can and makes her eat it with crackers. 'I've never been much of a cook,' she says, apologetic and slightly defiant. 'But you've lost blood.'

'It's good,' Gracie says, and eats. When she's finished she says politely, 'Thank you for dinner.'

Pearl puts her to bed in the room with the porthole. She goes to close the window; the night air has a bite to it at this time of year. 'Leave it open,' Gracie says. 'I like the noises the stones make. Hooting. It sounds like owls.'

'I suppose it does,' Pearl says. 'I never thought of it like that before.' All this time she thought the stones sounded like mourning or destruction. But maybe they've sounded like owls all along.

*

Pearl wakes completely in an instant. The house is quiet and at first she can't think what disturbed her. But then it comes again.

The unmistakeable ding of her laptop. The sound it makes when you scroll to the end of a document. It's irritating but Pearl has never been able to work out how to stop it.

She gets up silently, moves down the corridor lightly on the balls of her feet. For a moment, oddly, she thinks – *Wilder?* But he's dead.

Gracie's head is silhouetted by the bright screen. She's hunched, reading. Pearl can see what it is on the screen, what she's reading with such absorption. It's the manuscript of *Looking Glass Sound*.

'What the fuck are you doing?' Pearl asks, cold.

Gracie jumps, startled. 'I didn't hear you coming,' she says.

'I can see that.'

'I know I shouldn't have – I know—'

'I think you'd better get out.'

'Please, let me explain.'

'People like you should be ashamed of themselves.' Pearl gets them, occasionally, these people. They make their way out here to see it for themselves, the real-life inspiration for Looking Glass Cottage, for *The Sound and the Dagger*. At first, she had been flattered. Then she was annoyed and eventually, after someone quietly removed some of her laundry from the line outside and took it away with them, she was scared. She had the sign for Whistler Cottage taken down, the one that used to point up the sandy path to the house. It sort of worked. In Castine they don't answer questions about her anymore, won't direct people to the house. She's become a source of pride to them, something to be protected. Like a favourite pet, maybe.

The girl's eyes are glassy with tears. But there's also an air of resignation to her, which affects Pearl more. She's used to being kicked out into the cold night.

Pearl sits down. Gracie hovers, uncertain of her fate.

'Is Gracie really your name?' Pearl asks.

'Yes!'

'Did you come here to meet me?'

'No. I mean, I hoped—'

'Did you fake all that, being trapped, to make me bring you here?' She knows it doesn't make sense, Gracie couldn't have engineered it all. But she's scared, angry. She took this girl into her home.

'No,' Gracie is in tears. 'I came here because of my dad,' she says. 'My dad was from here. He was – he had something to do with that old house. I wanted to see it.'

The world slows down for Pearl, as it does in moments of shock. She curses herself. How stupid she has been, how blind. 'Your mother,' she says. 'Who was she?'

Gracie looks up slowly and for a second Pearl is terrified. There seems to be a flicker of light behind her eyes. She just shakes her head at Pearl.

'Who – *is* she?' Pearl asks.

'I think you already know,' says Gracie. A strand of hair falls over her cheek and Pearl sees how it's red in the lamplight, as red as an alarm. Pearl sees Gracie's mouth tighten up into a bud. She's trying not to cry.

'She won't see me,' Gracie says, loud and heartbroken, her face red. 'She told me not to come here.'

Pearl pushes Gracie gently away. 'You have to leave in the morning,' she says, making her tone as cool as she can. 'First thing.'

Before Pearl knows what's happening Gracie is crying on her shoulder. Her head is cornsilk under Pearl's hand. She feels Gracie's snot and tears sinking into the shoulder of her cotton pyjamas. Gracie's back heaves with sobs; Pearl can feel her heartbeat and the breath moving through her thin ribs. She's touched Gracie more in the last day and night than she has touched another person in years. *No*, she thinks, fierce – *I didn't come all this way, build all this armour for myself, only to feel this now.*

'I'm sorry I looked,' Gracie says. 'I know it was wrong. I just wanted to read what you were writing about him. And her. All I have is this – this *asking* inside me. Like a pulse, every second. Would he maybe have loved me? Even if he was bad,' Gracie wipes her red eyes hard with the back of her hand. 'Bad people can still, like, love you. I would have taken that, maybe. It would have been better than this.'

Pearl lies awake most of the night, listening. She wonders if Gracie will try to leave in the night, maybe with her wallet or laptop. She almost hopes she will. Wallets and laptops can be replaced. She would prefer that to having to act.

She recalls the doll she made all those years ago out of Harper's hair, Wilder's gum. A pearl from her mother's earring as round as a little bellybutton. Wrapped in the letter from Alton Pelletier, from Wilder's stolen folder. Did she really think she could bring back the dead, with witchcraft? It isn't real and never has been. Ghosts are just that: traces, memory. Nothing lasts.

When she ventures out of her room into the kitchen in the early, grey morning, Gracie is there, crutches and backpack leaning against the kitchen table.

'You can take some food with you,' Pearl says. She wonders what she has. She offers Gracie the box of pop tarts.

'I want to make you a deal,' Gracie says, determined.

'There's no deal here,' Pearl replies. 'You go.'

'I read your book last night,' Gracie says. 'Most of it. It's weird.'

'Great, thanks,' says Pearl.

'I mean it's weird to write a book that's all about your first book.'

'It's just what happened,' Pearl says. 'I mean, I tried to see it from his side.' Why is she justifying herself?

'What happened to him in real life, your friend?'

'I don't want to talk about that.'

'You need your ending.'

'The book has an ending. Sky and Wilder are happy together. The end.'

'I mean you need an ending for you. I have something I think you'll want.'

Pearl walks to the door and opens it. The day is grey, blustering. A wind whistles in. 'Time to go.'

'It's good, I promise,' Gracie says. 'It's something my mother left me. It's the only thing she sent with me to my adoptive parents. She wrote that I deserved to know about my dad.' She takes a deep breath. 'It's my only precious thing but I'll give it to you if you let me stay.'

Feeling pulses through Pearl. She tells herself it's shock, but she knows, really, that it's excitement. 'Fine,' she says, reckless. What is she agreeing to? 'Show it to me. You can stay for a couple days.'

Gracie takes an envelope out of the front pocket of her backpack. It's grubby and soft with much handling. She opens it carefully, slowly. Pearl wants to grab it from her but she doesn't. Instead she wipes her hands carefully with a cloth and takes the picture by its edges.

Pearl recognises it from Wilder's description – this picture, which once lived in Nathaniel Pelletier's wallet. She looks at the woman in the bar with her hair a shock of shaggy blonde, that her son will later share. She's pink with beer and the warmth of the room. She looks happy. She doesn't know that she's going to disappear soon. Pearl knows who she is. It's the woman they never found. The one they think might be the missing oil-drum woman.

Nat's mom.

An anonymous arm drapes over her shoulder, hands and face both hidden from view. The photograph is a Polaroid, folded in half.

Pearl unfolds it with shaking fingers. There he is.

The man's face is obscured by a thumb, broad and blurry and pink. Pearl can guess at the identity of the photographer. Wilder's uncle Vernon never got much better at it.

The man's wrist is now visible, however. He's wearing cufflinks made of Coke-bottle caps. Pearl thinks of all Wilder's mom's insistence that Edith was not the first affair. She thinks of Wilder's instant affection for Nathaniel Pelletier, how they gravitated towards one another. They say siblings who were separated at birth, or never met, can recognise one another if they meet later in life. Even if they're only half-brothers.

She looks at Gracie, feeling wild.

She missed it at first because Gracie has that red hair – but Pearl can see it now. The pale eyes, almost the same colour as her skin. The eyes are large, slightly protuberant. The Harlow look.

'Go put your stuff back in the bedroom,' she says briefly to Gracie and turns away. Now it's her turn to make a call. She hopes Harper answers. They haven't spoken since that day the milk spilled all over the kitchen floor, the day Pearl set a fire.

Pearl has decided to call the book *Looking Glass Sound*.

She uses Wilder's memoir as a beginning. She still had it in the safe at her New York apartment – that binder with Aphrodite on the front, containing his careful handwriting, telling the story of that summer. So, once again, she went back to those dog-eared pages. This time, she typed it up word for word.

The college part is pretty accurate, she didn't change much there. Trying to imagine his feelings, looking out through his eyes – it was a kind of salt-sweet torture. She made herself go inside him. Reliving it was like catharsis, but also cannibalism. Going to see Alton Pelletier. Her flight, leaving him, disappearing with his writing. She changed her own gender, of course – became Sky. It made sense – after all, she did the same in *The Sound and the Dagger*, years ago, when she made herself into Skandar. It's a disguise, this change, it makes her feel safe. Otherwise those books are just windows into her pain.

Maybe she made Sky and Wilder too romantic. She wants Wilder to have some happiness, even if it's only imaginary – even if it's just in a book.

Wilder is dead. He never got old, never married, never became a professor. Pearl most enjoyed that part of writing the book; it gave her pleasure to give him those things. It was good imagining him three decades later, a slightly grumpy older man. Pearl had a harder time imagining the technology in twelve years' time – she's never been much good at all that science-fiction stuff, all the critics say so.

In *Looking Glass Sound* she uses actual passages from her first novel, *The Sound and the Dagger*, to haunt her fictional Wilder. Just as the events that inspired it haunted him, all those years ago.

Wilder's story ended here, on Whistler Bay. Or up in the meadow on the hill above the house, anyhow. He must have got the idea from Harper all those years ago – hemlock. It grows up there. She has imagined it a thousand times – his last moments.

She forces herself not to think of what she knows about hemlock. The burning, the pain, the loss of muscle control, the drooling and convulsions.

Pearl still remembers the last thing Harper ever said to her, before she hung up, which was the last time they ever spoke.

'You did this.'

Pearl gave him a better ending. Wilder goes to the meadow surrounded by summer flowers. But in her version he finds Sky beneath the earth, and there's a happy ending.

And since she has been writing, it feels as if this version – though she knows that this doesn't make sense – has become true. She can imagine Wilder happy in this house, with Sky. She has felt – no, known – these past couple months, that he's really OK. Through some thin membrane, in another world, Wilder is alive and well. At times when the barriers are thin she feels him here. In the kitchen, pushing past her, absentminded, to get a can from the store cupboard. Lying by her in the night, breathing. Sometimes when she wakes up just before dawn, she even thinks she hears the clack, clack, clack of his old Remington in the kitchen.

But this is mere wishful thinking of course. Pearl's new book is just that. A book. And Wilder is dead. Gone these nineteen years. Some days Pearl doesn't even think about him at all. Not once.

She saw it in his face that morning in the lodge, with the bath with the feet. The night they spent together after seeing Alton Pelletier. She saw that what she felt was not returned. It wasn't that he didn't like women. But he didn't love Pearl, not like that.

Sometimes she tries to persuade herself that what she did to him wasn't payment for this fact.

Sandra Harlow left the final pages of Wilder's journal on the table at Whistler Cottage. They were the first thing Pearl saw when she opened the door to her new house. Pearl doesn't know whether

Sandra left them as a comfort for Pearl, or an accusation.

Pearl used them, too. Over the years she has pored over every word. Now she's using them in her new book. *Monsters, aren't we all, writers*, she thinks. *We eat everything we see.* The end of Wilder's memoir has always struck her as odd. He says he's coming back to Whistler Bay – which he did. He doesn't sound sad, but angry. He must have found he couldn't write his revenge novel. Writers' block follows you everywhere, as Pearl knows.

Sometimes she wonders what happened to that typed draft of *The Sound and the Dagger* she sent to Wilder. Her fictional Wilder burns it, in *Looking Glass Sound* – but really, it's never been found.

The fire roars and licks at the night sky. The quiet sea is full of stars. Somewhere in the dark, a seal barks.

Pearl waits, looking out for her – but of course the moment she takes her eyes off the path, bends to pour herself a drink, Harper appears silently. Suddenly she's just there, behind the fire.

She's older, of course she is. Red hair streaked with grey. But her face is unlined, as wicked-looking as ever. Firelight plays on it, makes holes of her eyes. All the beginnings to this conversation that Pearl had ready are gone from her head.

'Hello, Pearl,' Harper says. 'It's been a while.'

Pearl takes a deep breath. 'I thought you had an abortion, Harper,' she says. 'Back at school, you always let me think that—'

Harper goes pale and still. 'She's here, isn't she?'

Pearl nods. There's such sorrow in Harper's face. 'I found her wandering round the old Pelletier place.'

'I told her not to come.' Harper sits down suddenly in the sand. 'I can't see her,' she says. 'This is a trap. How could you do this to me?'

'Have a drink,' Pearl says. 'You need it.' Then she flushes, remembering.

But Harper isn't listening. 'I should have known she'd find me.'

'There's more.' Pearl hands Harper the Polaroid. It's in a clear plastic bag, now. Like an evidence bag, Pearl supposes.

Harper looks briefly and says, 'She's a girl in a tight spot. She wants somewhere to stay. Maybe she just saw what you needed and gave it to you.'

It's been years, but Harper and Pearl still see to the heart of each other. Maybe if you know someone this deeply once you can never lose it. 'No more lies, Harper,' Pearl says gently. 'Nat's gone. You don't need to keep his secrets anymore. Is this the picture Wilder saw in Nathaniel Pelletier's wallet?'

Harper nods. 'Vernon gave Nat the photograph, said it was of his mother and his real father. Vernon always thought it was wrong that Nat didn't know who his dad was – but he'd promised his brother never to tell anyone. So he kept giving Nat these little hints. When Nat saw Wilder's father wearing those bottle-cap cufflinks that evening at the cottage, he realised. He stole the cufflinks and hid them with his Polaroids behind the skirting board.' Harper takes a deep breath. 'The last time I ever saw him was at the hospital that day – the day I told him I was pregnant. I think he wanted our child to have something from their past. But of course the police found the cufflinks. All he had left to give was the photograph.'

'Did anyone else know?' Pearl's heart beats fast and strong.

Harper shakes her head. 'Nat was afraid of what Alton might do if he realised. But he knew his time was running out, one way or another.' Harper wipes her eyes fiercely. 'So that day in the hospital, he asked me to tell Wilder that they were brothers. And I was going to, I swear I was. But I waited, and waited, then it was too late.' Harper pauses. 'I found him. Wilder. Did you know that?'

315

'No,' Pearl says, shaken. 'I'm sorry. How did he seem to you, before—' She's trying to find a way to ask whether Wilder seemed likely to kill himself. 'From what he wrote in his memoir, it seemed like he was coming back here to write his revenge novel. But I guess something changed his mind.'

'He was angry,' Harper says.

'With me.'

'With you. But very – alive.'

'He might have a niece,' Pearl says. 'We'll be certain once we have the DNA. Gracie's agreed to it – I have some of Wilder's hair.'

Some strong feeling comes from Harper. 'Where did you get that?'

'I took it the morning after we—'

'You should have told me you had it,' Harper says. In the firelight she's pale with anger.

'What does it matter?' Pearl asks, her own anger rising. 'The things you keep to yourself, Harper! Did you never want to find her? Your daughter?'

'Don't you judge me, Pearl.'

'You're the one judging me,' says Pearl. 'You've blamed me for his death for so long – years, Harper, nearly twenty years – but it wasn't my fault!'

'You took a vulnerable, traumatised boy and used him,' Harper says. She ticks the items off on her fingers. 'You pumped him for information, you slept with him, you made him relive that traumatic past, just for your book – just like you tried to do to me.' Their faces are so close that Pearl thinks, *will she bite me?*

There is the sound of footsteps on the cliff path and they both turn their heads sharply. A slim figure comes out of the dark.

'I didn't know where you were,' Gracie says to Pearl.

'We decided to have a fire on the beach,' Pearl says. She breathes deeply, trying to calm herself. 'This is my fr— this is Harper.'

Pearl feels the air move and change as Gracie and Harper look at one another.

'I don't have anything to say to her,' Gracie says. She grabs a marshmallow from the bag and skewers it.

'These things take time,' Pearl says. The hurt on Gracie's face is too much to bear. 'You two need to get used to each other. You can do that, can't you, Harper?'

But Harper isn't listening. She's watching Gracie's features dancing in the firelight, watching her eat the long pink strings of marshmallow. Feeling eyes on her, Gracie looks up. For a moment Wilder looks out, pale, through Gracie's eyes. How could Pearl not have seen it before? Then Gracie tips her head back and he's gone, instead it's Nathaniel Pelletier who turns a leonine head up to look at the moon overhead.

Pearl is about to say, *do you see now? Harper, did you see that?* But there's no need. Harper's face gleams with tears. 'It worked,' she whispers. 'The magic. All three of us made it back here in the end.'

Gracie goes to bed after three hotdogs and most of the marshmallows.

'I'm going to credit him, you know,' Pearl says to Harper. 'He wrote some of it. I might even say he co-wrote it.'

'What are you going to do about her?' Harper asks.

'I don't know,' Pearl says. 'I thought maybe she could stay here when I go back to New York. For a time, anyway.' She doesn't know how Harper will react to this.

'If she does decide to stay,' Harper says, 'I'll look in on her.'

'You could have her to stay some night,' Pearl says.

'Maybe.'

'OK,' Pearl says.

Harper looks at Pearl in surprise. Pearl tries to stem the tears, push it all back in, but the ugly things are bulging up from the depths, closing her throat.

'I loved him,' Pearl says. 'I wanted him, and oh god, I was so fucked up back then. I didn't know how to deal with it all. I did it, I killed him like you said.'

'No,' Harper says quietly. 'I was angry when I said that. You were young. You were grieving. It was Alton Pelletier who killed Wilder. He never got over what happened. He never got over Nat.'

'I like to walk up there sometimes,' Pearl says, after a moment. 'Do you want to come?'

The path winds ahead like a snake's back, cinder-black and silver. Harper and Pearl stumble a little, laughing some. Pearl feels light as a feather, unlike herself. They could be back at school, walking across the hockey field under the bright moon.

The meadow is white-lit and broad. The moon is a lamp, glowing under the sea.

Pearl doesn't know exactly where they found him. She has never wanted to know. But now she sees Harper looking, staring really hard at the ground beneath a handsome beech tree. She thinks, *oh, there*, and she starts to cry all over again because it's a peaceful-looking place, comfortable, with some pale stars of night jasmine opening just now, nearby, and she's glad it happened in a peaceful place. There's so little to be glad about but there is this – this one small thing – that he died surrounded by flowers with the sea shining blue before him.

'Why did he come up here to do it?' Pearl asks. She has often wondered this. 'I thought he hated this place.'

'Maybe that's why he chose it,' Harper says. 'It's difficult to leave if you're surrounded by the things you love.' Harper breathes deeply; the night air is filled with spring. 'We would have done magic here, once, wouldn't we?'

'Being old kind of takes the magic out of things,' Pearl says. 'It's sad.'

'But also a relief.'

'Also that.'

'I gave up witchcraft, after Wilder died,' Harper says. 'It was too hard to keep hoping it would help. Too hard to take every time it failed. Part of me died with him. I know it's the same for you.' Harper touches Pearl lightly on the arm. 'It's good to see you again.'

Pearl is moved. She squeezes Harper's hand. Harper goes tense and Pearl thinks, *I've gone too far*, but Harper's attention is elsewhere. She calls suddenly, 'You can come out, Gracie!'

The girl comes out from the dappled shadow of the beech trees.

'I heard you talking about magic,' she says. 'I'm a witch too, you know.'

Gracie dances down the path ahead, surefooted in the moonlight. *I've gotten old*, Pearl thinks enviously – *old and afraid before my time*. Harper stays close to Pearl. Every so often, Pearl swears her feet leave the path. She glides beside Pearl, toes grazing the sandy shale.

I need some sleep, Pearl thinks. She's seeing things.

'I want you to have something,' Pearl says to Harper when they reach the house. 'Just a second. Wait here.'

She goes to her bedroom and takes the lock of hair from the locket where she keeps it, in the drawer with her mother's pearl, the blackened sphere that was once set into her mother's earring.

She recalls Wilder's expression of sleepy bewilderment and annoyance as she tugged the hair out of his head.

There's not much left but Pearl divides the dark, silky strands into two. Strange that this slender strand of hair can provide answers to so many questions. She'll keep half for the DNA testing, but half should go to Harper. On impulse she opens the box where she has kept the pearl for thirty-two years. She looks at it in moments of high tension. She finds it calming.

The pearl is not there.

Pearl breathes. Gracie, maybe. Or maybe not. Perhaps Pearl didn't put it back one night. Maybe it rolled down the back of a drawer. Not everything is someone's fault. She thinks for a moment, tests the old deep wounds – and realises, to her surprise, that it's all right. She doesn't need it anymore. Maybe Gracie needs it more. Time for new things.

Harper and Gracie are standing together, silhouetted against the moonlit sea. Gracie is whispering urgently to Harper. Their heads part quickly as Pearl comes back.

'Here.' Harper's hand is soft, smaller than Pearl remembers. She expects everything about Harper to be tough and hard but it's not, of course. Harper lost a lot, too.

'You must miss him,' she says. 'Both of them.'

She folds Wilder's hair into Harper's palm. 'For you,' she says. She pauses. 'You know, after you called me that day, the day he died – I tried to do magic with his hair. Like that stuff we used to do at school. I thought I could bring Wilder back to life with it. I burnt my mother's pearl. The only thing of hers I had left.'

'Well,' Harper says comfortingly, after a pause. 'Maybe it will work. Maybe you'll be together again one day.'

Pearl laughs and hugs her, and after a moment Harper returns the hug.

'He'll be waiting for you when you're ready,' Harper says. 'Wilder.' Pearl is surprised. She hadn't thought Harper religious. But they've both changed.

'I'm glad we're friends again,' Pearl says. 'You're the best friend I ever had. I'm sorry I didn't know it, back then.'

'Oh god,' Harper says. 'Neither of us knew anything. We were idiots. But sometimes we do get second chances.'

It's odd, Pearl thinks, how you can feel things, in the darkness. She can tell that Harper is smiling. She feels a great weight lifted, a burden she has carried for many years.

'Please don't go yet,' Gracie says to Harper, and it's so strong, the longing in her voice, that Pearl can almost see it on the night air like a colour.

'I'll leave you two to talk,' Pearl says.

Pearl tries to sleep but her mind is a lightning storm. She can hear the low murmur, out on the cliff, of Harper and Gracie talking. In the end Pearl gets up. She gets the Aphrodite binder out of the closet and sets it down on the kitchen table, strokes it gently with her fingers. It feels different now, something to be treasured, not a reminder of guilt. She opens it and spreads the pages of *The Dagger Man of Whistler Bay* out over the kitchen table. That broken type-writer key – it drives her nuts every time.

I don't think people should live by the ocean. It's too big to understand.

But what else can we do, Pearl thinks, *except keep coming back here again and again and again, trying to understand?*

Pearl reads, sinking into the blue and gold of that summer.

*

Her attention is snapped by a raised voice out in the night. 'I don't know if I can do it.' There is such suffering in Harper's voice.

Gracie says something back. Pearl can't make out the words but there are tears in them. She hastily focuses on the pages before her. Some things are private.

Later when the eastern sky is touched with the first gauzy light, Pearl hears Harper's steps fade away past the cottage and down the hill. A moment later Gracie comes quietly into the kitchen. She has been crying and her cheeks are red, but her eyes are bright stars.

'I'll make you a hot chocolate.' Pearl can't think of anything else to say but it seems to be the right thing because Gracie holds her tight and buries her face in Pearl's shoulder.

Pearl wakes with a gasp. Blue snowlight is coming through the porthole window. Someone is breathing beside her.

Ah, there you are, she says, and flings her arm over him, stroking his chest. Tap tap, she goes, as in, *follow me*. He turns towards her, but as he does he is gone.

Waking is like being torn apart.

It's not Wilder, she reminds herself. And he's definitely not a ghost. Ghosts don't exist. It's a dream she has sometimes, that's all, of a night twenty years ago, when she was young and Wilder was alive. She hardly knew him, really. It's been so long since they talked, since they touched – and what did it all mean anyway?

One day I'll be an eighty-year-old woman, Pearl thinks. *And I'll still be sad, missing this nineteen-year-old boy.*

*

Pearl stands under the maple, looking out at the Sound. *No*, she corrects herself. *Whistler Bay.* It's easy to get confused. The water looks back at her in a sheen of steel. The stones are quiet. It's time to get back to life.

'You OK?' Harper asks.

'Do you love her?' Pearl asks in a rush. 'I know I'm hardly the maternal type but please, don't let her stay like this, for you, if you know you can never really love her back.'

'That's my daughter, Pearl,' Harper says softly. 'Don't interfere.'

'OK,' Pearl says. 'I won't.'

Harper and Gracie have been growing closer, these last few weeks. Long walks along the coast path. Every so often Pearl comes home to find the kitchen haunted by faint scents – woodsmoke, resin, herbs. Harper is back to her old tricks, then. It's harmless enough, Pearl supposes. Wicca, white witching, whatever you call it – polite magic, stripped of the urgency and blood of bygone ages.

Sometimes Gracie and Harper go out at night under the waning moon. Once or twice Pearl has woken to faint screams coming up from the bay. Pearl is glad that Harper is reclaiming that part of herself. And it's good that she shares it with Gracie.

Gracie will stay and look after the cottage when Pearl's gone – it suits everyone. Mother and daughter can continue to weave the delicate web of their relationship, and Pearl gets a resident caretaker.

Gracie wanders out of the front door, chicken leg in one hand. She has the manuscript of *Looking Glass Sound* in the other. Pearl printed out two copies, one for Gracie and one for Harper. She can see that the title page has smears of chicken grease on it.

'Won't you be lonely?' Pearl asks Gracie again.

Gracie still puts everything she owns in her backpack each night and uses it as a pillow. Not because she's afraid that Pearl will steal things, but because she's used to doing it. She needs time to get used to being safe.

'I'll be alone,' Gracie says. 'Not the same. Anyway, I have Harper.'

Harper looks over at her daughter briefly and a quiet ripple of feeling passes between them.

'All set?' Gracie asks Pearl.

'All set,' she says, trying not to ask what Gracie thought of the book.

Gracie grins. She's good at hearing what people don't say. Survival instinct, Pearl supposes.

'I don't understand,' she says. 'You made Wilder do stuff for you for the book. You kind of used him.'

'Yes,' Pearl says.

'But he was your friend. You like, loved him. That didn't stop you?'

'Why should it?' Pearl asks, genuinely puzzled.

Gracie thinks about this. 'I like how they find her. My grandmother. The last barrel woman, hiding under this cliff. Can you imagine if it was true?'

'I don't think they'll ever find her now,' Pearl says gently. 'We don't even really know if that's what happened to her. That cave under this hill doesn't exist. I made it up.'

Gracie shrugs. 'I like the little chapters you put in that are only word games.'

Harper turns, looks at Gracie with a smile.

'What?' asks Pearl.

'You put in chapters that are just, like, words.'

'No,' Pearl says. 'I mean, I mention the word game I used to play with my dad but—'

'Well you put columns of words in,' Gracie says, puzzled and a little hurt. She seems to feel that she's being accused of lying, somehow. 'It's right there. And you made it look like a typewriter wrote them. That's cool too.'

'Gracie, you have to stop.' Sometimes Gracie gets anxious when Pearl's about to leave a room or the house, and she invents excuses for her to stay. 'I have to go, I'll miss the New York flight.'

'No.' Gracie shoves the bundle of pages into Pearl's hands. 'I mean it. You must have forgotten, or something. Take it. Look, you'll see that I'm right.'

Pearl takes the pages from her.

'Can I have the other chicken leg?' Gracie does this too, she asks for permission to eat food, as though it were being rationed.

'Of course,' Pearl says, absent, flipping through the pages. Gracie dances back into the cottage.

Pearl stops flipping. Her heart stops too.

```
Won't
Don't

Moss
Muss
Must
Rust
Trust

Hem
Them

Whelp
Help
```

```
He l d
He l p

He a p
He l p
```

She didn't write this. She knows she didn't.

According to Pearl's dad's rules, the game had a structure. The last word of each group should make a message.

Don't trust them
Help
Help
Help

'I must have written it and forgotten,' she says aloud, wild. 'I must have done.'

But the top of the *'l'* is missing, leaving it looking like a drunken 'i'. The letters are slightly greenish, as though the typewriter ribbon is running out.

'Wilder?' Pearl whispers, looking around her in a flood of – what? The sea and the sky shimmer, as though about to answer back.

Harper is watching her. 'Yes, he's in there,' she says. 'I put him there. I used the hair you gave me.'

The sky goes dark as dusk. Harper's eyes are as silver as the last of the light on the sea.

Pearl sees that she has never really known her at all because the look on her face is not of the woman she knew, or even really a person at all.

'You wanted to live forever,' Harper says gently. 'You both did, you and Wilder. That's all writers really want, whatever they say. Now, you can – here, in the book. I have your blood so after you die you'll go in too. You'll be together forever, walking through the pages.'

'How do you have my blood?' Pearl's flesh moves like the sea around her bones.

'Gracie. You bled on her jeans when she was trapped in the house, the day you took her in here. And she brought it to me – as well as your mother's pearl.'

'Gracie wouldn't. I tried to help her—'

'You tried to make yourself feel better. And she was using you to be near me. She's my daughter, mine.' Harper pauses. 'You're a monstrous person, but books are cages for monsters. You both deserve it, you and Wilder. You put all my pain there on the page without a thought. Those women who died – they don't deserve to be used by you. It was stealing, Pearl. She was your own mother, but you left her out of the story. You focused on the killer and his son instead.'

'This doesn't make sense,' Pearl says, desperate. 'Wilder died years ago. I only gave you his hair a couple of weeks ago.'

'If I had used a stone or a tree to trap him in – no, it wouldn't have worked. But books don't work like that. They are outside time. They are everywhere.'

'But—' Pearl's mind is a furnace. She feels the black pulse that comes from Harper. Every part of her shouts, *danger, get away.*

Harper sees. She smiles. 'That's right,' she says, gentle. 'Get in the car and drive. And don't come back here. This is my place. I thought you understood that. Why did you come back? You thought it was all about you, but this story has been about me, the whole time. You never thought about me, any of you. The things I had to – no one knows what I had to do, what I went through.'

Harper's face is pink and twisted with tears.

'Nat would have hated prison,' she says though clenched jaws. 'I couldn't let that happen to him. He took those pictures of those children. He told me, I made him tell me. He wanted forgiveness, so I gave him that – then I fed him. It was best.'

Harper looks up at Pearl. Her face is a screen of tears. 'Do you know what it's like – to kill someone you love?' Her voice is strangled, wet with tears. 'It's more than love can stand. I found a way we can all be together again. Nat, Wilder and I. We can go back to before it all happened.' Harper takes a deep, gulping breath. 'I messed up badly before, but I've finally fixed it.'

Harper

Fall 1992

She's almost ready.

The bay glistens, the meadow is golden in the low light. Harper smells the warm earth. It's been a dry summer. That's good. Hemlock grows stronger in the sunshine. Her heart is drier than the earth. Harper knows she has to take herself to the edge for this one. The last one.

The windows of Whistler Cottage were open as she passed. Some visitor. She ducked her head and hurried by. She doesn't want to attract attention.

She unpacks the items one by one. The silver knife, the gleaming fresh seabass she bought in Castine. There has to be something from the sea and Nat liked to catch striper. Carefully, she unwraps the sweater that swaddles the jar of tincture. The liquid is blood red, for some reason, she doesn't know why; maybe she did something wrong.

She found it in the *King's American Dispensatory* in her father's library – the instructions.

. . . pack it moderately in a conical glass percolator, and grad-
ually pour diluted alcohol upon it, until one thousand grammes of
tincture are obtained . . .

Luckily, she was always OK at science. Harper didn't have a
percolator so she used a coffee pot. She broke it afterwards and hid
the pieces in the trash, enclosed in three layers of garbage bags.

She unscrews the jar and carefully stands the knife in the liquid.
The whole blade should be covered in it.

Harper came back to watch over the bay as its guardian. She
has the strong impression – this could be wrong, though, so much
magic is guesswork– that it asked her to. Sometimes she thinks it's
watching her back. Or else she's mad. Either way, she's been here
since Fairview, in that empty white house. It's like time stopped
for Harper. Even Pearl has gone and done something with her life.
Harper read about it in the paper – the book. Harper hasn't drunk,
though. There is that. Not for two years.

'Haven't I done well, Natty?' she says aloud. She talks to him
sometimes. Maybe someday he'll answer.

'Harper?'

Harper turns, flesh thrilling. She hasn't even started yet – but
she knows that voice.

Wilder stands knee deep in the nodding grass, looking hesitant.
He has a leather satchel slung over his chest. Harper opens her
mouth to say hello. Instead, she says, 'Someone has fallen in love
with you since we met last. I can see it.' And she can, the gleaming
light of it all over him. 'I didn't know you were back.'

'I just got here,' Wilder says. 'I was looking at the sea and thinking about you – about the past. Then I looked up and there you
were outside. So I followed. Forgot my glasses on the table, but I
wanted to catch up with you. I didn't realise you were coming here.'

'You still hate this meadow?' she says, smiling. 'You used to say it was like someone died here.'

'Weirdly, I don't feel like that today.' He smiles too. 'I've grown up, I think.'

He looks at the fire she's built. The knife. She carved the handle herself, from walnut. The pattern of fish on the walnut handle is a little clumsier than the original. But it looks very similar.

'What are you doing?' Wilder asks slowly.

'I'm practising,' Harper says. She takes a deep breath. 'I think I can bring Nat back. But there's something else I need, and I can't get it yet. So I'm doing a trial run.

'Of?'

'You think all this is rubbish.'

'It doesn't matter what I think.'

She sighs. And she does want to tell someone; she worked really hard at getting this just right.

'Here's the knife – it's not the one Nat used but it's as close as I could make it. We're in a place where Nat gave his blood, remember? The forfeits. So the spells will be linked by blood and place and ownership. But I need to have the object to put it in. And it has to be this specific one. It's a book about you know, everything that happened, written by – well, that doesn't matter. It's called *The Sound and the Dagger* – it's published next year. Until then, I'm going to practise the rest of it. I have to get everything right. I think there's only one chance.' Harper looks out to sea. She doesn't want him to see her crying.

'I know it's stupid,' she says. 'I know I can't change anything. But I have to have some purpose. Some hope.'

Wilder looks at her. Silently, he opens his satchel and takes out a wad of pages. The title page reads: *The Sound and the Dagger*. 'You can do it now,' he says.

'How did you—' Harper feels the world disintegrate around her.

'She heard it from me,' Wilder says. 'Our story. We ended up at the same college.' He shakes his head. 'Pretty strange, right? That I turn up here with exactly the thing you need, just when you need it.'

'That's how it works,' Harper says. 'Magic. Is it – what are we like, in the book?'

'It's more about her than us, I think. You're called Helen, in it. Look. Here. I'm Wiley. She put herself in it, too – a character called Skandar.'

'Ugh,' Harper says.

'She's a low-down thief. I came up here to find her.'

'Are you going to kill her?' Harper is interested.

'I'm going to forgive her,' Wilder says with dignity.

Harper bursts out laughing. She laughs even harder at the look on his face. 'You don't change. I've got a better plan.' She holds out her hand. 'Give it to me.'

He hesitates.

Something breaks inside her. 'Give it to me, Wilder! Even if you think this is all crap, even if you think I'm insane – just humour me. OK?'

Her hands shake as she takes the manuscript. 'You'll enjoy this next part. I'm going to burn it.'

'Harper . . .'

She smiles and squeezes his hand. 'We can talk afterwards,' she says. 'There are things you should know, things I promised Nat I'd tell you.' She has failed to keep so many promises. But she can make it right.

Harper places the manuscript on the pyre. She takes the knife out of the jar and shakes it free of liquid, careful not to let the drops fall near her. She pours the rest of the tincture on the kindling at the base of the pile. It's mostly alcohol, it will act as an accelerant. She drops the match, and flame leaps up, pale in the sunshine, as though it's been waiting eagerly for this moment.

She raises the knife to her throat. A scratch would be enough, she thinks, but she's not taking chances.

'What the hell are you doing?' Wilder says, horrified. He lunges for her, she ducks out of his grasp. 'Harper, don't!'

'Don't try and stop me, Wilder,' she says, shoving him away. 'It needs my blood. I can bring Nat back in the book. I'll still be alive, I'll just be – in there. I'll be Helen.'

Wilder doesn't answer. He stares down at the long, deep bloody scratch that has opened his forearm.

Harper goes cold with horror. 'I'm sorry,' she says. 'Oh, Wilder. I'm so sorry.'

'It doesn't hurt,' he says. 'It should hurt. What's on the knife, Harper?'

'Tincture of hemlock,' she whispers.

'Oh god,' he says. 'Call 911. You can run down to the cottage . . .'

She knows there isn't time. The tincture is already in his body, riding on his blood.

'I'm scared. What's going to happen?'

'It'll be fine. I can fix this.' Harper's heart pounds. He's messed up the spell, she doesn't know what to do now. She can't fix this. Around them, red, burning fragments of paper float on the air.

'I don't want to die,' Wilder looks young and very afraid.

'Sit down,' Harper says. There's a handsome young beech tree nearby and she helps him sit with his back against the trunk. She hopes that keeping him still will slow the poison.

Wilder starts to cry. Harper reaches for him but he flinches away from her. He can feel her true self now, the vast darkness of her. 'Don't touch me,' he whispers.

'Whatever you want,' Harper says, smiling. She keeps the smile pinned to her face and the tears far, far back, stinging her throat. There must be a way – there must.

'Wait,' she says to Wilder.

She runs to the pyre. The book is nearly gone, it is roaring flame. She holds her breath and reaches in, manages to grab a white fragment of page. She stamps on its glowing edges. It's a scene between Wiley and the guy called Skandar. *Messy russet hair, big nose. Kind.*

How creative, Pearl, she thinks. *Making your main character a male version of you. Ugh, fine.* It will have to do.

She sharpens her mind and heart. To her terror and amazement, the feeling is coming upon her. Witchcraft is about to happen. The world goes blue and blurry at the edges.

She smears the singed page with blood from Wilder's wound. She bites the inside of her cheek until it bleeds, then spits that onto the page too.

When she's ready she says, 'Open your eyes.'

Wilder's eyes are vast, dark, pupils fully dilated by the poison. 'Who are you?' he asks. 'Am I dead?'

'You're Wiley.' Harper hears her voice, deep. She touches her throat, feels the stubble, the unfamiliar bump of an Adam's apple. Her shoulders are broad now. Powerful. Is this what it's like? She tries not to think. She has to believe it, he has to believe it. They have to get into the book.

She leans in, lets him feel her breath on his mouth, parts her lips. She gently touches them with hers. The gasp he takes is as long as her soul; they breathe each other in. She tastes his tongue, clean like minerals. When she grasps Wilder's hand she sees her own is unfamiliar – large, long-fingered.

'Put your hand on my heart,' she says.

Wilder thrusts his hand inside her shirt, buttons fly through the air. He places his hand on the strange flatness of her chest, over her heart. Harper stops thinking and lets the magic take over, lets it batter her like an avalanche. The world is a mess of colour around the fixed point of one another. Every part of her is focused on Wilder's breath, his mouth, his heartbeat. She tries to push their breathing, beating hearts into the book.

For a moment, the meadow shivers around them. The bay below is a different shape, there are seals on the warm rocks. *It's working*, she thinks. She and Wilder aren't beneath a beech tree, but standing in a sunlit brown stream. She's Skandar, and he's Wiley.

It only lasts for a moment. Wilder's lips spasm and go cold under hers. She feels it as he begins to die.

Harper pushes harder but it's no good. The blue light at the edges of things begins to dim. She feels her hair lengthen, her face narrow and smooth. She returns to herself.

Wilder is looking up at her, mouth frozen, eyes glassy with fear. The tiniest spark of life remains – and he's gone, his eyes are blank. She knows it didn't work. The page she holds is just a page.

Even though she knows it's useless, Harper shakes and calls to Wilder. She screams and beats his dead chest with a fist. The body that housed him grows slowly cool.

Harper strokes his dark hair. 'It'll be all right,' she whispers into his ear. 'I swear I'll fix it.'

Pearl

'I thought it was me who killed him,' Pearl says blankly. 'But it was you.'

'It was an accident,' Harper whispers.

'A life wasted for something that didn't even work,' Pearl says, her heart clenched with sorrow.

'I think you can only do it with a book that's not completely finished.' Harper almost sounds pleading. 'But most of all, I think it needed Gracie. She's all three of us, you see. Me, Nat and Wilder. Blood of our blood. Now we can all be together, do it all over again.'

'But that would be awful, to go through it all again,' Pearl says.

'I can't wait to see them,' Harper says.

Pearl says slowly, 'You put my mother's pearl in.' Her breath is short.

'Yes, you'll see your mother.'

Pearl thinks she might faint. She groans.

'I don't understand you, Pearl. You should be thanking me—'

'It means she'll die again, Harper. And again and again.'

'You'll get used to it. Though it's a shame you made Rebecca come back as a ghost in this book – her ghost suffers so much.'

Pearl looks at her hands and thinks of them wrapped about Harper's throat.

No. Harper's voice thunders in Pearl's skull. Pearl clutches her head.

Harper wipes her tears away, businesslike. 'Don't write about Whistler Bay anymore,' she says. 'It's not for you. That's two books we'll all have to live through, now. Try writing something different. Try writing lots of different things. Live and love – listen and watch. Then put it all into the worlds on the paper. That will give you more room to roam – when the time comes. You write them, so you're in all of them. We're just in the ones you decide to put us into.'

'This isn't possible,' Pearl says, weak. 'You're trying to scare me.'

'Maybe,' Harper says. 'Maybe not. Since you don't want to join us here, I would try to live as long as possible and make as many worlds to live in as you can.'

Her smile stretches slowly into a grin. It grows wider as she reaches for Pearl, who tries to scream but she can't get the breath. Harper's arms enclose her and Pearl feels it, the great dark smiling power of her, the old suns and moons and constellations turning within. How could she once have thought her harmless?

'Let me go,' she whispers, her insides twisting. 'Please, I'll do what you want. I'll go and never come back. I'll write about other places.'

'Pearl?' Gracie is saying, worried. 'Harper?' She stands in the doorway, chicken leg in hand. Her teeth gnaw the bare bone. Pearl flinches.

'Harper is using you, Gracie,' Pearl says. 'She just wants your blood.' She knows it's a cruel thing to say.

Gracie shakes her head. 'She's my mother,' she says, simply.

Harper watches Gracie with a slight smile – something burns in her eyes. Pearl sees, startled, that it's love. It passes between

337

mother and daughter, a bright, gleaming moment.

Harper turns back to Pearl. 'You're pretty low on gas,' she says politely, 'but you'll make it to the highway.' Pearl doesn't ask how she knows. That dark vastness pulses behind Harper's eyes – she taps Pearl lightly on the arm with one finger. The nail is dry, sharp and light.

Pearl gasps and flinches from the touch. She turns and runs down the hill, sliding and slipping on the shale path, feeling the weight of eyes on her back, her neck.

She slams the car door shut, sealing herself in. She breathes deeply, taking in the smell of leather, the comforting sweet tang of an old slushee in the cupholder. These are real, ordinary things. But power crawls on the back of her neck like flies.

The engine starts first try and Pearl sobs with relief. The car tears away in a spray of grit and shale. She reminds herself to breathe and the road steadies somewhat before her. *Don't look back*, she thinks, *do not, do not*, but in the end she can't resist, it's as if her neck is being cranked round by a handle. As she nears the turn she flings a glance behind her.

Up on the hill two figures are silhouetted, black against the sky. Pearl knows it must be Harper and Gracie, but for a moment the sun dazzles her eyes. It could be two boys on the cusp of manhood, standing arm in arm, to watch her leave.

[   ]

Wont
Won
Yon
You

Hart
Hare
Are

Fear
Ear
Hear
Her
Here

Tooth
Sooth
Soot
Toot
Too

Acknowledgements

My wonderful agents are fearless champions for my books and deserve far more praise than I can give them here. First thanks as always must go to the magical Jenny Savill, who always wields her power for good. Thank you to all at Andrew Nurnberg Associates: Michael Dean, Barbara Barbieri, Rory Clarke, Lucy Flynn, Juliana Galvis, Halina Koscia, Ylva Monsen, Andrew Nurnberg, Sabine Pfannenstiel and Marei Pittner.

To the wonderful Robin Straus and Danielle Metta at the Robin Straus Agency – thank you – you've changed everything for me.

All thanks go to my wonderful UK and US editors Miranda Jewess and Kelly Lonesome – I can't sing your praises highly enough. This book was quite the journey – thank you for your trust, your patience, your seemingly inexhaustible creativity and resourcefulness.

I am so grateful to the mighty Viper team for their brilliance and hard work – Andrew Franklin, Drew Jerrison, Flora Willis, Claire Beaumont and Niamh Murray in particular. In the copy edit, Hayley Shepherd's eagle eye saved me, as ever, from error.

To the amazing Nightfire coven in the US: Alexis Saarela

Devi Pillai, Michael Dudding, Jordan Hanley, Valeria Castorena, Kristin Temple and the rest of the fantastic team at Tor Nightfire and Tor Publishing Group – thank you. I feel very fortunate to be published by you.

The beautiful, dramatic covers for *Looking Glass Sound* were created by Steve Panton in the UK and Katie Klimowicz in the US.

For long talks, support and kindnesses too numerous to mention, my thanks to Emily Cavendish, Oriana Elia, Kate Griffin, Virginia Feito, Essie Fox, Lydia Leonard, Craig Leyenaar, Anna Mazzola, Andy Morwood, Thomas Olde Heuvelt, Natasha Pulley, Gillian Redfearn, Alice Slater, Holly Watt, Belinda Stewart-Wilson, Rachel Winterbottom and Anna Wood.

To my lovely parents Isabelle and Christopher, and to Antonia, Sam, Wolf and River – you are always in my heart.

My darling Eugene Noone, you are in every book I write, and you are missed.